CHAD

THE LITTLE SHEPHERD
OF KINGDOM COME

THE LITTLE SHEPHERD
OF KINGDOM COME

by JOHN FOX, JR.

WITH PICTURES BY
N.C.WYETH

NEW YORK
CHARLES SCRIBNER'S SONS
1931

TO

CURRIE DUKE

DAUGHTER OF THE CHIEF

AMONG

MORGAN'S MEN

K<small>ENTUCKY</small>, April, 1898

CONTENTS

[vii]

CONTENTS

ILLUSTRATIONS

THE
LITTLE SHEPHERD OF KINGDOM COME

THE
LITTLE SHEPHERD OF KINGDOM COME

I

TWO RUNAWAYS FROM LONESOME

THE days of that April had been days of mist and rain.
Sometimes, for hours, there would come a miracle of blue sky,
white cloud, and yellow light, but always between dark and
dark the rain would fall and the mist creep up the mountains
and steam from the tops—only to roll together from either
range, drip back into the valleys, and lift, straightway, as mist
again. So that, all the while Nature was trying to give lustier
life to every living thing in the lowland Bluegrass, all the
while a gaunt skeleton was stalking down the Cumberland—
tapping with fleshless knuckles, now at some unlovely cottage
of faded white and green, and now at a log cabin, stark and
gray. Passing the mouth of Lonesome, he flashed his scythe
into its unlifting shadows and went stalking on. High up, at
the source of the dismal little stream, the point of the shining
blade darted thrice into the open door of a cabin set deep into
a shaggy flank of Black Mountain, and three spirits, within,
were quickly loosed from aching flesh for the long flight into
the unknown.

It was the spirit of the plague that passed, taking with it
the breath of the unlucky and the unfit: and in the hut on
Lonesome three were dead—a gaunt mountaineer, a gaunt

daughter, and a gaunt son. Later, the mother, too, "jes' kind o' got tired," as little Chad said, and soon to her worn hands and feet came the well-earned rest. Nobody was left then but Chad and Jack, and Jack was a dog with a belly to feed and went for less than nothing with everybody but his little master and the chance mountaineer who had sheep to guard. So, for the fourth time, Chad, with Jack at his heels, trudged up to the point of a wooded spur above the cabin, where, at the foot of a giant poplar and under a wilderness of shaking June leaves, were three piles of rough boards, loosely covering three hillocks of rain-beaten earth; and, near them, an open grave. There was no service sung or spoken over the dead, for the circuit-rider was then months away; so, unnoticed, Chad stood behind the big poplar, watching the neighbors gently let down into the shallow trench a home-made coffin, rudely hollowed from the half of a bee-gum log, and, unnoticed, slipped away at the first muffled stroke of the dirt —doubling his fists into his eyes and stumbling against the gnarled bodies of laurel and rhododendron until, out in a clear sunny space, he dropped on a thick, velvet mat of moss and sobbed himself to sleep. When he awoke, Jack was licking his face and he sat up, dazed and yawning. The sun was dropping fast, the ravines were filling with blue shadows, luminous and misty, and a far drowsy tinkling from the valley told him that cows were starting homeward. From habit, he sprang quickly to his feet, but, sharply conscious on a sudden, dropped slowly back to the moss again, while Jack, who had started down the spur, circled back to see what the matter was, and stood with uplifted foot, much puzzled.

There had been a consultation about Chad early that morning among the neighbors, and old Nathan Cherry, who lived over on Stone Creek, in the next cove but one, said that he would take charge of the boy. Nathan did not wait for the burial, but went back home for his wagon, leaving word that Chad was to stay all night with a neighbor and meet him at the death-stricken cabin an hour by sun. The old man meant to have Chad bound to him for seven years by law—the boy had been told that—and Nathan hated dogs as much as Chad hated Nathan. So the lad did not lie long. He did not mean to be bound out, nor to have Jack mistreated, and he rose quickly and Jack sprang before him down the rocky path and toward the hut that had been a home to both. Under the poplar, Jack sniffed curiously at the new-made grave, and Chad called him away so sharply that Jack's tail drooped and he crept toward his master, as though to ask pardon for a fault of which he was not conscious. For one moment, Chad stood looking. Again the stroke of the falling earth smote his ears and his eyes filled; a curious pain caught him by the throat and he passed on, whistling—down into the shadows below to the open door of the cabin.

It was deathly still. The homespun bedclothes and hand-made quilts of brilliant colors had been thrown in a heap on one of the two beds of hickory withes; the kitchen utensils— a crane and a few pots and pans—had been piled on the hearth, along with strings of herbs and beans and red pepper-pods— all ready for old Nathan when he should come over for them, next morning, with his wagon. Not a living thing was to be heard or seen that suggested human life, and Chad sat down in the deepening loneliness, watching the shadows rise up the green walls that bound him in, and wondering what he should do, and where he should go, if he was not to go to old Nathan; while Jack, who seemed to know that some crisis was come, settled on his haunches a little way off, to wait, with perfect faith and patience, for the boy to make up his mind.

It was the first time, perhaps, that Chad had ever thought very seriously about himself, or wondered who he was, or whence he had come. Digging back into his memory as far as he could, it seemed to him that what had just happened now had happened to him once before, and that he had simply wandered away. He could not recollect where he had started from first, but he could recall many of the places where he had lived, and why he had left them—usually because somebody, like old Nathan, had wanted to have him bound out, or had misused Jack, or would not let the two stray off into the woods together, when there was nothing else to be done. He had stayed longest where he was now, because the old man and his son and his girl had all taken a great fancy to Jack, and had let the two guard cattle in the mountains and drive sheep and, if they stayed out in the woods over night, struck neither a stroke of hand nor tongue. The old mother had been his mother and, once more, Chad leaned his head against the worn lintel and wept silently. So far, nobody had seemed to care particularly who he was, or was not—nor had Chad. Most people were very kind to him, looking upon him as one of the wandering waifs that one finds throughout the Cumberland, upon whom the good folks of the mountains do not visit the father's sin. He knew what he was thought to be, and it mattered so little, since it made no discrimination against him, that he had accepted it without question. It did not matter now, except as it bore on the question as to where he should start his feet. It was a long time for him to have stayed in one place, and the roving memories, stirred within him now, took root, doubtless, in the restless spirit that had led his unknown ancestor into those mountain wilds after the Revolution.

All this while he had been sitting on the low threshold, with his elbows in the hollows of his thighs and his left hand across his mouth. Once more, he meant to be bound to no man's service and, at the final thought of losing Jack, the liberty-loving little tramp spat over his hand with sharp decision and rose.

Just above him and across the buck antlers over the door, lay a long flint-lock rifle; a bullet-pouch, a powder-horn, and a small raccoon-skin haversack hung from one of the prongs: and on them the boy's eyes rested longingly. Old Nathan, he knew, claimed that the dead man had owed him money; and he further knew that old Nathan meant to take all he could lay his hands on in payment: but he climbed resolutely upon a chair and took the things down, arguing the question, meanwhile:

"Uncle Jim said once he aimed to give this rifle gun to me. Mebbe he was foolin', but I don't believe he owed ole Nathan so much, an', anyways," he muttered grimly, "I reckon Uncle Jim 'ud kind o' like fer me to git the better of that ole devil— jes' a *leetle,* anyways."

The rifle, he knew, was always loaded; there was not much powder in the horn and there were not more than a dozen bullets in the pouch, but they would last him until he could get far away. No more would he take, however, than what he thought he could get along with—one blanket from the bed and, from the fireplace, a little bacon and a pone of corn-bread.

"An' I *know* Aunt Jane wouldn't 'a' keered about these

leetle fixin's, fer I have to have 'em, an' I know I've earned 'em anyways."

Then he closed the door softly on the spirits of the dead within, and caught the short, deer-skin latch-string to the wooden pin outside. With his Barlow knife, he swiftly stripped a bark string from a pawpaw bush near by, folded and tied his blanket, and was swinging the little pack to his shoulder, when the tinkle of a cow-bell came through the bushes, close at hand. Old Nance, lean and pied, was coming home; he had forgotten her, it was getting late, and he was anxious to leave for fear some neighbor might come; but there was no one to milk and, when she drew near with a low moo, he saw that her udders were full and dripping. It would hurt her to go unmilked, so Chad put his things down and took up a cedar piggin from a shelf outside the cabin and did the task thoroughly—putting the strippings in a cup and, so strong was the habit in him, hurrying with both to the rude spring-house and setting them in cool running water. A moment more and he had his pack and his rifle on one shoulder and was climbing the fence at the wood-pile. There he stopped once more with a sudden thought, and wrenching loose a short axe from the face of a hickory log, staggered under the weight of his weapons up the mountain. The sun was yet an hour high and, on the spur, he leaned his rifle against the big poplar and set to work with his axe on a sapling close by—talking frankly now to the God who made him:

"I reckon You know it, but I'm a-goin' to run away now. I hain't got no daddy an' no mammy, an' I hain't nuver had none as I knows—but Aunt Jane hyeh—she's been jes' like a mother to me an' I'm a-doin' fer her jes' whut I wish You'd

have somebody do fer my mother, ef You know whar she's
a-layin'."

Eight round sticks he cut swiftly—four long and four short
—and with these he built a low pen, as is the custom of the
mountaineers, close about the fresh mound, and, borrowing a
board or two from each of the other mounds, covered the grave
from the rain. Then he sunk the axe into the trunk of the
great poplar as high up as he could reach—so that it could
easily be seen—and, brushing the sweat from his face, he knelt
down:

"God!" he said, simply, "I hain't nothin' but a boy, but I
got to ack like a man now. I'm a-goin' now. I don't believe
You keer much and seems like I bring ever'body bad luck: an'
I'm a-goin' to live up hyeh on the mountain jes' as long as I
can. I don't want you to think I'm a-complainin'—fer I ain't.
Only hit does seem sort o' curious that You'd let me be down
hyeh—with me a-keerin' fer nobody now, an' nobody a-keerin' fer me. But Thy ways is inscrutable—leastwise, that's
whut the circuit-rider says—an' I ain't got a word more to say
—Amen."

Chad rose then and Jack, who had sat perfectly still, with
his head cocked to one side, and his ears straight forward in
wonder over this strange proceeding, sprang into the air, when
Chad picked up his gun, and, with a joyful bark, circled a
clump of bushes and sped back, leaping as high as the little
fellow's head and trying to lick his face—for Jack was a rover,
too.

The sun was low when the two waifs turned their backs
upon it, and the blue shadows in valley and ravine were darkening fast. Down the spur they went swiftly—across the river

and up the slope of Pine Mountain. As they climbed, Chad heard the last faint sound of a cow-bell far below him and he stopped short, with a lump in his throat that hurt. Soon darkness fell, and, on the very top, the boy made a fire with his flint and steel, cooked a little bacon, warmed his corn-pone, munched them and, wrapping his blanket around him and letting Jack curl into the hollow of his legs and stomach, turned his face to the kindly stars and went to sleep.

II

FIGHTING THEIR WAY

Twice, during the night, Jack roused him by trying to push himself farther under the blanket and Chad rose to rebuild the fire. The third time he was awakened by the subtle prescience of dawn and his eyes opened on a flaming radiance in the east. Again from habit he started to spring hurriedly to his feet and, again sharply conscious, he lay down again. There was no wood to cut, no fire to rekindle, no water to carry from the spring, no cow to milk, no corn to hoe; there was nothing to do—nothing. Morning after morning, with a day's hard toil at a man's task before him, what would he not have given, when old Jim called him, to have stretched his aching little legs down the folds of the thick feather-bed and slipped back into the delicious rest of sleep and dreams? Now he was his own master and, with a happy sense of freedom, he brushed the dew from his face and, shifting the chunk under his head, pulled his old cap down a little more on one side and closed his eyes. But sleep would not come and Chad had his first wonder over the perverse result of the full choice to do, or not to do. At once, the first keen savor of freedom grew less sweet to his nostrils and, straightway, he began to feel the first pressure of the chain of duties that was to be forged for him out of his perfect liberty, link by link, and he lay vaguely wondering.

Meanwhile, the lake of dull red behind the jagged lines of rose and crimson that streaked the east began to glow and look angry. A sheen of fiery vapor shot upward and spread swiftly over the miracle of mist that had been wrought in the night. An ocean of it and, white and thick as snow-dust, it filled valley, chasm, and ravine with mystery and silence up to the dark jutting points and dark waving lines of range after range that looked like breakers, surged up by some strange new law from an under-sea of foam; motionless, it swept down the valleys, poured swift torrents through high gaps in the hills and one long noiseless cataract over a lesser range—all silent, all motionless, like a great white sea stilled in the fury of a storm. Morning after morning, the boy had looked upon just such glory, calmly watching the mist part, like the waters, for the land, and the day break, with one phrase, "Let there be light," ever in his mind—for Chad knew his Bible. And, most often, in soft splendor, trailing cloud-mist, and yellow light leaping from crest to crest, and in the singing of birds and the shining of leaves and dew—there was light.

But that morning there was a hush in the woods that Chad understood. On a sudden, a light wind scurried through the trees and showered the mistdrops down. The smoke from his fire shot through the low undergrowth, without rising, and the starting mists seemed to clutch with long, white fingers at the tree-tops, as though loath to leave the safe, warm earth for the upper air. A little later, he felt some great shadow behind him, and he turned his face to see black clouds marshalling on either flank of the heavens and fitting their black wings together, as though the retreating forces of the night were gathering for a last sweep against the east. A sword flashed blindingly from the dome high above them and, after it, came one shaking peal that might have been the command to charge, for Chad saw the black hosts start fiercely. Afar off, the wind was coming; the trees began to sway above him, and the level sea of mist below began to swell, and the wooded breakers seemed to pitch angrily.

Challenging tongues ran quivering up the east, and the lake of red coals under them began to heave fiercely in answer. On either side the lightning leaped upward and forward, striking straight and low, sometimes, as though it were ripping up the horizon to let into the conflict the host of dropping stars. Then the artillery of the thunder crashed in earnest through the shaking heavens, and the mists below pitched like smoke belched from gigantic unseen cannon. The coming sun answered with upleaping swords of fire and, as the black thunder hosts swept overhead, Chad saw, for one moment, the whole east in a writhing storm of fire. A thick darkness rose from the first crash of battle and, with the rush of wind and rain, the mighty conflict went on unseen.

Chad had seen other storms at sunrise, but something happened now and he could never recall the others nor ever forget this. All it meant to him, young as he was then, was unrolled slowly as the years came on—more than the first great rebellion of the powers of darkness when, in the beginning, the Master gave the first command that the seven days' work of His hand should float through space, smitten with the welcoming rays of a million suns; more than the beginning thus of light—of life; more even than the first birth of a spirit in a living thing: for, long afterward, he knew that it meant the dawn of a new consciousness to him—the birth of a new spirit within him, and the foreshadowed pain of its slow mastery over his passion-racked body and heart. Never was there a crisis, bodily or spiritual, on the battle-field or alone under the stars, that this storm did not come back to him. And, always, through all doubt, and, indeed, in the end, when it came to him for the last time on his bed of death, the slow and sullen dispersion of wind and rain on the mountain that morning far, far back in his memory, and the quick coming of the Sun-king's victorious light over the glad hills and trees held out to him the promise of a final victory to the Sun-king's King over the darkness of all death and the final coming to his own brave spirit of peace and rest.

So Chad, with Jack drawn close to him, lay back, awe-stricken and with his face wet from mysterious tears. The comfort of the childish self-pity that came with every thought of himself, wandering, a lost spirit along the mountain-tops, was gone like a dream and ready in his heart was the strong new purpose to strike into the world for himself. He even took it as a good omen, when he rose, to find his fire quenched, the stopper of his powder-horn out, and the precious black grains scattered hopelessly on the wet earth. There were barely more than three charges left, and something had to be done at once. First, he must get farther away from old Nathan: the neighbors might search for him and find him and take him back.

So he started out, brisk and shivering, along the ridge path with Jack bouncing before him. An hour later, he came upon a hollow tree, filled with doty wood which he could tear out with his hands, and he built a fire and broiled a little more bacon. Jack got only a bit this time and barked reproachfully for more; but Chad shook his head and the dog started out, with both eyes open, to look for his own food. The sun was high enough now to make the drenched world flash like an emerald and its warmth felt good, as Chad tramped the topmost edge of Pine Mountain, where the brush was not thick and where, indeed, he often found a path running a short way and turning into some ravine—the trail of cattle and sheep and the pathway between one little valley settlement and another. He must have made ten miles and more by noon—for he was a sturdy walker and as tireless almost as Jack—and ten miles is a long way in the mountains, even now. So, already, Chad was far enough away to have no fear of pursuit, even if old Nathan wanted him back, which was doubtful. On the top of the next point, Jack treed a squirrel and Chad took a rest and brought him down, shot through the head and, then and there, skinned and cooked him and divided with Jack squarely.

"Jack," he said, as he reloaded his gun, "we can't keep this up much longer. I hain't got more'n two more loads o' powder here."

And, thereupon, Jack leaped suddenly in the air and, turning quite around, lighted with his nose pointed, as it was before he sprang. Chad cocked the old gun and stepped forward. A low hissing whir rose a few feet to one side of the path and, very carefully, the boy climbed a fallen trunk and edged his way, very carefully, toward the sound: and there, by a dead limb and with his ugly head reared three inches above his coil of springs, was a rattlesnake. The sudden hate in the boy's face was curious—it was instinctive, primitive, deadly. He must shoot off-hand now and he looked down the long barrel, shaded with tin, until the sight caught on one of the beady, unblinking eyes, and pulled the trigger. Jack leaped with the sound, in spite of Chad's yell of warning, which was useless, for the ball had gone true and the poison was set loose in the black, crushed head.

"Jack," said Chad, "we just *got* to go down now."

So they went on swiftly through the heat of the early afternoon. It was very silent up there. Now and then, a brilliant blue-jay would lilt from a stunted oak with the flute-like love-notes of spring; or a lonely little brown fellow would hop with a low chirp from one bush to another as though he had been lost up there for years and had grown quite hopeless about seeing his kind again. When there was a gap in the mountains, he could hear the querulous, senseless love-quarrel of flickers going on below him; passing a deep ravine, the note of the wood-thrush—that shy lyrist of the hills—might rise to him from a dense covert of maple and beech: or, with a startling call, a red-crested cock of the woods would beat his white-striped wings from spur to spur, as though he were keeping close to the long swells of an unseen sea. Several times, a pert flicker squatting like a knot to a dead limb, or the crimson plume of a cock of the woods, as plain as a splash of blood on a wall of vivid green, tempted him to let loose his last load, but he withstood them. A little later, he saw a fresh bear-track near a spring below the head of a ravine; and, later still, he heard the far-away barking of a hound and a deer leaped lightly into an open sunny spot and stood with uplifted hoof and pointed ears. This was too much and the boy's gun followed his heart to his throat, but the buck sprang lightly into the bush and vanished noiselessly.

The sun had dropped midway between the zenith and the blue bulks rolling westward. At the next gap, a broader path ran through and down the mountain. This, Chad knew, led to a settlement and, with a last look of choking farewell to his own world, he turned down. At once, the sense of possible

human companionship was curiously potent: at once, the boy's
half-wild manner changed and, though alert and still watchful,
he whistled cheerily to Jack, threw his gun over his shoulder,
and walked erect and confident. His pace slackened. Carelessly now his feet tramped beds of soft exquisite moss and lone
little settlements of forget-me-nots, and his long rifle-barrel
brushed laurel blossoms down in a shower behind him. Once
even, he picked up one of the pretty bells and looked idly at it,
turning it bottom upward. The waxen cup might have blos-
somed from a tiny waxen star. There was a little green star
for a calyx; above this, a little white star with its prongs out-
stretched—tiny arms to hold up the pink-flecked chalice for
the rain and dew. There came a time when he thought of it as
a star-blossom; but now his greedy tongue swept the honey
from it and he dropped it without another thought to the
ground. At the first spur down which the road turned, he could
see smoke in the valley. The laurel blooms and rhododendron
bells hung in thicker clusters and of a deeper pink. Here and
there was a blossoming wild cucumber and an umbrella-tree
with huger flowers and leaves; and, sometimes, a giant mag-
nolia with a thick creamy flower that the boy could not have
spanned with both hands and big, thin oval leaves, a man's
stride from tip to stem. Soon, he was below the sunlight and
in the cool shadows where the water ran noisily and the air
hummed with the wings of bees. On the last spur, he came
upon a cow browsing on sassafras-bushes right in the path and
the last shadow of his loneliness straightway left him. She was
old, mild, and unfearing, and she started down the road in
front of him as though she thought he had come to drive her
home, or as though she knew he was homeless and was leading

him to shelter. A little farther on, the river flashed up a welcome to him through the trees, and at the edge of the water, her mellow bell led him down stream and he followed. In the next hollow, he stooped to drink from a branch that ran across the road and, when he rose to start again, his bare feet stopped as though riven suddenly to the ground; for, half way up the next low slope, was another figure as motionless as his—with a bare head, bare feet, a startled face and wide eyes—but motionless only until the eyes met his: then there was a flash of bright hair and scarlet homespun, and the little feet, that had trod down the centuries to meet his, left the earth as though they had wings and Chad saw them, in swift flight, pass silently over the hill. The next moment, Jack came too near the old brindle and, with a sweep of her horns at him and a toss of tail and heels in the air, she, too, swept over the slope and on, until the sound of her bell passed out of hearing. Even to-day, in lonely parts of the Cumberland, the sudden coming of a stranger may put women and children to flight—something like this had happened before to Chad—but the sudden desertion and the sudden silence drew him in a flash back to the lonely cabin he had left and the lonely graves under the big poplar and, with a quivering lip, he sat down. Jack, too, dropped to his haunches and sat hopeless, but not for long. The chill of night was coming on and Jack was getting hungry. So he rose presently and trotted ahead and squatted again, looking back and waiting. But still Chad sat irresolute and, in a moment, Jack heard something that disturbed him, for he threw his ears toward the top of the hill and, with a growl, trotted back to Chad and sat close to him, looking up the slope. Chad rose then with his thumb on the lock of his gun, and over the hill came a tall figure and a short one, about Chad's size; and a dog, with white feet and white face, that was bigger than Jack; and behind them, three more figures, one of which was the tallest of the group. All stopped when they saw Chad, who dropped the butt of his gun at once to the ground. At once the strange dog, with a low snarl, started down toward the two little strangers, his yellow ears pointed, the hair bristling along his back, and his teeth in sight. Jack answered the challenge with an eager whimper, but dropped his tail, at Chad's sharp command—for Chad did not care to meet the world as an enemy, when he was looking for a friend. The group stood dumb with astonishment for a moment and the small boy's mouth was wide-open with surprise, but the strange dog came on with his tail rigid, and lifting his feet high.

"Begone!" said Chad, sharply, but the dog would not be-gone; he still came on as though bent on a fight.

"Call yo' dog off," Chad called aloud. "My dog'll kill him. You better call him off," he called again, in some concern, but the tall boy in front laughed scornfully.

"Let's see him," he said, and the small one laughed, too.

Chad's eyes flashed—no boy can stand an insult to his dog —and the curves of his open lips snapped together in a straight red line. "All right," he said, placidly, and, being tired, he dropped back on a stone by the wayside to await results. The very tone of his voice struck all shackles of restraint from Jack, who, with a springy trot, went forward slowly, as though he were making up a definite plan of action; for Jack had a fight-ing way of his own, which Chad knew.

"Sick him, Whizzer!" shouted the tall boy, and the group of five hurried eagerly down the hill and halted in a half circle about Jack and Chad: so that it looked an uneven conflict, indeed, for the two waifs from over Pine Mountain.

The strange dog was game and wasted no time. With a bound he caught Jack by the throat, tossed him several feet away, and sprang for him again. Jack seemed helpless against such strength and fury, but Chad's face was as placid as though it had been Jack who was playing the winning game. Jack himself seemed little disturbed; he took his punishment without an outcry of rage or pain. You would have thought he had quietly come to the conclusion that all he could hope to do was to stand the strain until his opponent had worn himself out. But that was not Jack's game, and Chad knew it. The tall boy was chuckling, and his brother of Chad's age was bent almost double with delight.

"Kill my dawg, will he?" he cried, shrilly.

"Oh, Lawdy!" groaned the tall one.

Jack was much bitten and chewed by this time, and, while his pluck and purpose seemed unchanged, Chad had risen to his feet and was beginning to look anxious. The three silent spectators behind pressed forward and, for the first time, one of these—the tallest of the group—spoke:

"Take yo' dawg off, Daws Dillon," he said, with quiet authority; but Daws shook his head, and the little brother looked indignant.

"He said he'd kill him," said Daws, tauntingly.

"Yo' dawg's bigger and hit ain't fair," said the other again and, seeing Chad's worried look, he pressed suddenly forward; but Chad had begun to smile, and was sitting down on his stone again. Jack had leaped this time, with his first growl during the fight, and Whizzer gave a sharp cry of surprise and pain.

Jack had caught him by the throat, close behind the jaws, and the big dog shook and growled and shook again. Sometimes Jack was lifted quite from the ground, but he seemed clamped to his enemy to stay. Indeed he shut his eyes, finally, and seemed to go quite to sleep. The big dog threshed madly and swung and twisted, howling with increasing pain and terror and increasing weakness, while Jack's face was as peaceful as though he were a puppy once more and hanging to his mother's neck instead of her breast, asleep. By and by, Whizzer ceased to shake and began to pant; and, thereupon, Jack took his turn at shaking, gently at first, but with maddening regularity and without at all loosening his hold. The big dog was too weak to resist soon and, when Jack began to jerk savagely, Whizzer began to gasp.

"You take *yo'* dawg off," called Daws, sharply.

Chad never moved.

"Will you say 'nough for him?" he asked, quietly; and the tall one of the silent three laughed.

"Call him off, I tell ye," repeated Daws, savagely; but again Chad never moved, and Daws started for a club. Chad's new friend came forward.

"Hol' on, now, hol' on," he said, easily. "None o' that, I reckon."

Daws stopped with an oath. "Whut you got to do with this, Tom Turner?"

"You started this fight," said Tom.

"I don't keer ef I did—take him off," Daws answered, savagely.

"Will you say 'nough fer him?" said Chad again, and again Tall Tom chuckled. The little brother clinched his fists and turned white with fear for Whizzer and fury for Chad, while Daws looked at the tall Turner, shook his head from side to side, like a balking steer, and dropped his eyes:

"Y-e-s," he said, sullenly.

"Say it, then," said Chad, and this time Tall Tom roared aloud, and even his two silent brothers laughed. Again Daws, with a furious oath, started for the dogs with his club, but Chad's ally stepped between.

"You say 'nough, Daws Dillon," he said, and Daws looked into the quiet half-smiling face and at the stalwart two grinning behind.

"Takin' up agin yo' neighbors fer a wood-colt, air ye?"

"I'm a-takin' up fer what's right and fair. How do you know he's a wood-colt—an' suppose he is? You say 'nough now, or——"

Again Daws looked at the dogs. Jack had taken a fresh grip and was shaking savagely and steadily. Whizzer's tongue was out—once his throat rattled.

" 'Nough!" growled Daws, angrily, and the word was hardly jerked from his lips before Chad was on his feet and prying Jack's jaws apart. "He ain't much hurt," he said, looking at the bloody hold which Jack had clamped on his enemy's throat, "but he'd a-killed him though, he al'ays does. Thar ain't no chance fer *no* dog, when Jack gits *that* holt."

Then he raised his eyes and looked into the quivering face of the owner of the dog—the little fellow—who, with the bellow of a yearling bull, sprang at him. Again Chad's lips took a straight red line and being on one knee was an advantage, for, as he sprang up, he got both underholds and there was a mighty tussle, the spectators yelling with frantic delight.

[22]

"Stick to him, little un," shouted Tom.

"Trip him, Tad," shouted Daws, fiercely.

"Stick to him, little un," shouted Tom, and his brothers, stoical Dolph and Rube, danced about madly. Even with underholds, Chad, being much the shorter of the two, had no advantage that he did not need, and, with a sharp thud, the two fierce little bodies struck the road side by side, spurting up a cloud of dust.

"Dawg—fall!" cried Rube, and Dolph rushed forward to pull the combatants apart.

"He don't fight fair," said Chad, panting, and rubbing his right eye which his enemy had tried to "gouge"; "but lemme at him—I can fight thataway, too." Tall Tom held them apart.

"You're too little, and he don't fight fair. I reckon you better go on home—you two—an' yo' mean dawg," he said to Daws; and the two Dillons—the one sullen and the other crying with rage—moved away with Whizzer slinking close to the ground after them. But at the top of the hill both turned with bantering yells, derisive wriggling of their fingers at their noses, and with other rude gestures. And, thereupon, Dolph and Rube wanted to go after them, but the tall brother stopped them with a word.

"That's about all they're fit fer," he said, contemptuously, and he turned to Chad.

"Whar you from, little man, an' whar you goin', an' what mought yo' name be?"

Chad told his name, and where he was from, and stopped.

"Whar you goin'?" said Tom again, without a word or look of comment.

Chad knew the disgrace and the suspicion that his answer was likely to generate, but he looked his questioner in the face fearlessly.

"I don't know whar I'm goin'."

The big fellow looked at him keenly, but kindly.

"You ain't lyin' an' I reckon you better come with us." He turned for the first time to his brothers and the two nodded.

"You an' yo' dawg, though Mammy don't like dawgs much; but you air a stranger an' you ain't afeerd, an' you can fight— you an' yo' dawg—an' I know Dad'll take ye both in."

So Chad and Jack followed the long strides of the three Turners over the hill and to the bend of the river, where were three long cane fishing-poles with their butts stuck in the mud —the brothers had been fishing, when the flying figure of the little girl told them of the coming of a stranger into those lonely wilds. Taking these up, they strode on—Chad after them and Jack trotting, in cheerful confidence, behind. It is probable that Jack noticed, as soon as Chad, the swirl of smoke rising from a broad ravine that spread into broad fields, skirted by the great sweep of the river, for he sniffed the air sharply, and trotted suddenly ahead. It was a cheering sight for Chad. Two negro slaves were coming from work in a corn-field close by, and Jack's hair rose when he saw them, and, with a growl, he slunk behind his master. Dazed, Chad looked at them.

"Whut've them fellers got on their faces?" he asked. Tom laughed.

"Hain't you nuver seed a nigger afore?" he asked.

Chad shook his head.

"Lots o' folks from yo' side o' the mountains nuver have seed a nigger," said Tom. "Sometimes hit skeers 'em."

"Hit don't skeer me," said Chad.

At the gate of the barn-yard, in which was a long stable with a deeply sloping roof, stood the old brindle cow, who

turned to look at Jack, and, as Chad followed the three brothers through the yard gate, he saw a slim scarlet figure vanish
swiftly from the porch into the house.

In a few minutes, Chad was inside the big log-cabin and
before a big log-fire, with Jack between his knees and turning
his soft human eyes keenly from one to another of the group
about his little master as Chad told how the mountain cholera
had carried off the man and the woman who had been father
and mother to him, and their children; at which the old mother
nodded her head in growing sympathy, for there were two
fresh mounds in her own graveyard on the point of a low hill
not far away; how old Nathan Cherry, whom he hated, had
wanted to bind him out, and how, rather than have Jack mistreated and himself be ill-used, he had run away along the
mountain-top; how he had slept one night under a log with
Jack to keep him warm; how he had eaten sassafras and birch
bark and had gotten drink from the green water-bulbs of the
wild honeysuckle; and how, on the second day, being hungry,
and without powder for his gun, he had started, when the sun
sank, for the shadows of the valley at the mouth of Kingdom
Come. Before he was done, the old mother knocked the ashes
from her clay pipe and quietly went into the kitchen, and Jack,
for all his good manners, could not restrain a whine of eagerness when he heard the crackle of bacon in a frying-pan and
the delicious smell of it struck his quivering nostrils. After
dark, old Joel, the father of the house, came in—a giant in size
and a mighty hunter—and he slapped his big thighs and roared
until the rafters seemed to shake when Tall Tom told him about
the dog-fight and the boy-fight with the family in the next cove:
for already the clanship was forming that was to add the last

horror to the coming great war and prolong that horror for nearly half a century after its close.

By and by, the scarlet figure of little Melissa came shyly out of the dark shadows behind and drew shyly closer and closer, until she was crouched in the chimney corner with her face shaded from the fire by one hand and a tangle of yellow hair, listening and watching him with her big, solemn eyes, quite fearlessly. Already the house was full of children and dependents, but no word passed between old Joel and the old mother, for no word was necessary. Two waifs who had so suffered and who could so fight could have a home under that roof if they pleased, forever. And Chad's sturdy little body lay deep in a feather-bed, and the friendly shadows from a big fireplace flickered hardly thrice over him before he was asleep. And Jack, for that night at least, was allowed to curl up by the covered coals, or stretch out his tired feet, if he pleased, to a warmth that in all the nights of his life, perhaps, he had never known before.

III

A "BLAB SCHOOL" ON KINGDOM COME

CHAD was awakened by the touch of a cold nose at his ear, the rasp of a warm tongue across his face, and the tug of two paws at his cover. "Git down, Jack!" he said, and Jack, with a whimper of satisfaction, went back to the fire that was roaring up the chimney, and a deep voice laughed and called:

"I reckon you better git *up*, little man!"

Old Joel was seated at the fire with his huge legs crossed and a pipe in his mouth. It was before dawn, but the household was busily astir. There was the sound of tramping in the frosty air outside and the noise of getting breakfast ready in the kitchen. As Chad sprang up, he saw Melissa's yellow hair drop out of sight behind the foot of the bed in the next corner, and he turned his face quickly, and, slipping behind the foot of his own bed and into his coat and trousers, was soon at the fire himself, with old Joel looking him over with shrewd kindliness.

"Yo' dawg's got a heap o' sense," said the old hunter, and Chad told him how old Jack was, and how a cattle-buyer from the "settlements" of the Bluegrass had given him to Chad when Jack was badly hurt and his owner thought he was going to die, and how Chad had nursed him, and how the two had always been together ever since. Through the door of the kitchen, Chad could see the old mother with her crane and pots and cooking-pans; outside, he could hear the moo of the old brindle, the bleat of her calf, the nicker of a horse, one lusty sheep-call, and the hungry bellow of young cattle at the barn, where Tall Tom was feeding the stock. Presently Rube stamped in with a back log and Dolph came through with a milk-pail.

"I can milk," said Chad, eagerly, and Dolph laughed.

"All right, I'll give ye a chance," he said, and old Joel looked pleased, for it was plain that the little stranger was not going to be a drone in the household, and, taking his pipe from his mouth but without turning his head, he called out:

"Git up thar, Melissy."

Getting no answer, he looked around to find Melissa standing at the foot of the bed.

"Come here to the fire, little gal, nobody's a-goin' to eat ye."

Melissa came forward, twisting her hands in front of her, and stood, rubbing one bare foot over the other, on the hearth-stones. She turned her face with a blush when Chad suddenly looked at her, and, thereafter, the little man gazed steadily into the fire in order to embarrass her no more.

With the breaking of light over the mountain, breakfast was over and the work of the day began. Tom was off to help a neighbor "snake" logs down the mountain and into Kingdom Come, where they would be "rafted" and floated on down the river to the capital—if a summer tide should come—to be turned into fine houses for the people of the Bluegrass. Dolph and Rube disappeared at old Joel's order to "go meet them sheep." Melissa helped her mother clear away the table and wash the dishes; and Chad, out of the tail of his eye, saw her surreptitiously feeding greedy Jack, while old Joel still sat by the fire, smoking silently. Chad stepped outside. The air was chill, but the mists were rising and a long band of rich, warm light lay over a sloping spur up the river, and where this met the blue morning shadows, the dew was beginning to drip and to sparkle. Chad could not stand inaction long, and his eye lighted up when he heard a great bleating at the foot of the spur and the shouts of men and boys. Just then the old mother called from the rear of the cabin:

"Joel, them sheep air comin'!"

The big form of the old hunter filled the doorway and Jack bounded out between his legs, while little Melissa appeared with two books, ready for school. Down the road came the flock of lean mountain-sheep, Dolph and Rube driving them. Behind, slouched the Dillon tribe—Daws and Whizzer and little Tad; Daws's father, old Tad, long, lean, stooping, crafty; and two new ones—cousins to Daws—Jake and Jerry, the giant twins.

"Joel Turner," said old Tad, sourly, "here's yo' sheep!"

Joel had bought the Dillons' sheep and meant to drive them to the county-seat ten miles down the river. There had evidently been a disagreement between the two when the trade was made, for Joel pulled out a gray pouch of coonskin, took from it a roll of bills, and, without counting them, held them out.

"Tad Dillon," he said, shortly, "here's yo' money!"

The Dillon father gave possession with a gesture and the Dillon faction, including Whizzer and the giant twins, drew aside together—the father morose; Daws watching Dolph and Rube with a look of much meanness; little Tad behind him, watching Chad, his face screwed up with hate; and Whizzer, pretending not to see Jack, but darting a surreptitious glance at him now and then, for then and there was starting a feud that was to run fiercely on, long after the war was done.

"Git my hoss, Rube," said old Joel, and Rube turned to the stable, while Dolph kept an eye on the sheep, which were lying on the road or straggling down the river. As Rube opened the stable-door, a dirty white object bounded out, and Rube, with a loud curse, tumbled over backward into the mud, while a fierce old ram dashed with a triumphant bleat for the open gate. Beelzebub, as the Turner mother had christened the mischievous brute, had been placed in the wrong stall and Beelzebub was making for freedom. He gave another triumphant baa as he swept between Dolph's legs and through the gate, and, with an answering chorus, the silly sheep sprang to their feet and followed. A sheep hates water, but not more than he loves a leader, and Beelzebub feared nothing. Straight for the water of the low ford the old conqueror made and, in the wake of his masterful summons, the flock swept, like a Mormon household, after him. Then was there a commotion indeed. Old Joel shouted and swore; Dolph shouted and swore, and Rube shouted and swore. Old Dillon smiled grimly, Daws and little Tad shouted with derisive laughter, and the big twins grinned. The mother came to the door, broom in hand, and, with a frowning face, watched the sheep splash through the water and into the woods across the river. Little Melissa looked frightened. Whizzer, losing his head, had run down after the sheep, barking and hastening their flight, until called back with a mighty curse from old Joel, while Jack sat on his haunches looking at Chad and waiting for orders.

"Goddlemighty!" said Joel, "how air we goin' to git them sheep back?" Up and up rose the bleating and baaing, for Beelzebub, like the prince of devils that he was, seemed bent on making all the mischief possible.

"How *air* we goin' to git 'em back?"

Chad nodded then, and Jack with an eager yelp made for the river—Whizzer at his heels. Again old Joel yelled furiously, as did Dolph and Rube, and Whizzer stopped and turned back with a drooping tail, but Jack plunged in. He knew but one voice behind him and Chad's was not in the chorus.

"Call yo' dawg back, boy," said Joel, sternly, and Chad opened his lips with anything but a call for Jack to come back —it was instead a fine high yell of encouragement and old Joel was speechless.

"That dawg'll kill them sheep," said Daws Dillon aloud.

Joel's face was red and his eyes rolled.

"Call that damned feist back, I tell ye," he shouted at last. "Hyeh, Rube, git my gun, git my gun!"

Rube started for the house, but Chad laughed. Jack had reached the other bank now, and was flashing like a ball of gray light through the weeds and up into the woods; and Chad slipped down the bank and into the river, hieing him on excitedly.

Joel was beside himself and he, too, lumbered down to the river, followed by Dolph, while the Dillons roared from the road.

"Boy!" he roared. "Eh, boy, eh! what's his name, Dolph? Call him back, Dolph, call the little devil back. If I don't wear him out with a hickory; holler fer 'em, damn 'em! Heh-o-oo-ee!" The old hunter's bellow rang through the woods like a dinner-horn. Dolph was shouting, too, but Jack and Chad seemed to have gone stone-deaf; and Rube, who had run down with the gun, started with an oath into the river himself, but Joel halted him.

"Hol' on, hol' on!" he said, listening. "By the eternal, he's a-roundin' 'em up!" The sheep were evidently much scattered, to judge from the bleating; but here, there, and everywhere, they could hear Jack's bark, while Chad seemed to have stopped in the woods and, from one place, was shouting orders to his dog. Plainly, Jack was no sheep-killer and by and by Dolph and Rube left off shouting, and old Joel's face became placid; and all of them from swearing helplessly fell to waiting quietly. Soon the bleating became less and less, and began to concentrate on the mountain-side. Not far below, they could hear Chad:

"Coo-oo-sheep! Coo-oo-sh'p-cooshy-cooshy-coo-oo-sheep!"

The sheep were answering. They were coming down a ravine, and Chad's voice rang out above:

"Somebody come across, an' stand on each side o' the holler."

Dolph and Rube waded across then, and soon the sheep came crowding down the narrow ravine with Jack barking behind them and Chad shooing them down. But for Dolph and Rube, Beelzebub would have led them up or down the river, and it was hard work to get him into the water until Jack, who seemed to know what the matter was, sharply nipped several sheep near him. These sprang violently forward, the whole flock in front pushed forward, too, and Beelzebub was thrust from the bank. Nothing else being possible, the old ram settled himself with a snort into the water and made for the other shore. Chad and Jack followed and, when they reached the road, Beelzebub was again a prisoner; the sheep, swollen like sponges, were straggling down the river, and Dillons and Turners were standing around in silence. Jack shook himself and dropped panting in the dust at his master's feet, without so much as an upward glance or a lift of his head for a pat of praise. As old Joel raised one foot heavily to his stirrup, he grunted, quietly:

"Well, I be damned." And when he was comfortably in his saddle he said again, with unction:

"I *do* be damned. I'll just take that dawg to help drive them sheep down to town. Come on, boy."

Chad started joyfully, but the old mother called from the door: "Who's a-goin' to take this gal to school, I'd like to know?"

Old Joel pulled in his horse, straightened one leg, and looked all around—first at the Dillons, who had started away, then at Dolph and Rube, who were moving determinedly after the sheep (it was Court Day in town and they could not miss Court Day), and then at Chad, who halted.

"Boy," he said, "don't you want to go to school—you ought to go to school?"

"Yes," said Chad, obediently, though the trip to town— and Chad had never been to a town—was a sore temptation.

"Go on, then, an' tell the teacher I sent ye. Here, Mammy —eh, what's yo' name, boy? Oh, Mammy—Chad, here, 'll take her. Take good keer o' that gal, boy, an' learn yo' a-b-abs like a man now."

Melissa came shyly forward from the door and Joel whistled to Jack and called him, but Jack, though he liked nothing better than to drive sheep, lay still, looking at Chad.

"Go 'long, Jack," said Chad, and Jack sprang up and was off, though he stopped again and looked back, and Chad had to tell him again to go on. In a moment dog, men, and sheep were moving in a cloud of dust around a bend in the road and little Melissa was at the gate.

"Take good keer of 'Lissy," said the mother from the porch, kindly; and Chad, curiously touched all at once by the trust shown him, stalked ahead like a little savage, while Melissa with her basket followed silently behind. The boy never thought of taking the basket himself—that is not the way of men with women in the hills—and not once did he look around or speak on the way up the river and past the blacksmith's shop and the grist-mill just beyond the mouth of Kingdom Come; but when they arrived at the log school-house it was his turn to be shy and he hung back to let Melissa go in first. Within, there was no floor but the bare earth, no window but the cracks between the logs, and no desks but the flat sides of slabs, held up by wobbling pegs. On one side were girls in linsey and homespun —some thin, undersized, underfed, and with weak, dispirited eyes and yellow tousled hair; others, round-faced, round-eyed, dark, and sturdy; most of them large-waisted and round-shouldered—especially the older ones—from work in the fields; but, now and then, one like Melissa, the daughter of a valley-farmer, erect, agile, spirited, intelligent. On the other side were the boys, in physical characteristics the same and suggesting the same social divisions: at the top the farmer—now and then a slave-holder and perhaps of gentle blood—who had dropped by the way on the westward march of civilization and had cleared some rich river-bottom and a neighboring summit of the mountains, where he sent his sheep and cattle to graze; where a creek opened into this valley some free-settler, whose grandfather had fought at King's Mountain—usually of Scotch-Irish descent, often English, but sometimes German or sometimes even Huguenot—would have his rude home of logs; under him, and in wretched cabins at the head of the creek or on the washed spur of the mountain above, or in some "deadenin'" still higher up and swept by mists and low-trailing clouds, the poor white trash—worthless descendants of the servile and sometimes criminal class who might have traced their origin back to the slums of London—hand-to-mouth tenants of the valley-aristocrat, hewers of wood for him in the lowlands and upland guardians of his cattle and sheep. And finally, walking up and down the earth floor—stern and smooth of face and of a preternatural dignity hardly to be found elsewhere—the mountain school-master.

It was a "blab school," as the mountaineers characterize a school in which the pupils study aloud, and the droning chorus —as shrill as locust cries—ceased suddenly when Chad came in, and every eye was turned on him with a sexless gaze of curiosity that made his face redden and his heart throb. But he forgot them when the school-master pierced him with eyes that seemed to shoot from under his heavy brows like a strong light from deep darkness. Chad met them, nor did his chin droop, and Caleb Hazel saw that the boy's face was frank and honest, and that his eye was fearless and kind, and, without question, he motioned to a seat—with one wave of his hand setting Chad on the corner of a slab and the studious drone to vibrating again. When the boy ventured to glance around, he saw Daws Dillon in one corner, making a face at him, and little Tad scowling from behind a book: and on the other side, among the girls, he saw another hostile face—next little Melissa—which had the pointed chin and the narrow eyes of the "Dillon breed," as old Joel called the family, whose farm was at the mouth of

Kingdom Come and whose boundary touched his own. When the first morning recess came—"little recess," as it was called —the master kept Chad in and asked him his name; if he had ever been to school, and whether he knew his A B C's; and he showed no surprise when Chad, without shame, told him no. So the master got Melissa's spelling-book and pointed out the first seven letters of the alphabet, and made Chad repeat them three times—watching the boy's earnest, wrinkling brow closely and with growing interest. When school "took up" again, Chad was told to say them aloud in concert with the others—which he did, until he could repeat them without looking at his book, and the master saw him thus saying them while his eyes roved around the room, and he nodded to himself with satisfaction— for he was accustomed to visible communion with himself, in school and out. At noon—"big recess"—Melissa gave Chad some corn-bread and bacon, and the boys gathered around him, while the girls looked at him curiously, merely because he was a stranger, and some of them—especially the Dillon girl—whispered, and Chad blushed and was uncomfortable, for once the Dillon girl laughed unkindly. The boys had no games, but they jumped and threw "rocks" with great accuracy at a little birch-tree, and Daws and Tad always spat on their stones and pointed with the forefinger of the left hand first at what they were going to throw at, while Chad sat to one side and took no part, though he longed to show them what he could do. By and by they fell to wrestling, and finally Tad bantered him for a trial. Chad hesitated, and his late enemy misunderstood.

"I'll give ye both underholts agin," he said, loftily, "you're afeerd!"

This was too much, and Chad sprang to his feet and grappled, disdaining the proffered advantage, and got hurled to the ground, his head striking the earth violently, and making him so dizzy that the brave smile with which he took his fall looked rather sickly and pathetic.

"Yes, an' Whizzer can whoop yo' dawg, too," said Tad, and Chad saw that he was going to have trouble with those Dillons, for Daws winked at the other boys, and the Dillon girl laughed again scornfully—at which Chad saw Melissa's eyes flash and her hands clinch as, quite unconsciously, she moved toward him to take his part; and all at once he was glad that he had nobody else to champion him.

"You wouldn' dare tech him if one of my brothers was here," she said, indignantly, "an' don't you dare tech him again, Tad Dillon. An' you—" she said, witheringly, "you—" she repeated and stopped helpless for the want of words, but her eyes spoke with the fierce authority of the Turner clan, and its dominant power for half a century, and Nancy Dillon shrank, though she turned and made a spiteful face, when Melissa walked toward the school-house alone.

That afternoon was the longest of Chad's life—it seemed as though it would never come to an end; for Chad had never sat so still for so long. His throat got dry repeating the dreary round of letters over and over and his head ached and he fidgeted in his chair while the slow hours passed and the sun went down behind the mountain and left the school-house in rapidly cooling shadow. His heart leaped when the last class was heard and the signal was given that meant freedom for the little prisoners; but Melissa sat pouting in her seat—she had missed her lesson and must be kept in for a while. So Chad, too, kept his seat and the master heard him say his letters, without the book, and nodded his head as though to say to himself that such quickness was exactly what he had looked for. By the time Chad had learned down to the letter O, Melissa was ready, for she was quick, too, and it was her anger that made her miss—and the two started home, Chad stalking ahead once more. To save him, he could not say a word of thanks, but how he wished that a bear or a wild-cat would spring into the road! He would fight it with teeth and naked hands to show her how he felt and to save her from harm.

The sunlight still lay warm and yellow far under the crest of Pine Mountain, and they had not gone far when Caleb Hazel overtook them and with long strides forged ahead. The schoolmaster "boarded around" and it was his week with the Turners, and Chad was glad, for he already loved the tall, gaunt, awkward man who asked him question after question so kindly —loved him as much as he revered and feared him—and the boy's artless, sturdy answers in turn pleased Caleb Hazel. And when Chad told who had given him Jack, the master began to talk about the far-away, curious country of which the cattle-dealer had told Chad so much: where the land was level and there were no mountains at all; where on one farm might be more sheep, cattle, and slaves than Chad had seen in all his life; where the people lived in big houses of stone and brick—what brick was Chad could not imagine—and rode along hard, white roads in shiny covered wagons, with two "niggers" on a high seat in front and one little "nigger" behind to open gates, and were proud and very high-heeled indeed; where there were towns that had more people than a whole county in the mountains, with rock roads running through them in every direction and narrow rock paths along these roads—like rows of hearthstones—for the people to walk on—the land of the bluegrass —the "settlemints of old Kaintuck."

And there were churches everywhere as tall as trees and school-houses a-plenty; and big schools, called colleges, to which the boys went when they were through with the little schools. The master had gone to one of these colleges for a year, and he was trying to make enough money to go again. And Chad must go some day, too; there was no reason why he shouldn't, since any boy could do anything he pleased if he only made up his mind and worked hard and never gave up. The master was an orphan, too, he said with a slow smile; he had been an orphan for a long while, and indeed the lonely struggle of his own boyhood was what was helping to draw him to Chad. This college, he said, was a huge brown house as big as a cliff that the master pointed out, that, gray and solemn, towered high above the river; and with a rock porch bigger than a great bowlder that hung just under the cliff, with twenty long, long stone steps to climb before one came to the big double front door.

"How do you git thar?" Chad asked so breathlessly that Melissa looked quickly up with a sudden foreboding that she might lose her little playfellow some day. The master had walked, and it took him a week. A good horse could make the trip in four days, and the river-men floated logs down the river to the capital in eight or ten days, according to the "tide." "When did they go? In the spring, when the 'tides' came. The Turners went down, didn't they, Melissa?" And Melissa said that her brother Tom had made one trip, and that Dolph and Rube were "might' nigh crazy" to go that coming spring; and, thereupon, a mighty resolution filled Chad's heart to the brim and steadied his eyes, but he did not open his lips then.

THE LITTLE SHEPHERD OF KINGDOM COME

Dusk was settling when the Turner cabin came in sight. None of the men-folks had come home yet, and the mother was worried; there was wood to cut and the cows to milk, and Chad's friend, old Betsey the brindle, had strayed off again; but she was glad to see Caleb Hazel, who, without a word, went out to the wood-pile, took off his coat, and swung the axe with mighty arms, while Chad carried in the wood and piled it in the kitchen; and then the two went after the old brindle together.

When they got back there was a great tumult at the cabin. Tom had brought some friends from over the mountain, and had told the neighbors as he came along that there was going to be a party at his house that night.

So there was a great bustle about the barn where Rube was getting the stock fed and the milking done; and around the kitchen, where Dolph was cutting more wood and piling it up at the door. Inside, the mother was hurrying up supper with Sintha, an older daughter, who had just come home from a visit, and Melissa helping her, while old Joel sat by the fire in the sleeping-room and smoked, with Jack lying on the hearth, or anywhere he pleased, for Jack, with his gentle ways, was winning the household one by one. He sprang up when he heard Chad's voice, and flew at him, jumping up and pawing him affectionately and licking his face while Chad hugged him and talked to him as though he were human and a brother; never before had the two been separated for a day. So, while the master helped Rube at the barn and Chad helped Dolph at the wood-pile, Jack hung about his master—tired and hungry as he was and much as he wanted to be by the fire or waiting in the kitchen for a sly bit from Melissa, whom he knew at once as the best of his new friends.

After supper, Dolph got out his banjo and played "Shady Grove," and "Blind Coon Dog," and "Sugar Hill," and "Gamblin' Man," while Chad's eyes glistened and his feet shuffled under his chair. And when Dolph put the rude thing down on the bed and went into the kitchen, Chad edged toward it and, while old Joel was bragging about Jack to the schoolmaster, he took hold of it with trembling fingers and touched the strings timidly. Then he looked around cautiously: nobody was paying any attention to him and he took it up into his lap and began to pick, ever so softly. Nobody saw him but Melissa, who slipped quietly to the back of the room and drew near him. Softly and swiftly Chad's fingers worked and Melissa could scarcely hear the sound of the banjo under her father's loud voice, but she could make out that he was playing a tune that still vibrates unceasingly from the Pennsylvania border to the pine-covered hills of Georgia—"Sourwood Mountain." Melissa held her breath while she listened—Dolph could not play like that—and by and by she slipped quietly to her father and pulled his sleeve and pointed to Chad. Old Joel stopped talking, but Chad never noticed; his head was bent over the neck of the banjo, his body was swaying rhythmically, his chubby fingers were going like lightning, and his eyes were closed—the boy was fairly lost to the world. The tune came out in the sudden silence, clean-cut and swinging:

Heh-o-dee-um-dee-eedle-dahdee-dee!

rang the strings and old Joel's eyes danced.

"Sing it, boy!" he roared, "sing it!" And Chad sprang from the bed, on fire with confusion and twisting his fingers helplessly. He looked almost frightened when Dolph ran back into the room and cried:

"Who was that a-pickin' that banjer?"

It was not often that Dolph showed such excitement, but he had good cause, and, when he saw Chad standing, shamefaced and bashful, in the middle of the floor, and Melissa joyously pointing her finger at him, he caught up the banjo from the bed and put it into the boy's hands. "Here, you just play that tune agin!"

Chad shrank back, half distressed and half happy, and only a hail outside from the first of the coming guests saved him from utter confusion. Once started, they came swiftly, and in half an hour all were there. Each got a hearty welcome from old Joel, who, with a wink and a laugh and a nod to the old mother, gave a hearty squeeze to some buxom girl, while the fire roared a heartier welcome still. Then was there a dance indeed—no soft swish of lace and muslin, but the active swing of linsey and simple homespun; no French fiddler's bows and scrapings, no intricate lancers, no languid waltz; but neat shuffling forward and back, with every note of the music beat; floor-thumping "cuttings of the pigeon's wing," and jolly jigs, two by two, and a great "swinging of corners," and "caging the bird," and "fust lady to the right *cheat* an' swing"; no flirting from behind fans and under stairways and little nooks, but honest, open courtship—strong arms about healthy waists, and a kiss taken now and then, with everybody to see and nobody to care who saw. If a chair was lacking, a pair of brawny knees made one chair serve for two, but never, if you please, for two men. Rude, rough, semi-barbarous, if you will, but simple, natural, honest, sane, earthy—and of the earth whence springs the oak and in time, maybe, the flower of civilization.

[42]

Softly and swiftly Chad's fingers worked.

A "BLAB SCHOOL" ON KINGDOM COME

At the first pause in the dance, old Joel called loudly for Chad. The boy tried to slip out of the door, but Dolph seized him and pulled him to a chair in the corner and put the banjo in his hands. Everybody looked on with curiosity at first, and for a little while Chad suffered; but when the dance turned attention from him, he forgot himself again and made the old thing hum with all the rousing tunes that had ever swept its string. When he stopped at last, to wipe the perspiration from his face, he noticed for the first time the school-master, who was yet divided between the church and the law, standing at the door—silent, grave, disapproving. And he was not alone in his condemnation; in many a cabin up and down the river, stern talk was going on against the ungodly "carryings on" under the Turner roof, and, far from accepting them as proofs of a better birth and broader social ideas, these Calvinists of the hills set the merry-makers down as the special prey of the devil, and the dance and the banjo as sly plots of the same to draw their souls to hell.

Chad felt the master's look, and he did not begin playing again, but put the banjo down by his chair and the dance came to an end. Once more Chad saw the master look, this time at Sintha, who was leaning against the wall with a sturdy youth in a fringed hunting-shirt bending over her—his elbow against a log directly over her shoulder. Sintha saw the look, too, and she answered with a little toss of her head, but when Caleb Hazel turned to go out the door, Chad saw that the girl's eyes followed him. A little later, Chad went out too, and found the master at the corner of the fence and looking at a low red star whose rich, peaceful light came through a gap in the hills. Chad shyly drew near him, hoping in some way to get a kindly word, but the master was so absorbed that he did not see or hear the boy and Chad, awed by the stern, solemn face, withdrew and, without a word to anybody, climbed into the loft and went to bed. He could hear every stroke on the floor below, every call of the prompter, and the rude laughter and banter, but he gave little heed to it all. For he lay thinking of Caleb Hazel and listening again to the stories he and the cattle-dealer had told him about the wonderful settlements. "God's Country," the dealer always called it, and such it must be, if what he and the master said was true. By and by the steady beat of feet under him, the swift notes of the banjo, the calls of the prompter and the laughter fused, became inarticulate, distant—ceased. And Chad, as he was wont to do, journeyed on to "God's Country" in his dreams.

IV

THE COMING OF THE TIDE

WHILE the corn grew, school went on and, like the corn, Chad's schooling put forth leaves and bore fruit rapidly. The boy's mind was as clear as his eye and, like a mountain-pool, gave back every image that passed before it. Not a word dropped from the master's lips that he failed to hear and couldn't repeat, and, in a month, he had put Dolph and Rube, who, big as they were, had little more than learned the alphabet, to open shame; and he won immunity with his fists from gibe and insult from every boy within his inches in school— including Tad Dillon, who came in time to know that it was good to let the boy alone. He worked like a little slave about the house, and, like Jack, won his way into the hearts of old Joel and his wife, and even of Dolph and Rube, in spite of their soreness over Chad's having spelled them both down before the whole school. As for Tall Tom, he took as much pride as the school-master in the boy, and in town, at the grist-mill, the cross-roads, or blacksmith shop, never failed to tell the story of the dog and the boy, whenever there was a soul to listen. And as for Melissa, while she ruled him like a queen and Chad paid sturdy and uncomplaining homage, she would have scratched out the eyes of one of her own brothers had he dared to lay a finger on the boy. For Chad had God's own gift—to win love from all but enemies and nothing but respect and fear from them. Every morning, soon after daybreak, he stalked ahead of the little girl to school, with Dolph and Rube lounging along behind, and, an hour before sunset, stalked back in the same way home again. When not at school, the two fished and played together—inseparable.

Corn was ripe now, and school closed and Chad went with the men into the fields and did his part, stripping the gray blades from the yellow stalks, binding them into sheaves, stowing them away under the low roof of the big barn, or stacking them tent-like in the fields—leaving each ear perched like a big roosting bird on each lone stalk. And when the autumn came, there were husking parties and dances and much merriment; and, night after night, Chad saw Sintha and the school-master in front of the fire—"settin' up"—close together with their arms about each other's necks and whispering. And there were quilting parties and house-warmings and house-raisings—one that was of great importance to Caleb Hazel and to Chad. For, one morning, Sintha disappeared and came back with the tall young hunter in the deerskin leggings—blushing furiously —a bride. At once old Joel gave them some cleared land at the head of a creek; the neighbors came in to build them a cabin, and among them all, none worked harder than the school-master; and no one but Chad guessed how sorely hit he was.

Meanwhile, the woods high and low were ringing with the mellow echoes of axes, and the thundering crash of big trees along the mountain-side; for already the hillsmen were felling trees while the sap was in the roots, so that they could lie all winter, dry better and float better in the spring, when the rafts were taken down the river to the little capital in the Blue-grass. And Caleb Hazel said that he would go down on a raft in the spring and perhaps Chad could go with him—who knew? For the school-master had now made up his mind finally—he would go out into the world and make his way out there; and nobody but Chad noticed that his decision came only after, and only a little while after, the house-raising at the head of the creek.

When winter came, school opened again, and on Saturdays and Sundays and cold snowy nights, Chad and the school-mas-ter—for he too lived at the Turners' now—sat before the fire in the kitchen, and the school-master read to him from "Ivan-hoe" and "The Talisman," which he had brought from the Bluegrass, and from the Bible which had been his own since he was a child. And the boy drank in the tales until he was drunk with them and learned the conscious scorn of a lie, the con-scious love of truth, and pride in courage, and the conscious reverence for women that make the essence of chivalry as dis-tinguished from the unthinking code of brave, simple people. He adopted the master's dignified phraseology as best he could; he watched him, as the master stood before the fire with his hands under his coat-tails, his chin raised, and his eyes dream-ily upward, and Tall Tom caught the boy in just this attitude one day and made fun of him before all the others. He tried some high-sounding phrases on Melissa, and Melissa told him he must be crazy. Once, even, he tried to kiss her hand gal-lantly and she slapped his face. Undaunted, he made a lance of white ash, threaded some loose yarn into Melissa's colors, as he told himself, sneaked into the barn, where Beelzebub was tied, got on the sheep's back and, as the old ram sprang for-ward, couched his lance at the trough and shattered it with a thrill that left him trembling for half an hour. It was too good to give up that secret joust and he made another lance and essayed another tournament, but this time Beelzebub butted the door open and sprang with a loud ba-a-a into the yard and charged for the gate—in full view of old Joel, the three brothers, and the school-master, who was standing in the road. Instinctively, Chad swung on in spite of the roar of laughter and astonishment that greeted him and, as Tom banged the gate, the ram swerved and Chad shot off sidewise as from a catapult and dropped, a most unheroic little knight, in the mire. That ended Chad's chivalry in the hills, for in the roars of laughter that greeted him, Chad recognized Caleb Hazel's as the loudest. If *he* laughed, chivalry could never thrive there, and Chad gave it up; but the seeds were sown.

The winter passed, and what a time Chad and Jack had, snaking logs out of the mountains with two, four, six—yes, even eight yoke of oxen, when the log was the heart of a monarch oak or poplar—snaking them to the chute; watching them roll and whirl and leap like jack-straws from end to end down the steep incline and, with one last shoot in the air, roll, shaking, quivering, into a mighty heap on the bank of Kingdom Come. And then the "rafting" of those logs—dragging them into the pool of the creek, lashing them together with saplings driven to the logs with wooden pins in auger-holes—wading about, meanwhile, waist deep in the cold water: and the final lashing of the raft to a near-by tree with a grape-vine cable—to await the coming of a "tide."

Would that tide never come? It seemed not. The spring ploughing was over, the corn planted; there had been rain after rain, but gentle rains only. There had been prayers for rain:

"O Lord," said the circuit-rider, "we do not presume to dictate to Thee, but we need rain, an' need it mighty bad. We do not presume to dictate, but, if it pleases Thee, send us, not a gentle sizzle-sozzle, but a sod-soaker, O Lord, a gully-washer. Give us a tide, O Lord!" Sunrise and sunset, old Joel turned his eye to the east and the west and shook his head. Tall Tom did the same, and Dolph and Rube studied the heavens for a sign. The school-master grew visibly impatient and Chad was in a fever of restless expectancy. The old mother had made him a suit of clothes—mountain-clothes—for the trip. Old Joel gave him a five-dollar bill for his winter's work. Even Jack seemed to know that something unusual was on hand, and hung closer about the house, for fear he might be left behind.

Softly at last, one night, came the patter of little feet on the roof and passed—came again and paused; and then there was a rush and a steady roar that wakened Chad and thrilled him as he lay listening. It did not last long, but the river was muddy enough and high enough for the Turner brothers to float the raft slowly out from the mouth of Kingdom Come and down in front of the house, where it was anchored to a huge sycamore in plain sight. At noon the clouds gathered and old Joel gave up his trip to town.

"Hit'll begin in about an hour, boys," he said, and in an hour it did begin. There was to be no doubt about this flood. At dusk, the river had risen two feet and the raft was pulling at its cable like an awakening sea-monster. Meanwhile, the mother had cooked a great pone of corn-bread, three feet in diameter, and had ground coffee and got sides of bacon ready. All night it poured and the dawn came clear, only to darken into gray again. But the river—the river! The roar of it filled the woods. The frothing hem of it swished through the tops of the trees and through the underbrush, high on the mountain-side. Arched slightly in the middle, for the river was still rising, it leaped and surged, tossing tawny mane and fleck and foam as it thundered along—a mad, molten mass of yellow struck into gold by the light of the sun. And there the raft, no longer the awkward monster it was the day before, floated like a lily-pad, straining at the cable as lightly as a greyhound leaping against its leash.

The neighbors were gathered to watch the departure—old Jerry Budd, blacksmith and "yarb doctor," and his folks; the Cultons and Middletons, and even the Dillons—little Tad and Whizzer—and all. And a bright picture of Arcadia the simple folk made, the men in homespun and the women with their brilliant shawls, as they stood on the bank laughing, calling to one another, and jesting like children. All were aboard now and there was no kissing nor shaking hands in the farewell. The good old mother stood on the bank, with Melissa holding to her apron and looking at Chad gravely.

"Take good keer o' yo'self, Chad," she said kindly, and then she looked down at the little girl. "He's a-comin' back, honey—Chad's a-comin' back." And Chad nodded brightly, but Melissa drew her apron across her mouth, dropped her eyes to the old rifle in the boy's lap, and did not smile.

All were aboard now—Dolph and Rube, old Squire Middleton, and the school-master, all except Tall Tom, who stood by the tree to unwind the cable.

"Hold on!" shouted the Squire.

A raft shot suddenly around the bend above them and swept past with the Dillon brothers, Jake and Jerry, nephews of old Tad Dillon, at bow and stern—passed with a sullen wave from Jerry and a good-natured smile from stupid Jake.

"All right," Tom shouted, and he unwound the great brown pliant vine from the sycamore and leaped aboard. Just then there was a mad howl behind the house and a gray streak of light flashed over the bank and Jack, with a wisp of rope around his neck, sprang through the air from a rock ten feet high and landed lightly on the last log as the raft shot forward. Chad gulped once and his heart leaped with joy, for he had agreed to leave Jack with old Joel, and old Joel had tied the dog in the barn.

"Hi there!" shouted the old hunter. "Throw that dawg off, Chad—throw him off."

But Chad shook his head and smiled.

"He won't go back," he shouted, and, indeed, there was Jack squatted on his haunches close by his little master and looking gravely back as though he were looking a last good-by.

"Hi!" shouted old Joel again. "How am I goin' to git along without that dawg? Throw him off, boy—throw him off, I tell ye!" Chad seized the dog by the shoulders, but Jack braced himself and, like a child, looked up in his master's face. Chad let go and shook his head.

A frantic yell from Tall Tom at the bow oar drew every eye to him. The current was stronger than anyone guessed and the raft was being swept by an eddy straight for the point of the opposite shore where there was a sharp turn in the river.

"Watch out thar," shouted old Joel, "you're goin' to 'bow'!" Dolph and Rube were slashing the stern oar forward and back through the swift water, but straight the huge craft made for that deadly point. Every man had hold of an oar and was tussling in silence for life. Every man on shore was yelling directions and warning, while the women shrank back with frightened faces. Chad scarcely knew what the matter was, but he gripped his rifle and squeezed Jack closer to him. He heard Tom roar a last warning as the craft struck, quivered a moment, and the stern swept around. The craft had "bowed."

"Watch out—jump, boys, jump! Watch when she humps! Watch yo' legs!" These were the cries from the shore, and still Chad did not understand. He saw Tom leap from the bow, and, as the stern swung to the other shore, Dolph, too, leaped. Then the stern struck. The raft humped in the middle like a bucking horse—the logs ground savagely together. Chad heard a cry of pain from Jack and saw the dog fly up in the air and drop in the water. He and his gun had gone up, too, but he came back on the raft with one leg in between two logs, and he drew it up in time to keep the limb from being smashed to a pulp as the logs crashed together again, but not quickly enough to save the foot from a painful squeeze. Then he saw Tom and Dolph leap back again, the raft whirled on and steadied in its course, and behind him he saw Jack swimming feebly for the shore—fighting the waves for his life, for the dog was hurt. Twice he turned his eyes despairingly toward Chad, and the boy would have leaped in the water to save him if Tom had not caught him by the arm.

"Tell him to git to shore," he said quickly, and Chad motioned, when Jack looked again, and the dog obediently made for land. Old Joel was calling tenderly:

"Come on, Jack; come on, ole feller!"

Chad watched with a thumping heart. Once Jack went under, but gave no sound. Again he disappeared, and when he came up he gave a cry for help, but when he heard Chad's answering cry he fought on stroke by stroke until Chad saw old

Joel reach out from the bushes and pull him in. And Chad could see that one of his hind legs hung limp. Then the raft swung around the curve out of sight.

Behind, the whole crowd rushed down to the water's edge. Jack tried to get away from old Joel and scramble after Chad on his broken leg, but old Joel held him, soothing him, and carried him back to the house, where the old "yarb doctor" put splints on the leg and bound it up tightly, just as though it had been the leg of a child. Melissa was crying and the old man put his hand on her head.

"He'll be all right, honey. That leg'll be as good as the other one in two or three weeks. It's all right, little gal."

Melissa stopped weeping with a sudden gulp. But when Jack was lying in the kitchen by the fire alone, she slipped in and put her arm around the dog's head, and, when Jack began to lick her face, she bent her own head down and sobbed.

V

OUT OF THE WILDERNESS

On the way to God's Country at last!

Already Chad had schooled himself for the parting with Jack, and but for this he must—little man that he was—have burst into tears. As it was, the lump in his throat stayed there a long while, but it passed in the excitement of that mad race down the river. The old Squire had never known such a tide.

"Boys," he said, gleefully, "we're goin' to make a *re*cord on this trip—you jus' see if we don't. That is, if we ever git thar alive."

All the time the old man stood in the middle of the raft yelling orders. Ahead was the Dillon raft, and the twin brothers—the giants, one mild, the other sour-faced—were gesticulating angrily at each other from bow and stern. As usual, they were quarrelling. On the Turner raft, Dolph was at the bow, the school-master at the stern, while Rube—who was cook —and Chad, in spite of a stinging pain in one foot, built an oven of stones, where coffee could be boiled and bacon broiled, and started a fire, for the air was chill on the river, especially when they were running between the hills and no sun could strike them.

When the fire blazed up, Chad sat by it watching Tall Tom and the school-master at the stern oar and Rube at the bow. When the turn was sharp, how they lashed the huge white blades through the yellow water—with the handle across their broad chests, catching with their toes in the little notches that had been chipped along the logs, and tossing the oars down and up with a mighty swing that made the blades quiver and bend like the tops of pliant saplings! Then, on a run, they would rush back to start the stroke again, while the old Squire yelled:

"Hit her up thar now—easy—easy! *Now!* Hit her up! Hit her up—*Now!*"

Now they passed between upright, wooded, gray mountainsides, threaded with faint lines of the coming green; now between gray walls of rock streaked white with water-falls, and now past narrow little valleys which were just beginning to sprout with corn. At the mouth of the creeks they saw other rafts making ready and, now and then, a raft would shoot out in the river from some creek ahead or behind them. In an hour, they struck a smooth run of several hundred yards where the men at the oars could sit still and rest, while the raft shot lightly forward in the middle of the stream; and down the river they could see the big Dillons making the next sharp turn and, even that far away, they could hear Jerry yelling and swearing at his patient brother.

"Some o' these days," said the old Squire, "that fool Jake's a-goin' to pick up somethin' an' knock that mean Jerry's head off. I wonder he hain't done it afore. Hit's funny how brothers can hate when they do git to hatin'."

That night, they tied up at Jackson—to be famous long after the war as the seat of a bitter mountain-feud. At noon, the next day, they struck "the Nahrrers" (Narrows), where the river ran like a torrent between high steep walls of rock, and where the men stood to the oars watchfully and the old Squire stood upright, watching every movement of the raft;

for "bowing" there would have meant destruction to the raft and the death of them all. That night they were in Beattyville, whence they floated next day, along lower hills and, now and then, past a broad valley. Once Chad looked at the schoolmaster—he wondered if they were approaching the Bluegrass —but Caleb Hazel smiled and shook his head. And had Chad waited another half hour, he would not have asked the question, even with his eyes, for they swept between high cliffs again—higher than he had yet seen.

That night they ran from dark to dawn, for the river was broader and a brilliant moon was high; and, all night, Chad could hear the swish of the oars, as they floated in mysterious silence past the trees and the hills and the moonlit cliffs, and he lay on his back, looking up at the moon and the stars, and thinking about the land to which he was going, and of Jack back in the land he had left; and of little Melissa. She had behaved very strangely during the last few days before the boy had left. She had not been sharp with him, even in play. She had been very quiet—indeed, she scarcely spoke a word to him, but she did little things for him that she had never done before, and she was unusually kind to Jack. Once, Chad found her crying behind the barn, and then she was very sharp with him, and told him to go away, and cried more than ever. Her little face looked very white, as she stood on the bank, and, somehow, Chad saw it all that night in the river and among the trees and up among the stars, but he little knew what it all meant to him or to her. He thought of the Turners back at home, and he could see them sitting around the big fire—Joel with his pipe, the old mother spinning flax, Jack asleep on the hearth, and Melissa's big solemn eyes shining from the dark corner where she lay wide-awake in bed and, when he went to sleep, her eyes followed him in his dreams.

When he awoke, the day was just glimmering over the hills, and the chill air made him shiver, as he built up the fire and began to get breakfast ready. At noon, that day, though the cliffs were still high, the raft swung out into a broader current, where the water ran smoothly and, once, the hills parted and, looking past a log-cabin on the bank of the river, Chad saw a stone house—relic of pioneer days—and, farther out, through a gap in the hills, a huge house with great pillars around it and, on the hill-side, many sheep and fat cattle, and a great barn. There dwelt one of the lords of the Bluegrass land, and again Chad looked to the school-master and, this time, the school-master smiled and nodded as though to say:

"We're getting close now, Chad." So Chad rose to his feet thrilled, and watched the scene until the hills shut it off again. One more night and one more dawn, and, before the sun rose, the hills had grown smaller and smaller and the glimpses between them more frequent and, at last, far down the river, Chad saw a column of smoke and all the men on the raft took off their hats and shouted. The end of the trip was near, for that black column meant the capital!

Chad trembled on his feet and his heart rose into his throat, while Caleb Hazel seemed hardly less moved. His hat was off and he stood motionless, with his face uplifted, and his grave eyes fastened on that dark column as though it rose from the pillar of fire that was leading him to some promised land.

As they rounded the next curve, some monster swept out of the low hills on the right, with a shriek that startled the boy almost into terror and, with a mighty puffing and rumbling, shot out of sight again. The school-master shouted to Chad, and the Turner brothers grinned at him delightedly:

"Steam-cars!" they cried, and Chad nodded back gravely, trying to hold in his wonder.

Sweeping around the next curve, another monster hove in sight with the same puffing and a long "h-o-o-ot!" A monster on the river and moving up stream steadily, with no oar and no man in sight, and the Turners and the school-master shouted again. Chad's eyes grew big with wonder as he ran forward to see the rickety little steamboat approach and, with wide eyes, devoured it, as it wheezed and labored up-stream past them— watched the thundering stern-wheel threshing the water into a wake of foam far behind it and flashing its blades, water-dripping in the sun—watched it till it puffed and wheezed and labored on out of sight. Great Heavens! to think that he— Chad—was seeing all that!

About the next bend, more but thinner columns of smoke were visible. Soon the very hills over the capital could be seen, with little green wheat-fields dotting them and, as the raft drew a little closer, Chad could see houses on the hills—more strange houses of wood and stone, and porches, and queer towers on them from which glistened shining points.

"What's them?" he asked.

"Lightnin'-rods," said Tom, and Chad understood, for the school-master had told him about them back in the mountains. Was there anything that Caleb Hazel had not told him? The haze over the town was now visible, and soon they swept past tall chimneys puffing out smoke, great warehouses covered on the outside with weather-brown tin, and, straight ahead— Heavens, what a bridge!—arching clear over the river and covered like a house, from which people were looking down on them as they swept under. There were the houses, in two rows on the streets, jammed up against each other and without any yards. And people! Where had so many people come from? Close to the river and beyond the bridge was another great mansion, with tall pillars; about it was a green yard, as smooth as a floor, and negroes and children were standing on the out-skirting stone wall and looking down at them as they floated by. And another great house still, and a big garden with little paths running through it, and more patches of that strange green grass. Was that bluegrass? It was, but it didn't look blue and it didn't look like any other grass Chad had ever seen. Below this bridge was another bridge, but not so high, and, while Chad looked, another black monster on wheels went crashing over it.

Tom and the school-master were working the raft slowly to the shore now, and, a little farther down, Chad could see more rafts tied up—rafts, rafts, nothing but rafts on the river, everywhere! Up the bank a mighty buzzing was going on, amid a cloud of dust, and little cars with logs on them were shooting about amid the gleamings of many saws, and, now and then, a log would leap from the river and start up toward that dust-cloud with two glistening iron teeth sunk in one end and a long iron chain stretching up along a groove built of boards —and Heaven only knew what was pulling it up. On the bank was a stout, jolly-looking man, whose red, kind face looked fa-miliar to Chad, as he ran down shouting a welcome to the Squire. Then the raft slipped along another raft, Tom sprang aboard it with the grape-vine cable, and the school-master leaped aboard with another cable from the stern.

"Why, boy," cried the stout man. "Where's yo' dog?" Then Chad recognized him, for he was none other than the cattle-dealer who had given him Jack.

"I left him at home."

"Is he all right?"

"Yes—I reckon."

"Then I'd like to have him back again."

Chad smiled and shook his head.

"Not much."

"Well, he's the best sheep-dog on earth."

The raft slowed up, creaking—slower—straining and creaking, and stopped. The trip was over, and the Squire had made his "*re*cord," for the red-faced man whistled incredulously when the old man told him what day he had left Kingdom Come.

An hour later the big Dillon twins hove in sight, just as the Turner party was climbing the sawdust hill into the town, where Dolph and Rube were for taking the middle of the street like other mountaineers, who were marching thus ahead of them, single file, but Tom and the school-master laughed at them and drew them over to the sidewalk. Bricks and stones laid down for people to walk on—how wonderful! And all the houses were of brick or were weather-boarded—all built together, wall against wall. And the stores with the big glass windows all filled with wonderful things! Then a pair of swinging green shutters through which, while Chad and the school-master waited outside, Tom insisted on taking Dolph and Rube and giving them their first drink of Bluegrass whiskey—red liquor, as the hill-men call it. A little farther on, they all stopped still on a corner of the street, while the school-master pointed out to Chad and Dolph and Rube, the Capitol—a mighty structure of massive stone, with majestic stone columns, where people went to the Legislature. How they looked with wondering eyes at the great flag floating lazily over it, and at the wonderful fountain tossing water in the air, and with the water, three white balls which leaped and danced in the jet of shining spray and never flew away from it. How did they stay there? The school-master laughed—Chad had asked him a question at last that he couldn't answer. And the tall spiked iron fence that ran all the way around the yard, which was full of trees—how wonderful that was, too! As they stood looking, law-makers and visitors poured out through the doors —a brave array—some of them in tight trousers, high hats, and blue coats with brass buttons, and, as they passed, Caleb Hazel reverently whispered the names of those he knew—distinguished lawyers, statesmen, and Mexican veterans: witty Tom Marshall; Roger Hanson, bulky, brilliant; stately Preston; eagle-eyed Buckner; and Breckenridge, the magnificent, forensic in bearing. Chad was thrilled.

A little farther on, they turned to the left, and the school-master pointed out the Governor's mansion, and there, close by, was a high gray wall—a wall as high as a house, with a wooden box taller than a man on each corner, and, inside, another big gray building in which, visible above the walls were grated windows—the penitentiary! Every mountaineer has heard that word, and another—the "Legislatur'."

Chad shivered as he looked, for he could recall that sometimes down in the mountains a man would disappear for years and turn up again at home, whitened by confinement; and, during his absence, when anyone asked about him, the answer was —"penitentiary." He wondered what those boxes on the walls were for, and he was about to ask, when a guard stepped from one of them with a musket and started to patrol the wall, and he had no need to ask. Tom wanted to go up on the hill and look at the Armory and the graveyard, but the school-master said they did not have time, and, on the moment, the air was startled with whistles far and near—six o'clock! At once Caleb Hazel led the way to supper in the boarding-house, where a kind-faced old lady spoke to Chad in a motherly way, and where the boy saw his first hot biscuit and was almost afraid to eat anything at the table for fear he might do something wrong. For the first time in his life, too, he slept on a mattress without any feather-bed, and Chad lay wondering, but unsatisfied still. Not yet had he been out of sight of the hills, but the master had told him that they would see the Bluegrass next day, when they were to start back to the mountains by train as far as Lexington. And Chad went to sleep, dreaming his old dream still.

VI

LOST AT THE CAPITAL

It had been arranged by the school-master that they should all meet at the railway station to go home, next day at noon, and, as the Turner boys had to help the Squire with the logs at the river, and the school-master had to attend to some business of his own, Chad roamed all morning around the town. So engrossed was he with the people, and the sights and sounds of the little village, that he came to himself with a start and trotted back to the boarding-house for fear that he might not be able to find the station alone. The old lady was standing in the sunshine at the gate.

Chad panted—"Where's——?"

"They're gone."

"Gone!" echoed Chad, with a sinking heart.

"Yes, they've been gone—" But Chad did not wait to listen; he whirled into the hall-way, caught up his rifle, and, forgetting his injured foot, fled at full speed down the street. He turned the corner, but could not see the station, and he ran on about another corner and still another, and, just when he was about to burst into tears, he saw the low roof that he was looking for, and hot, panting, and tired, he rushed to it, hardly able to speak.

"Has that en*jine* gone?" he asked breathlessly. The man who was whirling trunks on their corners into the baggage-room did not answer. Chad's eyes flashed, and he caught the man by the coat-tail.

"Has that en*jine* gone?" he cried.

The man looked over his shoulder.

"Leggo my coat, you little devil. Yes, that en*jine's* gone," he added, mimicking. Then he saw the boy's unhappy face and he dropped the trunk and turned to him.

"What's the matter?" he asked, kindly.

Chad had turned away with a sob.

"They've lef' me—they've lef' me," he said, and then, controlling himself:

"Is thar another goin'?"

"Not till to-morrow mornin'."

Another sob came, and Chad turned away—he did not want anybody to see him cry. And this was no time for crying, for Chad's prayer back at the grave under the poplar flashed suddenly back to him.

"I got to ack like a man now." And, sobered at once, he walked on up the hill—thinking. He could not know that the school-master was back in the town, looking for him. If he waited until the next morning, the Turners would probably have gone on; whereas, if he started out now on foot, and walked all night, he might catch them before they left Lexington next morning. And if he missed the Squire and the Turner boys, he could certainly find the school-master there. And if not, he could go on to the mountains alone. Or he might stay in the "settle-mints"—what had he come for? He might—he would—oh, he'd get along somehow, he said to himself, wagging his head—he always had, and he always would. He could always go back to the mountains. If he only had Jack—if he only had Jack! Nothing would make any difference then, and he would never be lonely, if he only had Jack. But, cheered with his determination, he rubbed the tears from his eyes with his coat-sleeve and climbed the long hill. There was the Armory, which, years later, was to harbor Union troops in the great war, and beyond it was the little city of the dead that sits on top of the hill far above the shining river. At the great iron gates he stopped a moment, peering through. He saw a wilderness of white slabs and, not until he made his way across the thick green turf and spelled out the names carved on them, could he make out what they were for. How he wondered when he saw the innumerable green mounds, for he hardly knew there were as many people in the world living as he saw there must be in that place, dead. But he had no time to spare, and he turned quickly back to the pike—saddened—for his heart went back, as his faithful heart was always doing, to the lonely graves under the big poplar back in the mountains.

When he reached the top of the slope, he saw a rolling country of low hills stretching out before him, greening with spring; with far stretches of thick grass and many woodlands under a long, low sky, and he wondered if this was the Bluegrass. But he "reckoned" not—not yet. And yet he looked in wonder at the green slopes, and the woods, and the flashing creek, and nowhere in front of him—wonder of all—could he see a mountain. It was as Caleb Hazel had told him, only Chad was not looking for any such mysterious joy as thrilled his sensitive soul. There had been a light sprinkle of snow— such a fall as may come even in early April—but the noon sun had let the wheat-fields and the pastures blossom through it, and had swept it from the gray moist pike until now there were patches of white only in gully and along north hill-sides under little groups of pines and in the woods, where the sunlight

could not reach; and Chad trudged sturdily on in spite of his
heavy rifle and his lame foot, keenly alive to the new sights
and sounds and smells of the new world—on, until the shadows
lengthened and the air chilled again; on, until the sun began
to sink close to the far-away haze of the horizon. Never had
the horizon looked so far away. His foot began to hurt, and
on the top of a hill he had to stop and sit down for a while in
the road, the pain was so keen. The sun was setting now in a
glory of gold, rose, pink, and crimson. Over him, the still
clouds caught the divine light which swept swiftly through the
heavens until the little pink clouds over the east, too, turned
golden pink and the whole heavens were suffused with green
and gold. In the west, cloud was piled on cloud like vast cathe-
drals that must have been built for worship on the way straight
to the very throne of God. And Chad sat thrilled, as he had
been at the sunrise on the mountains the morning after he ran
away. There was no storm, but the same loneliness came to
him now, and he wondered what he should do. He could not get
much farther that night—his foot hurt too badly. He looked
up—the clouds had turned to ashes and the air was growing
chill—and he got to his feet and started on. At the bottom of
the hill and down a little creek he saw a light, and he turned
toward it. The house was small, and he could hear the crying
of a child inside and could see a tall man cutting wood, so he
stopped at the bars and shouted:

"Hello!"

The man stopped his axe in mid-air and turned. A woman,
with a baby in her arms, appeared in the light of the door with
children crowding about her.

"Hello!" answered the man.

"I want to git to stay all night." The man hesitated.

"We don't keep people all night."

"Not keep people all night," thought Chad with wonder.

"Oh, I reckon you will," he said. Was there anybody in the world who wouldn't take in a stranger for the night? From the doorway the woman saw that it was a boy who was asking shelter and the trust in his voice appealed vaguely to her.

"Come in!" she called, in a patient, whining tone. "You can stay, I reckon."

But Chad changed his mind suddenly. If they were in doubt about wanting him—he was in no doubt as to what he would do.

"No, I reckon I'd better git on," he said sturdily, and he turned and limped back up the hill to the road—still wondering, and he remembered that, in the mountains, when people wanted to stay all night, they usually stopped before sundown. Travelling after dark was suspicious in the mountains, and perhaps it was in this land, too. So, with this thought, he had half a mind to go back and explain, but he pushed on. Half a mile farther, his foot was so bad that he stopped with a cry of pain in the road and, seeing a barn close by, he climbed the fence and into the loft and burrowed himself under the hay. From under the shed he could see the stars rising. It was very still and very lonely, and he was hungry—hungrier and lonelier than he had ever been in his life, and a sob of helplessness rose to his lips—if he only had Jack—but he held it back.

"I got to ack like a man now." And, saying this over and over to himself, he went to sleep.

VII

A FRIEND ON THE ROAD

RAIN fell that night—gentle rain and warm, for the south wind rose at midnight. At four o'clock a shower made the shingles over Chad rattle sharply, but without wakening the lad, and then the rain ceased; and when Chad climbed stiffly from his loft—the world was drenched and still, and the dawn was warm, for spring had come that morning, and Chad trudged along the road—unchilled. Every now and then he had to stop to rest his foot. Now and then he would see people getting breakfast ready in the farm-houses that he passed, and, though his little belly was drawn with pain, he would not stop and ask for something to eat—for he did not want to risk another rebuff. The sun rose, and the light leaped from every wet blade of grass and bursting leaf to meet it—leaped as though flashing back gladness that the spring was come. For a little while Chad forgot his hunger and forgot his foot—like the leaf and grass-blade his stout heart answered with gladness, too, and he trudged on.

Meanwhile, far behind him, an old carriage rolled out of a big yard and started toward him and toward Lexington. In the driver's seat was an old gray-haired, gray-bearded negro with knotty hands and a kindly face; while, on the oval-shaped seat behind the lumbering old vehicle, sat a little darky with his bare legs dangling down. In the carriage sat a man who might have been a stout squire straight from merry England,

[68]

except that there was a little tilt to the brim of his slouch hat that one never sees except on the head of a Southerner, and in his strong, but easy, good-natured mouth was a pipe of corn-cob with a long cane stem. The horses that drew him were a handsome pair of half thorough-breds, and the old driver, with his eyes half closed, looked as though, even that early in the morning, he were dozing.

An hour later, the pike ran through an old wooden-covered bridge, to one side of which a road led down to the water, and the old negro turned the carriage to the creek to let his horses drink. The carriage stood still in the middle of the stream and presently the old driver turned his head:

"Mars Cal!" he called in a low voice. The Major raised his head. The old negro was pointing with his whip ahead and the Major saw something sitting on the stone fence, some twenty yards beyond, which stirred him sharply from his mood of contemplation.

"Shades of Dan'l Boone!" he said, softly. It was a minia-ture pioneer—the little still figure watching him solemnly and silently. Across the boy's lap lay a long rifle—the Major could see that it had a flintlock—and on his tangled hair was a coon-skin cap—the scalp above his steady dark eyes and the tail hanging down the lad's neck. And on his feet were—mocca-sins! The carriage moved out of the stream and the old driver got down to hook the check-reins over the shining bit of metal that curved back over the little saddles to which the boy's eyes had swiftly strayed. Then they came back to the Major.

"Howdye!" said Chad.

"Good-mornin', little man," said the Major pleasantly, and Chad knew straightway that he had found a friend. But there was silence. Chad scanned the horses and the strange vehicle, and the old driver and the little pickaninny who, hearing the boy's voice, had stood up on his seat and was grinning over one of the hind wheels, and then his eyes rested on the Major with a simple confidence and unconscious appeal that touched the Major at once.

"Are you goin' my way?" The Major's nature was too mellow and easy-going to pay any attention to final g's. Chad lifted his old gun and pointed up the road.

"I'm a-goin' thataway."

"Well, don't you want to ride?"

"Yes," he said, simply.

"Climb right in, my boy."

So Chad climbed in, and, holding the old rifle upright between his knees, he looked straight forward, in silence, while the Major studied him with a quiet smile.

"Where are you from, little man?"

"I come from the mountains."

"The mountains?" said the Major.

The Major had fished and hunted in the mountains, and somewhere in that unknown region he owned a kingdom of wild mountain-land, but he knew as little about the people as he knew about the Hottentots, and cared hardly more.

"What are you doin' up here?"

"I'm goin' home," said Chad.

"How did you happen to come away?"

"Oh, I been wantin' to see the settle*mints.*"

"The settle*mints,*" echoed the Major, and then he understood. He recalled having heard the mountaineers call the Bluegrass region the "settlemints" before.

"Where are you from, little man?"

"I come down on a raft with Dolph and Tom and Rube and the Squire and the school-teacher, an' I got lost in Frankfort. They've gone on, I reckon, an' I'm tryin' to ketch 'em."

"What will you do if you don't?"

"Foller 'em," said Chad, sturdily.

"Does your father live down in the mountains?"

"No," said Chad, shortly.

The Major looked at the lad gravely.

"Don't little boys down in the mountains ever say 'sir' to their elders?"

"No," said Chad. "No, sir," he added gravely, and the Major broke into a pleased laugh—the boy was quick as lightning.

"I ain't got no daddy. An' no mammy—I ain't got—nothin'." It was said quite simply, as though his purpose merely was not to sail under false colors, and the Major's answer was quick and apologetic:

"Oh!" he said, and for a moment there was silence again. Chad watched the woods, the fields, and the cattle, the strange grain growing about him, and the birds and the trees. Not a thing escaped his keen eye, and, now and then, he would ask a question which the Major would answer with some surprise and wonder. His artless ways pleased the old fellow.

"You haven't told me your name."

"You hain't axed me."

"Well, I axe you now," laughed the Major, but Chad saw nothing to laugh at.

"Chad," he said.

"Chad what?"

Now it had always been enough in the mountains, when

anybody asked his name, for him to answer simply—Chad. He hesitated now and his brow wrinkled as though he were thinking hard.

"I don't know," said Chad.

"What? Don't know your own name?" The boy looked up into the Major's face with eyes that were so frank and unashamed, and at the same time so vaguely troubled, that the Major was abashed.

"Of course not," he said kindly, as though it were the most natural thing in the world that a boy should not know his own name. Presently the Major said, reflectively:

"Chadwick."

"Chad," corrected the boy.

"Yes, I know"; and the Major went on thinking that Chadwick happened to be an ancestral name in his own family.

Chad's brow was still wrinkled—he was trying to think what old Nathan Cherry used to call him.

"I reckon I hain't thought o' my name since I left old Nathan," he said. Then he told briefly about the old man, and lifting his lame foot suddenly, he said: "Ouch!" The Major looked around and Chad explained:

"I hurt my foot comin' down the river an' hit got wuss walkin' so much." The Major noticed then that the boy's face was pale, and that there were dark hollows under his eyes, but it never occurred to him that the lad was hungry, for, in the Major's land, nobody ever went hungry for long. But Chad was suffering now, and he leaned back in his seat and neither talked nor looked at the passing fields. By and by, he spied a cross-roads store.

"I wonder if I can't git somethin' to eat in that store."

The Major laughed: "You ain't gettin' hungry so soon, are you? You must have eaten breakfast pretty early."

"I ain't had no breakfast—an' I didn't hev no supper last night."

"What?" shouted the Major.

Chad stated the fact with brave unconcern, but his lip quivered slightly—he was weak.

"Well, I reckon we'll get something to eat there, whether they've got anything or not."

And then Chad explained, telling the story of his walk from Frankfort. The Major was amazed that anybody could have denied the boy food and lodging.

"Who were they, Tom?" he asked.

The old driver turned:

"They wus some po' white trash down on Cane Creek, I reckon, suh. Must 'a' been." There was a slight contempt in the negro's words that made Chad think of hearing the Turners call the Dillons white trash—though they never said "po' white trash."

"Oh!" said the Major. So the carriage stopped, and when a man in a black slouch hat came out, the Major called:

"Jim, here's a boy who ain't had anything to eat for twenty-four hours. Get him a cup of coffee right away, and I reckon you've got some cold ham handy."

"Yes, indeed, Major," said Jim, and he yelled to a negro girl who was standing on the porch of his house behind the store.

Chad ate ravenously and the Major watched him with genuine pleasure. When the boy was through, he reached in his pocket and brought out his old five-dollar bill, and the Major laughed aloud and patted him on the head.

"You can't pay for anything while you are with me, Chad."

The whole earth wore a smile when they started out again. The swelling hills had stretched out into gentler slopes. The sun was warm, the clouds were still, and the air was almost drowsy. The Major's eyes closed and everything lapsed into silence. That was a wonderful ride for Chad. It was all true, just as the school-master had told him; the big, beautiful houses he saw now and then up avenues of blossoming locusts; the endless stone fences, the whitewashed barns, the woodlands and pastures; the meadow-larks flitting in the sunlight and singing everywhere; fluting, chattering blackbirds, and a strange new black bird with red wings, at which Chad wondered very much, as he watched it balancing itself against the wind and singing as it poised. Everything seemed to sing in that wonderful land. And the seas of bluegrass stretching away on every side, with the shadows of clouds passing in rapid succession over them, like mystic floating islands—and never a mountain in sight. What a strange country it was.

"Maybe some of your friends are looking for you in Frankfort," said the Major.

"No, sir, I reckon not," said Chad—for the man at the station had told him that the men who had asked about him were gone.

"All of them?" asked the Major.

Of course, the man at the station could not tell whether all of them had gone, and perhaps the school-master had stayed behind—it was Caleb Hazel if anybody.

"Well, now, I wonder," said Chad—"the school-teacher might 'a' stayed."

Again the two lapsed into silence—Chad thinking very

hard. He might yet catch the school-master in Lexington, and he grew very cheerful at the thought.

"You ain't told me yo' name," he said, presently. The Major's lips smiled under the brim of his hat.

"You hain't axed me."

"Well, I axe you now." Chad, too, was smiling.

"Cal," said the Major.

"Cal what?"

"I don't know."

"Oh, yes, you do, now—you foolin' me"—the boy lifted one finger at the Major.

"Buford—Calvin Buford."

"Buford—Buford—Buford," repeated the boy, each time with his forehead wrinkled as though he were trying to recall something.

"What is it, Chad?"

"Nothin'—nothin'."

And then he looked up with bewildered face at the Major, and broke into the quavering voice of an old man.

"Chad Buford, you little devil, come hyeh this minute or I'll beat the life outen you!"

"What—what!" said the Major excitedly. The boy's face was as honest as the sky above him. "Well, that's funny— very funny."

"Well, that's it," said Chad, "that's what ole Nathan used to call me. I reckon I hain't nuver thought o' my name agin tell you axed me." The Major looked at the lad keenly and then dropped back in his seat ruminating.

Away back in 1778 a linchpin had slipped in a wagon on the Wilderness Road and his grandfather's only brother, Chadwick Buford, had concluded to stop there for a while and hunt and come on later—thus ran an old letter that the Major had in his strong box at home—and that brother had never turned up again, and the supposition was that he had been killed by Indians. Now it would be strange if he had wandered up in the mountains and settled there, and if this boy were a descendant of his. It would be very, very strange, and then the Major almost laughed at the absurdity of the idea. The name Buford was all over the State. The boy had said, with amazing frankness and without a particle of shame, that he was a waif—a "woodscolt," he said, with paralyzing candor. And so the Major dropped the matter out of his mind, except in so far that it was a peculiar coincidence—again saying, half to himself:

"It certainly is very odd."

VIII

HOME WITH THE MAJOR

AHEAD of them, it was Court Day in Lexington. From
the town, as a centre, white turnpikes radiated in every direction like the strands of a spider's web. Along them, on the day
before, cattle, sheep, and hogs had made their slow way. Since
dawn, that morning, the fine dust had been rising under hoof
and wheel on every one of them, for Court Day is yet the great
day of every month throughout the Bluegrass. The crowd had
gone ahead of the Major and Chad. Only now and then would
a laggard buggy or carriage turn into the pike from a pasture-
road or locust-bordered avenue. Only men were occupants,
for the ladies rarely go to town on court days—and probably
none would go on that day. Trouble was expected. An abolitionist, one Brutus Dean—not from the North, but a Kentuckian, a slave-holder and a gentleman—would probably start a
paper in Lexington to exploit his views in the heart of the Bluegrass; and his quondam friends would shatter his press and
tear his office to pieces. So the Major told Chad, and he
pointed out some "hands" at work in a field.

"An', mark my words, some day there's goin' to be the
damnedest fight the world ever saw over these very niggers.
An' the day ain't so far away."

It was noon before they reached the big cemetery on the
edge of Lexington. Through a rift in the trees the Major
pointed out the grave of Henry Clay, and told him about the
big monument that was to be reared above his remains. The

grave of Henry Clay! Chad knew all about him. He had heard Caleb Hazel read the great man's speeches aloud by the hour—had heard him intoning them to himself as he walked the woods to and fro from school. Would wonders never cease? There seemed to be no end to the houses and streets and people in this big town, and Chad wondered why everybody turned to look at him and smiled, and, later in the day, he came near getting into a fight with another boy who seemed to be making fun of him to his companions. He wondered at that, too, until it suddenly struck him that he saw nobody else carrying a rifle and wearing a coonskin cap—perhaps it was his cap and his gun. The Major was amused and pleased, and he took a certain pride in the boy's calm indifference to the attention he was drawing to himself. And he enjoyed the little mystery which he and his queer little companion seemed to create as they drove through the streets.

On one corner was a great hemp factory. Through the windows Chad could see negroes, dusty as millers, bustling about, singing as they worked. Before the door were two men—one on horseback. The Major drew up a moment.

"How are you, John? Howdye, Dick?" Both men answered heartily, and both looked at Chad—who looked intently at them—the graceful, powerful man on foot, and the slender, wiry man with wonderful dark eyes on horseback.

"Pioneering, Major?" asked John Morgan.

"This is a namesake of mine from the mountains. He's come up to see the settlements."

Richard Hunt turned on his horse. "How do you like 'em?"

"Never seed nothin' like 'em in my life," said Chad, gravely.

Morgan laughed and Richard Hunt rode on with them down the street.

"Was that Captain Morgan?" asked Chad.

"Yes," said the Major. "Have you heard of him before?"

"Yes, sir. A feller on the road tol' me, if I was lookin' fer somethin' to do hyeh in Lexington to go to Captin Morgan."

The Major laughed: "That's what everybody does."

At once, the Major took the boy to an old inn and gave him a hearty meal; and while the Major attended to some business, Chad roamed the streets.

"Don't get into trouble, my boy," said the Major, "an' come back here an hour or two by sun."

Naturally, the lad drifted where the crowd was thickest—to Cheapside. Cheapside—at once the market-place and the forum of the Bluegrass from pioneer days to the present hour—the platform that knew Clay, Crittenden, Marshall, Breckenridge, as it knows the lesser men of to-day, who resemble those giants of old as the woodlands of the Bluegrass to-day resemble the primeval forests from which they sprang.

Cheapside was thronged that morning with cattle, sheep, hogs, horses, farmers, aristocrats, negroes, poor whites. The air was a babel of cries from auctioneers—head, shoulders, and waistband above the crowd—and the cries of animals that were changing owners that day—one of which might now and then be a human being. The Major was busy, and Chad wandered where he pleased—keeping a sharp lookout everywhere for the school-master, but though he asked right and left, he could find nobody, to his great wonder, who knew even the master's name. In the middle of the afternoon the country people began to leave town and Cheapside was cleared, but, as Chad walked past the old inn, he saw a crowd gathered within and about the wide doors of a livery-stable, and in a circle outside that lapped half the street. The auctioneer was in plain sight above the heads of the crowd, and the horses were led out one by one from the stable. It was evidently a sale of considerable moment, and there were horse-raisers, horse-trainers, jockeys, stable-boys, gentlemen—all eager spectators or bidders. Chad edged his way through the outer rim of the crowd and to the edge of the sidewalk, and, when a spectator stepped down from a dry-goods box from which he had been looking on, Chad stepped up and took his place. Straightway, he began to wish he could buy a horse and ride back to the mountains. What fun that would be, and how he would astonish the folks on Kingdom Come. He had his five dollars still in his pocket, and when the first horse was brought out, the auctioneer raised his hammer and shouted in loud tones:

"How much am I offered for this horse?"

There was no answer, and the silence lasted so long that before he knew it Chad called out in a voice that frightened him:

"Five dollars!" Nobody heard the bid, and nobody paid any attention to him.

"One hundred dollars," said a voice.

"One hundred and twenty-five," said another, and the horse was knocked down for two hundred dollars.

A black stallion with curving neck and red nostrils and two white feet walked proudly in.

"How much am I offered?"

"Five dollars," said Chad, promptly. A man who sat near heard the boy and turned to look at the little fellow, and was hardly able to believe his ears. And so it went on. Each time a horse was put up Chad shouted out:

"Five dollars," and the crowd around him began to smile and laugh and encourage him and wait for his bid. The auctioneer, too, saw him, and entered into the fun himself, addressing himself to Chad at every opening bid.

"Keep it up, little man," said a voice behind him. "You'll get one by and by." Chad looked around. Richard Hunt was smiling to him from his horse on the edge of the crowd.

The last horse was a brown mare—led in by a halter. She was old and a trifle lame, and Chad, still undispirited, called out this time louder than ever:

"Five dollars!"

He shouted out this time loudly enough to be heard by everybody, and a universal laugh rose; then came silence, and, in that silence, an imperious voice shouted back:

"Let him have her!" It was the owner of the horse who spoke—a tall man with a noble face and long iron-gray hair. The crowd caught his mood, and as nobody wanted the old mare very much, and the owner would be the sole loser, nobody bid against him, and Chad's heart thumped when the auctioneer raised his hammer and said:

"Five dollars, five dollars—what am I offered? Five dollars, five dollars, going at five dollars, five dollars—going at five dollars—going—going, last bid, gentlemen—gone!" The hammer came down with a blow that made Chad's heart jump, and brought a roar of laughter from the crowd.

"What is the name, please?" said the auctioneer, bending forward with great respect and dignity toward the diminutive purchaser.

"Chad."

The auctioneer put his hand to one ear:

"I beg your pardon—Dan'l Boone did you say?"

"No!" shouted Chad indignantly—he began to feel that fun was going on at his expense. "You heerd me—*Chad.*"

"Ah, Mr. Chad."

Not a soul knew the boy, but they liked his spirit, and several followed him when he went up and handed his five dollars, and took the halter of his new treasure—trembling so that he could scarcely stand. The owner of the horse placed his hand on the little fellow's head.

"Wait a minute," he said, and, turning to a negro boy: "Jim, go bring a bridle." The boy brought out a bridle, and the tall man slipped it on the old mare's head, and Chad led her away—the crowd watching him. Just outside he saw the Major, whose eyes opened wide:

"Where'd you get that old horse, Chad?"

"Bought her," said Chad.

"What? What'd you give for her?"

"Five dollars."

The Major looked pained, for he thought the boy was lying, but Richard Hunt called him aside and told the story of the purchase; and then how the Major did laugh—laughed until the tears rolled down his face.

And then and there he got out of his carriage and went into a saddler's shop and bought a brand-new saddle with a red blanket, and put it on the old mare and hoisted the boy to his seat. Chad was to have no little honor in his day, but he never knew a prouder moment than when he clutched the reins in his left hand and squeezed his short legs against the fat sides of that old brown mare.

[82]

HOME WITH THE MAJOR

He rode down the street and back again, and then the Major told him he had better put the black boy on the mare, to ride her home ahead of him, and Chad reluctantly got off and saw the little darky on his new saddle and his new horse.

"Take good keer o' that hoss, boy," he said, with a warning shake of his head, and again the Major roared.

First, the Major said, he would go by the old University and leave word with the faculty for the school-master when he should come there to matriculate; and so, at a turnstile that led into a mighty green yard, in the middle of which stood a huge gray mass of stone, the carriage stopped, and the Major got out and walked through the campus and up the great flight of stone steps, and disappeared. The mighty columns, the stone steps—where had Chad heard of them? And then the truth flashed. This was the college of which the school-master had told him down in the mountains, and, looking, Chad wanted to get closer.

"I wonder if it'll make any difference if I go up thar?" he said to the old driver.

"No," the old man hesitated—"no, suh, co'se not." And Chad climbed out and the old negro followed him with his eyes. He did not wholly approve of his master's picking up an unknown boy on the road. It was all right to let him ride, but to be taking him home—old Tom shook his head.

"Jess wait till Miss Lucy sees that piece o' white trash," he said, shaking his head. Chad was walking slowly with his eyes raised. It must be the college where the school-master had gone to school—for the building was as big as the cliff that he had pointed out down in the mountains, and the porch was as big as the black rock that he pointed out at the same time—the college where Caleb Hazel said Chad, too, must go some day. The Major was coming out when the boy reached the foot of the steps, and with him was a tall, gray man with spectacles and a white tie and very white hands, and the Major said:

"There he is now, Professor." And the Professor looked at Chad curiously, and smiled, and smiled again kindly, when he saw the boy's grave, unsmiling eyes fastened on him.

Then, out of the town and through the late radiant afternoon they went until the sun sank and the carriage stopped before a gate. While the pickaninny was opening it, another carriage went swiftly behind them, and the Major called out cheerily to the occupants—a quiet, sombre, dignified-looking man and two handsome boys and a little girl. "They're my neighbors, Chad," said the Major.

Not a sound did the wheels make on the thick turf as they drove toward the old-fashioned brick house (it had no pillars), with its windows shining through the firs and cedars that filled the yard. The Major put his hand on the boy's shoulder:

"Well, here we are, little man."

At the yard gate there was a great barking of dogs, and a great shout of welcome from the negroes who came forward to take the horses. To each of them the Major gave a little package, which each darky took with shining teeth and a laugh of delight—all looking with wonder at the curious little stranger with his rifle and coonskin cap, until a scowl from the Major checked the smile that started on each black face. Then the Major led Chad up a flight of steps and into a big hall and on into a big drawing-room, where there was a huge fireplace and a great fire that gave Chad a pang of homesickness at once. Chad was not accustomed to taking off his hat when he entered a house in the mountains, but he saw the Major take off his, and he dropped his own cap quickly. The Major sank into a chair.

"Here we are, little man," he said, kindly.

Chad sat down and looked at the books, and the portraits and prints, and the big mirrors and the carpets on the floor, none of which he had ever seen before, and he wondered at it all and what it all might mean. A few minutes later, a tall lady in black, with a curl down each side of her pale face, came in. Like old Tom, the driver, the Major, too, had been wondering what his sister, Miss Lucy, would think of his bringing so strange a waif home, and now, with sudden humor, he saw himself fortified.

"Sister," he said, solemnly, "here's a little kinsman of yours. He's a great-great-grandson of your great-great-uncle—Chadwick Buford. That's his name. What kin does that make us?"

"Hush, brother," said Miss Lucy, for she saw the boy reddening with embarrassment and she went across and shook hands with him, taking in with a glance his coarse strange clothes, and his soiled hands and face, and his tangled hair, but pleased at once with his shyness and his dark eyes. She was really never surprised at any caprice of her brother, and she did not show much interest when the Major went on to tell where he had found the lad—for she would have thought it quite possible that he might have taken the boy out of a circus. As for Chad, he was in awe of her at once—which the Major noticed with an inward chuckle, for the boy had shown no awe of him. Chad could hardly eat for shyness at supper and because everything was so strange and beautiful, and he scarcely opened his lips when they sat around the great fire, until Miss

Lucy was gone to bed. Then he told the Major all about himself and old Nathan and the Turners and the school-master, and how he hoped to come back to the Bluegrass, and go to that big college himself, and he amazed the Major when, glancing at the books, he spelled out the titles of two of Scott's novels, "The Talisman" and "Ivanhoe," and told how the school-master had read them to him. And the Major, who had a passion for Sir Walter, tested Chad's knowledge, and he could mention hardly a character or a scene in the two books that did not draw an excited response from the boy.

"Wouldn't you like to stay here in the Bluegrass now and go to school?"

Chad's eyes lighted up.

"I reckon I would; but how am I goin' to school, now, I'd like to know? I ain't got no money to buy books, and the school-teacher said you have to pay to go to school, up here."

"Well, we'll see about that," said the Major, and Chad wondered what he meant. Presently the Major got up and went to the sideboard and poured out a drink of whiskey and, raising it to his lips, stopped:

"Will you join me?" he asked, humorously, though it was hard for the Major to omit that formula even with a boy.

"I don't keer if I do," said Chad, gravely. The Major was astounded and amused, and thought that the boy was not in earnest, but he handed him the bottle and Chad poured out a drink that staggered his host, and drank it down without winking. At the fire, the Major pulled out his chewing-tobacco. This, too, he offered and Chad accepted, equalling the Major in the accuracy with which he reached the fireplace thereafter with the juice, carrying off his accomplishment, too, with per-

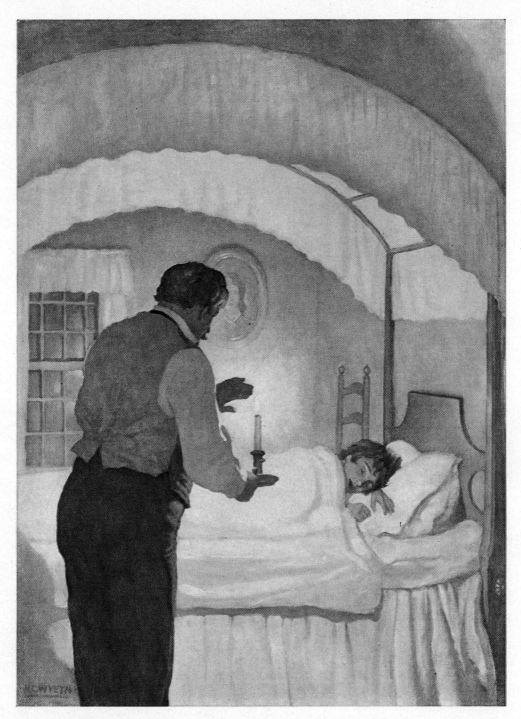

He looked at the boy a long time and fancied he could see some resemblance to the portrait.

fect and unconscious gravity. The Major was nigh to splitting with silent laughter for a few minutes, and then he grew grave.

"Does everybody drink and chew down in the mountains?"

"Yes, sir," said Chad. "Everybody makes his own licker where I come from."

"Don't you know it's very bad for little boys to drink and chew?"

"No, sir."

"Did nobody ever tell you it was very bad for little boys to drink and chew?"

"No, sir"—not once had Chad forgotten that "sir."

"Well, it is."

Chad thought for a minute. "Will it keep me from gittin' to be a *big* man?"

"Yes."

Chad quietly threw his quid into the fire.

"Well, I be damned," said the Major under his breath. "Are you goin' to quit?"

"Yes, sir."

Meanwhile, the old driver, whose wife lived on the next farm, was telling the servants over there about the queer little stranger whom his master had picked up on the road that day, and after Chad was gone to bed, the Major got out some old letters from a chest and read them over again. Chadwick Buford was his great-grandfather's twin brother, and not a word had been heard of him since the two had parted that morning on the old Wilderness Road, away back in the earliest pioneer days. So, the Major thought and thought—"suppose —suppose—" And at last he got up and with an uplifted candle, looked a long while at the portrait of his grandfather that hung on the southern wall. Then, with a sudden humor, he carried the light to the room where the boy was in sound sleep, with his head on one sturdy arm, his hair loose on the pillow, and his lips slightly parted and showing his white, even teeth; he looked at the boy a long time and fancied he could see some resemblance to the portrait in the set of the mouth, and the nose, and the brow, and he went back smiling at his fancies and thinking—for the Major was sensitive to the claim of any drop of the blood in his own veins—no matter how diluted. He was a handsome little chap.

"How strange! How strange!"

And he smiled when he thought of the boy's last question.

"Where's *yo'* mammy?"

It had stirred the Major.

"I am like you, Chad," he had said. "I've got no mammy— no nothin', except Miss Lucy, and she don't live here. I'm afraid she won't be on this earth long. Nobody lives here but me, Chad."

IX

MARGARET

THE Major was in town and Miss Lucy had gone to spend the day with a neighbor; so Chad was left alone.

"Look aroun', Chad, and see how you like things," said the Major. "Go anywhere you please."

And Chad looked around. He went to the barn to see his old mare and the Major's horses, and to the kennels, where the fox-hounds reared against the palings and sniffed at him curiously; he strolled about the quarters, where the little pickaninnies were playing, and out to the fields, where the servants were at work under the overseer, Jerome Conners, a tall, thin man with shrewd eyes, a sour, sullen face, and protruding upper teeth. One of the few smiles that ever came to that face came now when the overseer saw the little mountaineer. By and by Chad got one of the "hands" to let him take hold of the plough and go once around the field, and the boy handled the plough like a veteran, so that the others watched him, and the negro grinned, when he came back, and said:

"You sutinly can plough fer a fac'!"

He was lonesome by noon and had a lonely dinner, during which he could scarcely realize that it was really he—Chad—Chad sitting up at the table alone and being respectfully waited on by a kinky-headed little negro girl—called Thanky-ma'am because she was born on Thanksgiving day—and he wondered what the Turners would think if they could see him now—and the school-master. Where was the school-master? He began to

[89]

be sorry that he hadn't gone to town to try to find him. Perhaps the Major would see him—but how would the Major know the school-master? He was sorry he hadn't gone. After dinner he started out-doors again. Earth and sky were radiant with light. Great white tumbling clouds were piled high all around the horizon—and what a long length of sky it was in every direction! Down in the mountains, he had to look straight up, sometimes, to see the sky at all. Blackbirds chattered in the cedars as he went to the yard gate. The field outside was full of singing meadow-larks, and crows were cawing in the woods beyond. There had been a light shower, and on the dead top of a tall tree he saw a buzzard stretching his wings out to the sun. Past the edge of the woods ran a little stream with banks that were green to the very water's edge, and Chad followed it on through the woods, over a worm rail-fence, along a sprouting wheat-field, out into a pasture in which sheep and cattle were grazing, and on, past a little hill, where, on the next low slope, sat a great white house with big white pillars, and Chad climbed on top of the stone fence—and sat, looking. On the portico stood a tall man in a slouch hat and a lady in black. At the foot of the steps a boy—a head taller than Chad perhaps—was rigging up a fishing-pole. A negro boy was leading a black pony toward the porch, and, to his dying day, Chad never forgot the scene that followed. For, the next moment, a little figure in a long riding-skirt stood in the big doorway and then ran down the steps, while a laugh, as joyous as the water running at his feet, floated down the slope to his ears. He saw the negro stoop, the little girl bound lightly to her saddle; he saw her black curls shake in the sunlight, again the merry laugh tinkled in his ears, and then, with a white plume nodding from her black cap, she galloped off and disappeared among the trees; and Chad sat looking after her—thrilled, mysteriously thrilled—mysteriously saddened, straightway. Would he ever see her again?

The tall man and the lady in black went in-doors, the negro disappeared, and the boy at the foot of the steps kept on rigging his pole. Several times voices sounded under the high creek bank below him, but, quick as his ears were, Chad did not hear them. Suddenly there was a cry that startled him, and something flashed in the sun over the edge of the bank and flopped in the grass.

"Snowball!" an imperious young voice called below the bank, "get that fish!"

On the moment Chad was alert again—somebody was fishing down there—and he sprang from his perch and ran toward the fish just as a woolly head and a jet-black face peeped over the bank.

The pickaninny's eyes were stretched wide when he saw the strange figure in coonskin cap and moccasins running down on him, his face almost blanched with terror, and he loosed his hold and, with a cry of fright, rolled back out of sight. Chad looked over the bank. A boy of his own age was holding another pole, and, hearing the little darky slide down, he said, sharply:

"Get that fish, I tell you!"

"Look dar, Mars' Dan, look dar!"

The boy looked around and up and stared with as much wonder as his little body-servant, but with no fear.

"Howdye!" said Chad; but the white boy stared on silently.

"Fishin'?" said Chad.

"Yes," said Dan, shortly—he had shown enough curiosity

and he turned his eyes to his cork. "Get that fish, Snowball," he said again.

"I'll git him fer ye," Chad said; and he went to the fish and unhooked it and came down the bank with the perch in one hand and the pole in the other.

"Whar's yo' string?" he asked, handing the pole to the still trembling little darky.

"I'll take it," said Dan, sticking the butt of his cane-pole in the mud. The fish slipped through his wet fingers, when Chad passed it to him, dropped on the bank, flopped to the edge of the creek, and the three boys, with the same cry, scrambled for it—Snowball falling down on it and clutching it in both his black little paws.

"Dar now!" he shrieked. "I got him!"

"Give him to me," said Dan.

"Lemme string him," said the black boy.

"Give him to me, I tell you!" And, stringing the fish, Dan took the other pole and turned his eyes to his corks, while the pickaninny squatted behind him and Chad climbed up and sat on the bank—letting his legs dangle over. When Dan caught a fish he would fling it with a whoop high over the bank. After the third fish, the lad was mollified and got over his ill-temper. He turned to Chad:

"Want to fish?"

Chad sprang down the bank quickly.

"Yes," he said, and he took the other pole out of the bank, put on a fresh wriggling worm, and moved a little farther down the creek where there was an eddy.

"Ketchin' any?" said a voice above the bank and Chad looked up to see still another lad, taller by a head than either he or Dan—evidently the boy whom he had seen rigging a pole up at the big house on the hill.

"Oh, 'bout 'leven," said Dan, carelessly.

"Howdye!" said Chad.

"Howdye!" said the other boy, and he, too, stared curiously, but Chad had got used to people staring at him.

"I'm goin' over the big rock," added the new arrival, and he went down the creek and climbed around a steep little cliff, and out on a huge rock that hung over the creek, where he dropped his hook. He had no cork, and Chad knew that he was trying to catch catfish. Presently he jerked, and a yellow mudcat rose to the surface, fighting desperately for his life, and Dan and Snowball yelled crazily. Then Dan pulled out a perch.

"I got another one," he shouted. And Chad fished silently. They were making "a mighty big fuss," he thought, "over mighty little fish. If he just had a minnow an' had 'em down in the mountains, 'I Gonnies, he'd show 'em what fishin' was!" But he began to have good luck as it was. Perch after perch he pulled out quietly, and he kept Snowball busy stringing them until he had five on the string. The boy on the rock was watching him, and so was the boy near him—furtively—while Snowball's admiration was won completely, and he grinned and gurgled his delight, until Dan lost his temper again and spoke to him sharply. Dan did not like to be beaten at anything. Pretty soon there was a light thunder of hoofs on the turf above the bank. A black pony shot around the bank and was pulled in at the edge of the ford, and Chad was looking into the dancing black eyes of a little girl with a black velvet cap on her dark curls and a white plume waving from it.

"Howdye!" said Chad, and his heart leaped curiously, but the little girl did not answer. She, too, stared at him as all the others had done, and started to ride into the creek, but Dan stopped her sharply:

"Now, Margaret, don't you ride into that water. You'll skeer the fish."

"No, you won't," said Chad, promptly. "Fish don't keer nothin' about a hoss." But the little girl stood still, and her brother's face flushed. He resented the stranger's interference and his assumption of a better knowledge of fish.

"Mind your own business," trembled on his tongue, and the fact that he held the words back only served to increase his ill-humor and make a worse outbreak possible. But, if Chad did not understand, Snowball did, and his black face grew suddenly grave as he sprang more alertly than ever at any word from his little master. Meanwhile, all unconscious, Chad fished on, catching perch after perch, but he could not keep his eyes on his cork while the little girl was so near, and more than once he was warned by a suppressed cry from the pickaninny when to pull. Once, when he was putting on a worm, he saw the little girl watching the process with great disgust, and he remembered that Melissa would never bait her own hook. All girls were alike, he "reckoned" to himself, and when he caught a fish that was unusually big, he walked over to her.

"I'll give this un to you," he said, but she shrank from it.

"Go 'way!" she said, and she turned her pony. Dan was red in the face by this time. How did this piece of poor white trash dare to offer a fish to his sister? And this time the words came out like the crack of a whip:

"S'pose you mind your own business!"

Chad started as though he had been struck and looked around quickly. He said nothing, but he stuck the butt of his pole in the mud at once and climbed up on the bank again and sat there, with his legs hanging over; and his own face was not pleasant to see. The little girl was riding at a walk up the road. Chad kept perfect silence, for he realized that he had not been minding his own business; still he did not like to be told so, and in such a way. Both corks were shaking at the same time now.

"You got a bite," said Dan, but Chad did not move.

"You got a bite, I tell you," he said, in almost the tone he had used to Snowball, but Chad, when the small aristocrat looked sharply around, dropped his elbows to his knees and his chin into his hand—taking no notice. Once he spat dexterously into the creek. Dan's own cork was going under:

"Snowball!" he cried—"jerk!" A fish flew over Chad's head. Snowball had run for the other pole at command and jerked, too, but the fish was gone and with it the bait.

"You lost that fish!" said the boy, hotly, but Chad sat silent —still. If he would only say something! Dan began to think that the stranger was a coward. So presently, to show what a great little man he was, he began to tease Snowball, who was up on the bank unhooking the fish, of which Chad had taken no notice.

"What's your name?"

"Snowball!" shouted the black little henchman, obediently.

"Louder!"

"S-n-o-w-b-a-l-l!"

"Louder!" The little black fellow opened his mouth wide.

"S-N-O-W-B-A-L-L!" he shrieked.

"LOUDER!"

At last Chad spoke—quietly.

"He can't holler no louder."

"What do you know about it? Louder!" and Dan started menacingly after the little darky, but Chad stepped between.

"Don't hit him!"

Now Dan had never struck Snowball in his life, and he would as soon have struck his own brother—but he must not be told that he couldn't. His face flamed, and little Hotspur that he was, he drew his fist back and hit Chad full in the chest. Chad leaped back to avoid the blow, tumbling Snowball down the bank; the two clinched, and, while they tussled, Chad heard the other brother clambering over the rocks, the beat of hoofs coming toward him on the turf, and the little girl's cry:

"Don't you *dare* touch my brother!"

Both went down side by side with their heads just hanging over the bank, where both could see Snowball's black wool coming to the surface in the deep hole, and both heard his terrified shriek as he went under again. Chad was first to his feet.

"Git a rail!" he shouted and plunged in, but Dan sprang in after him. In three strokes, for the current was rather strong, Chad had the kinky wool in his hand, and, in a few strokes more, the two boys had Snowball gasping on the bank. Harry, the taller brother, ran forward to help them carry him up the bank, and they laid him, choking and bawling, on the grass. Whip in one hand and with the skirt of her long black riding-habit in the other, the little girl stood above, looking on —white and frightened. The hullabaloo had reached the house, and General Dean was walking swiftly down the hill, with Snowball's mammy, topped by a red bandanna handkerchief, rushing after him, and the kitchen servants following.

"What does this mean?" he said, sternly, and Chad was in a strange awe at once—he was so tall, and he stood so straight, and his eye was so piercing. Few people could lie into that eye. The little girl spoke first—usually she does speak first, as well as last.

"Dan and—and—that boy were fighting and they pushed Snowball into the creek."

"Dan was teasin' Snowball," said Harry the just.

"And that boy meddled," said Dan.

"Who struck first?" asked the General, looking from one boy to the other. Dan dropped his eyes sullenly and Chad did not answer.

"I wasn't goin' to hit Snowball," said Dan.

"I thought you wus," said Chad.

"Who struck first?" repeated the General, looking at Dan now.

"That boy meddled and I hit him."

Chad turned and answered the General's eyes steadily.

"I reckon I had no business meddlin'!"

"He tried to give sister a fish."

That was unwise in Dan—Margaret's chin lifted.

"Oh," she said, "that was it, too, was it? Well——"

"I didn't see no harm givin' the little gal a fish," said Chad. "Little gal," indeed! Chad lost the ground he might have gained. Margaret's eyes looked all at once like her father's.

"I'm a little *girl,* thank you."

Chad turned to her father now, looking him in the face straight and steadily.

"I reckon I had no business meddlin', but I didn't think hit was fa'r fer him to hit the nigger; the nigger was littler, an' I didn't think hit was right."

"I didn't mean to hit him—I was only playin'!"

"But I *thought* you was goin' to hit him," said Chad. He looked at the General again. "But I had no business meddlin'." And he picked up his old coonskin cap from the grass to start away.

"Hold on, little man," said the General.

"Dan, haven't I told you not to tease Snowball?" Dan dropped his eyes again.

"Yes, sir."

"You struck first, and this boy says he oughtn't to have meddled, but I think he did just right. Have you anything to say to him?" Dan worked the toe of his left boot into the turf for a moment.

"No, sir."

"Well, go up to your room and think about it awhile and see if you don't owe somebody an apology. Hurry up now an' change your clothes. You'd better come up to the house and get some dry clothes for yourself, my boy," he added to Chad. "You'll catch cold."

"Much obleeged," said Chad. "But I don't ketch cold."

He put on his old coonskin cap, and then the General recognized him.

"Why, aren't you the little boy who bought a horse from me in town the other day?" And then Chad recognized him as the tall man who had cried out:

"Let him have her."

"Yes, sir."

"Well, I know all about you," said the General, kindly. "You are staying with Major Buford. He's a great friend and neighbor of mine. Now you must come up and get some

[98]

clothes, Harry!"—But Chad, though he hesitated, for he knew now that the gentleman had practically given him the old mare, interrupted, sturdily,

"No, sir, I can't go—not while he's a-feelin' hard at me."

"Very well," said the General, gravely. Chad started off on a trot and stopped suddenly.

"I wish you'd please tell that little *gurl*"—Chad pronounced the word with some difficulty—"that I didn't mean nothin' callin' her a little gal. Ever'body calls gurls gals whar I come from."

"All right," laughed the General. Chad trotted all the way home, and there Miss Lucy made him take off his wet clothes at once, though the boy had to go to bed while they were drying, for he had no other clothes, and while he lay in bed the Major came up and listened to Chad's story of the afternoon, which Chad told him word for word just as it had all happened.

"You did just right, Chad," said the Major, and he went down the stairs, chuckling:

"Wouldn't go in and get dry clothes because Dan wouldn't apologize. Dear me! I reckon they'll have it out when they see each other again. I'd like to be on hand, and I'd bet my bottom dollar on Chad." But they did not have it out. Half an hour after supper somebody shouted "Hello!" at the gate, and the Major went out and came back smiling.

"Somebody wants to see you, Chad," he said. And Chad went out and found Dan there on the black pony with Snowball behind him.

"I've come over to say that I had no business hittin' you down at the creek, and—" Chad interrupted him:

"That's all right," he said, and Dan stopped and thrust out his hand. The two boys shook hands gravely.

"An' my papa says you are a man an' he wants you to come over and see us and I want you—and Harry and Margaret. We all want you."

"All right," said Chad. Dan turned his black pony and galloped off.

"An' come soon!" he shouted back.

Out in the quarters Mammy Ailsie, old Tom's wife, was having her own say that night.

"Ole Marse Cal Buford pickin' a piece o' white trash out de gutter an' not sayin' whar he come from an' nuttin' 'bout him. An' old Mars Henry takin' him jus' like he was quality. My Tom say dat boy don' know who is his mammy ner his daddy. I ain' gwine to let my little mistis play wid no sech trash, I tell you—'deed I ain't!" And this talk would reach the drawing-room by and by, where the General was telling the family, at just about the same hour, the story of the horse sale and Chad's purchase of the old brood mare.

"I knew where he was from right away," said Harry. "I've seen mountain-people wearing caps like his up at Uncle Brutus's, when they come down to go to Richmond."

The General frowned.

"Well, you won't see any more people like him up there again."

"Why, papa?"

"Because you aren't going to Uncle Brutus's any more."

"Why, papa?"

The mother put her hand on her husband's knee.

"Never mind, son," she said.

X

THE BLUEGRASS

God's Country!

No humor in that phrase to the Bluegrass Kentuckian! There never was—there is none now. To him, the land seems in all the New World, to have been the pet shrine of the Great Mother herself. She fashioned it with loving hands. She shut it in with a mighty barrier of mighty mountains to keep the mob out. She gave it the loving clasp of a mighty river, and spread broad, level prairies beyond that the mob might glide by, or be tempted to the other side, where the earth was level and there was no need to climb: that she might send priests from her shrine to reclaim Western wastes, or let the weak or the unloving—if such could be—have easy access to another land.

In the beginning, such was her clear purpose to the Kentuckian's eye, she filled it with flowers and grass and trees, and fish and bird and wild beast, just as she made Eden for Adam and Eve. The red men fought for the Paradise—fought till it was drenched with blood, but no tribe, without a mortal challenge from another straightway, could ever call a rood its own. Boone loved the land from the moment the eagle eye in his head swept its shaking wilderness from a mountain-top, and every man who followed him loved the land no less. And when the chosen came, they found the earth ready to receive them— lifted above the baneful breath of river-bottom and marshland, drained by rivers full of fish, filled with woods full of game, and underlaid—all—with thick, blue, limestone strata that, like some divine agent working in the dark, kept crumbling—ever crumbling—to enrich the soil and give bone-building virtue to every drop of water and every blade of grass. For those chosen people—such, too, seemed her purpose—the Mother went to the race upon whom she had smiled a benediction for a thousand years—the race that obstacle but strengthens, that thrives best under an alien effort to kill, that has ever conquered its conquerors, and that seems bent on the task of carrying the best ideals any age has ever known back to the Old World from which it sprang. The Great Mother knows! Knows that her children must suffer, if they stray too far from her great teeming breasts. And how she has followed close when this Saxon race—her youngest born—seemed likely to stray too far—gathering its sons to her arms in virgin lands that they might suckle again and keep the old blood fresh and strong. Who could know what danger threatened it when she sent her blue-eyed men and women to people the wilderness of the New World? To climb the Alleghanies, spread through the wastes beyond, and plant their kind across a continent from sea to sea. Who knows what dangers threaten now, when, this task done, she seems to be opening the eastern gates of the earth with a gesture that seems to say—"Enter, reclaim, and dwell therein!"

One little race of that race in the New World, and one only, has she kept flesh of her flesh, bone of her bone—to that race only did she give no outside aid. She shut it in with gray hill and shining river. She shut it off from the mother state and the mother nation and left it to fight its own fight with savage nature, savage beast, and savage man. And thus she gave the little race strength of heart and body and brain, and taught it to stand together as she taught each man of the race to stand alone, protect his women, mind his own business, and meddle not at all; to think his own thoughts and die for them if need be, though he divided his own house against itself; taught the man to cleave to one woman, with the penalty of death if he strayed elsewhere; to keep her—and even himself—in dark ignorance of the sins against Herself for which she has slain other nations, and in that happy ignorance keeps them to-day, even while she is slaying elsewhere still.

And Nature holds the Kentuckians close even to-day—suckling at her breasts and living after her simple laws. What further use she may have for them is hid by the darkness of to-morrow, but before the Great War came she could look upon her work and say with a smile, that it was good. The land was a great series of wooded parks such as one might have found in Merry England, except that worm fence and stone wall took the place of hedge along the highways. It was a land of peace and of a plenty that was close to easy luxury—for all. Poor whites were few, the beggar was unknown, and throughout the region there was no man, woman, or child, perhaps, who did not have enough to eat and to wear and a roof to cover his head, whether it was his own roof or not. If slavery had to be—then the fetters were forged light and hung loosely. And, broadcast, through the people, was the upright sturdiness of the Scotch-Irishman, without his narrowness and bigotry; the grace and chivalry of the Cavalier without his Quixotic sentiment and his weakness; the jovial good-nature of the English squire and the leavening spirit of a simple yeomanry that bore itself with unconscious tenacity to traditions that seeped from the very earth. And the wings of the eagle hovered over all.

For that land it was the flowering time of the age and the people; and the bud that was about to open into the perfect flower had its living symbol in the little creature racing over the bluegrass fields on a black pony, with a black velvet cap and a white nodding plume above her shaking curls, just as the little stranger who had floated down into those Elysian fields—with better blood in his veins than he knew—was a reincarnation perhaps of the spirit of the old race that had lain dormant in the hills. The long way from log-cabin to Greek portico had marked the progress of the generations before her; and, on this same way, the boy had set his sturdy feet.

XI

A TOURNAMENT

On Sunday, the Major and Miss Lucy took Chad to church —a country church built of red brick and overgrown with ivy —and the sermon was very short, Chad thought, for, down in the mountains, the circuit-rider would preach for hours—and the deacons passed around velvet pouches for the people to drop money in, and they passed around bread, of which nearly everybody took a pinch, and a silver goblet with wine, from which the same people took a sip—all of which Chad did not understand. Usually the Deans went to Lexington to church, for they were Episcopalians, but they were all at the country church that day, and with them was Richard Hunt, who smiled at Chad and waved his riding-whip. After church Dan came to him and shook hands. Harry nodded to him gravely, the mother smiled kindly, and the General put his hand on the boy's head. Margaret looked at him furtively, but passed him by. Perhaps she was still "mad" at him, Chad thought, and he was much worried. Margaret was not shy like Melissa, but her face was kind. The General asked them all over to take dinner, but Miss Lucy declined—she had asked people to take dinner with her. And Chad, with keen disappointment, saw them drive away.

It was a lonely day for him that Sunday. He got tired staying so long at the table, and he did not understand what the guests were talking about. The afternoon was long, and he wandered restlessly about the yard and the quarters. Jerome

Conners, the overseer, tried to be friendly with him for the first time, but the boy did not like the overseer and turned away from him. He walked down to the pike gate and sat on it, looking over toward the Deans'. He wished that Dan would come over to see him or, better still, that he could go over to see Dan and Harry and—Margaret. But Dan did not come and Chad could not ask the Major to let him go—he was too shy about it—and Chad was glad when bedtime came.

Two days more and spring was come in earnest. It was in the softness of the air, the tenderness of cloud and sky, and the warmth of the sunlight. The grass was greener and the trees quivered happily. Hens scratched and cocks crowed more lustily. Insect life was busier. A stallion nickered in the barn, and from the fields came the mooing of cattle. Field-hands going to work chaffed the maids about the house and quarters. It stirred dreamy memories of his youth in the Major, and it brought a sad light into Miss Lucy's faded eyes. Would she ever see another spring? It brought tender memories to General Dean, and over at Woodlawn, after he and Mrs. Dean had watched the children go off with happy cries and laughter to school, it led them back into the house hand in hand. And it set Chad's heart aglow as he walked through the dewy grass and amid the singing of many birds toward the pike gate. He, too, was on his way to school—in a brave new suit of clothes—and nobody smiled at him now, except admiringly, for the Major had taken him to town the preceding day and had got the boy clothes such as Dan and Harry wore. Chad was worried at first—he did not like to accept so much from the Major.

"I'll pay you back," said Chad. "I'll leave you my hoss when I go 'way, if I don't," and the Major laughingly said that was all right and he made Chad, too, think that it was all right. And so spring took the shape of hope in Chad's breast, that morning, and a little later it took the shape of Margaret, for he soon saw the Dean children ahead of him in the road and he ran to catch up with them.

All looked at him with surprise—seeing his broad white collar with ruffles, his turned-back, ruffled cuffs, and his boots with red tops; but they were too polite to say anything. Still Chad felt Margaret taking them all in and he was proud and confident. And, when her eyes were lifted to the handsome face that rose from the collar and the thick yellow hair, he caught them with his own in an unconscious look of fealty, that made the little girl blush and hurry on and not look at him again until they were in school, when she turned her eyes, as did all the other boys and girls, to scan the new "scholar." Chad's work in the mountains came in well now. The teacher, a gray, sad-eyed, thin-faced man, was surprised at the boy's capacity, for he could read as well as Dan, and in mental arithmetic even Harry was no match for him; and when in the spelling class he went from the bottom to the head in a single lesson, the teacher looked as though he were going to give the boy a word of praise openly, and Margaret was regarding him with a new light in her proud eyes. That was a happy day for Chad, but it passed after school when, as they went home together, Margaret looked at him no more; else Chad would have gone by the Deans' house when Dan and Harry asked him to go and look at their ponies and the new sheep that their father had just bought; for Chad was puzzled and awed and shy of the little girl. It was strange—he had never felt that way about Melissa. But his shyness kept him away from her day after day until, one morning, he saw her ahead of him going to school alone, and his heart thumped as he quietly and swiftly overtook her without calling to her; but he stopped running that she might not know that he had been running, and for the first time she was shy with him. Harry and Dan were threatened with the measles, she said, and would say no more. When they went through the fields toward the school-house, Chad stalked ahead as he had done in the mountains with Melissa, and, looking back, he saw that Margaret had stopped. He waited for her to come up, and she looked at him for a moment as though displeased. Puzzled, Chad gave back her look for a moment and turned without a word—still stalking ahead. He looked back presently and Margaret had stopped and was pouting.

"You aren't polite, little boy. My mamma says a *nice* little boy always lets a little *girl* go first." But Chad still walked ahead. He looked back presently and she had stopped again —whether angry or ready to cry, he could not make out—so he waited for her, and as she came slowly near, he stepped gravely from the path, and Margaret went on like a queen.

In town, a few days later, he saw a little fellow take off his hat when a lady passed him, and it set Chad to thinking. He recalled asking the school-master once what was meant when the latter read about a knight doffing his plume, and the school-master had told him that men, in those days, took off their hats in the presence of ladies just as they did in the Bluegrass now; but Chad had forgotten. He understood it all then and he surprised Margaret, next morning, by taking off his cap gravely when he spoke to her; and the little lady was greatly pleased, for her own brothers did not do that, at least, not to her, though she had heard her mother tell them that they must. All this must be chivalry, Chad thought, and when Harry and Dan got well, he revived his old ideas, but Harry laughed at him and Dan did, too, until Chad, remembering Beelzebub, suggested that they should have a tournament with two rams that the General had tied up in the stable. They would make spears and each would get on a ram. Harry would let them out into the lot and they would have "a real charge—sure enough." But Margaret received the plan with disdain, until Dan, at Chad's suggestion, asked the General to read them the tournament scene in "Ivanhoe," which excited the little lady a great deal; and when Chad said that she must be the "Queen of Love and Beauty" she blushed prettily and thought, after all, that it would be great fun. They would make lances of ashwood and helmets of tin buckets, and perhaps Margaret would make red sashes for them. Indeed, she would, and the tournament would take place on the next Saturday. But, on Saturday, one of the sheep was taken over to Major Buford's and the other was turned loose in the Major's back pasture and the great day had to be postponed.

It was on the night of the reading from "Ivanhoe" that Harry and Dan found out how Chad could play the banjo. Passing old Mammy's cabin that night before supper, the three boys had stopped to listen to old Tom play, and after a few tunes, Chad could stand it no longer.

"I foller pickin' the banjer a leetle," he said shyly, and thereupon he had taken the rude instrument and made the old negro's eyes stretch with amazement, while Dan rolled in the grass with delight, and every negro who heard ran toward the boy. After supper, Dan brought the banjo into the house and made Chad play on the porch, to the delight of them all. And there, too, the servants gathered, and even old Mammy was observed slyly shaking her foot—so that Margaret clapped her hands and laughed the old woman into great confusion. After that no Saturday came that Chad did not spend the night at the Deans', or Harry and Dan did not stay at Major Buford's. And not a Saturday passed that the three boys did not go coon-hunting with the darkies, or fox-hunting with the Major and the General. Chad never forgot that first starlit night when he was awakened by the near winding of a horn and heard the Major jump from bed. He jumped too, and when the Major reached the barn, a dark little figure was close at his heels.

"Can I go, too?" Chad asked, eagerly.

"Think you can stick on?"

"Yes, sir."

"All right. Get my bay horse. That old mare of yours is too slow."

The Major's big bay horse! Chad was dizzy with pride.

When they galloped out into the dark woods, there were the General and Harry and Dan and half a dozen neighbors, sitting silently on their horses and listening to the music of the hounds.

The General laughed.

"I thought you'd come," he said, and the Major laughed too, and cocked his ear. "Old Rock's ahead," he said, for he knew, as did everyone there, the old hound's tongue.

"He's been ahead for an hour," said the General with quiet satisfaction, "and I think he'll stay there."

Just then a dark object swept past them, and the Major with a low cry hied on his favorite hound.

"Not now, I reckon," he said, and the General laughed again.

Dan and Harry pressed their horses close to Chad, and all talked in low voices.

"Ain't it fun?" whispered Dan. Chad answered with a shiver of pure joy.

"He's making for the creek," said the Major, sharply, and he touched spurs to his horse. How they raced through the woods, cracking brush and whisking around trees, and how they thundered over the turf and clattered across the road and on! For a few moments the Major kept close to Chad, watching him anxiously, but the boy stuck to the big bay like a jockey, and he left Dan and Harry on their ponies far behind. All night they rode under the starlit sky, and ten miles away they caught poor Reynard. Chad was in at the kill, with the Major and the General, and the General gave Chad the brush with his own hand.

"Where did you learn to ride, boy?"

"I never learned," said Chad, simply, whereat the Major winked at his friends and patted Chad on the shoulder.

"I've got to let my boys ride better horses, I suppose," said the General; "I can't have a boy who does not know how to ride beating them this way."

Day was breaking when the Major and Chad rode into the stable-yard. The boy's face was pale, his arms and legs ached, and he was so sleepy that he could hardly keep his eyes open.

"How'd you like it, Chad?"

"I never knowed nothing like it in my life," said Chad.

"I'm going to teach you to shoot."

"Yes, sir," said Chad.

As they approached the house, a squirrel barked from the woods.

"Hear that, Chad?" said the Major. "We'll get him."

The following morning, Chad rose early and took his old rifle out into the woods, and when the Major came out on the porch before breakfast the boy was coming up the walk with six squirrels in his hand. The Major's eyes opened, and he looked at the squirrels when Chad dropped them on the porch. Every one of them was shot through the head.

"Well, I'm damned! How many times did you shoot, Chad?"

"Seven."

"What—missed only once?"

"I took a knot fer a squirrel once," said Chad.

The Major roared aloud.

"Did I say I was going to teach you to shoot, Chad?"

"Yes, sir."

The Major chuckled and that day he told about those squirrels and that knot to everybody he saw. With every day the Major grew fonder and prouder of the boy and more convinced than ever that the lad was of his own blood.

"There's nothing that I like that that boy don't take to like a duck to water." And when he saw the boy take off his hat to Margaret and observed his manner with the little girl, he said to himself that if Chad wasn't a gentleman born, he ought to have been, and the Major believed that he must be.

Everywhere, at school, at the Deans', with the darkies— with everybody but Conners, the overseer—Chad became a favorite, but, as to Napoleon, so to Chad, came Waterloo—with the long deferred tournament came Waterloo to Chad.

A TOURNAMENT

And it came after a certain miracle on May-day. The Major had taken Chad to the festival where the dance was on sawdust in the woodland—in the bottom of a little hollow, around which the seats ran as in an amphitheatre. Ready to fiddle for them stood none other than John Morgan himself, his gray eyes dancing and an arch smile on his handsome face; and, taking a place among the dancers, were Richard Hunt and—Margaret. The poised bow fell, a merry tune rang out, and Richard Hunt bowed low to his little partner, who, smiling and blushing, dropped him the daintiest of graceful courtesies. Then the miracle came to pass. Rage straightway shook Chad's soul—shook it as a terrier shakes a rat—and the look on his face and in his eyes went back a thousand years. And Richard Hunt, looking up, saw the strange spectacle, understood, and did not even smile. On the contrary, he went at once after the dance to speak to the boy and got for his answer fierce, white, staring silence and a clinched fist, that was almost ready to strike. Something else that was strange happened then to Chad. He felt a very firm and a very gentle hand on his shoulder, his own eyes dropped before the piercing dark eyes and kindly smile above him, and, a moment later, he was shyly making his way with Richard Hunt toward Margaret.

It was on Thursday of the following week that Dan told him the two rams were once more tied in his father's stable. On Saturday, then, they would have the tournament. To get Mammy's help, Margaret had to tell the plan to her, and Mammy stormed against the little girl taking part in any such undignified proceedings, but imperious Margaret forced her to keep silent and help make sashes and a tent for each of the two knights. Chad would be the "Knight of the Cumberland" and

Dan the "Knight of the Bluegrass." Snowball was to be Dan's squire and black Rufus, Harry's body-servant, would be squire to Chad. Harry was King John, the other pickaninnies would be varlets and vassals, and outraged Uncle Tom, so Dan told him, would, "by the beard of Abraham," have to be a "Dog of an Unbeliever." Margaret was undecided whether she would play Rebecca, or the "Queen of Love and Beauty," until Chad told her she ought to be both, so both she decided to be. So all was done—the spears fashioned of ash, the helmets battered from tin buckets, colors knotted for the spears, and shields made of sheepskins. On the stiles sat Harry and Margaret in royal state under a canopy of calico, with indignant Mammy behind them. At each end of the stable-lot was a tent of cotton, and before one stood Snowball and before the other black Rufus, each with his master's spear and shield. Near Harry stood Sam, the trumpeter, with a fox-horn to sound the charge, and four black vassals stood at the stable-door to lead the chargers forth.

Near the stiles were the neighbors' children, and around the barn was gathered every darky on the place, while behind the hedge and peeping through it were the Major and the General, the one chuckling, the other smiling indulgently.

The stable-doors opened, the four vassals disappeared and came forth, each pair leading a ram, one covered with red calico, the other with blue cotton, and each with a bandanna handkerchief around his neck. Each knight stepped forth from his tent, as his charger was dragged—ba-a-ing and butting—toward it, and, grasping his spear and shield and setting his helmet on more firmly, got astride gravely—each squire and vassal solemn, for the King had given command that no varlet must show unseemly mirth. Behind the hedge, the Major was hold-

Dan, nearly unseated, had dropped his lance to catch hold of his charger's wool.

ing his hands to his sides and the General was getting grave. It had just occurred to him that those rams would make for each other like tornadoes, and he said so.

"Of course they will," chuckled the Major. "Don't you suppose they know that? That's what they're doing it for. Bless my soul!"

The King waved his hand just then and his black trumpeter tooted the charge.

"Leggo!" said Chad.

"Leggo!" said Dan.

And Snowball and Rufus let go, and each ram ran a few paces and stopped with his head close to the ground, while each knight brandished his spear and dug with his spurred heels. One charger gave a ba-a! The other heard, raised his head, saw his enemy, and ba-a-ed an answering challenge. Then they started for each other with a rush that brought a sudden fearsome silence, quickly followed by a babel of excited cries, in which Mammy's was loudest and most indignant. Dan, nearly unseated, had dropped his lance to catch hold of his charger's wool, and Chad had gallantly lowered the point of his, because his antagonist was unarmed. But the temper of rams and not of knights was in that fight now, and they came together with a shock that banged the two knights into each other and hurled both violently to the ground. General Dean and the Major ran anxiously from the hedge. Several negro men rushed for the rams, who were charging and butting like demons. Harry tumbled from the canopy in a most unkingly fashion. Margaret cried and Mammy wrung her hands. Chad rose dizzily, but Dan lay still. Chad's elbow had struck him in the temple and knocked him unconscious.

The servants were thrown into an uproar when Dan was

carried back into the house. Harry was white and almost in tears.

"I did it, father, I did it," he said, at the foot of the steps.

"No," said Chad, sturdily, "I done it myself."

Margaret heard and ran from the hallway and down the steps, brushing away her tears with both hands.

"Yes, you did—you *did*," she cried. "I hate you."

"Why, Margaret," said General Dean.

Chad, startled and stung, turned without a word and, unnoticed by the rest, made his way slowly across the fields.

XII

BACK TO KINGDOM COME

It was the tournament that, at last, loosed Mammy's tongue. She was savage in her denunciation of Chad to Mrs. Dean—so savage and in such plain language that her mistress checked her sharply, but not before Margaret had heard, though the little girl, with an awed face, slipped quietly out of the room into the yard, while Harry stood in the doorway, troubled and silent.

"Don't let me hear you speak that way again, Mammy," said Mrs. Dean, so sternly that the old woman swept out of the room in high dudgeon. And yet she told her husband of Mammy's charge.

"I am rather surprised at Major Buford."

"Perhaps he doesn't know," said the General. "Perhaps it isn't true."

"Nobody knows anything about the boy."

"That's true."

"Well, I cannot have my children associating with a waif."

"He seems like a nice boy."

"He uses extraordinary language. I cannot have him teaching my children mischief. Why I believe Margaret is really fond of him. I know Harry and Dan are." The General looked thoughtful.

"I will speak to Major Buford about him," he said; and he did—no little to that gentleman's confusion—though he defended Chad stanchly—and the two friends parted with some heat.

Thereafter, the world changed for Chad, for is there any older and truer story than that Evil has wings, while Good goes a plodding way? Chad felt the change, in the negroes, in the sneering overseer, and could not understand. The rumor reached Miss Lucy's ears and she and the Major had a spirited discussion that rather staggered Chad's kind-hearted companion. It reached the school, and a black-haired youngster, named Georgie Forbes, who had long been one of Margaret's abject slaves, and who hated Chad, brought out the terrible charge in the presence of a dozen school-children at noon-recess one day. It had been no insult in the mountains, but Chad, dazed though he was, knew it was meant for an insult, and his hard fist shot out promptly, landing in his enemy's chin and bringing him bawling to the earth. Others gave out the cry then, and the boy fought right and left like a demon. Dan stood sullenly near, taking no part, and Harry, while he stopped the unequal fight, turned away from Chad coldly, calling Margaret, who had run up toward them, away at the same time, and Chad's three friends turned from him then and there, while the boy, forgetting all else, stood watching them with dumb wonder and pain. The school-bell clanged, but Chad stood still—with his heart wellnigh breaking. In a few minutes the last pupil had disappeared through the school-room door, and Chad stood under a great elm—alone. But only a moment, for he turned quickly away, the tears starting to his eyes, walked rapidly through the woods, climbed the worm fence beyond, and dropped, sobbing, in the thick bluegrass.

An hour later he was walking swiftly through the fields toward the old brick house that had sheltered him. He was very quiet at supper that night, and after Miss Lucy had gone to bed and he and the Major were seated before the fire, he was so quiet that the Major looked at him anxiously.

"What's the matter, Chad? Are you sick?"

"Nothin'—no, sir."

But the Major was uneasy, and when he rose to go to bed, he went over and put his hand on the boy's head.

"Chad," he said, "if you hear of people saying mean things about you, you mustn't pay any attention to them."

"No, sir."

"You're a good boy, and I want you to live here with me. Good-night, Chad," he added, affectionately. Chad nearly broke down, but he steadied himself.

"Good-by, Major," he said, brokenly. "I'm obleeged to you."

"Good-by?" repeated the Major. "Why——"

"Good-night, I mean," stammered Chad.

The Major stood inside his own door, listening to the boy's slow steps up the second flight. "I'm gettin' to love that boy," he said, wonderingly—"An' I'm damned if people who talk about him don't have me to reckon with"—and the Major shook his head from side to side. Several times he thought he could hear the boy moving around in the room above him, and while he was wondering why the lad did not go to bed, he fell asleep.

Chad was moving around. First, by the light of a candle, he laboriously dug out a short letter to the Major—scalding it with tears. Then he took off his clothes and got his old mountain-suit out of the closet—moccasins and all—and put them on. Very carefully he folded the pretty clothes he had taken off—just as Miss Lucy had taught him—and laid them on the bed. Then he picked up his old rifle in one hand and his old coonskin cap in the other, blew out the candle, slipped noiselessly down the stairs in his moccasined feet, out the unbolted door and into the starlit night. From the pike fence he turned once to look back to the dark, silent house amid the dark trees. Then he sprang down and started through the fields—his face set toward the mountains.

It so happened that mischance led General Dean to go over to see Major Buford about Chad next morning. The Major listened patiently—or tried ineffectively to listen—and when the General was through, he burst out with a vehemence that shocked and amazed his old friend.

"Damn those niggers!" he cried, in a tone that seemed to include the General in his condemnation, "that boy is the best boy I ever knew. I believe he is my own blood, he looks like that picture there"—pointing to the old portrait—"and if he is what I believe he is, by ——, sir, he gets this farm and all I have. Do you understand that?"

"I believe he told you what he was."

"He did—but I don't believe he knows, and, anyhow, whatever he is, he shall have a home under this roof as long as he lives."

The General rose suddenly—stiffly.

"He must never darken my door again."

"Very well." The Major made a gesture which plainly said, "In that event, you are darkening mine too long," and the General rose, slowly descended the steps of the portico, and turned:

"Do you really mean, Cal, that you are going to let a little brat that you picked up in the road only yesterday stand between *you* and *me?*"

The Major softened.

"Look here," he said, whisking a sheet of paper from his coat-pocket. While the General read Chad's scrawl, the Major watched his face.

"He's gone, by ——. A hint was enough for him. If he isn't the son of a gentleman, then I'm not, nor you."

"Cal," said the General, holding out his hand, "we'll talk this over again."

The bees buzzed around the honeysuckles that clambered over the porch. A crow flew overhead. The sound of a crying child came around the corner of the house from the quarters, and the General's footsteps died on the gravel-walk, but the Major heard them not. Mechanically he watched the General mount his black horse and canter toward the pike gate. The overseer called to him from the stable, but the Major dropped his eyes to the scrawl in his hand, and when Miss Lucy came out he silently handed it to her.

"I reckon you know what folks is a-sayin' about me. I tol' you myself. But I didn't know hit wus any harm, and anyways hit ain't my fault, I reckon, an' I don't see how folks can blame me. But I don' want nobody who don' want me. An' I'm leavin' 'cause I don't want to bother you. I never bring nothing but trouble nohow an' I'm goin' back to the mountains. Tell Miss Lucy good-by. She was mighty good to me, but I know she didn't like me. I left the hoss for you. If you don't have no use fer the saddle, I wish you'd give hit to Harry, 'cause he tuk up fer me at school when I was fightin', though he wouldn't speak to me no more. I'm mighty sorry to leave you. I'm obleeged to you 'cause you wus so good to me an' I'm goin' to see you agin some day, if I can. Good-by."

"Left that damned old mare to pay for his clothes and his board and his schooling," muttered the Major. "By the gods" —he rose suddenly and strode away—"I beg your pardon, Lucy."

A tear was running down each of Miss Lucy's faded cheeks.

Dawn that morning found Chad springing from a bed in a haystack—ten miles from Lexington. By dusk that day, he was on the edge of the Bluegrass and that night he stayed at a farm-house, going in boldly, for he had learned now that the wayfarer was as welcome in a Bluegrass farm-house as in a log-cabin in the mountains. Higher and higher grew the green swelling slopes, until, climbing one about noon next day, he saw the blue foothills of the Cumberland through the clear air —and he stopped and looked long, breathing hard from pure ecstasy. The plain-dweller never knows the fierce home hunger that the mountain-born have for hills.

Besides, beyond those blue summits were the Turners and the school-master and Jack, waiting for him, and he forgot hunger and weariness as he trod on eagerly toward them. That night, he stayed in a mountain-cabin, and while the contrast of the dark room, the crowding children, the slovenly dress, and the coarse food was strangely disagreeable, along with the strange new shock came the thrill that all this meant hills and home. It was about three o'clock of the fourth day that, tramping up the Kentucky River, he came upon a long, even stretch of smooth water, from the upper end of which two black bowlders were thrust out of the stream, and with a keener thrill he realized that he was nearing home. He recalled seeing those rocks as the raft swept down the river, and the old Squire had said that they were named after oxen—"Billy and Buck." Opposite the rocks he met a mountaineer.

"How fer is it to Uncle Joel Turner's?"

"A leetle the rise o' six miles, I reckon."

The boy was faint with weariness, and those six miles seemed a dozen. Idea of distance is vague among the mountaineers, and two hours of weary travel followed, yet nothing that he recognized was in sight. Once a bend of the river looked familiar, but when he neared it, the road turned steeply from the river and over a high bluff, and the boy started up with a groan. He meant to reach the summit before he stopped to rest, but in sheer pain, he dropped a dozen paces from the top and lay with his tongue, like a dog's, between his lips.

The top was warm, but a chill was rising from the fast-darkening shadows below him. The rim of the sun was about to brush the green tip of a mountain across the river, and the boy rose in a minute, dragged himself on to the point where, rounding a big rock, he dropped again with a thumping heart and a reeling brain. There it was—old Joel's cabin in the pretty valley below—old Joel's cabin—home! Smoke was rising from the chimney, and that far away it seemed that Chad could smell frying bacon. There was the old barn, and he could make out one of the boys feeding stock and another chopping wood— was that the school-master? There was the huge form of old Joel at the fence talking with a neighbor. He was gesticulating as though angry, and the old mother came to the door as the neighbor moved away with a shuffling gait that the boy knew belonged to the Dillon breed. Where was Jack? Jack!

Chad sprang to his feet and went down the hill on a run. He climbed the orchard fence, breaking the top-rail in his eagerness, and as he neared the house, he gave a shrill yell. A scarlet figure flashed like a flame out of the door, with an answering cry, and the Turners followed:

"Why, boy," roared old Joel. "Mammy, hit's Chad!"

Dolph dropped an armful of feed. The man with the axe left it stuck in a log, and each man shouted:

"Chad!"

The mountaineers are an undemonstrative race, but Mother Turner took the boy in her arms and the rest crowded around, slapping him on the back and all asking questions at once— Dolph and Rube and Tom. Yes, and there was the school-master—every face was almost tender with love for the boy. But where was Jack?

"Where's—where's Jack?" said Chad.

Old Joel changed face—looking angry; the rest were grave. Only the old mother spoke:

"Jack's all right."

"Oh," said Chad, but he looked anxious.

Melissa inside heard. He had not asked for *her,* and with the sudden choking of a nameless fear she sprang out the door to be caught by the school-master, who had gone around the corner to look for her.

"Lemme go," she said, fiercely, breaking his hold and darting away, but stopping, when she saw Chad in the doorway, looking at her with a shy smile.

"Howdye, Melissa!"

The girl stared at him mildly and made no answer, and a wave of shame and confusion swept over the boy as his thoughts flashed back to a little girl in a black cap and on a black pony, and he stood reddening and helpless. There was a halloo at the gate. It was old Squire Middleton and the circuit-rider, and old Joel went toward them with a darkening face.

"Why, hello, Chad," the Squire said. "You back again?"

He turned to Joel.

"Look hyeh, Joel. Thar hain't no use o' your buckin' agin yo' neighbors and harborin' a sheep-killin' dog." Chad started and looked from one face to another—slowly but surely making out the truth.

"You never seed the dawg afore last spring. You don't know that he hain't a sheep-killer."

"It's a lie—a lie," Chad cried, hotly, but the school-master stopped him.

"Hush, Chad," he said, and he took the boy inside and told him Jack was in trouble. A Dillon sheep had been found dead on a hill-side. Daws Dillon had come upon Jack leaping out of the pasture, and Jack had come home with his muzzle bloody. Even with this overwhelming evidence, old Joel stanchly refused to believe the dog was guilty and ordered old man Dillon off the place. A neighbor had come over, then another, and another, until old Joel got livid with rage.

"That dawg mought eat a dead sheep but he never would kill a live one, and if you kill him, by ——, you've got to kill me fust."

Now there is no more unneighborly or unchristian act for a farmer than to harbor a sheep-killing dog. So the old Squire and the circuit-rider had come over to show Joel the grievous error of his selfish, obstinate course, and, so far, old Joel had refused to be shown. All of his sons sturdily upheld him and little Melissa fiercely—the old mother and the school-master alone remaining quiet and taking no part in the dissension.

"Have they got Jack?"

"No, Chad," said the school-master. "He's safe—tied up in the stable." Chad started out, and no one followed but Melissa. A joyous bark that was almost human came from the stable as Chad approached, for the dog must have known the sound of his master's footsteps, and when Chad threw open the door, Jack sprang the length of his tether to meet him and was jerked to his back. Again and again he sprang, barking, as though beside himself, while Chad stood at the door, looking sorrowfully at him.

"Down, Jack!" he said sternly, and Jack dropped obediently, looking straight at his master with honest eyes and whimpering like a child.

"Jack," said Chad, "did you kill that sheep?" This was all strange conduct for his little master, and Jack looked wondering and dazed, but his eyes never wavered or blinked. Chad could not long stand those honest eyes.

"No," he said, fiercely—"no, little doggie, no—*no!*" And Chad dropped on his knees and took Jack in his arms and hugged him to his breast.

XIII

ON TRIAL FOR HIS LIFE

By degrees the whole story was told Chad that night. Now
and then the Turners would ask him about his stay in the Bluegrass, but the boy would answer as briefly as possible and come
back to Jack. Before going to bed, Chad said he would bring
Jack into the house:

"Somebody might pizen him," he explained, and when he
came back, he startled the circle about the fire:

"Whar's Whizzer?" he asked, sharply. "Who's seen Whizzer?"

Then it developed that no one had seen the Dillon dog—
since the day before the sheep was found dead near a ravine at
the foot of the mountain in a back pasture. Late that afternoon
Melissa had found Whizzer in that very pasture when she was
driving old Betsy, the brindle, home at milking-time. Since
then, no one of the Turners had seen the Dillon dog. That,
however, did not prove that Whizzer was not at home. And
yet,

"I'd like to know whar Whizzer is now!" said Chad, and,
after, at old Joel's command, he had tied Jack to a bedpost—
an outrage that puzzled the dog sorely—the boy threshed his
bed for an hour—trying to think out a defence for Jack and
wondering if Whizzer might not have been concerned in the
death of the sheep.

[127]

It is hardly possible that what happened, next day, could happen anywhere except among simple people of the hills. Briefly, the old Squire and the circuit-rider had brought old Joel to the point of saying, the night before, that he would give Jack up to be killed, if he could be proven guilty. But the old hunter cried with an oath:

"You've got to prove him guilty." And thereupon the Squire said he would give Jack every chance that he would give a man—*he would try him;* each side could bring in witnesses; old Joel could have a lawyer if he wished, and Jack's case would go before a jury. If pronounced innocent, Jack should go free: if guilty—then the dog should be handed over to the sheriff, to be shot at sundown. Joel agreed.

It was a strange procession that left the gate of the Turner cabin next morning. Old Joel led the way, mounted, with "ole Sal," his rifle, across his saddle-bow. Behind him came Mother Turner and Melissa on foot and Chad with his rifle over his left shoulder, and leading Jack by a string with his right hand. Behind them slouched Tall Tom with his rifle and Dolph and Rube, each with a huge old-fashioned horse-pistol swinging from his right hip. Last strode the school-master. The cabin was left deserted—the hospitable door held closed by a deer-skin latch caught to a wooden pin outside.

It was a strange humiliation to Jack thus to be led along the highway, like a criminal going to the gallows. There was no power on earth that could have moved him from Chad's side, other than the boy's own command—but old Joel had sworn that he would keep the dog tied and the old hunter always kept his word. He had sworn, too, that Jack should have a fair trial. Therefore, the guns—and the school-master walked with his hands behind him and his eyes on the ground: he feared trouble.

Half a mile up the river and to one side of the road, a space of some thirty feet square had been cut into a patch of rhododendron and filled with rude benches of slabs—in front of which was a rough platform on which sat a home-made, cane-bottomed chair. Except for the opening from the road, the space was walled with a circle of living green through which the sun dappled the benches with quivering disks of yellow light—and, high above, great poplars and oaks arched their mighty heads. It was an open-air "meeting-house" where the circuit-rider preached during his summer circuit and there the trial was to take place.

Already a crowd was idling, whittling, gossiping in the road, when the Turner cavalcade came in sight—and for ten miles up and down the river people were coming in for the trial.

"Mornin', gentlemen," said old Joel, gravely.

"Mornin'," answered several, among whom was the Squire, who eyed Joel's gun and the guns coming up the road.

"Squirrel-huntin'?" he asked and, as the old hunter did not answer, he added, sharply:

"Air you afeerd, Joel Turner, that you ain't a-goin' to git justice from *me?*"

"I don't keer whar it comes from," said Joel, grimly—"but I'm a-goin' to *have* it."

It was plain that the old man not only was making no plea for sympathy, but was alienating the little he had: and what he had was very little—for who but a lover of dogs can give full sympathy to his kind? And, then, Jack was believed to be guilty. It was curious to see how each Dillon shrank uncon-

sciously as the Turners gathered—all but Jerry, one of the
giant twins. He always stood his ground—fearing not man,
nor dog—nor devil.

Ten minutes later, the Squire took his seat on the platform,
while the circuit-rider squatted down beside him. The crowd,
men and women and children, took the rough benches. To one
side sat and stood the Dillons, old Tad and little Tad, Daws,
Nance, and others of the tribe. Straight in front of the Squire
gathered the Turners about Melissa and Chad and Jack as a
centre—with Jack squatted on his haunches foremost of all,
facing the Squire with grave dignity and looking at none else
save, occasionally, the old hunter or his little master.

To the right stood the sheriff with his rifle, and on the outskirts hung the school-master. Quickly the old Squire chose a
jury—giving old Joel the opportunity to object as he called
each man's name. Old Joel objected to none, for every man
called, he knew, was more friendly to him than to the Dillons:
and old Tad Dillon raised no word of protest, for he knew his
case was clear. Then began the trial, and any soul that was
there would have shuddered could he have known how that
trial was to divide neighbor against neighbor, and mean death
and bloodshed for half a century after the trial itself was long
forgotten.

The first witness, old Tad—long, lean, stooping, crafty—
had seen the sheep rushing wildly up the hill-side " 'bout crack
o' day," he said, and had sent Daws up to see what the matter
was. Daws had shouted back:

"That damned Turner dog has killed one o' our sheep.
Thar he comes now. Kill him!" And old Tad had rushed in-

Straight in front of the Squire gathered the Turners about Melissa and Chad and Jack as a centre.

doors for his rifle and had taken a shot at Jack as he leaped into the road and loped for home. Just then a stern, thick little voice rose from behind Jack:

"Hit was a God's blessin' fer you that you didn't hit him."

The Squire glared down at the boy and old Joel said, kindly:

"Hush, Chad."

Old Dillon had then gone down to the Turners and asked them to kill the dog, but old Joel had refused.

"Whar was Whizzer?" Chad asked, sharply.

"You can't axe that question," said the Squire. "Hit's er-er-irrelevant."

Daws came next. When he reached the fence upon the hillside he could see the sheep lying still on the ground. As he was climbing over, the Turner dog jumped the fence and Daws saw blood on his muzzle.

"How close was you to him?" asked the Squire.

" 'Bout twenty feet," said Daws.

"Humph!" said old Joel.

"Whar was Whizzer?" Again the old Squire glared down at Chad.

"Don't you axe that question again, boy. Didn't I tell you hit was irrelevant?"

"What's irrelevant?" the boy asked, bluntly.

The Squire hesitated. "Why—why, hit ain't got nothin' to do with the case."

"Hit ain't?" shouted Chad.

"Joel," said the Squire, testily, "ef you don't keep that boy still, I'll fine him fer contempt o' court."

Joel laughed, but he put his heavy hand on the boy's shoulder. Little Tad Dillon and Nance and the Dillon mother had all seen Jack running down the road. There was no doubt but that it was the Turner dog. And with this clear case against poor Jack, the Dillons rested. And what else could the Turners do but establish Jack's character and put in a plea of mercy —a useless plea, old Joel knew—for a first offence? Jack was the best dog old Joel had ever known, and the old man told wonderful tales of the dog's intelligence and kindness and how one night Jack had guarded a stray lamb that had broken its leg—until daybreak—and he had been led to the dog and the sheep by Jack's barking for help. The Turner boys confirmed this story, though it was received with incredulity.

How could a dog that would guard one lone helpless lamb all night long take the life of another?

There was no witness that had aught but kind words to say of the dog or aught but wonder that he should have done this thing—even back to the cattle-dealer who had given him to Chad. For at that time the dealer said—so testified Chad, no objection being raised to hearsay evidence—that Jack was the best dog he ever knew. That was all the Turners or anybody could do or say, and the old Squire was about to turn the case over to the jury when Chad rose:

"Squire," he said, and his voice trembled, "Jack's my dog. I lived with him night an' day for 'bout three years an' I want to axe some questions."

He turned to Daws:

"I want to axe you ef thar was any blood around that sheep."

"Thar was a great big pool o' blood," said Daws, indignantly. Chad looked at the Squire.

[132]

"Well, a sheep-killin' dog don't leave no great big pool o' blood, Squire, with the *fust* one he kills! *He sucks it!*" Several men nodded their heads.

"Squire! The fust time I come over these mountains, the fust people I seed was these Dillons—an' Whizzer. They sicked Whizzer on Jack hyeh and Jack whooped him. Then Tad thar jumped me and I whooped him." (The Turner boys were nodding confirmation.) "Sence that time they've hated Jack an' they've hated me and they hate the Turners partly fer takin' keer o' me. Now you said somethin' I axed just now was irrelevant, but I tell you, Squire, I know a sheep-killin' dawg, and jes' as I know Jack *ain't,* I know the Dillon dawg naturely *is,* and I tell you, if the Dillons' dawg killed that sheep and they could put it on Jack—they'd do it. They'd do it—Squire, an' I tell you, you—ortern't—to let—that—sheriff—thar—shoot my—dog—until the Dillons answers what I axed—" the boy's passionate cry rang against the green walls and out the opening and across the river—

"Whar's Whizzer?"

The boy startled the crowd and the old Squire himself, who turned quickly to the Dillons.

"Well, whar is Whizzer?"

Nobody answered.

"He ain't been seen, Squire, sence the evenin' afore the night o' the killin'!" Chad's statement seemed to be true. Not a voice contradicted.

"An' I want to know if Daws seed signs o' killin' on Jack's head when he jumped the fence, why them same signs didn't show when he got home."

Poor Chad! Here old Tad Dillon raised his hand.

"Axe the Turners, Squire," he said, and as the school-master on the outskirts shrank, as though he meant to leave the crowd, the old man's quick eye caught the movement and he added:

"Axe the school-teacher!"

Every eye turned with the Squire's to the master, whose face was strangely serious straightway.

"Did you see any signs on the dawg when he got home?" The gaunt man hesitated with one swift glance at the boy, who almost paled in answer.

"Why," said the school-master, and again he hesitated, but old Joel, in a voice that was without hope, encouraged him:

"Go on!"

"What wus they?"

"Jack had blood on his muzzle, and a little strand o' wool behind one ear."

There was no hope against that testimony. Melissa broke away from her mother and ran out to the road—weeping. Chad dropped with a sob to his bench and put his arms around the dog: then he rose up and walked out the opening while Jack leaped against his leash to follow. The school-master put out his hand to stop him, but the boy struck it aside without looking up and went on: he could not stay to see Jack condemned. He knew what the verdict would be, and in twenty minutes the jury gave it, without leaving their seats.

"Guilty!"

The Sheriff came forward. He knew Jack and Jack knew him, and wagged his tail and whimpered up at him when he took the leash.

"Well, by ——, this is a job I don't like, an' I'm damned

ef I'm agoin' to shoot this dawg afore he knows what I'm shootin' him fer. I'm goin' to show him that sheep fust. Whar's that sheep, Daws?"

Daws led the way down the road, over the fence, across the meadow, and up the hill-side where lay the slain sheep. Chad and Melissa saw them coming—the whole crowd—before they themselves were seen. For a minute the boy watched them. They were going to kill Jack where the Dillons said he had killed the sheep, and the boy jumped to his feet and ran up the hill a little way and disappeared in the bushes, that he might not hear Jack's death-shot, while Melissa sat where she was, watching the crowd come on. Daws was at the foot of the hill, and she saw him make a gesture toward her, and then the Sheriff came on with Jack—over the fence, past her, the Sheriff saying, kindly, "Howdy, Melissa. I shorely am sorry to have to kill Jack," and on to the dead sheep, which lay fifty yards beyond. If the Sheriff expected Jack to drop head and tail and look mean he was greatly mistaken. Jack neither hung back nor sniffed at the carcass. Instead he put one fore foot on it and, with the other bent in the air, looked without shame into the Sheriff's eyes—as much as to say:

"Yes, this is a wicked and shameful thing, but what have I got to do with it? Why are you bringing *me* here?"

The Sheriff came back greatly puzzled and shaking his head. Passing Melissa, he stopped to let the unhappy little girl give Jack a last pat, and it was there that Jack suddenly caught scent of Chad's tracks. With one mighty bound the dog snatched the rawhide string from the careless Sheriff's hand, and in a moment, with his nose to the ground, was speeding up toward the woods. With a startled yell and a frightful oath the

Sheriff threw his rifle to his shoulder, but the little girl sprang up and caught the barrel with both hands, shaking it fiercely up and down and hieing Jack on with shriek after shriek. A minute later Jack had disappeared in the bushes, Melissa was running like the wind down the hill toward home, while the whole crowd in the meadow was rushing up toward the Sheriff, led by the Dillons, who were yelling and swearing like madmen. Above them, the crestfallen Sheriff waited. The Dillons crowded angrily about him, gesticulating and threatening, while he told his story. But nothing could be done—nothing. They did not know that Chad was up in the woods or they would have gone in search of him—knowing that when they found him they would find Jack—but to look for Jack now would be like searching for a needle in a hay-stack. There was nothing to do, then, but to wait for Jack to come home, which he would surely do—to get to Chad—and it was while old Joel was promising that the dog should be surrendered to the Sheriff that little Tad Dillon gave an excited shriek.

"Look up thar!"

And up there at the edge of the wood was Chad standing and, at his feet, Jack sitting on his haunches, with his tongue out and looking as though nothing had happened or could ever happen to Chad or to him.

"Come up hyeh," shouted Chad.

"You come down hyeh," shouted the Sheriff, angrily. So Chad came down, with Jack trotting after him. Chad had cut off the rawhide string, but the Sheriff caught Jack by the nape of the neck.

"You won't git away from me agin, I reckon."

"Well, I reckon you ain't goin' to shoot him," said Chad. "Leggo that dawg."

"Don't be a fool, Jim," said old Joel. "The dawg ain't goin' to leave the boy." The Sheriff let go.

"Come on up hyeh," said Chad. "I got somethin' to show ye."

The boy turned with such certainty that without a word Squire, Sheriff, Turners, Dillons, and spectators followed. As they approached a deep ravine the boy pointed to the ground where were evidences of some fierce struggle—the dirt thrown up, and several small stones scattered about with faded stains of blood on them.

"Wait hyeh!" said the boy, and he slid down the ravine and appeared again dragging something after him. Tall Tom ran down to help him and the two threw before the astonished crowd the body of a black and white dog.

"Now I reckon you know whar Whizzer is," panted Chad vindictively to the Dillons.

"Well, what of it?" snapped Daws.

"Oh, nothin'," said the boy with fine sarcasm. "Only *Whizzer* killed that sheep and Jack killed Whizzer." From every Dillon throat came a scornful grunt.

"Oh, I reckon so," said Chad, easily. "Look thar!" He lifted the dead dog's head, and pointed at the strands of wool between his teeth. He turned it over, showing the deadly grip in the throat and close to the jaws, that had choked the life from Whizzer—Jack's own grip.

"Ef you will jes' rickollect, Jack had that same grip the time afore—when I pulled him off o' Whizzer."

"By ——, that's so," said Tall Tom, and Dolph and Rube

echoed him amid a dozen voices, for not only old Joel, but many of his neighbors knew Jack's method of fighting, which had made him a victor up and down the length of Kingdom Come.

There was little doubt that the boy was right—that Jack had come on Whizzer killing the sheep, and had caught him at the edge of the ravine, where the two had fought, rolling down and settling the old feud between them in the darkness at the bottom. And up there on the hill-side, the jury that pronounced Jack guilty pronounced him innocent, and, as the Turners started joyfully down the hill, the sun that was to have sunk on Jack stiff in death, sank on Jack frisking before them— home.

And yet another wonder was in store for Chad. A strange horse with a strange saddle was hitched to the Turner fence; beside it was an old mare with a boy's saddle, and as Chad came through the gate a familiar voice called him cheerily by name. On the porch sat Major Buford.

XIV

THE MAJOR IN THE MOUNTAINS

The quivering heat of August was giving way, and the golden peace of autumn was spreading through the land. The breath of mountain woods by day was as cool as the breath of valleys at night. In the mountains, boy and girl were leaving school for work in the fields, and from the Cumberland foot-hills to the Ohio, boy and girl were leaving happy holidays for school. Along a rough, rocky road and down a shining river, now sunk to deep pools with trickling riffles between—for a drouth was on the land—rode a tall, gaunt man on an old brown mare that switched with her tail now and then at a long-legged, rough-haired colt stumbling awkwardly behind. Where the road turned from the river and up the mountain, the man did a peculiar thing, for there, in that lonely wilderness, he stopped, dismounted, tied the reins to an overhanging branch and, leaving mare and colt behind, strode up the mountain, on and on, disappearing over the top. Half an hour later, a sturdy youth hove in sight, trudging along the same road with his cap in his hand, a long rifle over one shoulder and a dog trotting at his heels. Now and then the boy would look back and scold the dog, and the dog would drop his muzzle with shame, until the boy stooped to pat him on the head, when he would leap frisking before him, until another affectionate scolding was due. The old mare turned her head when she heard them coming, and nickered. Without a moment's hesitation the lad untied her, mounted and rode up the mountain. For two days the

man and the boy had been "riding and tying," as this way of
travel for two men and one horse is still known in the hills, and
over the mountain, they were to come together for the night.
At the foot of the spur on the other side, boy and dog came
upon the tall man sprawled at full length across a moss-covered
bowlder. The dog dropped behind, but the man's quick eye
caught him:

"Where'd that dog come from, Chad?" Jack put his belly
to the earth and crawled slowly forward—penitent, but deter-
mined.

"He broke loose, I reckon. He come tearin' up behind me
'bout an hour ago, like a house afire. Let him go." Caleb Hazel frowned.

"I told you, Chad, that we'd have no place to keep him."

"Well, we can send him home as easy from up thar as we
can from hyeh—let him go."

"All right!" Chad understood not a whit better than the
dog; for Jack leaped to his feet and jumped around the school-
master, trying to lick his hands, but the school-master was absorbed and would none of him. There, the mountain-path
turned into a wagon-road and the school-master pointed with
one finger.

"Do you know what that is, Chad?"

"No, sir." Chad said "sir" to the school-master now.

"Well, that's"—the school-master paused to give his words
effect—"that's the old Wilderness Road."

Ah, did he not know the old, old Wilderness Road! The
boy gripped his rifle unconsciously, as though there might yet
be a savage lying in ambush in some covert of rhododendron
close by. And, as they trudged ahead, side by side now, for it

was growing late, the school-master told him, as often before, the story of that road and the pioneers who had trod it—the hunters, adventurers, emigrants, fine ladies and fine gentlemen who had stained it with their blood; and how that road had broadened into the mighty way for a great civilization from sea to sea. The lad could see it all, as he listened, wishing that he had lived in those stirring days, never dreaming in how little was he of different mould from the stout-hearted pioneers who beat out the path with their moccasined feet; how little less full of danger were his own days to be; how little different had been his own life, and was his purpose now—how little different after all was the bourn to which his own restless feet were bearing him.

Chad had changed a good deal since that night after Jack's trial, when the kind-hearted old Major had turned up at Joel's cabin to take him back to the Bluegrass. He was taller, broader at shoulder, deeper of chest; his mouth and eyes were prematurely grave from much brooding and looked a little defiant, as though the boy expected hostility from the world and was prepared to meet it, but there was no bitterness in them, and luminous about the lad was the old atmosphere of brave, sunny cheer and simple self-trust that won people to him.

The Major and old Joel had talked late that night after Jack's trial. The Major had come down to find out who Chad was, if possible, and to take him back home, no matter who he might be. The old hunter looked long into the fire.

"Co'se I know hit 'ud be better fer Chad, but, Lawd, how we'd hate to give him up. Still, I reckon I'll have to let him go, but I can stand hit better, if you can git him to leave Jack hyeh." The Major smiled. Did old Joel know where Nathan

Cherry lived? The old hunter did. Nathan was a "damned old skinflint who lived across the mountain on Stone Creek—who stole other folks' farms and if he knew anything about Chad the old hunter would squeeze it out of his throat; and if old Nathan, learning where Chad now was, tried to pester him, he would break every bone in the skinflint's body." So the Major and old Joel rode over next day to see Nathan, and Nathan with his shifting eyes told them Chad's story in a high, cracked voice that, recalling Chad's imitation of it, made the Major laugh. Chad was a foundling, Nathan said: his mother was dead and his father had gone off to the Mexican War and never come back: he had taken the mother in himself, and Chad had been born in his own house, when he lived farther up the river, and the boy had begun to run away as soon as he was old enough to toddle. And with each sentence Nathan would call for confirmation on a silent, dark-faced daughter who sat inside: "Didn't he, Betsy?" or "Wasn't he, gal?" And the girl would nod sullenly, but say nothing. It seemed a hopeless mission except that, on the way back, the Major learned that there were one or two Bufords living down the Cumberland, and like old Joel, shook his head over Nathan's pharisaical philanthropy to a homeless boy and wondered what the motive under it was— but he went back with the old hunter and tried to get Chad to go home with him. The boy was rock-firm in his refusal.

"I'm obleeged to you, Major, but I reckon I better stay in the mountains." That was all Chad would say, and at last the Major gave up and rode back over the mountain and down the Cumberland alone, still on his quest. At a blacksmith's shop far down the river he found a man who had "heerd tell of a Chad Buford who had been killed in the Mexican War and whose daddy lived 'bout fifteen mile down the river." The Major found that Buford dead, but an old woman told him his name was Chad, that he had "fit in the War o' 1812 when he was nothin' but a chunk of a boy, and that his daddy, whose name, too, was Chad, had been killed by Injuns some'eres aroun' Cumberland Gap." By this time the Major was as keen as a hound on the scent, and, in a cabin at the foot of the sheer gray wall that crumbles into the Gap, he had the amazing luck to find an octogenarian with an unclouded memory who could recollect a queer-looking old man who had been killed by Indians—"a ole feller with the curiosest hair I ever did see," added the patriarch. His name was Colonel Buford, and the old man knew where he was buried, for he himself was old enough at the time to help bury him. Greatly excited, the Major hired mountaineers to dig into the little hill that the old man pointed out, on which there was, however, no sign of a grave, and, at last, they uncovered the skeleton of an old gentleman in a wig and peruke! There was little doubt now that the boy, no matter what the blot on his 'scutcheon, was of his own flesh and blood, and the Major was tempted to go back at once for him, but it was a long way, and he was ill and anxious to get back home. So he took the Wilderness Road for the Bluegrass, and wrote old Joel the facts and asked him to send Chad to him whenever he would come. But the boy would not go. There was no definite reason in his mind. It was a stubborn instinct merely—the instinct of pride, of stubborn independence—of shame that festered in his soul like a hornet's sting. Even Melissa urged him. She never tired of hearing Chad tell about the Bluegrass country, and when she knew that the Major wanted him to go back, she followed him out in the yard that night and found him on the fence whittling. A red star was sinking behind the mountains. "Why won't you go back no more, Chad?" she said.

" 'Cause I hain't got no daddy er mammy." Then Melissa startled him.

"Well, I'd go—an' *I* hain't got no daddy er mammy." Chad stopped his whittling.

"Whut'd you say, Lissy?" he asked, gravely.

Melissa was frightened—the boy looked so serious.

"Cross yo' heart an' body that you won't *nuver* tell *no* body." Chad crossed.

"Well, mammy said I mustn't ever tell nobody—but I *hain't* got no daddy er mammy. I heerd her a-tellin' the school-teacher." And the little girl shook her head over her frightful crime of disobedience.

"You *hain't?*"

"I *hain't!*"

Melissa, too, was a waif, and Chad looked at her with a wave of new affection and pity.

"Now, why won't you go back just because you hain't got no daddy an' mammy?"

Chad hesitated. There was no use making Melissa unhappy.

"Oh, I'd just ruther stay hyeh in the mountains," he said, carelessly—lying suddenly like the little gentleman that he was—lying as he knew, and as Melissa some day would come to know. Then Chad looked at the little girl a long while, and in such a queer way that Melissa turned her face shyly to the red star.

"I'm goin' to stay right hyeh. Ain't you glad, Lissy?"

The little girl turned her eyes shyly back again. "Yes, Chad," she said.

He would stay in the mountains and work hard; and when he grew up he would marry Melissa and they would go away where nobody knew him or her: or they would stay right there in the mountains where nobody blamed him for what he was nor Melissa for what she was; and he would study law like Caleb Hazel, and go to the Legislature—but Melissa! And with the thought of Melissa in the mountains came always the thought of dainty Margaret in the Bluegrass and the chasm that lay between the two—between Margaret and him, for that matter; and when Mother Turner called Melissa from him in the orchard next day, Chad lay on his back under an apple-tree, for a long while, thinking; and then he whistled for Jack and climbed the spur above the river where he could look down on the shadowed water and out to the clouded heaps of rose and green and crimson, where the sun was going down under one faint white star. Melissa was the glow-worm that, when darkness came, would be a watch-fire at his feet—Margaret, the star to which his eyes were lifted night and day—and so runs the world. He lay long watching that star. It hung almost over the world of which he had dreamed so long and upon which he had turned his back forever. Forever? Perhaps, but he went back home that night with a trouble in his soul that was not to pass, and while he sat by the fire, he awoke from the same dream to find Melissa's big eyes fixed on him, and in them was a vague trouble that was more than his own reflected back to him.

Still the boy went back sturdily to his old life, working in the fields, busy about the house and stable, going to school, reading and studying with the school-master at nights, and wandering in the woods with Jack and his rifle. And he hungered for spring to come again when he should go with the Turner boys to take another raft of logs down the river to the capital. Spring came, and going out to the back pasture one morning, Chad found a long-legged, ungainly creature stumbling awkwardly about his old mare—a colt! That, too, he owed the Major, and he would have burst with pride had he known that the colt's sire was a famous stallion in the Bluegrass. That spring he did go down the river again. He did not let the Major know he was coming and, through a nameless shyness, he could not bring himself to go to see his old friend and kinsman, but in Lexington, while he and the school-master were standing on Cheapside, the Major whirled around a corner on them in his carriage, and, as on the turnpike a year before, old Tom, the driver, called out:

"Look dar, Mars Cal!" And there stood Chad.

"Why, bless my soul! Chad—why, boy! How you have grown!" For Chad had grown, and his face was curiously aged and thoughtful. The Major insisted on taking him home, and the school-master, too, who went reluctantly. Miss Lucy was there, looking whiter and more fragile than ever, and she greeted Chad with a sweet kindliness that took the sting from his unjust remembrance of her. And what that failure to understand her must have been, Chad better knew when he saw the embarrassed awe, in her presence, of the school-master, for whom all in the mountains had so much reverence. At the table was Thankyma'am waiting. Around the quarters and the stable the pickaninnies and servants seemed to remember the boy in a kindly genuine way that touched him, and even Jerome

Conners, the overseer, seemed glad to see him. The Major was drawn at once to the grave school-master, and he had a long talk with him that night. It was no use, Caleb Hazel said, trying to persuade the boy to live with the Major—not yet. And the Major was more content when he came to know in what good hands the boy was, and, down in his heart, he loved the lad the more for his sturdy independence, and for the pride that made him shrink from facing the world with the shame of his birth; knowing that Chad thought of him, perhaps more than of himself. Such unwillingness to give others trouble seemed remarkable in so young a lad. Not once did the Major mention the Deans to the boy, and about them Chad asked no questions—not even when he saw their carriage passing the Major's gate. When they came to leave the Major said:

"Well, Chad, when that filly of yours is a year old, I'll buy 'em both from you, if you'll sell 'em, and I reckon you can come up and go to school then."

Chad shook his head. Sell that colt? He would as soon have thought of selling Jack. But the temptation took root, just the same, then and there, and grew steadily until, after another year in the mountains, it grew too strong. For, in that year, Chad grew to look the fact of his birth steadily in the face, and in his heart grew steadily a proud resolution to make his way in the world despite it. It was curious how Melissa came to know the struggle that was going on within him, and how Chad came to know that she knew—though no word passed between them: more curious still, how it came with a shock to Chad one day to realize how little was the tragedy of his life in comparison with the tragedy in hers, and to learn that the little girl with swift vision had already reached that truth and with sweet unselfishness had reconciled herself. He was a boy—he could go out in the world and conquer it, while her life was as rigid and straight before her as though it ran between close walls of rock as steep and sheer as the cliff across the river. One thing he never guessed—what it cost the little girl to support him bravely in his purpose, and to stand with smiling face when the first breath of one sombre autumn stole through the hills, and Chad and the school-master left the Turner home for the Bluegrass, this time to stay.

She stood in the doorway after they had waved good-by from the head of the river—the smile gone, and her face in a sudden dark eclipse. The wise old mother went in-doors. Once the girl started through the yard as though she would rush after them and stopped at the gate, clinching it hard with both hands. As suddenly she became quiet. She went in-doors to her work, and worked quietly and without a word. Thus she did all day while her mind and her heart ached. When she went after the cows before sunset she stopped at the barn where Beelzebub had been tied. She lifted her eyes to the hay-loft where she and Chad had hunted for hens' eggs and played hide-and-seek. She passed through the orchard where they had worked and played so many happy hours, and on to the back pasture where the Dillon sheep had been killed and she had kept the Sheriff from shooting Jack. And she saw and noted everything with a piteous pain and dry eyes. But she gave no sign that night, and not until she was in bed did she with covered head give way. Then the bed shook with her smothered sobs. This is the sad way with women. After the way of men, Chad proudly marched the old Wilderness Road that led to a big, bright, beautiful world where one had but to do and dare

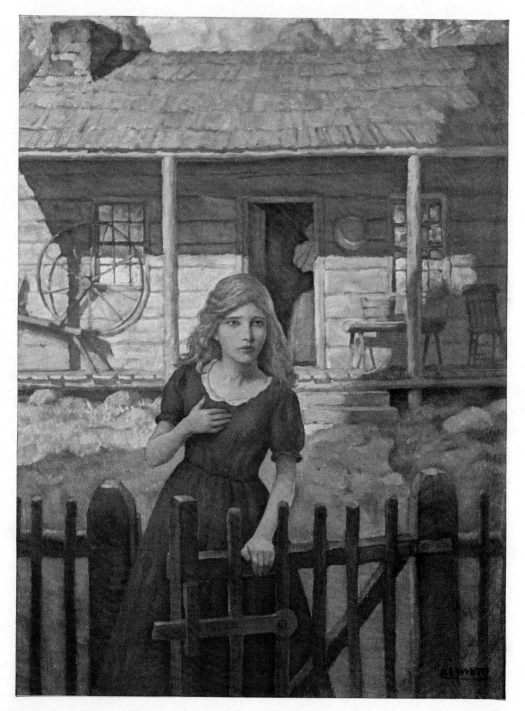

Once the girl started through the yard as though she would rush after them and stopped at the gate.

to reach the stars. The men who had trod that road had made that big world beyond, and their life Chad himself had lived so far. Only, where they had lived he had been born—in a log-cabin. Their weapons—the axe and the rifle—had been his. He had had the same fight with Nature as they. He knew as well as they what life in the woods in "a half-faced camp" was. Their rude sports and pastimes, their log-rollings, house-raisings, quilting parties, corn-huskings, feats of strength, had been his. He had the same lynx eyes, cool courage, swiftness of foot, readiness of resource, that had been trained into them. His heart was as stout and his life as simple and pure. He was taking their path and, in the far West, beyond the Bluegrass world where he was going, he could, if he pleased, take up the same life at the precise point where they had left off. At sunset, Chad and the school-master stood on the summit of the Cumberland foothills and looked over the rolling land with little less of a thrill, doubtless, than the first hunters felt when the land before them was as much a wilderness as the wilds through which they had made their way. Below them a farmhouse shrank half out of sight into a little hollow, and toward it they went down.

The outside world had moved swiftly during the two years that they had been buried in the hills, as they learned at the farm-house that night. Already the national storm was threatening, the air was electrically charged with alarms, and already here and there the lightning had flashed. The underground railway was busy with black freight, and John Brown, fanatic, was boldly lifting his shaggy head. Old Brutus Dean was even publishing an abolitionist paper at Lexington, the aristocratic heart of the State. He was making abolition speeches throughout the Bluegrass with a dagger thrust in the table before him —shaking his black mane and roaring defiance like a lion. The news thrilled Chad unaccountably, as did the shadow of any danger, but it threw the school-master into gloom. There was more. A dark little man by the name of Douglas, and a sinewy giant by the name of Lincoln, were thrilling the West. Phillips and Garrison were thundering in Massachusetts, and fiery tongues in the South were flashing back scornful challenges and threats that would imperil a nation. An invisible air-line shot suddenly between the North and the South, destined to drop some day and lie a dead-line on the earth, and on each side of it two hordes of brothers, who thought themselves two hostile peoples, were shrinking away from each other with the half-conscious purpose of making ready for a charge. In no other State in the Union was the fratricidal character of the coming war to be so marked as in Kentucky, in no other State was the national drama to be so fully played to the bitter end.

That night even, Brutus Dean was going to speak near by, and Chad and Caleb Hazel went to hear him. The fierce abolitionist first placed a Bible before him.

"This is for those who believe in religion," he said; then a copy of the Constitution: "this for those who believe in the laws and in freedom of speech. And this," he thundered, driving a dagger into the table and leaving it to quiver there, "is for the rest!" Then he went on and no man dared to interrupt.

And only next day came the rush of wind that heralds the storm. Just outside of Lexington Chad and the school-master left the mare and colt at a farm-house and with Jack went into town on foot. It was Saturday afternoon, the town was full of people, and an excited crowd was pressing along Main Street toward Cheapside. The man and the boy followed eagerly. Cheapside was thronged—thickest around a frame building that bore a newspaper sign on which was the name of Brutus Dean. A man dashed from a hardware store with an axe, followed by several others with heavy hammers in their hands. One swing of the axe, the door was crashed open and the crowd went in like wolves. Shattered windows, sashes and all, flew out into the street, followed by showers of type, chair-legs, table-tops, and then, piece by piece, the battered cogs, wheels, and forms of a printing-press. The crowd made little noise. In fifteen minutes the house was a shell with gaping windows, surrounded with a pile of chaotic rubbish, and the men who had done the work quietly disappeared. Chad looked at the school-master for the first time—neither of them had uttered a word. The school-master's face was white with anger, his hands were clinched, and his eyes were so fierce and burning that the boy was frightened.

XV

TO COLLEGE IN THE BLUEGRASS

As the school-master had foretold, there was no room at college for Jack. Several times Major Buford took the dog home with him, but Jack would not stay. The next morning the dog would turn up at the door of the dormitory where Chad and the school-master slept, and as a last resort the boy had to send Jack home. So, one Sunday morning Chad led Jack out of the town for several miles, and at the top of a high hill pointed toward the mountains and sternly told him to go home. And Jack, understanding that the boy was in earnest, trotted sadly away with a placard around his neck:

I own this dog. His name is Jack. He is on his way to Kingdom Come. Please feed him. Uncle Joel Turner will shoot any man who steels him.   CHAD.

It was no little consolation to Chad to think that the faithful sheep-dog would in no small measure repay the Turners for all they had done for him. But Jack was the closest link that bound him to the mountains, and dropping out of sight behind the crest of the hill, Chad crept to the top again and watched Jack until he trotted out of sight, and the link was broken. Then Chad went slowly and sorrowfully back to his room.

It was the smallest room in the dormitory that the school-master had chosen for himself and Chad, and in it were one closet, one table, one lamp, two chairs and one bed—no more. There were two windows in the little room—one almost swept by the branches of a locust-tree and overlooking the brown-gray sloping campus and the roofs and church-steeples of the town—the other opening to the east on a sweep of field and woodland over which the sun rose with a daily message from the unseen mountains far beyond, and toward which Chad had sent Jack trotting home. It was a proud day for Chad when Caleb Hazel took him to "matriculate"—leading him from one to another of the professors, who awed the lad with their pre-ternatural dignity, but it was a sad blow when he was told that in everything but mathematics he must go to the preparatory department until the second session of the term—the "kitchen," as it was called by the students. He bore it bravely, though, and the school-master took him down the shady streets to the busy thoroughfare, where the official book-store was, and where Chad, with pure ecstasy, caught his first new books under one arm and trudged back, bending his head now and then to catch the delicious smell of the fresh leaves and print. It was while he was standing with his treasures under the big elm at the turnstile, looking across the campus at the sundown, that two boys came down the gravel path. He knew them both at once as Dan and Harry Dean. Both looked at him curiously, as he thought, but he saw that neither knew him and no one spoke. The sound of wheels came up the street behind him just then, and a carriage halted at the turnstile to take them in. Turning, Chad saw a slender girl with dark hair and eyes and heard her call brightly to the boys. He almost caught his breath at the sound of her voice, but he kept sturdily on his way, and the girl's laugh rang in his ears as it rang the first time he heard it, was ringing when he reached his room, ringing when he went to bed that night, and as he lay sleepless, looking through his window at the quiet stars.

For some time, indeed, no one recognized him, and Chad was glad. Once he met Richard Hunt riding with Margaret, and the piercing dark eyes that the boy remembered so well turned again to look at him. Chad colored and bravely met them with his own, but there was no recognition. And he saw John Morgan—Captain John Morgan—at the head of the "Lexington Rifles," which he had just formed from the best blood of the town, as though in long preparation for that coming war—saw him and Richard Hunt, as lieutenant, drilling them in the campus, and the sight thrilled him as nothing else, except Margaret, had ever done. Many times he met the Dean brothers on the playground and in the streets, but there was no sign that he was known until he was called to the blackboard one day in geometry, the only course in which he had not been sent to the "kitchen." Then Chad saw Harry turn quickly when the professor called his name. Confused though he was for a moment, he gave his demonstration in his quaint speech with perfect clearness and without interruption from the professor, who gave the boy a keen look as he said, quietly:

"Very good, sir!" And Harry could see his fingers tracing in his class-book the figures that meant a perfect recitation.

"How are you, Chad?" he said in the hallway afterward.

"Howdye!" said Chad, shaking the proffered hand.

[154]

"I didn't know you—you've grown so tall. Didn't you know me?"

"Yes."

"Then why didn't you speak to me?"

" 'Cause you didn't know *me*."

Harry laughed. "Well, that isn't fair. See you again."

"All right," said Chad.

That very afternoon Chad met Dan in a foot-ball game—an old-fashioned game, in which there were twenty or thirty howling lads on each side and nobody touched the ball except with his foot—met him so violently that, clasped in each other's arms, they tumbled to the ground.

"Leggo!" said Dan.

"S'pose you leggo!" said Chad.

As Dan started after the ball he turned to look at Chad and after the game he went up to him.

"Why, aren't you the boy who was out at Major Buford's once?"

"Yes." Dan thrust out his hand and began to laugh. So did Chad, and each knew that the other was thinking of the tournament.

"In college?"

"Math'matics," said Chad. "I'm in the kitchen fer the rest."

"Oh!" said Dan. "Where you living?" Chad pointed to the dormitory, and again Dan said "Oh!" in a way that made Chad flush, but added, quickly:

"You better play on our side to-morrow."

Chad looked at his clothes—foot-ball seemed pretty hard on clothes—"I don't know," he said—"mebbe."

It was plain that neither of the boys was holding anything against Chad, but neither had asked the mountain lad to come to see him—an omission that was almost unforgivable according to Chad's social ethics. So Chad proudly went into his shell again, and while the three boys met often, no intimacy developed. Often he saw them with Margaret, on the street, in a carriage or walking with a laughing crowd of boys and girls; on the porticos of old houses or in the yards; and, one night, Chad saw, through the wide-open door of a certain old house on the corner of Mill and Market Streets, a party going on; and Margaret, all in white, dancing, and he stood in the shade of the trees opposite, with new pangs shooting through him, and went back to his room in desolate loneliness, but with a new grip on his resolution that his own day should yet come.

Steadily the boy worked, forging his way slowly but surely toward the head of his class in the "kitchen," and the schoolmaster helped him unwearyingly. And it was a great help—mental and spiritual—to be near the stern Puritan, who loved the boy as a brother and was ever ready to guide him with counsel and aid him with his studies. In time the Major went to the president to ask him about Chad, and that august dignitary spoke of the lad in a way that made the Major, on his way through the campus, swish through the grass with his cane in great satisfaction. He always spoke of the boy now as his adopted son and, whenever it was possible, he came in to take Chad out home to spend Sunday with him; but, being a wise man and loving Chad's independence, he let the boy have his own way. He had bought the filly—and would hold her, he said, until Chad could buy her back, and he would keep the old nag as a brood-mare and would divide profits with Chad—to all of

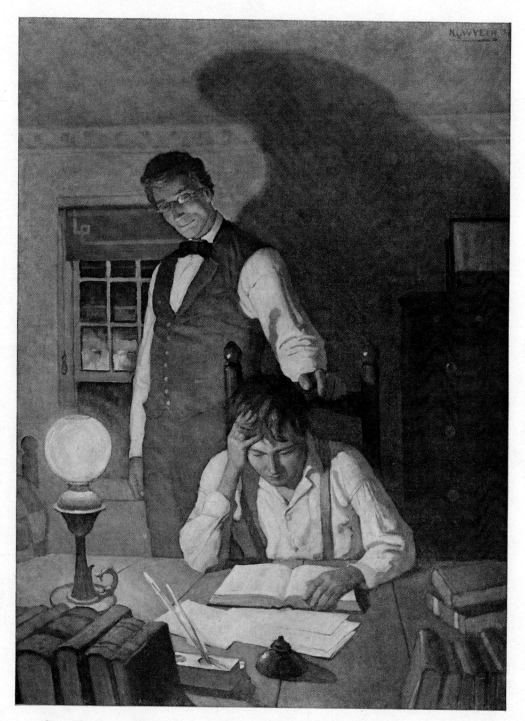

Steadily the boy worked,—and the schoolmaster helped him unwearyingly.

which the boy agreed. The question of the lad's birth was ignored between them, and the Major rarely spoke to Chad of the Deans, who were living in town during the winter, nor questioned him about Dan or Harry or Margaret. But Chad had found out where the little girl went to church, and every Sunday, despite Caleb Hazel's protest, he would slip into the Episcopal church, with a queer feeling—little Calvinist of the hills that he was—that it was not quite right for him even to enter that church; and he would watch the little girl come in with her family and, after the queer way of these "furriners," kneel first in prayer. And there, with soul uplifted by the dim rich light and the peal of the organ, he would sit watching her; rising when she rose, watching the light from the windows on her shining hair and sweet-spirited face, watching her reverent little head bend in obeisance to the name of the Master, though he kept his own held straight, for no Popery like that was for him. Always, however, he would slip out before the service was quite over, and never wait even to see her come out of church. He was too proud for that and, anyhow, it made him lonely to see the people greeting one another and chatting and going off home together when there was not a soul to speak to him. It was just one such Sunday that they came face to face for the first time. Chad had gone down the street after leaving the church, had changed his mind and was going back to his room. People were pouring from the church, as he went by, but Chad did not even look across. A clatter rose behind him and he turned to see a horse and rockaway coming at a gallop up the street, which was narrow. The negro driver, frightened though he was, had sense enough to pull his running horse away from the line of vehicles in front of the church so that the beast stumbled against the curb-stone, crashed into a tree, and dropped struggling in the gutter below another line of vehicles waiting on the other side of the street. Like lightning, Chad leaped and landed full length on the horse's head and was tossed violently to and fro, but he held on until the animal lay still.

"Unhitch the hoss," he called, sharply.

"Well, that was pretty quick work for a boy," said a voice across the street that sounded familiar, and Chad looked across to see General Dean and Margaret watching him. The boy blushed furiously when his eyes met Margaret's and he thought he saw her start slightly, but he lowered his eyes and hurried away.

It was only a few days later that, going up from town toward the campus, he turned a corner and there was Margaret alone and moving slowly ahead of him. Hearing his steps she turned her head to see who it was, but Chad kept his eyes on the ground and passed her without looking up. And thus he went on, although she was close behind him, across the street and to the turnstile. As he was passing through, a voice rose behind him:

"You aren't very polite, little boy." He turned quickly— Margaret had not gone around the corner: she, too, was coming through the campus and there she stood, grave and demure, though her eyes were dancing.

"My mamma says a *nice* little boy always lets a little *girl* go *first*."

"I didn't know you was comin' through."

"Was comin' through!" Margaret made a little face as though to say—"Oh, dear."

"I said I didn't know you *were* coming through this way."

Margaret shook her head. "No," she said; "no, you didn't."

"Well, that's what I meant to say." Chad was having a hard time with his English. He had snatched his cap from his head, had stepped back outside the stile, and was waiting to turn it for her. Margaret passed through and waited where the paths forked.

"Are you going up to the college?" she asked.

"I was—but I ain't now—if you'll let me walk a piece with you." He was scarlet with confusion—a tribute that Chad rarely paid his kind. His way of talking was very funny, to be sure, but had she not heard her father say that "the poor little chap had had no chance in life;" and Harry, that some day he would be the best in his class?

"Aren't you—Chad?"

"Yes—ain't you Margaret—Miss Margaret?"

"Yes, I'm Margaret." She was pleased with the hesitant title and the boy's halting reverence.

"An' I called you a little gal." Margaret's laugh tinkled in merry remembrance. "An' you wouldn't take my fish."

"I can't bear to touch them."

"I know," said Chad, remembering Melissa.

They passed a boy who knew Chad, but not Margaret. The lad took off his hat, but Chad did not lift his; then a boy and a girl and, when only the two girls spoke, the other boy lifted his hat, though he did not speak to Margaret. Still Chad's hat was untouched and when Margaret looked up, Chad's face was red with confusion again. But it never took the boy long to learn and, thereafter, during the walk his hat came off unfailingly. Everyone looked at the two with some surprise and Chad noticed that the little girl's chin was being lifted higher and higher. His intuition told him what the matter was, and when they reached the stile across the campus and Chad saw a crowd of Margaret's friends coming down the street, he halted as if to turn back, but the little girl told him imperiously to come on. It was a strange escort for haughty Margaret—the country-looking boy, in coarse homespun—but Margaret spoke cheerily to her friends and went on, looking up at Chad and talking to him as though he were the dearest friend she had on earth.

At the edge of town she suggested that they walk across a pasture and go back by another street, and not until they were passing through the woodland did Chad come to himself.

"You know I didn't rickollect when you called me 'little boy.'"

"Indeed!"

"Not at fust, I mean," stammered Chad.

Margaret grew mock-haughty and Chad grew grave. He spoke very slowly and steadily. "I reckon I rickollect ever'-thing that happened out thar a sight better'n you. I ain't forgot nothin'—anything."

The boy's sober and half-sullen tone made Margaret catch her breath with a sudden vague alarm. Unconsciously she quickened her pace, but, already, she was mistress of an art to which she was born and she said, lightly:

"Now, that's *much* better." A piece of pasteboard dropped from Chad's jacket just then, and, taking the little girl's cue to swerve from the point at issue, he picked it up and held it out for Margaret to read. It was the first copy of the placard which he had tied around Jack's neck when he sent him home, and it set Margaret to laughing and asking questions. Before he knew it Chad was telling her about Jack and the mountains; how he had run away; about the Turners, and about Melissa, and coming down the river on a raft—all he had done and all he meant to do. And from looking at Chad now and then, Margaret finally kept her eyes fixed on his—and thus they stood when they reached the gate, while crows flew cawing over them and the air grew chill.

"And did Jack go home?"

Chad laughed.

"No, he didn't. He come back, and I had to hide fer two days. Then, because he couldn't find me he did go, thinking I had gone back to the mountains, too. He went to look fer me."

"Well, if he comes back again I'll ask my papa to get them to let you keep Jack at college," said Margaret.

Chad shook his head.

"Then I'll keep him for you myself." The boy looked his gratitude, but shook his head again.

"He won't stay."

Margaret asked for the placard again as they moved down the street.

"You've got it spelled wrong," she said, pointing to "steel." Chad blushed. "I can't spell when I write," he said. "I can't even talk—right."

"But you'll learn," she said.

"Will you help me?"

"Yes."

"Tell me when I say things wrong?"

"Yes."

"Where'm I goin' to see you?"

Margaret shook her head thoughtfully; then the reason for her speaking first to Chad came out.

"Papa and I saw you on Sunday, and papa said you must be very strong, as well as brave, and that you knew something about horses. Harry told us who you were when papa described you, and then I remembered. Papa told Harry to bring you to see us. And you must come," she said, decisively.

They had reached the turnstile at the campus again.

"Have you had any more tournaments?" asked Margaret.

"No," said Chad, apprehensively.

"Do you remember the last thing I said to you?"

"I rickollect that better'n anything," said Chad.

"Well, I didn't hate you. I'm sorry I said that," she said, gently. Chad looked very serious.

"That's all right," he said. "I seed—I *saw* you on Sunday, too."

"Did you know me?"

"I reckon I did. And that wasn't the fust time." Margaret's eyes were opening with surprise.

"I been goin' to church ever' Sunday fer nothin' else but just to see you." Again his tone gave her vague alarm, but she asked:

"Why didn't you speak to me?"

They were nearing the turnstile across the campus now, and Chad did not answer.

"Why didn't you speak to me?"

Chad stopped suddenly, and Margaret looked quickly at him, and saw that his face was scarlet. The little girl started and her own face flamed. There was one thing she had forgotten, and even now she could not recall what it was—only that it was something terrible she must not know—old Mammy's words when Dan was carried in senseless after the tournament. Frightened and helpless, she shrank toward the turnstile, but Chad did not wait. With his cap in his hand, he turned abruptly, without a sound, and strode away.

XVI

AGAIN THE BAR SINISTER

AND yet, the next time Chad saw Margaret, she spoke to him shyly but cordially, and when he did not come near her, she stopped him on the street one day and reminded him of his promise to come and see them. And Chad knew the truth at once—that she had never asked her father about him, but had not wanted to know what she had been told she must not know, and had properly taken it for granted that her father would not ask Chad to his house, if there were a good reason why he should not come. But Chad did not go even to the Christmas party that Margaret gave in town, though the Major urged him. He spent Christmas with the Major, and he did go to a country party, where the Major was delighted with the boy's grace and agility, dancing the quadrille, and where the lad occasioned no little amusement with his improvisations in the way of cutting pigeon's wings and shuffling, which he had learned in the mountains. So the Major made him accept a loan and buy a suit for social purposes after Christmas, and had him go to Madam Blake's dancing school, and promise to go to the next party to which he was asked. And that Chad did —to the big gray house on the corner, through whose widespread doors his longing eyes had watched Margaret and her friends flitting like butterflies months before.

It intoxicated the boy—the lights, music, flowers, the little girls in white—and Margaret. For the first time he met her friends, Nellie Hunt, sister to Richard; Elizabeth Morgan, cousin to John Morgan; and Miss Jennie Overstreet, who, young as she was, wrote poems—but Chad had eyes only for Margaret. It was while he was dancing a quadrille with her, that he noticed a tall, pale youth with black hair, glaring at him, and he recognized Georgie Forbes, a champion of Margaret, and the old enemy who had caused his first trouble in his new home. Chad laughed with fearless gladness, and Margaret tossed her head. It was Georgie now who blackened and spread the blot on Chad's good name, and it was Georgie to whom Chad—fast learning the ways of gentlemen—promptly sent a pompous challenge, that the difficulty might be settled "in any way the gentleman saw fit." Georgie insultingly declined to fight with one who was not his equal, and Chad boxed his jaws in the presence of a crowd, floored him with one blow, and contemptuously twisted his nose. Thereafter open comment ceased. Chad was making himself known. He was the swiftest runner on the foot-ball field; he had the quickest brain in mathematics; he was elected to the Periclean Society, and astonished his fellow-members with a fiery denunciation of the men who banished Napoleon to St. Helena—so fiery was it, indeed, that his opponents themselves began to wonder how that crime had ever come to pass. He would fight at the drop of a hat, and he always won; and by-and-by the boy began to take a fierce joy in battling his way upward against a block that would have crushed a weaker soul. It was only with Margaret that that soul was in awe. He began to love her with a pure reverence that he could never know at another age. Every Saturday night, when dusk fell, he was mounting the steps of her house. Every Sunday morning he was waiting to take her home from church. Every afternoon he looked for her, hoping

to catch sight of her on the streets, and it was only when Dan
and Harry got indignant, and after Margaret had made a passionate defence of Chad in the presence of the family, that the
General and Mrs. Dean took the matter in hand. It was a
childish thing, of course; a girlish whim. It was right that they
should be kind to the boy—for Major Buford's sake, if not for
his own; but they could not have even the pretence of more than
a friendly intimacy between the two, and so Margaret was told
the truth. Immediately, when Chad next saw her, her honest
eyes sadly told him that she knew the truth, and Chad gave up
then. Thereafter he disappeared from sports and from his
kind in every way, except in the classroom and in the debating
hall. Sullenly he stuck to his books. From five o'clock in the
morning until ten o'clock at night, he was at them steadily, in
his room, or at recitation—except for an hour's walk with the
school-master and the three half-hours that his meals kept him
away. He grew so pale and thin that the Major and Caleb
Hazel were greatly worried, but protest from both was useless.
Before the end of the term he had mounted into college in every
study, and was holding his own. At the end he knew his power
—knew what he *could* do, and his face was set, for his future,
dauntless. When vacation came, he went at once to the Major's
farm, but not to be idle. In a week or two he was taking some
of the reins into his own hands as a valuable assistant to the
Major. He knew a good horse, could guess the weight of a
steer with surprising accuracy, and was a past master in knowledge of sheep. By instinct he was canny at a trade—what
mountaineer is not?—and he astonished the Major with the
shrewd deals he made. Authority seemed to come naturally to
him, and the Major swore that he could get more work out of

the "hands" than the overseer himself, who sullenly resented
Chad's interference, but dared not open his lips. Not once did
he go to the Deans', and neither Harry nor Dan came near him.
There was little intercourse between the Major and the General, as well; for, while the Major could not, under the cir-
cumstances, blame the General, inconsistently, he could not
quite forgive him, and the line of polite coolness between the
neighbors was never overstepped. At the end of July, Chad
went to the mountains to see the Turners and Jack and Melissa.
He wore his roughest clothes, put on no airs, and, to all eyes,
save Melissa's, he was the same old Chad. But feminine sub-
tlety knows no social or geographical lines, and while Melissa
knew what had happened as well as Chad, she never let him see
that she knew. Apparently she was giving open encouragement
to Dave Hilton, a tawny youth from down the river, who was
hanging, dog-like, about the house, and foolish Chad began to
let himself dream of Margaret with a light heart. On the third
day before he was to go back to the Bluegrass, a boy came from
over Black Mountain with a message from old Nathan Cherry.
Old Nathan had joined the church, had fallen ill, and, fearing
he was going to die, wanted to see Chad. Chad went over with
curious premonitions that were not in vain, and he came back
with a strange story that he told only to old Joel, under promise
that he should never make it known to Melissa. Then he started
for the Bluegrass, going over Pine Mountain and down
through Cumberland Gap. He would come back every year of
his life, he told Melissa and the Turners, but Chad knew he was
bidding a last farewell to the life he had known in the mountains. At Melissa's wish and old Joel's, he left Jack behind,
though he sorely wanted to take the dog with him. It was little

enough for him to do in return for their kindness, and he could see that Melissa's affection for Jack was even greater than his own: and how incomparably lonelier than his life was the life that she must lead! This time Melissa did not rush to the yard gate when he was gone. She sank slowly where she stood to the steps of the porch, and there she sat stone-still. Old Joel passed her on the way to the barn. Several times the old mother walked to the door behind her, and each time starting to speak, stopped and turned back, but the girl neither saw nor heard them. Jack trotted by, whimpering. He sat down in front of her, looking up at her unseeing eyes, and it was only when he crept to her and put his head in her lap, that she put her arms around him and bent her own head down; but no tears came.

XVII

CHADWICK BUFORD, GENTLEMAN

AND so, returned to the Bluegrass, the mid-summer of that year, Chadwick Buford, gentleman. A youth of eighteen, with the self-poise of a man, and a pair of level, clear eyes, that looked the world in the face as proudly as ever, but with no defiance and no secret sense of shame. It was a curious story that Chad brought back and told to the Major, on the porch under the honeysuckle vines, but it seemed to surprise the Major very little: how old Nathan had sent for him to come to his death-bed and had told Chad that he was no foundling; that one of his farms belonged to the boy; that he had lied to the Major about Chad's mother, who was a lawful wife, in order to keep the land for himself; how old Nathan had offered to give back the farm, or pay him the price of it in live stock, and how, at old Joel's advice, he had taken the stock and turned the stock into money. How, after he had found his mother's grave, his first act had been to take up the rough bee-gum coffin that held her remains, and carry it down the river, and bury her where she had the right to lie, side by side with her grandfather and his—the old gentleman who slept in wig and peruke on the hill-side—that her good name and memory should never again suffer insult from any living tongue. It was then that Major took Chad by the shoulders roughly, and, with tears in his eyes, swore that he would have no more nonsense from the boy; that Chad was flesh of his flesh and bone of his bone; that he would adopt him and make him live where he belonged, and break his

[169]

damned pride. And it was then that Chad told him how gladly he would come, now that he could bring him an untarnished name. And the two walked together down to the old family graveyard, where the Major said that the two in the mountains should be brought some day and where the two brothers who had parted nearly fourscore years ago could, side by side, await Judgment Day.

When they went back into the house, the Major went to the sideboard.

"Have a drink, Chad?"

Chad laughed: "Do you think it will stunt my growth?"

"Stand up here, and let's see," said the Major.

The two stood up, back to back, in front of a long mirror, and Chad's shaggy hair rose at least an inch above the Major's thin locks of gray. The Major turned and looked at him from head to foot with affectionate pride.

"Six feet in your socks, to the inch, without that hair. I reckon it won't stunt you—not now."

"All right," laughed Chad, "then I'll take that drink." And together they drank.

Thus, Chadwick Buford, gentleman, after the lapse of three-quarters of a century, came back to his own: and what that own, at that day and in that land, was!

It was the rose of Virginia, springing, in full bloom, from new and richer soil—a rose of a deeper scarlet and a stronger stem: and the big village where the old University reared its noble front was the very heart of that rose. There were the proudest families, the stateliest homes, the broadest culture, the most gracious hospitality, the gentlest courtesies, the finest chivalry, that the State has ever known. There lived the political idols; there, under the low sky, rose the memorial shaft to Clay. There had lived beaux and belles, memories of whom hang still about the town, people it with phantom shapes, and give an individual or a family here and there a subtle distinction to-day. There the grasp of Calvinism was most lax. There were the dance, the ready sideboard, the card table, the love of the horse and the dog, and but little passion for the game-cock. There were as manly virtues, as manly vices, as the world has ever known. And there, love was as far from lust as heaven from hell.

It was on the threshold of this life that Chad stood. Kentucky had given birth to the man who was to uphold the Union —birth to the man who would seek to shatter it. Fate had given Chad the early life of one, and like blood with the other; and, curiously enough, in his own short life, he already epitomized the social development of the nation, from its birth in a log cabin to its swift maturity behind the columns of a Greek portico. Against the uncounted generations of gentlepeople that ran behind him to sunny England, how little could the short sleep of three in the hills count! It may take three generations to make a gentleman, but one is enough, if the blood be there, the heart be right, and the brain and hand come early under discipline.

It was to General Dean that the Major told Chad's story first. The two old friends silently grasped hands, and the cloud between them passed like mist.

"Bring him over to dinner on Saturday, Cal—you and Miss Lucy, won't you? Some people are coming out from town." In making amends, there was no half-way with General Dean.

"I will," said the Major, "gladly."

[171]

The cool of the coming autumn was already in the air that Saturday when Miss Lucy and the Major and Chad, in the old carriage, with old Tom as driver and the pickaninny behind, started for General Dean's. The Major was beautiful to behold, in his flowered waistcoat, his ruffled shirt, white trousers strapped beneath his highly polished, high-heeled boots, high hat and frock coat, with only the lowest button fastened, in order to give a glimpse of that wonderful waistcoat, just as that, too, was unbuttoned at the top that the ruffles might peep out upon the world. Chad's raiment, too, was a Solomon's— for him. He had protested, but in vain; and he, too, wore white trousers with straps, high-heeled boots, and a wine-colored waistcoat and slouch hat, and a brave, though very conscious, figure he made, with his tall body, well-poised head, strong shoulders and thick hair. It was a rare thing for Miss Lucy to do, but the old gentlewoman could not resist the Major, and she, too, rode in state with them, smiling indulgently at the Major's quips, and now, kindly, on Chad. A drowsy peace lay over the magnificent woodlands, unravaged then except for firewood; the seared pastures, just beginning to show green again for the second spring; the flashing creek, the seas of still hemp and yellow corn. And Chad saw a wistful shadow cross Miss Lucy's pale face, and a darker one anxiously sweep over the Major's jesting lips.

Guests were arriving, when they entered the yard gate, and guests were coming behind them. General and Mrs. Dean were receiving them on the porch, and Harry and Dan were helping the ladies out of their carriages, while, leaning against one of the columns, in pure white, was the graceful figure of Margaret. That there could ever have been any feeling in any member of the family other than simple, gracious kindliness toward him, Chad could neither see nor feel. At once every trace of embarrassment in him was gone, and he could but wonder at the swift justice done him in a way that was so simple and effective. Even with Margaret there was no trace of consciousness. The past was wiped clean of all save courtesy and kindness. There were the Hunts—Nellie, and the Lieutenant of the Lexington Rifles, Richard Hunt, a dauntless-looking daredevil, with the ready tongue of a coffee-house wit and the grace of a cavalier. There was Elizabeth Morgan, to whom Harry's grave eyes were always wandering, and Miss Jennie Overstreet, who was romantic and openly now wrote poems for the *Observer,* and who looked at Chad with no attempt to conceal her admiration of his appearance and her wonder as to who he was. And there were the neighbors roundabout—the Talbotts, Quisenberrys, Clays, Prestons, Morgans—surely no less than forty strong, and all for dinner. It was no little trial for Chad in that crowd of fine ladies, judges, soldiers, lawyers, statesmen —but he stood it well. While his self-consciousness made him awkward, he had pronounced dignity of bearing; his diffidence emphasized his modesty, and he had the good sense to stand and keep still. Soon they were at table—and what a table and what a dinner that was! The dining-room was the biggest and sunniest room in the house; its walls covered with hunting prints, pictures of game and stag heads. The table ran the length of it. The snowy tablecloth hung almost to the floor. At the head sat Mrs. Dean, with a great tureen of calf's head soup in front of her. Before the General was the saddle of venison that was to follow, drenched in a bottle of ancient Madeira, and flanked by flakes of red-currant jelly. Before the Major rested broiled wild ducks, on which he could show his carving skill—on game as well as men. A great turkey supplanted the venison, and last to come, and before Richard Hunt, Lieutenant of the Rifles, was a Kentucky ham. That ham! Mellow, aged, boiled in champagne, baked brown, spiced deeply, rosy pink within, and of a flavor and fragrance to shatter the fast of a Pope; and without, a brown-edged white layer, so firm that the lieutenant's deft carving knife, passing through, gave no hint to the eye that it was delicious fat. There had been merry jest and laughter and banter and gallant compliment before, but it was Richard Hunt's turn now, and story after story he told, as the rose-flakes dropped under his knife in such thin slices that their edges coiled. It was full half an hour before the carver and story-teller were done. After that ham, the tablecoth was lifted, and the dessert spread on another lying beneath; then that, too, was raised, and the nuts and wines were placed on a third—red damask this time.

Then came the toasts: to the gracious hostess from Major Buford; to Miss Lucy from General Dean; from valiant Richard Hunt to blushing Margaret, and then the ladies were gone, and the talk was politics—the election of Lincoln, slavery, disunion.

"If Lincoln is elected, no power but God's can avert war," said Richard Hunt, gravely.

Dan's eyes flashed. "Will you take me?"

The lieutenant lifted his glass. "Gladly, my boy."

"Kentucky's convictions are with the Union; her kinship and sympathies with the South," said a deep-voiced lawyer. "She must remain neutral."

"Straddling the fence," said the Major, sarcastically.

"No; to avert the war, if possible, or to act the peacemaker when the tragedy is over."

"Well, I can see Kentuckians keeping out of a fight," laughed the General, and he looked around. Three out of five of the men present had been in the Mexican war. The General had been wounded at Cerro Gordo, and the Major had brought his dead home in leaden coffins.

"The fanatics of Boston, the hot-heads of South Carolina— they are making the mischief."

"And New England began with slavery," said the lawyer again.

"And naturally, with that conscience that is a national calamity, was the first to give it up," said Richard Hunt, "when the market price of slaves fell to sixpence a pound in the open Boston markets." There was an incredulous murmur.

"Oh, yes," said Hunt, easily, "I can show you advertisements in Boston papers of slaves for sale at sixpence a pound."

Perhaps it never occurred to a soul present that the word "slave" was never heard in that region except in some such way. With Southerners, the negroes were "our servants" or "our people"—never slaves. Two lads at that table were growing white—Chad and Harry—and Chad's lips opened first.

"I don't think slavery has much to do with the question, really," he said, "not even with Mr. Lincoln." The silent surprise that followed the boy's embarrassed statement ended in a gasp of astonishment when Harry leaned across the table and said, hotly:

"Slavery has *everything* to do with the question."

The Major looked bewildered; the General frowned, and the keen-eyed lawyer spoke again:

"The struggle was written in the Constitution. The framers evaded it. Logic leads one way as well as another and no man can logically blame another for the way he goes."

"No more politics now, gentlemen," said the General quickly. "We will join the ladies. Harry," he added, with some sternness, "lead the way!"

As the three boys rose, Chad lifted his glass. His face was pale and his lips trembled.

"May I propose a toast, General Dean?"

"Why, certainly," said the General, kindly.

"I want to drink to one man but for whom I might be in a log-cabin now, and might have died there for all I know—my friend and, thank God! my kinsman—Major Buford."

It was irregular and hardly in good taste, but the boy had waited till the ladies were gone, and it touched the Major that he should want to make such a public acknowledgment that there should be no false colors in the flag he meant henceforth to bear.

The startled guests drank blindly to the confused Major, though they knew not why, but as the lads disappeared the lawyer asked:

"Who is that boy, Major?"

Outside, the same question had been asked among the ladies and the same story told. The three girls remembered him vaguely, they said, and when Chad reappeared, in the eyes of the poetess at least, the halo of romance floated above his head.

She was waiting for Chad when he came out on the porch, and she shook her curls and flashed her eyes in a way that almost alarmed him. Old Mammy dropped him a curtsey, for she had had her orders, and, behind her, Snowball, now a tall, fine-looking coal-black youth, grinned a welcome. The three girls were walking under the trees, with their arms mysteriously twined about one another's waists, and the poetess walked down toward them with the three lads, Richard Hunt following. Chad could not know how it happened, but, a moment later, Dan was walking away with Nellie Hunt one way; Harry with Elizabeth Morgan the other; the Lieutenant had Margaret alone, and Miss Overstreet was leading him away, raving meanwhile about the beauty of field and sky. As they went toward the gate he could not help flashing one look toward the pair under the fir tree. An amused smile was playing under the Lieutenant's beautiful mustache, his eyes were dancing with mischief, and Margaret was blushing with anything else than displeasure.

"Oho!" he said, as Chad and his companion passed on. "Sits the wind in that corner? Bless me, if looks could kill, I'd have a happy death here at your feet, Mistress Margaret. *See* the young man! It's the second time he has almost slain me."

Chad could scarcely hear Miss Jennie's happy chatter, scarcely saw the shaking curls, the eyes all but in a frenzy of rolling. His eyes were in the back of his head, and his backward-listening ears heard only Margaret's laugh behind him.

"Oh, I do love the autumn"—it was at the foot of those steps, thought Chad, that he first saw Margaret springing to the back of her pony and dashing off under the fir trees—"and it's coming. There's one scarlet leaf already"—Chad could see the rock fence where he had sat that spring day—"it's curious and mournful that you can see in any season a sign of the next to come." And there was the creek where he found Dan fishing, and there the road led to the ford where Margaret had spurned his offer of a slimy fish—ugh! "I do love the autumn. It makes me feel like the young woman who told Emerson that she had such mammoth thoughts she couldn't give them utterance—why, wake up, Mr. Buford, wake up!" Chad came to with a start.

"Do you know you aren't very polite, Mr. Buford?" Mr. Buford! That did sound funny.

"But I know what the matter is," she went on. "I saw you look"—she nodded her head backward. "Can you keep a secret?" Chad nodded; he had not yet opened his lips.

"That's going to be a match back there. He's only a few years older. The French say that a woman should be half a man's age plus seven years. That would make her only a few years too young, and she can wait." Chad was scarlet under the girl's mischievous torture, but a cry from the house saved him. Dan was calling them back.

"Mr. Hunt has to go back early to drill the Rifles. Can you keep another secret?" Again Chad nodded gravely. "Well, he is going to drive *me* back. I'll tell him what a dangerous rival he has." Chad was dumb; there was much yet for him to learn before he could parry with a tongue like hers.

"He's very good-looking," said Miss Jennie, when she joined the girls, "but oh, so stupid."

Margaret turned quickly and unsuspiciously. "Stupid! Why, he's the first man in his class."

"Oh," said Miss Jennie, with a demure smile, "perhaps *I* couldn't draw him out," and Margaret flushed to have caught the deftly tossed bait so readily.

A moment later the Lieutenant was gathering up the reins, with Miss Jennie by his side. He gave a bow to Margaret, and Miss Jennie nodded to Chad.

"Come see me when you come to town, Mr. Buford," she called, as though to an old friend, and still Chad was dumb, though he lifted his hat gravely.

At no time was Chad alone with Margaret, and he was not sorry—her manner so puzzled him. The three lads and three girls walked together through Mrs. Dean's garden with its grass walks and flower beds and vegetable patches surrounded with rose bushes. At the lower edge they could see the barn with sheep in the yard around it, and there were the very stiles where Harry and Margaret had sat in state when Dan and Chad were charging in the tournament. The thing might never have happened for any sign from Harry or Dan or Margaret, and Chad began to wonder if his past or his present were a dream.

How fine this courtesy was Chad could not realize. Neither could he know that the favor Margaret had shown him when he was little more than outcast he must now, as an equal, win for himself. Miss Jennie had called him "Mr. Buford." He wondered what Margaret would call him when he came to say good-by. She called him nothing. She only smiled at him.

"You must come to see us soon again," she said, graciously, and so said all the Deans.

The Major was quiet going home, and Miss Lucy drowsed. All evening the Major was quiet.

"If a fight does come," he said, when they were going to bed, "I reckon I'm not too old to take a hand."

"And I reckon I'm not too young," said Chad.

XVIII

THE SPIRIT OF '76 AND THE SHADOW OF '61

ONE night, in the following April, there was a great dance in Lexington. Next day the news of Sumter came. Chad pleaded to be let off from the dance, but the Major would not hear of it. It was a fancy-dress ball, and the Major had a pet purpose of his own that he wanted gratified, and Chad had promised to aid him. That fancy was that Chad should go in regimentals, as the stern, old soldier on the wall, of whom the Major swore the boy was the "spit and image." The Major himself helped Chad dress in wig, peruke, stock, breeches, boots, spurs, cocked hat, sword, and all. And then he led the boy down into the parlor, where Miss Lucy was waiting for them, and stood him up on one side of the portrait. To please the old fellow, Chad laughingly struck the attitude of the pictured soldier, and the Major cried:

"What'd I tell you, Lucy!" Then he advanced and made a low bow.

"General Buford," he said, "General Washington's compliments, and will General Buford plant the flag on that hill where the left wing of the British is entrenched?"

"Hush, Cal," said Miss Lucy, laughing.

"General Buford's compliments to General Washington. General Buford will plant that flag on *any* hill that *any* enemy holds against it."

The lad's face paled as the words, by some curious impulse, sprang to his lips, but the unsuspecting Major saw no lurking

[180]

significance in his manner, nor in what he said, and then there
was a rumble of carriage wheels at the door.

The winter had sped swiftly. Chad had done his work in
college only fairly well, for Margaret had been a disturbing
factor. The girl was an impenetrable mystery to him, for the
past between them was not only wiped clean—it seemed quite
gone. Once only had he dared to open his lips about the old
days, and the girl's flushed silence made a like mistake forever
impossible. He came and went at the Deans' as he pleased.
Always they were kind, courteous, hospitable—no more, no
less, unvaryingly. During the Christmas holidays he and Margaret had had a foolish quarrel, and it was then that Chad took
his little fling at his little world—a fling that was foolish, but
harmful, chiefly in that it took his time and his mind and his
energy from his work. He not only neglected his studies, but
he fell in with the wild young bucks of the town, learned to
play cards, took more wine than was good for him sometimes,
was on the verge of several duels, and night after night raced
home in his buggy against the coming dawn. Though Miss
Lucy looked worried, the indulgent old Major made no protest. Indeed he was rather pleased. Chad was sowing his
wild oats—it was in the blood, and the mood would pass. It
did pass, naturally enough, on the very day that the breach between him and Margaret was partly healed; and the heart of
Caleb Hazel, whom Chad, for months, had not dared to face,
was made glad when the boy came back to him remorseful and
repentant—the old Chad once more.

They were late in getting to the dance. Every window in
the old Hunt home was brilliant with light. Chinese lanterns
swung in the big yard. The scent of early spring flowers smote

the fresh night air. Music and the murmur of nimble feet and happy laughter swept out the wide-open doors past which white figures flitted swiftly. Scarcely anybody knew Chad in his regimentals, and the Major, with the delight of a boy, led him around, gravely presenting him as General Buford here and there. Indeed, the lad made a noble figure with his superb height and bearing, and he wore sword and spurs as though born to them. Margaret was dancing with Richard Hunt when she saw his eyes searching for her through the room, and she gave him a radiant smile that almost stunned him. She had been haughty and distant when he went to her to plead forgiveness: she had been too hard, and Margaret, too, was repentant.

"Why, who's that?" asked Richard Hunt. "Oh, yes," he added, getting his answer from Margaret's face. "Bless me, but he's fine—the very spirit of '76. I must have him in the Rifles."

"Will you make him a lieutenant?" asked Margaret.

"Why, yes, I will," said Mr. Hunt, decisively. "I'll resign myself in his favor, if it pleases you."

"Oh, no, no—no one could fill your place."

"Well, he can, I fear—and here he comes to do it. I'll have to retreat some time, and I suppose I'd as well begin now." And the gallant gentleman bowed to Chad.

"Will you pardon me, Miss Margaret? My mother is calling me."

"You must have keen ears," said Margaret; "your mother is upstairs."

"Yes; but she wants me. Everybody wants me, but——" he bowed again with an imperturbable smile and went his way.

Margaret looked demurely into Chad's eager eyes.

"And how is the spirit of '76?"

"The spirit of '76 is unchanged."

"Oh, yes, he is; I scarcely knew him."

"But he's unchanged; he never will change."

Margaret dropped her eyes and Chad looked around.

"I wish we could get out of here."

"We can," said Margaret, demurely.

"We will!" said Chad, and he made for a door, outside which lanterns were swinging in the wind. Margaret caught up some flimsy garment and wound it about her pretty round throat—they call it a "fascinator" in the South.

Chad looked down at her.

"I wish you could see yourself; I wish I could tell you how you look."

"I have," said Margaret, "every time I passed a mirror. And other people have told me. Mr. Hunt did. He didn't seem to have much trouble."

"I wish I had his tongue."

"If you had, and nothing else, you wouldn't have me"—Chad started as the little witch paused a second, drawling—"leaving my friends and this jolly dance to go out into a freezing yard and talk to an aged Colonial who doesn't appreciate his modern blessings. The next thing you'll be wanting, I suppose—will be——"

"You, Margaret; you—*you!*"

It had come at last and Margaret hardly knew the choked voice that interrupted her. She had turned her back to him to sit down. She paused a moment, standing. Her eyes closed; a slight tremor ran through her, and she sank with her face in her hands. Chad stood silent, trembling. Voices murmured about them, but like the music in the house, they seemed strangely far away. The stirring of the wind made the sudden damp on his forehead icy-cold. Margaret's hands slowly left her face, which had changed as by a miracle. Every trace of coquetry was gone. It was the face of a woman who knew her own heart, and had the sweet frankness to speak it, that was lifted now to Chad.

"I'm so glad you are what you are, Chad; but had you been otherwise—that would have made no difference to me. You believe that, don't you, Chad? They might not have let me marry you, but I should have cared, just the same. They may not now, but that, too, will make no difference." She turned her eyes from his for an instant, as though she were looking far backward. "Ever since that day," she said, slowly, "when I heard you say, 'Tell the little gurl I didn't mean nothin' callin' her a little gal' "—there was a low, delicious gurgle in the throat as she tried to imitate his odd speech, and then her eyes suddenly filled with tears, but she brushed them away, smiling brightly. "Ever since then, Chad——" she stopped—a shadow fell across the door of the little summer house.

"Here I am, Mr. Hunt," she said, lightly; "is this your dance?" She rose and was gone. "Thank you, Mr. Buford," she called back, sweetly.

For a moment Chad stood where he was, quite dazed—so quickly, so unexpectedly had the crisis come. The blood had rushed to his face and flooded him with triumph and happiness. A terrible doubt chilled him as quickly. Had he heard aright —could he have misunderstood her? Had the dream of years really come true? What was it she had said? He stumbled

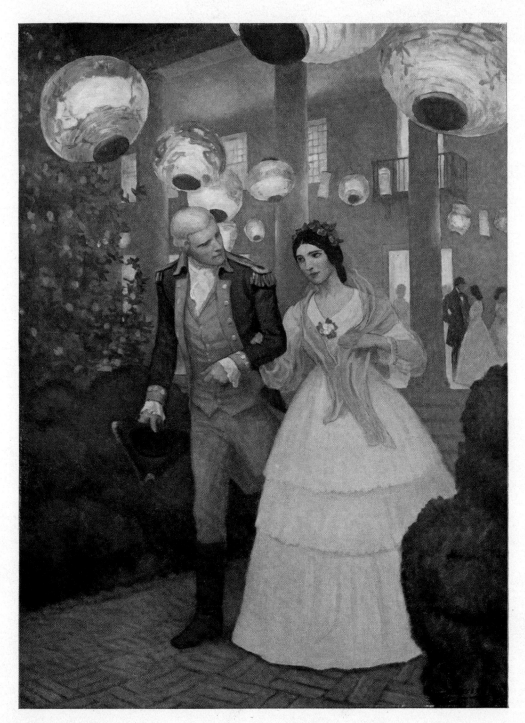

"I wish you could see yourself; I wish I could tell you how you look."

around in the half darkness, wondering. Was this another phase of her unceasing coquetry? How quickly her tone had changed when Richard Hunt's shadow came. At that moment, he neither could nor would have changed a hair had some genie dropped them both in the midst of the crowded ball-room. He turned swiftly toward the dancers. He must see, know—now!

The dance was a quadrille and the figure was "Grand right and left." Margaret had met Richard Hunt opposite, halfway, when Chad reached the door, and was curtseying to him with a radiant smile. Again the boy's doubts beat him fiercely; and then Margaret turned her head, as though she knew he must be standing there. Her face grew so suddenly serious and her eyes softened with such swift tenderness when they met his, that a wave of guilty shame swept through him. And when she came around to him and passed, she leaned from the circle toward him, merry and mock-reproachful:

"You mustn't look at me like that," she whispered, and Hunt, close at hand, saw, guessed and smiled. Chad turned quickly away again.

That happy dawn—going home! The Major drowsed and fell asleep. The first coming light, the first cool breath that was stealing over the awakening fields, the first spring leaves with their weight of dew, were not more fresh and pure than the love that was in the boy's heart. He held his right hand in his left, as though he were imprisoning there the memory of the last little clasp that she had given it. He looked at the Major, and he wondered how anybody on earth, at that hour, could be asleep. He thought of the wasted days of the past few months; the silly, foolish life he had led, and thanked God that, in the memory of them, there was not one sting of shame.

[185]

How he would work for her now! Little guessing how proud she already was, he swore to himself how proud she should be of him some day. He wondered where she was, and what she was doing. She could not be asleep, and he must have cried aloud could he have known—could he have heard her on her knees at her bedside, whispering his name for the first time in her prayers; could he have seen her, a little later, at her open window, looking across the fields, as though her eyes must reach him through the morning dusk.

That happy dawn—for both, that happy dawn!

It was well that neither, at that hour, could see beyond the rim of his own little world. In a far Southern city another ball, that night, had been going on. Down there the air was charged with the prescience of dark trouble, but, while the music moaned to many a heart like a god in pain, there was no brooding—only a deeper flush to the cheek, a brighter sparkle to the eye, a keener wit to the tongue; to the dance, a merrier swing. And at that very hour of dawn, ladies, slippered, bare of head, and in evening gowns, were fluttering like white moths along the streets of old Charleston, and down to the Battery, where Fort Sumter lay, gray and quiet in the morning mist—to await with jest and laughter the hissing shriek of one shell that lighted the fires of a four years' hell in a happy land of God-fearing peace and God-given plenty, and the hissing shriek of another that Anderson, Kentuckian, hurled back, in heroic defence of the flag struck for the first time by other than an alien hand.

XIX

THE BLUE OR THE GRAY

In the far North, as in the far South, men had but to drift
with the tide. Among the Kentuckians, the forces that moulded
her sons—Davis and Lincoln—were at war in the State, as
they were at war in the nation. By ties of blood, sympathies,
institutions, Kentucky was bound fast to the South. Yet, ten
years before, Kentuckians had demanded the gradual eman-
cipation of the slave. That far back, they had carved a pledge
on a block of Kentucky marble, which should be placed in the
Washington monument, that Kentucky would be the last to
give up the Union. For ten years, they had felt the shadow of
the war creeping toward them. In the dark hours of that dismal year, before the dawn of final decision, the men, women,
and children of Kentucky talked of little else save war, and
the skeleton of war took its place in the closet of every home
from the Ohio to the crest of the Cumberland. When the dawn
of that decision came, Kentucky spread before the world a
record of independent-mindedness, patriotism, as each side saw
the word, and sacrifice that has no parallel in history. She sent
the flower of her youth—forty thousand strong—into the Confederacy; she lifted the lid of her treasury to Lincoln, and in
answer to his every call, sent him a soldier, practically without
a bounty and without a draft. And when the curtain fell on
the last act of the great tragedy, half of her manhood was be-

hind it—helpless from disease, wounded, or dead on the battle-field.

So, on a gentle April day, when the great news came, it came like a sword that, with one stroke, slashed the State in twain, shearing through the strongest bonds that link one man to another, whether of blood, business, politics or religion, as though they were no more than threads of wool. Nowhere in the Union was the National drama so played to the bitter end in the confines of a single State. As the nation was rent apart, so was the commonwealth; as the State, so was the county; as the county, the neighborhood; as the neighborhood, the family; and as the family, so brother and brother, father and son. In the nation the kinship was racial only. Brother knew not the face of brother. There was distance between them, antagonism, prejudice, a smouldering dislike easily fanned to flaming hatred. In Kentucky the brothers had been born in the same bed, slept in the same cradle, played under the same roof, sat side by side in the same schoolroom, and stood now on the threshold of manhood arm in arm, with mutual interests, mutual love, mutual pride in family that made clan feeling peculiarly intense. For anti-slavery fanaticism, or honest unionism, one needed not to go to the far North; as, for imperious, hot-headed, non-interference or pure State sovereignty, one needed not to go to the far South. They were all there in the State, the county, the family—under the same roof. Along the border alone did feeling approach uniformity—the border of Kentucky hills. There unionism was free from prejudice as nowhere else on the continent save elsewhere throughout the Southern mountains. Those Southern Yankees knew nothing about the valley aristocrat, nothing about his slaves, and cared as little for one as for the other. Since '76 they had known but one flag, and one flag only, and to that flag instinctively they rallied. But that the State should be swept from border to border with horror, there was division even here: for, in the Kentucky mountains, there was, here and there, a patriarch like Joel Turner who owned slaves, and he and his sons fought for them as he and his sons would have fought for their horses, or their cattle, or their sheep.

It was the prescient horror of such a condition that had no little part in the neutral stand that Kentucky strove to maintain. She knew what war was—for every fireside was rich in memories that men and women had of kindred who had fallen on numberless battle-fields—back even to St. Clair's defeat and the Raisin massacre; and though she did not fear war for its harvest of dangers and death, she did look with terror on a conflict between neighbors, friends, and brothers. So she refused troops to Lincoln; she refused them to Davis. Both pledged her immunity from invasion, and, to enforce that pledge, she raised Home Guards as she had already raised State Guards for internal protection and peace. And there—as a State—she stood: but the tragedy went on in the Kentucky home—a tragedy of peculiar intensity and pathos in one Kentucky home —the Deans'.

Harry had grown up tall, pale, studious, brooding. He had always been the pet of his Uncle Brutus—the old Lion of White Hall. Visiting the Hall, he had drunk in the poison, or consecration, as was the point of view, of abolitionism. At the first sign he was never allowed to go again. But the poison had gone deep. Whenever he could, he went to hear old Brutus speak. Eagerly he heard stories of the fearless abolitionist's hand-to-hand fights with men who sought to skewer his fiery tongue. Deeply he brooded on every word that his retentive ear had caught from the old man's lips, and on the wrongs he endured in behalf of his cause and for freedom of speech.

One other hero did he place above him—the great commoner after whom he had been christened, Henry Clay Dean. He knew how Clay's life had been devoted to averting the coming war, and how his last days had been darkly shadowed by the belief that, when he was gone, the war must come. At times he could hear that clarion voice as it rang through the Senate with the bold challenge to his own people that paramount was his duty to the nation—subordinate his duty to his State. Who can tell what the nation owed, in Kentucky, at least, to the passionate allegiance that was broadcast through the State to Henry Clay? It was not in the boy's blood to be driven an inch, and no one tried to drive him. In his own home he was a spectre of gnawing anguish to his mother and Margaret, of unspeakable bitterness and disappointment to his father, and an impenetrable sphinx to Dan. For in Dan there was no shaking doubt. He was the spirit, incarnate, of the young, unquestioning, unthinking, generous, reckless, hot-heated, passionate South.

And Chad? The news reached Major Buford's farm at noon, and Chad went to the woods and came in at dusk, haggard and spent. Miserably now he held his tongue and tortured his brain. Purposely, he never opened his lips to Harry Dean. He tried to make known to the Major the struggle going on within him, but the iron-willed old man brushed away all argument with an impatient wave of his hand. With Margaret he talked once, and straightway the question was dropped like a living coal. So, Chad withdrew from his fellows. The social life of the town, gayer than ever now, knew him no more. He kept up his college work, but when he was not at his books, he walked the fields, and many a moonlit midnight found him striding along a white turnpike, or sitting motionless on top of a fence along the border of some woodland, his chin in both hands, fighting his fight out in the cool stillness alone. He himself little knew the unmeant significance there was in the old Continental uniform he had worn to the dance. Even his old rifle, had he but known it, had been carried with Daniel Morgan from Virginia to Washington's aid in Cambridge. His earliest memories of war were rooted in thrilling stories of King's Mountain. He had heard old men tell of pointing deadly rifles at red-coats at New Orleans, and had absorbed their own love of Old Hickory. The school-master himself, when a mere lad, had been with Scott in Mexico. The spirit of the backwoodsman had been caught in the hills, and was alive and unchanged at that very hour. The boy was practically born in Revolutionary days, and that was why, like all mountaineers, Chad had little love of State and only love of country— was first, last and all the time, simply American. It was not reason—it was instinct. The heroes the school-master had taught him to love and some day to emulate, had fought under one flag, and, like them, the mountaineers never dreamed there could be another. And so the boy was an unconscious reincarnation of that old spirit, uninfluenced by temporary apostasies in the outside world, untouched absolutely by sectional prejudice or the appeal of the slave. The mountaineer had no hatred of the valley aristocrat, because he knew nothing of him, and envied no man what he was, what he had, or the life he led. So, as for slavery, that question, singularly enough, never troubled his soul. To him slaves were hewers of wood and drawers of water. The Lord had made them so, and the Bible said that it was right. That the school-master had taught Chad. He had read "Uncle Tom's Cabin," and the story made him smile. The tragedies of it he had never known and he did not believe. Slaves were sleek, well-fed, well-housed, loved and trusted, rightly inferior and happy; and no aristocrat ever moved among them with a more lordly, righteous air of authority than did this mountain lad who had known them little more than half a dozen years. Unlike the North, the boy had no prejudice, no antagonism, no jealousy, no grievance to help him in his struggle. Unlike Harry, he had no slave sympathy to stir him to the depths, no stubborn, rebellious pride to prod him on. In the days when the school-master thundered at him some speech of the Prince of Kentuckians, it was always the national thrill in the fiery utterance that had shaken him even then. So that unconsciously the boy was the embodiment of pure Americanism, and for that reason he and the people among whom he was born stood among the millions on either side, quite alone.

What was he fighting then—ah, what? If the bed-rock of his character was not loyalty, it was nothing. In the mountains the Turners had taken him from the Wilderness. In the Bluegrass the old Major had taken him from the hills. His very life he owed to the simple, kindly mountaineers, and what he valued more than his life he owed to the simple gentleman who had picked him up from the roadside and, almost without question, had taken him to his heart and to his home. The Turners, he knew, would fight for their slaves as they would have fought Dillon or Devil had either proposed to take from them a cow, a hog, or a sheep. For that Chad could not blame them. And the Major was going to fight, as he believed, for his liberty, his State, his country, his property, his fireside. So in the eyes of both, Chad must be the snake who had warmed his frozen body on their hearthstones and bitten the kindly hands that had warmed him back to life. What would Melissa say? Mentally he shrank from the fire of her eyes and the scorn of her tongue when she should know. And Margaret—the thought of her brought always a voiceless groan. To her, he had let his doubts be known, and her white silence closed his own lips then and there. The simple fact that he had doubts was an entering wedge of coldness between them that Chad saw must force them apart; for he knew that the truth must come soon, and what would be the bitter cost of that truth. She could never see him as she saw Harry. Harry was a beloved and erring brother. Hatred of slavery had been cunningly planted in his heart by her father's own brother, upon whose head the blame for Harry's sin was set. The boy had been taunted until his own father's scorn had stirred his proud independence into stubborn resistance and intensified his resolution to do what he pleased and what he thought was right. But Chad—she would never understand him. She would never understand his love for the Government that had once abandoned her people to savages and forced her State and his to seek aid from a foreign land. In her eyes, too, he would be rending the hearts that had been tenderest to him in all the world: and that was all. Of what fate she would deal out to him he dared not think. If he lifted his hand against the South, he must strike at the heart of all he loved best, to which he owed most. If against the Union, at the heart of all that was best in himself. In him the pure spirit that gave birth to the nation was fighting for life. Ah, God! what should he do— what should he do?

XX

OFF TO THE WAR

THROUGHOUT that summer Chad fought his fight, daily swaying this way and that—fought it in secret until the phantom of neutrality faded and gave place to the grim spectre of war—until with each hand Kentucky drew a sword and made ready to plunge both into her own stout heart. When Sumter fell, she shook her head resolutely to both North and South. Crittenden, in the name of Union lovers and the dead Clay, pleaded with the State to take no part in the fratricidal crime. From the mothers, wives, sisters and daughters of thirty-one counties came piteously the same appeal. Neutrality, to be held inviolate, was the answer to the cry from both the North and the South; but armed neutrality, said Kentucky. The State had not the moral right to secede; the Nation, no constitutional right to coerce: if both the North and the South left their paths of duty and fought—let both keep their battles from her soil. Straightway State Guards went into camp and Home Guards were held in reserve, but there was not a fool in the Commonwealth who did not know that, in sympathy, the State Guards were already for the Confederacy and the Home Guards for the Union cause. This was in May.

In June, Federals were enlisting across the Ohio; Confederates, just over the border of Dixie which begins in Tennessee. Within a month Stonewall Jackson sat on his horse, after Bull Run, watching the routed Yankees, praying for fresh men that he might go on and take the Capitol, and, from the Federal dream of a sixty-days' riot, the North woke with a gasp. A week or two later, Camp Dick Robinson squatted down on the edge of the Bluegrass, the first violation of the State's neutrality, and beckoned with both hands for Yankee recruits. Soon an order went round to disarm the State Guards, and on that very day the State Guards made ready for Dixie. On that day the crisis came at the Deans', and on that day Chad Buford made up his mind. When the Major and Miss Lucy went to bed that night, he slipped out of the house and walked through the yard and across the pike, following the little creek half unconsciously toward the Deans', until he could see the light in Margaret's window, and there he climbed the worm fence and sat leaning his head against one of the forked stakes with his hat in his lap. He would probably not see her again. He would send her word next morning to ask that he might, and he feared what the result of that word would be. Several times his longing eyes saw her shadow pass the curtain, and when her light was out, he closed his eyes and sat motionless—how long he hardly knew; but, when he sprang down, he was stiffened from the midnight chill and his unchanged posture. He went back to his room then, and wrote Margaret a letter and tore it up and went to bed. There was little sleep for him that night, and when the glimmer of morning brightened at his window, he rose listlessly, dipped his hot head in a bowl of water and stole out to the barn. His little mare whinnied a welcome as he opened the barn door. He patted her on the neck.

"Good-by, little girl," he said. He started to call her by name and stopped. Margaret had named the beautiful creature "Dixie." The servants were stirring.

"Good-mawnin', Mars Chad," said each, and with each he

shook hands, saying simply that he was going away that morning. Only old Tom asked him a question.

"Foh Gawd, Mars Chad," said the old fellow, "old Mars Buford can't git along widout you. You gwine to come back soon?"

"I don't know, Uncle Tom," said Chad, sadly.

"Whar you gwine, Mars Chad?"

"Into the army."

"De ahmy?" The old man smiled. "You gwine to fight de Yankees?"

"I'm going to fight *with* the Yankees."

The old driver looked as though he could not have heard aright.

"You foolin' this ole nigger, Mars Chad, ain't you?"

Chad shook his head, and the old man straightened himself a bit.

"I'se sorry to heah it, suh," he said, with dignity, and he turned to his work.

Miss Lucy was not feeling well that morning and did not come down to breakfast. The boy was so pale and haggard that the Major looked at him anxiously.

"What's the matter with you, Chad? Are you sick?"

"I didn't sleep very well last night, Major."

The Major chuckled. "I reckon you ain't gettin' enough sleep these days. I reckon I wouldn't, either, if I were in your place."

Chad did not answer. After breakfast he sat with the Major on the porch in the fresh, sunny air. The Major smoked his pipe, taking the stem out of his mouth now and then to shout some order as a servant passed under his eye.

"What's the news, Chad?"

"Mr. Crittenden is back."

"What did old Lincoln say?"

"That Camp Dick Robinson was formed for Kentuckians by Kentuckians, and he did not believe that it was the wish of the State that it should be removed."

"Well, by ——! after his promise. What did Davis say?"

"That if Kentucky opened the Northern door for invasion, she must not close the Southern door to entrance for defence."

"And dead right he is," growled the Major with satisfaction.

"Governor Magoffin asked Ohio and Indiana to join in an effort for a peace Congress," Chad added.

"Well?"

"Both governors refused."

"I tell you, boy, the hour has come."

The hour had come.

"I'm going away this morning, Major."

The Major did not even turn his head.

"I thought this was coming," he said quietly. Chad's face grew even paler, and he steeled his heart for the revelation.

"I've already spoken to Lieutenant Hunt," the Major went on. "He expects to be a captain, and he says that, maybe, he can make you a lieutenant. You can take that boy Brutus as a body servant." He brought his fist down on the railing of the porch. "God, but I'd give the rest of my life to be ten years younger than I am now."

"Major, I'm *going into the Union army.*"

The Major's pipe almost dropped from between his lips. Catching the arms of his chair with both hands, he turned

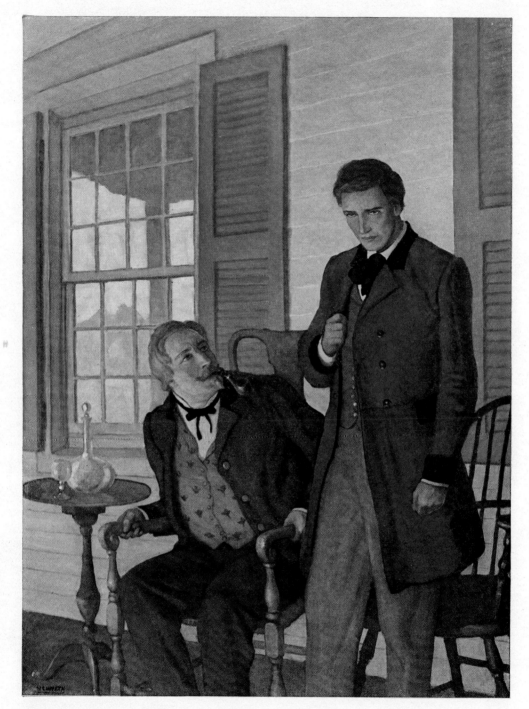

"*Major, I'm going into the Union army.*"

heavily and with dazed wonder, as though the boy had struck him with his fist from behind, and, without a word, stared hard into Chad's tortured face. The keen old eye had not long to look before it saw the truth, and then, silently, the old man turned back. His hands trembled on the chair, and he slowly thrust them into his pockets, breathing hard through his nose. The boy expected an outbreak, but none came. A bee buzzed above them. A yellow butterfly zigzagged by. Blackbirds chattered in the firs. The screech of a peacock shrilled across the yard, and a ploughman's singing wailed across the fields:

> Trouble, O Lawd!
> Nothin' but trouble in de lan' of Canaan.

The boy knew he had given his old friend a mortal hurt.

"Don't, Major," he pleaded. "You don't know how I have fought against this. I tried to be on your side. I thought I was. I joined the Rifles. I found first that I couldn't fight *with* the South, and—then—I—found that I had to fight *for* the North. It almost kills me when I think of all you have done——"

The Major waved his hand imperiously. He was not the man to hear his favors recounted, much less refer to them himself. He straightened and got up from his chair. His manner had grown formal, stately, coldly courteous.

"I cannot understand, but you are old enough, sir, to know your own mind. You should have prepared me for this. You will excuse me a moment." Chad rose and the Major walked toward the door, his step not very steady, and his shoulders a bit shrunken—his back, somehow, looked suddenly old.

"Brutus!" he called sharply to a black boy who was training rosebushes in the yard. "Saddle Mr. Chad's horse." Then, without looking again at Chad, he turned into his office, and Chad, standing where he was, with a breaking heart, could hear, through the open window, the rustling of papers and the scratching of a pen.

In a few minutes he heard the Major rise and he turned to meet him. The old man held a roll of bills in one hand and a paper in the other.

"Here is the balance due you on our last trade," he said, quietly. "The mare is yours—Dixie," he added, grimly. "The old mare is in foal. I will keep her and send you your due when the time comes. We are quite even," he went on in a level tone of business. "Indeed, what you have done about the place more than exceeds any expense that you have ever caused me. If anything, I am still in your debt."

"I can't take it," said Chad, choking back a sob.

"You will have to take it," the Major broke in, curtly, "unless——" the Major held back the bitter speech that was on his lips and Chad understood. The old man did not want to feel under any obligations to him.

"I would offer you Brutus, as was my intention, except that I know you would not take him——" again he added, grimly, "and Brutus would run away from you."

"No, Major," said Chad, sadly, "I would not take Brutus," and he stepped down one step of the porch backward.

"I tried to tell you, Major, but you wouldn't listen. I don't wonder, for I couldn't explain to you what I couldn't understand myself. I——" the boy choked and tears filled his eyes. He was afraid to hold out his hand.

"Good-by, Major," he said, brokenly.

"Good-by, sir," answered the Major, with a stiff bow, but the old man's lip shook and he turned abruptly within.

Chad did not trust himself to look back, but, as he rode through the pasture to the pike gate, his ears heard, never to forget, the chatter of the blackbirds, the noises around the barn, the cry of the peacock, and the wailing of the ploughman:

> Trouble, O Lawd!
> Nothin' but trouble——

At the gate the little mare turned her head toward town and started away in the easy swinging lope for which she was famous. From a cornfield Jerome Conners, the overseer, watched horse and rider for a while, and then his lips were lifted over his protruding teeth in one of his ghastly, infrequent smiles. Chad Buford was out of his way at last. At the Deans' gate, Snowball was just going in on Margaret's pony and Chad pulled up.

"Where's Mr. Dan, Snowball?—and Mr. Harry?"

"Mars Dan he gwine to de wah—an' I'se gwine wid him."

"Is Mr. Harry going, too?" Snowball hesitated. He did not like to gossip about family matters, but it was a friend of the family who was questioning him.

"Yessuh! But Mammy say Mars Harry's teched in de haid. He gwine to fight wid de po' white trash."

"Is Miss Margaret at home?"

"Yessuh."

Chad had his note to Margaret, unsealed. He little felt like seeing her now, but he had just as well have it all over at once. He took it out and looked it over once more—irresolute.

"I'm going away to join the Union army, Margaret. May I come to tell you good-by? If not, God bless you always.

CHAD."

"Take this to Miss Margaret, Snowball, and bring me an answer here as soon as you can."

"Yessuh."

The black boy was not gone long. Chad saw him go up the steps, and in a few moments he reappeared and galloped back.

"Ole Mistis say dey ain't no answer."

"Thank you, Snowball." Chad pitched him a coin and loped on toward Lexington with his head bent, his hands folded on the pommel, and the reins flapping loosely. Within one mile of Lexington he turned into a cross-road and set his face toward the mountains.

An hour later, the General and Harry and Dan stood on the big portico. Inside, the mother and Margaret were weeping in each other's arms. Two negro boys were each leading a saddled horse from the stable, while Snowball was blubbering at the corner of the house. At the last moment Dan had decided to leave him behind. If Harry could have no servant, Dan, too, would have none. Dan was crying without shame. Harry's face was as white and stern as his father's. As the horses drew near, the General stretched out the sabre in his hand to Dan.

"This should belong to you, Harry."

"It is yours to give, father," said Harry, gently.

"It shall never be drawn against my roof and your mother." The boy was silent.

"You are going far North?" asked the General, more gently. "You will not fight on Kentucky soil?"

"You taught me that the first duty of a soldier is obedience. I must go where I'm ordered."

"God grant that you two may never meet."

"Father!" It was a cry of horror from both the lads.

The horses were waiting at the stiles. The General took Dan in his arms and the boy broke away and ran down the steps, weeping.

"Father," said Harry, with trembling lips, "I hope you won't be too hard on me. Perhaps the day will come when you won't be so ashamed of me. I hope you and mother will forgive me. I *can't* do otherwise than I *must*. Will you shake hands with me, father?"

"Yes, my son. God be with you both."

And then, as he watched the boys ride side by side to the gate, he added:

"I could kill my own brother with my own hand for this."

He saw them stop a moment at the gate; saw them clasp hands and turn opposite ways—one with his face set for Tennessee, the other making for the Ohio. Dan waved his cap in a last sad good-by. Harry rode over the hill without turning his head. The General stood rigid, with his hands clasped behind his back, staring across the gray fields between them. Through the window came the low sound of sobbing.

XXI

MELISSA

Shortly after dusk, that night, two or three wagons moved quietly out of Lexington, under a little guard with guns loaded and bayonets fixed. Back at the old Armory—the home of the "Rifles"—a dozen youngsters drilled vigorously with faces in a broad grin, as they swept under the motto of the company—"Our laws the commands of our Captain." They were following out those commands most literally. Never did Lieutenant Hunt give his orders more sonorously—he could be heard for blocks away. Never did young soldiers stamp out manœuvres more lustily—they made more noise than a regiment. Not a man carried a gun, though ringing orders to "Carry arms" and "Present arms" made the windows rattle. It was John Morgan's first ruse. While that mock-drill was going on, and listening Unionists outside were laughing to think how those Rifles were going to be fooled next day, the guns of the company were moving in those wagons toward Dixie—toward mocking-bird-haunted Bowling Green, where the underfed, unclothed, unarmed body of Albert Sydney Johnston's army lay, with one half-feathered wing stretching into the Cumberland hills and the frayed edge of the other touching the Ohio.

Next morning, the Home Guards came gayly around to the Armory to seize those guns, and the wily youngsters left temporarily behind (they, too, fled for Dixie, that night) gibed them unmercifully; so that, then and there, a little interchange of powder-and-ball civilities followed; and thus, on the very first day, Daniel Dean smelled the one and heard the other whistle right harmlessly and merrily. Straightway, more guards were called out; cannon were planted to sweep the principal streets, and from that hour the old town was under the rule of a Northern or Southern sword for the four years' reign of the war.

Meanwhile, Chad Buford was giving a strange journey to Dixie. Whenever he dismounted, she would turn her head toward the Bluegrass, as though it surely were time they were starting for home. When they reached the end of the turnpike, she lifted her feet daintily along the muddy road, and leaped pools of water like a cat. Climbing the first foot-hills, she turned her beautiful head to right and left, and with pointed ears, snorted now and then at the strange dark woods on either side, and the tumbling water-falls. The red of her wide nostrils was showing when she reached the top of the first mountain, and from that high point of vantage she turned her wondering eyes over the wide rolling stretch that waved homeward, and whinnied with distinct uneasiness when Chad started her down into the wilderness beyond. Distinctly that road was no path for a lady to tread, but Dixie was to know it better in the coming war.

Within ten miles of the Turners', Chad met the first man that he knew—Hence Sturgill from Kingdom Come. He was driving a wagon.

"Howdye, Hence!" said Chad, reining in.

"Whoa!" said Hence, pulling in and staring at Chad's horse and at Chad from hat to spur.

"Don't you know me, Hence?"

"Well, God—I—may—die, if it ain't Chad! How air ye, Chad? Goin' up to ole Joel's?"

"Yes. How are things on Kingdom Come?"

Hence spat on the ground and raised one hand high over his head:

"God—I—may—die, if thar hain't hell to pay on Kingdom Come. You better keep off o' Kingdom Come," and then he stopped with an expression of quick alarm, looked around him into the bushes and dropped his voice to a whisper:

"But I hain't sayin' a word—rickollect now—not a word!"

Chad laughed aloud. "What's the matter with you, Hence?"

Hence put one finger on one side of his nose—still speaking in a low tone:

"Whut'd I say, Chad? D'I say one word?" He gathered up his reins. "You rickollect Jake and Jerry Dillon?" Chad nodded. "You know Jerry was al'ays a-runnin' over Jake 'cause Jake didn't have good sense. Jake was drapped when he was a baby. Well, Jerry struck Jake over the head with a fence-rail 'bout two months ago, an' when Jake come to, he had just as good sense as anybody, and now he hates Jerry like pizen, an' Jerry's half afeared of him. An' they do say as how them two brothers air a-goin'——" Again Hence stopped abruptly and clucked to his team. "But I ain't a-sayin' a word, now, mind ye—not a word!"

Chad rode on, amused, and thinking that Hence had gone daft, but he was to learn better. A reign of forty years' terror was starting in those hills.

Not a soul was in sight when he reached the top of the hill from which he could see the Turner home below—about the house, or the orchard, or in the fields. No one answered his halloo at the Turner gate, though Chad was sure that he saw a woman's figure flit past the door. It was a full minute before Mother Turner cautiously thrust her head outside the door and peered at him.

"Why, Aunt Betsey," called Chad, "don't you know me?"

At the sound of his voice Melissa sprang out the door with a welcoming cry, and ran to him, Mother Turner following with a broad smile on her kind old face. Chad felt the tears almost come—these were friends indeed. How tall Melissa had grown, and how lovely she was, with her tangled hair and flashing eyes and delicately modelled face. She went with him to the stable to help him put up his horse, blushing when he looked at her, and talking very little, while the old mother, from the fence, followed him with her dim eyes. At once Chad began to ply both with questions—where was Uncle Joel and the boys and the school-master? And, straightway, Chad felt a reticence in both—a curious reticence even with him. On each side of the fireplace, on each side of the door, and on each side of the window, he saw narrow blocks fixed to the logs. One was turned horizontal, and through the hole under it Chad saw daylight—portholes they were. At the door were oaken blocks as catches for a piece of upright wood nearby, which was plainly used to bar the door. The cabin was a fortress. By degrees the story came out. The neighborhood was in a turmoil of bloodshed and terror. Tom and Dolph had gone off to the war— Rebels. Old Joel had been called to the door one night, a few weeks since, and had been shot down without warning. They had fought all night. Melissa herself had handled a rifle at one of the portholes. Rube was out in the woods now, with Jack guarding and taking care of his wounded father. A

Home Guard had been organized, and Daws Dillon was captain. They were driving out of the mountains every man who owned a negro, for nearly every man who owned a negro had taken, or was forced to take, the Rebel side. The Dillons were all Yankees, except Jerry, who had gone off with Tom; and the giant brothers, Rebel Jerry and Yankee Jake—as both were already known—had sworn to kill each other on sight. Bushwhacking had already begun. When Chad asked about the school-master, the old woman's face grew stern, and Melissa's lip curled with scorn.

"Yankee!" The girl spat the word out with such vindictive bitterness that Chad's face turned slowly scarlet, while the girl's keen eyes pierced him like a knife and narrowed as, with pale face and heaving breast, she rose suddenly from her chair and faced him—amazed, bewildered, burning with sudden hatred. "And you're another!" The girl's voice was like a hiss.

"Why, Lissy!" cried the old mother, startled, horrified.

"Look at him!" said the girl. The old woman looked; her face grew hard and frightened, and she rose feebly, moving toward the girl as though for protection against him. Chad's very heart seemed suddenly to turn to water. He had been dreading the moment to come when he must tell. He knew it would be hard, but he was not looking for this.

"You better git away!" quavered the old woman, "afore Joel and Rube come in."

"Hush!" said the girl, sharply, her hands clinched like claws, her whole body stiff, like a tigress ready to attack, or awaiting attack.

"Mebbe he come hyeh to find out whar they air—don't tell him!"

"Lissy!" said Chad, brokenly.

"Then whut did you come fer?"

"To tell you good-by, I came to see all of you, Lissy."

The girl laughed scornfully, and Chad knew he was help-less. He could not explain, and they could not understand—nobody had understood.

"Aunt Betsey," he said, "you took Jack and me in, and you took care of me just as though I had been your own child. You know I'd give my life for you or Uncle Joel, or any one of the boys"—his voice grew a little stern—"and you know it, too, Lissy——"

"You're makin' things wuss," interrupted the girl, stridently, "an' now you're goin' to do all you can to kill us. I reckon you can see that door. Why don't you go over to the Dillons?" she panted. "They're friends o' your'n. An' don't let Uncle Joel or Rube ketch you anywhar round hyeh!"

"I'm not afraid to see Uncle Joel or Rube, Lissy."

"You must git away, Chad," quavered the old woman. "They mought hurt ye!"

"I'm sorry not to see Jack. He's the only friend I have now."

"Why, Jack would snarl at ye," said the girl, bitterly. "He hates a Yankee." She pointed again with her finger. "I reckon you can see that door."

They followed him, Melissa going on the porch and the old woman standing in the doorway. On one side of the walk Chad saw a rose-bush that he had brought from the Bluegrass for Melissa. It was dying. He took one step toward it, his foot sinking in the soft earth where the girl had evidently been working around it, and broke off the one green leaf that was left.

"Here, Lissy! You'll be sorry you were so hard on me. I'd never get over it if I didn't think you would. Keep this, won't you, and let's be friends, not enemies."

He held it out, and the girl angrily struck the rose-leaf from his hand to her feet.

Chad rode away at a walk. Two hundred yards below, where the hill rose, the road was hock-deep with sand, and Dixie's feet were as noiseless as a cat's. A few yards beyond a ravine on the right, a stone rolled from the bushes into the road. Instinctively Chad drew rein, and Dixie stood motionless. A moment later, a crouching figure, with a long squirrel rifle, slipped out of the bushes and started noiselessly across the ravine. Chad's pistol flashed.

"Stop!"

The figure crouched more, and turned a terror-stricken face —Daws Dillon's.

"Oh, it's you, is it? Well, drop that gun and come down here."

The Dillon boy rose, leaving his gun on the ground, and came down, trembling.

"What're you doin' sneaking around in the brush?"

"Nothin'!" The Dillon had to make two efforts before he could speak at all. "Nothin', jes' a-huntin'!"

"Huntin'!" repeated Chad. He lowered his pistol and looked at the sorry figure silently.

"I know what you were huntin', you rattlesnake! I understand you are captain of the Home Guard. I reckon you don't know that nobody *has* to go into this war. That a man has the right to stay peaceably at home, and nobody has the right to bother him. If you don't know it, I tell you now. I believe you had something to do with shooting Uncle Joel."

The Dillon shook his head, and fumbled with his hands.

"If I knew it, I'd kill you where you stand, now. But I've got one word to say to you, you hell-pup. I hate to think it, but you and I are on the same side—that is, if you have any side. But in spite of that, if I hear of any harm happening to Aunt Betsey, or Melissa, or Uncle Joel, or Rube, while they are all peaceably at home, I'm goin' to hold you and Tad responsible, whether you are or not, and I'll kill you"—he raised one hand to make the Almighty a witness to his oath—"I'll kill you, if I have to follow you both to hell for doin' it. Now, you take keer of 'em! Turn 'round!"

The Dillon hesitated.

"Turn!" Chad cried, savagely, raising his pistol. "Go back to that gun, an' if you turn your head I'll shoot you where you're sneakin' aroun' to shoot Rube or Uncle Joel—in the back, you cowardly feist. Pick up that gun! Now, let her off! See if you can hit that beech-tree in front of you. Just imagine that it's me."

The rifle cracked and Chad laughed.

"Well, you ain't much of a shot. I reckon you must have chills and fever. Now, come back here. Give me your powder-horn. You'll find it on top of the hill on the right-hand side of the road. Now, you trot—home!"

The Dillon stared.

"Double-quick!" shouted Chad. "You ought to know what that means if you are a soldier—a soldier!" he repeated, contemptuously.

The Dillon disappeared on a run.

Chad rode all that night. At dawn he reached the foot-hills, and by noon he drew up at the road which turned to Camp

Dick Robinson. He sat there a long time thinking, and then pushed on toward Lexington. If he could, he would keep from fighting on Kentucky soil.

Next morning he was going at an easy "running-walk" along the old Maysville road toward the Ohio. Within three miles of Major Buford's, he leaped the fence and struck across the fields that he might go around and avoid the risk of a painful chance meeting with his old friend or any of the Deans.

What a land of peace and plenty it was—the woodlands, meadows, pasture lands! Fat cattle raised their noses from the thick grass and looked with mild inquiry at him. Sheep ran bleating toward him, as though he were come to salt them. A rabbit leaped from a thorn-bush and whisked his white flag into safety in a hemp-field. Squirrels barked in the big oaks, and a covey of young quail fluttered up from a fence corner and sailed bravely away. 'Possum signs were plentiful, and on the edge of the creek he saw a coon solemnly searching under a rock with one paw for crawfish. Every now and then Dixie would turn her head impatiently to the left, for she knew where home was. The Deans' house was just over the hill; he would have but the ride to the top to see it and, perhaps, Margaret. There was no need. As he sat looking up the hill, Margaret herself rode slowly over it, and down, through the sunlight slanting athwart the dreaming woods, straight toward him. Chad sat still. Above him the road curved, and she could not see him until she turned a little thicket just before him. Her pony was more startled than was she. A little leap of color to her face alone showed her surprise.

"Did you get my note?"

"I did. You got my mother's message?"

"I did." Chad paused. "That is why I am passing around you."

The girl said nothing.

"But I'm glad I came so near. I wanted to see you once more. I wish I could make you understand. But nobody understands. I hardly understand myself. But please try to believe that what I say is true. I'm just back from the mountains, and listen, Margaret—" He halted a moment to steady his voice. "The Turners down there took me in when I was a ragged outcast. They clothed me, fed me, educated me. The Major took me when I was little more; and he fed me, clothed me, educated me. The Turners scorned me—Melissa told me to go herd with the Dillons. The Major all but turned me from his door. Your father was bitter toward me, thinking that I had helped turn Harry to the Union cause. But let me tell you! If the Turners died, believing me a traitor; if Lissy died with a curse on her lips for me; if the Major died without, as he believed, ever having polluted his lips again with my name; if Harry were brought back here dead, and your father died, believing that his blood was on my hands; and if I lost you and your love, and you died, believing the same thing—I must still go. Oh, Margaret, I can't understand—I have ceased to reason. I only know I must go!"

The girl in the mountains had let her rage and scorn loose like a storm, but the gentlewoman only grew more calm. Every vestige of color left her, but her eyes never for a moment wavered from his face. Her voice was quiet and even and passionless:

"Then, why don't you go?"

The lash of an overseer's whip across his face could not

[213]

have made his soul so bleed. Even then he did not lose himself.

"I am in your way," he said, quietly. And backing Dixie from the road, and without bending his head or lowering his eyes, he waited, hat in hand, for Margaret to pass.

. . . .

All that day Chad rode, and, next morning, Dixie climbed the Union bank of the Ohio and trotted into the recruiting camp of the Fourth Ohio Cavalry. The first man Chad saw was Harry Dean—grave, sombre, taciturn, though he smiled and thrust out his hand eagerly. Chad's eyes dropped to the sergeant's stripes on Harry's sleeves, and again Harry smiled.

"You'll have 'em yourself in a week. These fellows ride like a lot of meal-bags over here. Here's my captain," he added, in a lower voice.

A pompous officer rode slowly up. He pulled in his horse when he saw Chad.

"You want to join the army?"

"Yes," said Chad.

"All right. That's a fine horse you've got."

Chad said nothing.

"What's his name?"

"*Her* name is Dixie."

The captain stared. Some soldiers behind laughed in a smothered fashion, sobering their faces quickly when the captain turned upon them, furious.

"Well, change her name!"

"I'll not change her name," said Chad, quietly.

"What!" shouted the officer. "How dare you—" Chad's eyes looked ominous.

"Don't you give any orders to me—not yet. You haven't the right; and when you have, you can save your breath by not giving that one. This horse comes from Kentucky, and so do I; her name will stay Dixie as long as I straddle her, and I propose to straddle her until one of us dies, or"—he smiled and nodded across the river—"somebody over there gets her who won't object to her name as much as you do."

The astonished captain's lips opened, but a quiet voice behind interrupted him:

"Never mind, Captain." Chad turned and saw a short, thick-set man with a stubbly brown beard, whose eyes were twinkling, though his face was grave. "A boy who wants to fight for the Union, and insists on calling his horse Dixie, must be all right. Come with me, my lad."

As Chad followed, he heard the man saluted as Colonel Grant, but he paid no heed. Few people at that time did pay heed to the name of Ulysses Grant.

XXII

MORGAN'S MEN

Boots and saddles at daybreak!

Over the border, in Dixie, two videttes in gray trot briskly from out a leafy woodland, side by side, and looking with keen eyes right and left; one, erect, boyish, bronzed; the other, slouching, bearded, huge—the boy, Daniel Dean; the man, Rebel Jerry Dillon, one of the giant twins.

Fifty yards behind them emerges a single picket; after him come three more videttes, the same distance apart. Fifty yards behind the last rides "the advance"—a guard of twenty-five picked men. No commission among "Morgan's Men" was more eagerly sought than a place on that guard of hourly risk and honor. Behind it trot still three more videttes, at intervals of one hundred yards, and just that interval behind the last of these ride Morgan's Men, the flower of Kentucky's youth, in columns of fours—Colonel Hunt's regiment in advance, the colors borne by Renfrew the Silent in a brilliant Zouave jacket studded with buttons of red coral. In the rear rumble two Parrot guns, affectionately christened the "Bull Pups."

Skirting the next woodland ran a cross-road. Down one way gallops Dan, and down the other lumbers Rebel Jerry, each two hundred yards. A cry rings from vidette to vidette behind them and back to the guard. Two horsemen spur from the "advance" and take the places of the last two videttes, while the videttes in front take and keep the original formation until the column passes that cross-road, when Dean and Dillon gallop up to their old places in the extreme front again. Far in front, and on both flanks, are scouting parties, miles away.

This was the way Morgan marched.

Yankees ahead! Not many, to be sure—no more numerous than two or three to one; so back fall the videttes and forward charges that advance guard like a thunderbolt, not troubling the column behind. Wild yells, a clattering of hoofs, the crack of pistol-shots, a wild flight, a merry chase, a few riderless horses gathered in from the fleeing Yankees, and the incident is over.

Ten miles more, and many hostile bayonets gleam ahead. A serious fight, this, perhaps—so back drops the advance, this time as a reserve; up gallops the column into single rank and dismounts, while the flank companies, deploying as skirmishers, cover the whole front, one man out of each set of fours and the corporals holding the horses in the rear. The "Bull Pups" bark and the Rebel yell rings as the line—the files two yards apart—"a long flexible line curving forward at each extremity"—slips forward at a half run. This time the Yankees charge.

From every point of that curving line pours a merciless fire, and the charging men in blue recoil—all but one. (War is full of grim humor.) On comes one lone Yankee, hatless, red-headed, pulling on his reins with might and main, his horse beyond control, and not one of the enemy shoots as he sweeps helplessly into their line. A huge rebel grabs his bridle-rein.

"I don't know whether to kill you now," he says, with pretended ferocity, "or wait till the fight is over."

[217]

"For God's sake, don't kill me at all!" shouts the Yankee. "I'm a dissipated character, and not prepared to die."

Shots from the right flank and rear, and that line is thrown about like a rope. But the main body of the Yankees is to the left.

"Left face! Double-quick!" is the ringing order, and, by magic, the line concentrates in a solid phalanx and sweeps forward.

This was the way Morgan fought.

And thus, marching and fighting, he went his triumphant way into the land of the enemy, without sabres, without artillery, without even the "Bull Pups," sometimes—fighting infantry, cavalry, artillery with only muzzle-loading rifles, pistols, and shotguns; scattering Home Guards like turkeys; destroying railroads and bridges; taking towns and burning Government stores, and encompassed, usually, with forces treble his own.

This was what Morgan did on a raid, was what he had done, what he was starting out now to do again.

Darkness threatens, and the column halts to bivouac for the night on the very spot where, nearly a year before, Morgan's Men first joined Johnston's army, which, like a great, lean, hungry hawk, guarded the Southern border.

Daniel Dean was a war-worn veteran now. He could ride twenty hours out of the twenty-four; he could sleep in his saddle or anywhere but on picket duty, and there was no trick of the trade in camp, or on the march, that was not at his finger's end.

Fire first! Nobody had a match, the leaves were wet and the twigs sobby, but by some magic a tiny spark glows under some shadowy figure, bites at the twigs, snaps at the branches, and wraps a log in flames.

Water next! A tin cup rattles in a bucket, and another shadowy figure steals off into the darkness, with an instinct as unerring as the skill of a water-witch with a willow wand. The Yankees chose open fields for camps, but your rebel took to the woods. Each man and his chum picked a tree for a home, hung up canteens and spread blankets at the foot of it. Supper— Heavens, what luck—fresh beef! One man broils it on coals, pinning pieces of fat to it to make gravy; another roasts it on a forked stick, for Morgan carried no cooking utensils on a raid.

Here, one man made up bread in an oilcloth (and every Morgan's man had one soon after they were issued to the Federals) ; another worked up corn-meal into dough in the scooped-out half of a pumpkin; one baked bread on a flat rock, another on a board, while a third had twisted his dough around his ramrod; if it were spring-time, a fourth might be fitting his into a cornshuck to roast in ashes. All this Dan Dean could do.

The roaring fire thickens the gloom of the woods where the lonely pickets stand. Pipes are out now. An oracle outlines the general campaign of the war as it will be and as it should have been. A long-winded, innocent braggart tells of his personal prowess that day. A little group is guying the new recruit. A wag shaves a bearded comrade on one side of his face, pockets his razor and refuses to shave the other side. A poet, with a bandaged eye, and hair like a wind-blown hay-stack, recites "I am dying, Egypt—dying," and then a pure, clear, tenor voice starts through the forest-aisles, and there is sudden silence. Every man knows that voice, and loves the boy who owns it—little Tom Morgan, Dan's brother-in-arms, the General's seventeen-year-old brother—and there he stands leaning against a tree, full in the light of the fire, a handsome, gallant figure—a song like a seraph's pouring from his lips. One bearded soldier is gazing at him with curious intentness, and when the song ceases, lies down with a suddenly troubled face. He has seen the "death-look" in the boy's eyes—that prophetic death-look in which he has unshaken faith. The night deepens, figures roll up in blankets, quiet comes, and Dan lies wide awake and deep in memories, and looking back on those early helpless days of the war with a tolerant smile.

He was a war-worn veteran now, but how vividly he could recall that first night in the camp of a big army, in the very woods where he now lay—dusk settling over the Green River country, which Morgan's Men grew to love so well; a mocking-bird singing a farewell song from the top of a stunted oak to the dead summer and the dying day; Morgan seated on a cracker-box in front of his tent, contemplatively chewing one end of his mustache; Lieutenant Hunt swinging from his horse, smiling grimly.

"It would make a horse laugh—a Yankee cavalry horse, anyhow—to see this army."

Hunt had been over the camp that first afternoon on a personal tour of investigation. There were not a thousand Springfield and Enfield rifles at that time in Johnston's army. Half of the soldiers were armed with shotguns and squirrel rifles, and the greater part of the other half with flintlock muskets. But nearly every man, thinking he was in for a rough-and-tumble fight, had a bowie-knife and a revolver swung to his belt.

"Those Arkansas and Texas fellows have got knives that would make a Malay's blood run cold."

"Well, they'll do to hew firewood and cut meat," laughed Morgan.

The troops were not only badly armed. On his tour, Hunt had seen men making blankets of a piece of old carpet, lined on one side with a piece of cotton cloth; men wearing ox-hide buskins, or complicated wrapping of rags, for shoes; orderly sergeants making out reports on shingles; surgeons using a twisted handkerchief instead of a tourniquet. There was a total lack of medicine, and camp diseases were already breaking out—measles, typhoid fever, pneumonia, bowel troubles—each fatal, it seemed, in time of war.

"General Johnston has asked Richmond for a stand of thirty thousand arms," Morgan had mused, and Hunt looked up inquiringly.

"Mr. Davis can only spare a thousand."

"That's lucky," said Hunt, grimly.

And then the military organization of that army, so characteristic of the Southerner! An officer who wanted to be more than a colonel, and couldn't be a brigadier, would have a "legion"—a hybrid unit between a regiment and a brigade. Sometimes there was a regiment whose roll-call was more than two thousand men, so popular was its colonel. Companies would often refuse to designate themselves by letter, but by the thrilling titles they had given themselves. How Morgan and Hunt had laughed over "The Yellow Jackets," "The Dead Shots," "The Earthquakes," "The Chickasha Desperadoes," and "The Hell Roarers"! Regiments would bear the names of their commanders—a singular instance of the Southerner's passion for individuality, as a man, a company, a regiment, or a brigade. And there was little or no discipline, as the word is understood among the military elect, and with no army that the world has ever seen, Richard Hunt always claimed, was there so little need of it. For Southern soldiers, he argued, were, from the start, obedient, zealous, and tolerably patient, from good sense and a strong sense of duty. They were born fighters; a spirit of emulation induced them to learn the drill; pride and patriotism kept them true and patient to the last, but they could not be made, by punishment or the fear of it, into machines. They read their chance of success, not in opposing numbers, but in the character and reputation of their commanders, who, in turn, believed, as a rule, that "the unthinking automaton, formed by routine and punishment, could no more stand before the high-strung young soldier with brains and good blood, and some practice and knowledge of warfare, than a tree could resist a stroke of lightning." So that with Southern soldiers discipline came to mean "the pride which made soldiers learn their duties rather than incur disgrace; the subordination that came from self-respect and respect for the man whom they thought worthy to command them."

Boots and saddles again at daybreak! By noon the column reached Green River, over the Kentucky line, where Morgan, even on his way down to join Johnston, had begun the operations which were to make him famous. No picket duty that infantry could do as well, for Morgan's cavalry! He wanted it kept out on the front or the flanks of an army, and as close as possible upon the enemy. Right away, there had been thrilling times for Dan in the Green River country—setting out at dark, chasing countrymen in Federal pay or sympathy, prowling all night around and among pickets and outposts; entrapping the unwary; taking a position on the line of retreat at daybreak, and turning leisurely back to camp with prisoners and information. How memories thronged! At this very turn of the road, Dan remembered, they had their first brush with the enemy. No plan of battle had been adopted, other than to hide on both sides of the road and send their horses to the rear.

"I think we ought to charge 'em," said Georgie Forbes, Chad's old enemy. Dan saw that his lip trembled, and, a moment later, Georgie, muttering something, disappeared.

The Yankees had come on, and, discovering them, halted. Morgan himself stepped out in the road and shot the officer riding at the head of the column. His men fell back without returning the fire, deployed and opened up. Dan recognized the very tree behind which he had stood, and again he could almost hear Richard Hunt chuckling from behind another close by.

"We would be in bad shape," said Richard Hunt, as the bullets whistled high overhead, "if we were in the tops of these trees instead of behind them." There had been no manœuvring, no command given among the Confederates. Each man fought his own fight. In ten minutes a horse-holder ran up from the rear, breathless, and announced that the Yankees were flanking. Every man withdrew, straightway, after his own fashion, and in his own time. One man was wounded and several were shot through the clothes.

"That was like a camp-meeting or an election row," laughed Morgan, when they were in camp.

"Or an affair between Austrian and Italian outposts," said Hunt.

A chuckle rose behind them. A lame colonel was limping past.

"I got your courier," he said.

"I sent no courier," said Morgan.

"It was Forbes who wanted to charge 'em," said Dan.

Again the Colonel chuckled.

"The Yankees ran when you did," he said, and limped, chuckling, away.

But it was great fun, those moonlit nights, burning bridges and chasing Home Guards who would flee fifteen or twenty miles sometimes to "rally." Here was a little town through which Dan and Richard Hunt had marched with nine prisoners in a column—taken by them alone—and a captured United States flag, flying in front, scaring Confederate sympathizers and straggling soldiers, as Hunt reported, horribly. Dan chuckled at the memory, for the prisoners were quartered with different messes, and, that night, several bottles of sparkling Catawba happened, by some mystery, to be on hand. The prisoners were told that this was regularly issued by their commissaries, and thereupon they plead, with tears, to be received into the Confederate ranks.

This kind of service was valuable training for Morgan's later work. Slight as it was, it soon brought him thirty old, condemned artillery-horses—Dan smiled now at the memory of those ancient chargers—which were turned over to Morgan to be nursed until they would bear a mount, and, by and by, it gained him a colonelcy and three companies, superbly mounted and equipped, which, as "Morgan's Squadron," became known far and near. Then real service began.

In January, the right wing of Johnston's hungry hawk had been broken in the Cumberland Mountains. Early in February, Johnston had withdrawn it from Kentucky before Buell's hosts, with its beak always to the foe. By the middle of the month, Grant had won the Western border States to the Union, with the capture of Fort Donelson. In April, the sun of Shiloh rose and set on the failure of the first Confederate aggressive campaign at the West; and in that fight Dan saw his first real battle, and Captain Hunt was wounded. In May, Buell had pushed the Confederate lines south and east toward Chattanooga. To retain a hold on the Mississippi valley, the Confederates must make another push for Kentucky, and it was this great Southern need that soon put John Morgan's name on the lips of every rebel and Yankee in the middle South. In June, provost-marshals were appointed in every county in Kentucky; the dogs of war began to be turned loose on the "secesh sympathizers" throughout the State; and Jerome Conners, overseer, began to render sly service to the Union cause.

For it was in June that Morgan paid his first memorable little visit to the Bluegrass, and Daniel Dean wrote his brother Harry the short tale of the raid.

"We left Dixie with nine hundred men," the letter ran, "and got back in twenty-four days with twelve hundred. Travelled over one thousand miles, captured seventeen towns, destroyed all Government supplies and arms in them, scattered fifteen hundred Home Guards, and paroled twelve hundred regular troops. Lost of the original nine hundred, in killed, wounded, and missing, about ninety men. How's that? We kept twenty thousand men busy guarding Government posts or chasing us, and we're going back often. Oh, Harry, I *am* glad that you are with Grant."

But Harry was not with Grant—not now. While Morgan was marching up from Dixie to help Kirby Smith in the last great effort that the Confederacy was about to make to win Kentucky—down from the yellow river marched the Fourth Ohio Cavalry to go into camp at Lexington; and with it marched Chadwick Buford and Harry Dean, who, too, were veterans now—who, too, were going home. Both lads wore a second lieutenant's empty shoulder-straps, which both yet meant to fill with bars, but Chad's promotion had not come as swiftly as Harry had predicted; the Captain, whose displeasure he had incurred, prevented that. It had come, in time, however, and with one leap he had landed, after Shiloh, at Harry's side. In the beginning, young Dean had wanted to go to the Army of the Potomac, as did Chad, but one quiet word from the taciturn colonel with the stubbly reddish-brown beard and the perpetual black cigar, kept both where they were.

"Though," said Grant to Chad, as his eye ran over beautiful Dixie from tip of nose to tip of tail, and came back to Chad, slightly twinkling, "I've a great notion to put *you* in the infantry just to get hold of that horse."

So it was no queer turn of fate that had soon sent both the lads to help hold Zollicoffer at Cumberland Gap, that stopped them at Camp Dick Robinson to join forces with Wolford's cavalry, and brought Chad face to face with an old friend. Wolford's cavalry was gathered from the mountains and the hills, and when some scouts came in that afternoon, Chad, to his great joy, saw, mounted on a gaunt sorrel, none other than his old school-master, Caleb Hazel, who, after shaking hands with both Harry and Chad, pointed silently at a great, strange figure following him on a splendid horse some fifty yards behind. The man wore a slouch hat, tow linen breeches, home-made suspenders, a belt with two pistols, and on his naked heels were two huge Texan spurs. Harry broke into a laugh, and Chad's puzzled face cleared when the man grinned; it was Yankee Jake Dillon, one of the giant twins. Chad looked at him curiously; that blow on the head that his brother, Rebel Jerry, had given him, had wrought a miracle. The lips no longer hung apart, but were set firmly, and the eye was almost keen; the face was still rather stupid, but not foolish—and it was still kind. Chad knew that, somewhere in the Confederate lines, Rebel Jerry was looking for Jake, as Yankee Jake, doubtless, was now looking for Jerry, and he began to think that it might be well for Jerry if neither was ever found. Daws Dillon, so he learned from Caleb Hazel and Jake, was already making his name a watchword of terror along the border of Virginia and Tennessee, and was prowling, like a wolf, now and then, along the edge of the Bluegrass. Old Joel Turner had died of his wound, Rube had gone off to the war, and Mother Turner and Melissa were left at home, alone.

"Daws fit fust on one side and then on t'other," said Jake, and then he smiled in a way that Chad understood; "an' sence you was down thar last, Daws don't seem to hanker much atter meddlin' with the Turners, though the two women did have to run over into Virginny, once in a while. Melissy," he added, "was a-goin' to marry Dave Hilton, so folks said; and he reckoned they'd already hitched most likely, sence Chad thar——"

A flash from Chad's eyes stopped him, and Chad, seeing Harry's puzzled face, turned away. He was glad that Melissa was going to marry—yes, he was glad; and how he did pray that she might be happy!

Fighting Zollicoffer, only a few days later, Chad and

Harry had their baptism of fire, and strange battle orders they heard, that made them smile even in the thick of the fight.

"Huddle up thar!" "Scatter out, now!" "Form a line of fight!" "Wait till you see the shine of their eyes!"

"I see 'em!" shouted a private, and "bang" went his gun. That was the way the fight opened. Chad saw Harry's eyes blazing like stars from his pale face, which looked pained and half sick, and Chad understood—the lads were fighting their own people, and there was no help for it. A voice bellowed from the rear, and a man in a red cap loomed in the smoke-mist ahead:

"Now, now! Git up and git, boys!"

That was the order for the charge, and the blue line went forward. Chad never forgot that first battle-field when he saw it a few hours later strewn with dead and wounded, the dead lying, as they dropped, in every conceivable position, features stark, limbs rigid; one man with a half-smoked cigar on his breast; the faces of so many beardless; some frowning, some as if asleep and dreaming; and the wounded—some talking pitifully, some in delirium, some courteous, patient, anxious to save trouble, others morose, sullen, stolid, independent; never forgot it, even the terrible night after Shiloh, when he searched heaps of wounded and slain for Caleb Hazel, who lay all through the night wounded almost to death.

Later, the Fourth Ohio followed Johnston, as he gave way before Buell, and many times did they skirmish and fight with ubiquitous Morgan's Men. Several times Harry and Dan sent each other messages to say that each was still unhurt, and both were in constant horror of some day coming face to face. Once, indeed, Harry, chasing a rebel and firing at him, saw him lurch

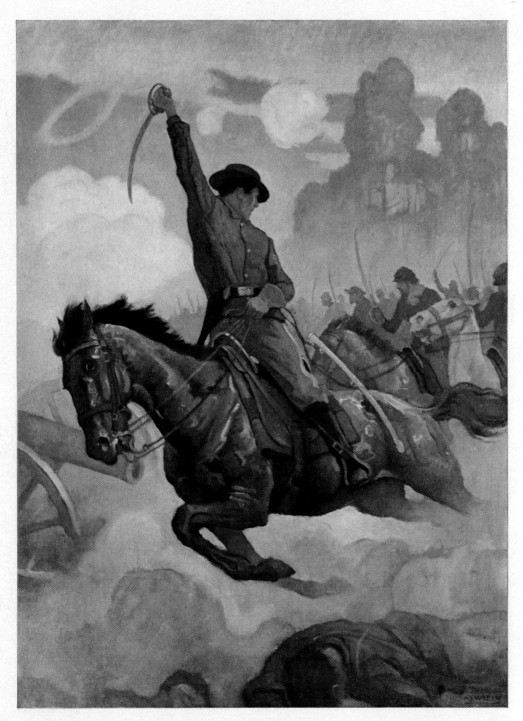

It was not until Shiloh that Chad got his shoulder-straps, leading a charge.

in his saddle, and Chad, coming up, found the lad on the ground, crying over a canteen which the rebel had dropped. It was marked with the initials D. D., the strap was cut by the bullet Harry had fired, and not for a week of agonizing torture did Harry learn that the canteen, though Dan's, had been carried that day by another man.

It was on these scouts and skirmishes that the four—Harry and Chad, and Caleb Hazel and Yankee Jake Dillon, whose dog-like devotion to Chad soon became a regimental joke—became known, not only among their own men, but among their enemies, as the shrewdest and most daring scouts in the Federal service. Every Morgan's man came to know the name of Chad Buford; but it was not until Shiloh that Chad got his shoulder-straps, leading a charge under the very eye of General Grant. After Shiloh, the Fourth Ohio went back to its old quarters across the river, and no sooner were Chad and Harry there than Kentucky was put under the Department of the Ohio; and so it was also no queer turn of fate that now they were on their way to new head-quarters in Lexington.

Straight along the turnpike that ran between the Dean and the Buford farms, the Fourth Ohio went in a cloud of thick dust that rose and settled like a gray choking mist on the seared fields. Side by side rode Harry and Chad, and neither spoke when, on the left, the white columns of the Dean house came into view, and, on the right, the red brick of Chad's old home showed through the dusty leaves; not even when both saw on the Dean porch the figures of two women who, standing motionless, were looking at them. Harry's shoulders drooped, and he stared stonily ahead, while Chad turned his head quickly. The front door and shutters of the Buford house were closed, and there were few signs of life about the place. Only at the gate was the slouching figure of Jerome Conners, the overseer, who, waving his hat at the column, recognized Chad, as he rode by, and spoke to him, Chad thought, with a covert sneer. Farther ahead, and on the farthest boundary of the Buford farm, was a Federal fort, now deserted, and the beautiful woodland that had once stood in perfect beauty around it was sadly ravaged and nearly gone, as was the Dean woodland across the road. It was plain that some people were paying the Yankee piper for the death-dance in which a mighty nation was shaking its feet.

On they went, past the old college, down Broadway, wheeling at Second Street—Harry going on with the regiment to camp on the other edge of the town; Chad reporting with his colonel at General Ward's head-quarters, a columned brick house on one corner of the college campus, and straight across from the Hunt home, where he had first danced with Margaret Dean.

That night the two lay on the edge of the Ashland woods, looking up at the stars, the ripened bluegrass—a yellow, moon-lit sea—around them and the woods dark and still behind them. Both smoked and were silent, but each knew that to the other his thoughts were known; for both had been on the same errand that day, and the miserable tale of the last ten months both had learned.

Trouble had soon begun for the ones who were dear to them, when both left for the war. At once General Anderson had promised immunity from arrest to every peaceable citizen in the State, but at once the shiftless, the prowling, the lawless, gathered to the Home Guards for self-protection, to mask deviltry and to wreak vengeance for private wrongs. At once mischief began. Along the Ohio, men with Southern sympathies were clapped into prison. Citizens who had joined the Confederates were pronounced guilty of treason, and Breckinridge was expelled from the Senate as a traitor. Morgan's great raid in June, '61, spread consternation through the land and, straightway, every district and county were at the mercy of a petty local provost. No man of Southern sympathies could stand for office. Courts in session were broken up with the bayonet. Civil authority was overthrown. Destruction of property, indemnity assessments on innocent men, arrests, imprisonment, and murder became of daily occurrence. Ministers were jailed and lately prisons had even been prepared for disloyal women. Major Buford, forced to stay at home on account of his rheumatism and the serious illness of Miss Lucy, had been sent to prison once and was now under arrest again. General Dean, old as he was, had escaped and had gone to Virginia to fight with Lee; and Margaret and Mrs. Dean, with a few servants, were out on the farm alone.

But neither spoke of the worst that both feared was yet to come—and "Taps" sounded soft and clear on the night air.

XXIII

CHAD CAPTURES AN OLD FRIEND

MEANWHILE Morgan was coming on—led by the two vi- dettes in gray—Daniel Dean and Rebel Jerry Dillon—coming on to meet Kirby Smith in Lexington after that general had led the Bluegrass into the Confederate fold. They were taking short cuts through the hills now, and Rebel Jerry was guide, for he had joined Morgan for that purpose. Jerry had long been notorious along the border. He never gave quarter on his expeditions for personal vengeance, and it was said that not even he knew how many men he had killed. Every Morgan's man had heard of him, and was anxious to see him; and see him they did, though they never heard him open his lips except in answer to a question. To Dan he seemed to take a strange fancy right away, but he was as voiceless as the grave, except for an occasional oath, when bush-whackers of Daws Dillon's ilk would pop at the advance guard—sometimes from a rock directly overhead, for chase was useless. It took a roundabout climb of one hundred yards to get to the top of that rock, so there was nothing for videttes and guards to do but pop back, which they did to no purpose. On the third day, however, after a skirmish in which Dan had charged with a little more dare- deviltry than usual, the big Dillon ripped out an oath of pro- test. An hour later he spoke again:

"I got a brother on t'other side."

Dan started. "Why, so have I," he said. "What's your brother with?"

"Wolford's cavalry."

"That's curious. So was mine—for a while. He's with Grant now." The boy turned his head away suddenly.

"I might meet him, if he were with Wolford now," he said, half to himself, but Jerry heard him and smiled viciously.

"Well, that's what I'm goin' with you fellers fer—to meet mine."

"What!" said Dan, puzzled.

"We've been lookin' fer each other sence the war broke out. I reckon he went on t'other side to keep me from killin' him."

Dan shrank away from the giant with horror; but next day the mountaineer saved the boy's life in a fight in which Dan's chum—gallant little Tom Morgan—lost his; and that night, as Dan lay sleepless and crying in his blanket, Jerry Dillon came in from guard-duty and lay down by him.

"I'm goin' to take keer o' you."

"I don't need you," said Dan, gruffly, and Rebel Jerry grunted, turned over on his side and went to sleep. Night and day thereafter he was by the boy's side.

A thrill ran through the entire command when the column struck the first Bluegrass turnpike, and a cheer rang from front to rear. Near Midway, a little Bluegrass town some fifteen miles from Lexington, a halt was called, and another deafening cheer arose in the extreme rear and came forward like a rushing wind, as a coal-black horse galloped the length of the column—its rider, hat in hand, bowing with a proud smile to the flattering storm—for the idolatry of the man and his men was mutual—with the erect grace of an Indian, the air of a courtier, and the bearing of a soldier in every line of the six feet and more of his tireless frame. No man who ever saw John Morgan on horseback but had the picture stamped forever on his brain, as no man who ever saw that coal-black horse ever forgot Black Bess. Behind him came his staff, and behind them came a wizened little man, whose nickname was "Lightning"—telegraph operator for Morgan's Men. There was need of Lightning now, so Morgan sent him on into town with Dan and Jerry Dillon, while he and Richard Hunt followed leisurely.

The three troopers found the station operator seated on the platform—pipe in mouth, and enjoying himself hugely. He looked lazily at them.

"Call up Lexington," said Lightning, sharply.

"Go to hell!" said the operator, and then he nearly toppled from his chair. Lightning, with a vicious gesture, had swung a pistol on him.

"Here—here!" he gasped, "what'd you mean?"

"Call up Lexington," repeated Lightning. The operator seated himself.

"What do you want in Lexington?" he growled.

"Ask the time of day?" The operated stared, but the instrument clicked.

"What's your name?" asked Lightning.

"Woolums."

"Well, Woolums, you're a 'plug.' I wanted to see how you handled the key. Yes, Woolums, you're a plug."

Then Lightning seated himself, and Woolums' mouth flew open—Lightning copied his style with such exactness. Again the instrument clicked and Lightning listened, smiling:

CHAD CAPTURES AN OLD FRIEND

"Will there be any danger coming to Midway?" asked a railroad conductor in Lexington. Lightning answered, grinning:

"None. Come right on. No sign of rebels here." Again a click from Lexington.

"General Ward orders General Finnell of Frankfort to move his forces. General Ward will move toward Georgetown, to which Morgan with eighteen hundred men is marching."

Lightning caught his breath—this was Morgan's force and his intention exactly. He answered:

"Morgan with upward of two thousand men has taken the road to Frankfort. This is reliable." Ten minutes later, Lightning chuckled.

"Ward orders Finnell to recall his regiment to Frankfort."

Half an hour later another idea struck Lightning. He clicked as though telegraphing from Frankfort:

"Our pickets just driven in. Great excitement. Force of enemy must be two thousand."

Then Lightning laughed. "I've fooled 'em," said Lightning.

There was turmoil in Lexington. The streets thundered with the tramp of cavalry going to catch Morgan. Daylight came and nothing was done—nothing known. The afternoon waned, and still Ward fretted at head-quarters, while his impatient staff sat on the piazza talking, speculating, wondering where the wily raider was. Leaning on the campus-fence near by were Chadwick Buford and Harry Dean.

It had been a sad day for those two. The mutual tolerance that prevailed among their friends in the beginning of the war had given way to intense bitterness now. There was no thrill for them in the flags fluttering a welcome to them from the windows of loyalists, for under those flags old friends passed them in the street with no sign of recognition, but a sullen, averted face, or a stare of open contempt. Elizabeth Morgan had met them, and turned her head when Harry raised his cap, though Chad saw tears spring to her eyes as she passed. Sad as it was for him, Chad knew what the silent torture in Harry's heart must be, for Harry could not bring himself, that day, even to visit his own home. And now Morgan was coming, and they might soon be in a death-fight, Harry with his own blood-brother and both with boyhood friends.

"God grant that you two may never meet!"

That cry from General Dean was beating ceaselessly through Harry's brain now, and he brought one hand down on the fence, hardly noticing the drop of blood that oozed from the force of the blow.

"Oh, I wish I could get away from here!"

"I shall the first chance that comes," said Chad, and he lifted his head sharply, staring down the street. A phaeton was coming slowly toward them and in it were a negro servant and a girl in white. Harry was leaning over the fence with his back toward the street, and Chad, the blood rushing to his face, looked in silence, for the negro was Snowball and the girl was Margaret. He saw her start and flush when she saw him, her hands giving a little convulsive clutch at the reins; but she came on, looking straight ahead. Chad's hand went unconsciously to his cap, and when Harry rose, puzzled to see him bareheaded, the phaeton stopped, and there was a half-broken cry:

"Harry!"

CHAD CAPTURES AN OLD FRIEND

Cap still in hand, Chad strode away as the brother, with an answering cry, sprang toward her.

. . . .

When he came back, an hour later, at dusk, Harry was seated on the portico, and the long silence between them was broken at last.

"She—they oughtn't to come to town at a time like this," said Chad, roughly.

"I told her that," said Harry, "but it was useless. She will come and go just as she pleases."

Harry rose and leaned for a moment against one of the big pillars, and then he turned impulsively, and put one hand lightly on the other's shoulder.

"I'm sorry, old man," he said, gently.

A pair of heels clicked suddenly together on the grass before them, and an orderly stood at salute.

"General Ward's compliments, and will Lieutenant Buford and Lieutenant Dean report to him at once?"

The two exchanged a swift glance, and the faces of both grew grave with sudden apprehension.

Inside, the General looked worried, and his manner was rather sharp.

"Do you know General Dean?" he asked, looking at Harry.

"He is my father, sir."

The General wheeled in his chair.

"What!" he exclaimed. "Well—um—I suppose one of you will be enough. You can go."

When the door closed behind Harry, he looked at Chad.

"There are two rebels at General Dean's house to-night,"

he said, quietly. "One of them, I am told—why, he must be that boy's brother," and again the General mused; then he added, sharply:

"Take six good men out there right away and capture them. And watch out for Daws Dillon and his band of cut-throats. I am told he is in this region. I've sent a company after him. But you capture the two at General Dean's."

"Yes, sir," said Chad, turning quickly, but the General had seen the lad's face grow pale.

"It is very strange down here—they may be his best friends," he thought, and, being a kind-hearted man, he reached out his hand toward a bell to summon Chad back, and drew it in again.

"I cannot help that; but that boy must have good stuff in him."

Harry was waiting for him outside. He knew that Dan would go home if it was possible, and what Chad's mission must be.

"Don't hurt him, Chad."

"You don't have to ask that," answered Chad, sadly.

.   .   .   .

So Chad's old enemy, Daws Dillon, was abroad. There was a big man with the boy at the Deans', General Ward had said, but Chad little guessed that it was another old acquaintance, Rebel Jerry Dillon, who, at that hour, was having his supper brought out to the stable to him, saying that he would sleep there, take care of the horses, and keep on the look-out for Yankees. Jerome Conners's hand must be in this, Chad thought, for he never for a moment doubted that the overseer had brought the news to General Ward. He was playing a fine game of loyalty to both sides, that overseer, and Chad grimly made up his mind that, from one side or the other, his day would come. And this was the fortune of war—to be trotting, at the head of six men, on such a mission, along a road that, at every turn, on every little hill, and almost in every fence-corner, was stored with happy memories for him; to force entrance as an enemy under a roof that had showered courtesy and kindness down on him like rain, that in all the world was most sacred to him; to bring death to an old playmate, the brother of the woman whom he loved, or capture, which might mean a worse death in a loathsome prison. He thought of that dawn when he drove home after the dance at the Hunts' with the old Major asleep at his side and his heart almost bursting with high hope and happiness, and he ran his hand over his eyes to brush the memory away. He must think only of his duty now, and that duty was plain.

Across the fields they went in a noiseless walk, and leaving their horses in the woods, under the care of one soldier, slipped into the yard. Two men were posted at the rear of the house, one was stationed at each end of the long porch to command the windows on either side, and, with a sergeant at his elbow, Chad climbed the long steps noiselessly and knocked at the front door. In a moment it was thrown open by a woman, and the light fell full in Chad's face.

"You—you—*you!*" said a voice that shook with mingled terror and contempt, and Margaret shrank back, step by step. Hearing her, Mrs. Dean hurried into the hallway. Her face paled when she saw the Federal uniform in her doorway, but her chin rose haughtily, and her voice was steady and most courteous:

"What can we do for you?" she asked, and she, too, recognized Chad, and her face grew stern as she waited for him to answer.

"Mrs. Dean," he said, half choking, "word has come to head-quarters that two Confederate soldiers are spending the night here, and I have been ordered to search the house for them. My men have surrounded it, but if you will give me your word that they are not here, not a man shall cross your threshold—not even myself."

Without a word Mrs. Dean stood aside.

"I am sorry," said Chad, motioning to the Sergeant to follow him. As he passed the door of the drawing-room, he saw, under the lamp, a pipe with ashes strewn about its bowl. Chad pointed to it.

"Spare me, Mrs. Dean." But the two women stood with clinched hands, silent. Dan had flashed into the kitchen, and was about to leap from the window when he saw the gleam of a rifle-barrel, not ten feet away. He would be potted like a rat if he sprang out there, and he dashed noiselessly up the back stairs, as Chad started up the front stairway toward the garret, where he had passed many a happy hour playing with Margaret and Harry and the boy whom he was after as an enemy, now. The door was open at the first landing, and the creak of the stairs under Dan's feet, heard plainly, stopped. The Sergeant, pistol in hand, started to push past his superior.

"Keep back," said Chad, sternly, and as he drew his pistol, a terrified whisper rose from below.

"Don't, don't!" And then Dan, with hands up, stepped into sight.

"I'll spare you," he said, quietly. "Not a word, mother.

They've got me. You can tell him there is no one else in the house, though."

Mrs. Dean's eyes filled with tears, and a sob broke from Margaret.

"There is no one else," she said, and Chad bowed. "In the house," she added, proudly, scorning the subterfuge.

"Search the barn," said Chad, "quick!" The Sergeant ran down the steps.

"I reckon you are a little too late, my friend," said Dan. "Why, bless me, it's my old friend Chad—and a lieutenant! I congratulate you," he added, but he did not offer to shake hands.

Chad had thought of the barn too late. Snowball had seen the men creeping through the yard, had warned Jerry Dillon, and Jerry had slipped the horses into the woodland, and had crept back to learn what was going on.

"I will wait for you out here," said Chad. "Take your time."

"Thank you," said Dan.

He came out in a moment and Mrs. Dean and Margaret followed him. At a gesture from the Sergeant, a soldier stationed himself on each side of Dan, and, as Chad turned, he took off his cap again. His face was very pale and his voice almost broke:

"You will believe, Mrs. Dean," he said, "that this was something I *had* to do."

Mrs. Dean bent her head slightly.

"Certainly, mother," said Dan. "Don't blame Lieutenant Chad. Morgan will have Lexington in a few days and then I'll be free again. Maybe I'll have Lieutenant Chad a prisoner—no telling!"

Chad smiled faintly, and then, with a flush, he spoke again —warning Mrs. Dean, in the kindliest way, that, henceforth, her house would be under suspicion, and telling her of the severe measures that had been inaugurated against rebel sympathizers.

"Such sympathizers have to take oath of allegiance and give bonds to keep it."

"If they don't?"

"Arrest and imprisonment."

"And if they give the oath and violate it?"

"The penalty is death, Mrs. Dean."

"And if they aid their friends?"

"They are to be dealt with according to military law."

"Anything else?"

"If loyal citizens are hurt or damaged by guerillas, disloyal citizens of the locality must make compensation."

"Is it true that a Confederate sympathizer will be shot down if on the streets of Lexington?"

"There was such an order, Mrs. Dean."

"And if a loyal citizen is killed by one of these so-called guerillas, for whose acts nobody is responsible, prisoners of war are to be shot in retaliation?"

"Mother!" cried Margaret.

"No, Mrs. Dean—not prisoners of war—guerillas."

"And when will you begin war on women?"

"Never, I hope." His hesitancy brought a scorn into the searching eyes of his pale questioner that Chad could not face, and without daring even to look at Margaret he turned away.

Such retaliatory measures made startling news to Dan. He grew very grave while he listened, but as he followed Chad he chatted and laughed and joked with his captors. Morgan would have Lexington in three days. He was really glad to get a chance to fill his belly with Yankee grub. It hadn't been full more than two or three times in six months.

All the time he was watching for Jerry Dillon, who, he knew, would not leave him if there was the least chance of getting him out of the Yankee's clutches. He did not have to wait long. Two men had gone to get the horses, and as Dan stepped through the yard-gate with his captors, two figures rose out of the ground. One came with head bent like a battering-ram. He heard Snowball's head strike a stomach on one side of him, and with an astonished groan the man went down. He saw the man on his other side drop from some crashing blow, and he saw Chad trying to draw his pistol. His own fist shot out, catching Chad on the point of the chin. At the same instant there was a shot and the Sergeant dropped.

"Come on, boy!" said a hoarse voice, and then he was speeding away after the gigantic figure of Jerry Dillon through the thick darkness, while a harmless volley of shots sped after them. At the edge of the woods they dropped. Jerry Dillon had his hand over his mouth to keep from laughing aloud.

"The hosses ain't fer away," he said. "Oh, Lawd!"

"Did you kill him?"

"I reckon not," whispered Jerry. "I shot him on the wrong side. I'm al'ays a-fergettin' which side a man's heart's on."

"What became of Snowball?"

"He run jes' as soon as he butted the feller on his right. He said he'd git *one,* but I didn't know what he was doin' when I seed him start like a sheep. Listen!"

There was a tumult at the house—moving lights, excited

cries, and a great hurrying. Black Rufus was the first to appear with a lantern, and when he held it high as the fence, Chad saw Margaret in the light, her hands clinched and her eyes burning.

"Have you killed him?" she asked, quietly but fiercely. "You nearly did once before. Have you succeeded this time?" Then she saw the Sergeant writhing on the ground, his right forearm hugging his breast, and her hands relaxed and her face changed.

"Did Dan do that? Did Dan do that?"

"Dan was unarmed," said Chad, quietly.

"Mother," called the girl, as though she had not heard him, "send someone to help. Bring him to the house," she added, turning. As no movement was made, she turned again.

"Bring him up to the house," she said, imperiously, and when the hesitating soldiers stooped to pick up the wounded man, she saw the streak of blood running down Chad's chin and she stared open-eyed. She made one step toward him, and then she shrank back out of the light.

"Oh!" she said. "Are you wounded, too? Oh!"

"No!" said Chad, grimly. "Dan didn't do that"—pointing to the Sergeant—"he did this—with his fist. It's the second time Dan has done this. Easy, men," he added, with low-voiced authority.

Mrs. Dean was holding the door open.

"No," said Chad, quickly. "That wicker lounge will do. He will be cooler on the porch." Then he stooped, and loosening the Sergeant's blouse and shirt examined the wound.

"It's only through the shoulder, Lieutenant," said the man, faintly. But it was under the shoulder, and Chad turned.

CHAD CAPTURES AN OLD FRIEND

"Jake," he said, sharply, "go back and bring a surgeon—and an officer to relieve me. I think he can be moved in the morning, Mrs. Dean. With your permission I will wait here until the Surgeon comes. Please don't disturb yourself further"—Margaret had appeared at the door, with some bandages that she and her mother had been making for Confederates and behind her a servant followed with towels and a pail of water—"I am sorry to trespass."

"Did the bullet pass through?" asked Mrs. Dean, simply.

"No, Mrs. Dean," said Chad.

Margaret turned indoors. Without another word, her mother knelt above the wounded man, cut the shirt away, staunched the trickling blood, and deftly bound the wound with lint and bandages, while Chad stood, helplessly watching her.

"I am sorry," he said again, when she rose, "sorry——"

"It is nothing," said Mrs. Dean, quietly. "If you need anything, you will let me know. I shall be waiting inside."

She turned and a few moments later Chad saw Margaret's white figure swiftly climb the stairs—but the light still burned in the noiseless room below.

.   .   .   .

Meanwhile Dan and Jerry Dillon were far across the fields on their way to rejoin Morgan. When they were ten miles away, Dan, who was leading, turned.

"Jerry, that Lieutenant was an old friend of mine. General Morgan used to say he was the best scout in the Union Army. He comes from your part of the country, and his name is Chad Buford. Ever heard of him?"

[245]

"I've knowed him sence he was a chunk of a boy, but I don't rickollect ever hearin' his last name afore. I nuver knowed he had any."

"Well, I heard him call one of his men Jake—and he looked exactly like you." The giant pulled in his horse.

"I'm goin' back."

"No, you aren't," said Dan; "not now—it's too late. That's why I didn't tell you before." Then he added, angrily: "You are a savage and you ought to be ashamed of yourself harboring such hatred against your own blood-brother."

Dan was perhaps the only one of Morgan's Men who would have dared to talk that way to the man, and Jerry Dillon took it only in sullen silence.

A mile farther they struck a pike, and, as they swept along, a brilliant light glared into the sky ahead of them, and they pulled in. A house was in flames on the edge of a woodland, and by its light they could see a body of men dash out of the woods and across the field on horseback, and another body dash after them in pursuit—the pursuers firing and the pursued sending back defiant yells. Daws Dillon was at his work again, and the Yankees were after him.

.   .   .   .

Long after midnight Chad reported the loss of his prisoner. He was much chagrined—for failure was rare with him—and his jaw and teeth ached from the blow Dan had given him, but in his heart he was glad that the boy had got away. When he went to his tent, Harry was awake and waiting for him.

"It's I who have escaped," he said; "escaped again. Four times now we have been in the same fight. Somehow fate

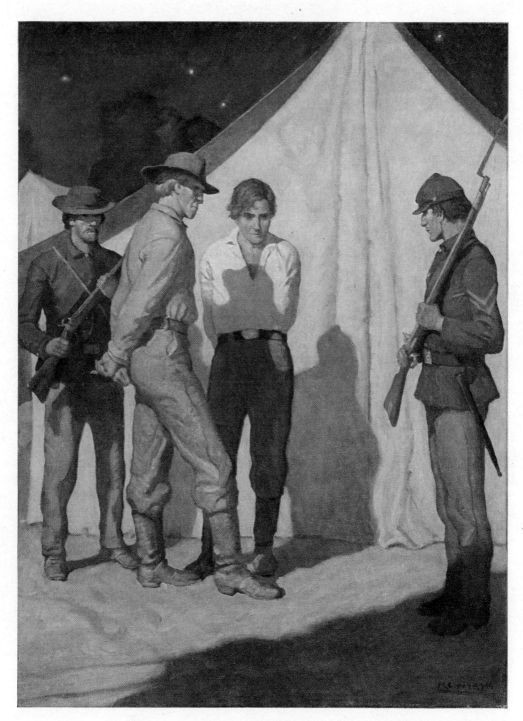

"Two prisoners, sir. We captured 'em with Daws Dillon."

seems to be pointing always one way—always one way. Why, night after night, I dream that either he or I—" Harry's voice trembled—he stopped short, and, leaning forward, stared out the door of his tent. A group of figures had halted in front of the Colonel's tent opposite, and a voice called, sharply:

"Two prisoners, sir. We captured 'em with Daws Dillon. They are guerillas, sir."

"It's a lie, Colonel," said an easy voice, that brought both Chad and Harry to their feet, and plain in the moonlight both saw Daniel Dean, pale but cool, and near him, Rebel Jerry Dillon—both with their hands bound behind them.

XXIV

A RACE BETWEEN DIXIE AND DAWN

But the sun sank next day from a sky that was aflame with rebel victories. It rose on a day rosy with rebel hopes, and the prophetic coolness of autumn was in the early morning air when Margaret in her phaeton moved through the front pasture on her way to town—alone. She was in high spirits and her head was lifted proudly. Dan's boast had come true. Kirby Smith had risen swiftly from Tennessee, had struck the Federal Army on the edge of the Bluegrass the day before, and sent it helter-skelter to the four winds. Only that morning she had seen a regiment of the hated Yankees move along the turnpike in flight for the Ohio. It was the Fourth Ohio Cavalry, and Harry and one whose name never passed her lips were among those dusty cavalrymen; but she was glad, and she ran down to the stile and, from the fence, waved the Stars and Bars at them as they passed—which was very foolish, but which brought her deep content. Now the rebels did hold Lexington. Morgan's Men were coming that day and she was going into town to see Dan and Colonel Hunt and General Morgan and be fearlessly happy and triumphant. At the Major's gate, whom should she see coming out but the dear old fellow himself, and, when he got off his horse and came to her, she leaned forward and kissed him, because he looked so thin and pale from confinement, and because she was so glad to see him. Morgan's Men were really coming, that very day, the Major said, and he told her much thrilling news. Jackson had obliterated Pope at the second battle of Manassas. Eleven thousand prisoners had been taken at Harper's Ferry and Lee had gone on into Maryland on the flank of Washington. Recruits were coming into the Confederacy by the thousands. Bragg had fifty-five thousand men and an impregnable stronghold in front of Buell, who had but few men more—not enough to count a minute, the Major said.

"Lee has routed 'em out of Virginia," cried the old fellow, "and Buell is doomed. I tell you, little girl, the fight is almost won."

Jerome Conners rode to the gate and called to the Major in a tone that arrested the girl's attention. She hated that man and she had noted a queer change in his bearing since the war began. She looked for a flash of anger from the Major, but none came, and she began to wonder what hold the overseer could have on his old master. She drove on, puzzled, wondering, and disturbed; but her cheeks were flushed—the South was going to win, the Yankees were gone, and she must get to town in time to see the triumphant coming of Morgan's Men. They were coming in when she reached the Yankee head-quarters, which, she saw, had changed flags—thank God—coming proudly in, amid the waving of the Stars and Bars and frenzied shouts of welcome. Where were the Bluegrass Yankees now? The Stars and Stripes that had fluttered from their windows had been drawn in and they were keeping very quiet, indeed—Oh! it was joy! There was gallant Morgan himself swinging from Black Bess to kiss his mother, who stood waiting for him at her gate, and there was Colonel Hunt, gay, debonair, jesting, shaking hands right and left, and crowding the streets, Morgan's Men—the proudest blood in the land— every gallant trooper getting his welcome from the lips and arms of mother, sister, sweetheart, or cousin of farthest degree. But where was Dan? She had heard nothing of him since the night he had escaped capture, and while she looked right and left for him to dash toward her and swing from his horse, she heard her name called, and turning she saw Richard Hunt at the wheel of her phaeton. He waved his hand toward the happy reunions going on around them.

"The enforced brotherhood, Miss Margaret," he said, his eyes flashing, "I belong to that, you know."

For once the subtle Colonel made a mistake. Perhaps the girl in her trembling happiness and under the excitement of the moment might have welcomed him, as she was waiting to welcome Dan, but she drew back now.

"Oh! no, Colonel—not on that ground."

Her eyes danced, she flushed curiously, as she held out her hand, and the Colonel's brave heart quickened. Straightway he began to wonder—but a quick shadow in Margaret's face checked him.

"But where's Dan? Where *is* Dan?" she repeated, impatiently.

Richard Hunt looked puzzled. He had just joined his command and something must have gone wrong with Dan. So he lied swiftly.

"Dan is out on a scout. I don't think he has got back yet. I'll find out."

Margaret watched him ride to where Morgan stood with his mother in the midst of a joyous group of neighbors and friends, and, a moment later, the two officers came toward her on foot.

"Don't worry, Miss Margaret," said Morgan, with a smile.

"The Yankees have got Dan and have taken him away as prisoner—but don't worry, we'll get him exchanged in a week. I'll give three brigadier-generals for him."

Tears came to the girl's eyes, but she smiled through them bravely.

"I must go back and tell mother," she said, brokenly. "I hoped——"

"Don't worry, little girl," said Morgan again. "I'll have him if I have to capture the whole State of Ohio."

Again Margaret smiled, but her heart was heavy, and Richard Hunt was unhappy. He hung around her phaeton all the while she was in town. He went home with her, cheering her on the way and telling her of the Confederate triumph that was at hand. He comforted Mrs. Dean over Dan's capture, and he rode back to town slowly, with his hands on his saddle-bow—wondering again. Perhaps Margaret had gotten over her feeling for that mountain boy—that Yankee—and there Richard Hunt checked his own thoughts, for that mountain boy, he had discovered, was a brave and chivalrous enemy, and to such, his own high chivalry gave salute always.

He was very thoughtful when he reached camp. He had an unusual desire to be alone, and that night, he looked long at the stars, thinking of the girl whom he had known since her babyhood—knowing that he would never think of her except as a woman again.

So the Confederates waited now in the Union hour of darkness for Bragg to strike his blow. He did strike it, but it was at the heart of the South. He stunned the Confederacy by giving way before Buell. He brought hope back with the bloody battle of Perryville. Again he faced Buell at Harrodsburg, and then he wrought broadcast despair by falling back without battle, dividing his forces and retreating into Tennessee. The dream of a battle-line along the Ohio with a hundred thousand more men behind it was gone, and the last and best chance to win the war was lost forever. Morgan, furious with disappointment, left Lexington. Kentucky fell under Federal control once more; and Major Buford, dazed, dismayed, unnerved, hopeless, brought the news out to the Deans.

"They'll get me again, I suppose, and I can't leave home on account of Lucy."

"Please do, Major," said Mrs. Dean. "Send Miss Lucy over here and make your escape. We will take care of her." The Major shook his head sadly and rode away.

Next day Margaret sat on the stile and saw the Yankees coming back to Lexington. On one side of her the Stars and Bars were fixed to the fence from which they had floated since the day she had waved the flag at them as they fled. She saw the advance guard come over the hill and jog down the slope and then the regiment slowly following after. In the rear she could see two men, riding unarmed. Suddenly three cavalrymen spurred forward at a gallop and turned in at her gate. The soldier in advance was an officer, and he pulled out a handkerchief, waved it once, and, with a gesture to his companions, came on alone. She knew the horse even before she recognized the rider, and her cheeks flushed, her lips were set, and her nostrils began to dilate. The horseman reined in and took off his cap.

"I come under a flag of truce," he said, gravely, "to ask this garrison to haul down its colors—and—to save useless effusion of blood," he added, still more gravely.

"Your war on women has begun, then?"

"I am obeying orders—no more, no less."

"I congratulate you on your luck or your good judgment always to be on hand when disagreeable duties are to be done."

Chad flushed.

"Won't you take the flag down?"

"No, make your attack. You will have one of your usual victories—with overwhelming numbers—and it will be safe and bloodless. There are only two negroes defending this garrison. They will not fight, nor will we."

"Won't you take the flag down?"

"No!"

Chad lifted his cap and wheeled. The Colonel was waiting at the gate.

"Well, sir?" he asked, frowning.

"I shall need help, sir, to take that flag down," said Chad.

"What do you mean, sir?"

"A woman is defending it."

"What!" shouted the Colonel.

"That is my sister, Colonel," said Harry Dean. The Colonel smiled and then grew grave.

"You should warn her not to provoke the authorities. The Government is advising very strict measures now with rebel sympathizers." Then he smiled again.

"Fours! Left wheel! Halt! Present—sabres!"

A line of sabres flashed in the sun, and Margaret, not understanding, snatched the flag from the fence and waved it back in answer. The Colonel laughed aloud. The column moved on, and each captain, following, caught the humor of the situation and each company flashed its sabres as it went by, while Margaret stood motionless.

In the rear rode those two unarmed prisoners. She could see now that their uniforms were gray and she knew that they were prisoners, but she little dreamed that they were her brother Dan and Rebel Jerry Dillon, nor did Chad Buford or Harry Dean dream of the purpose for which, just at that time, they were being brought back to Lexington. Perhaps one man who saw them did know: for Jerome Conners, from the woods opposite, watched the prisoners ride by with a malicious smile that nothing but impending danger to an enemy could ever bring to his face; and with the same smile he watched Margaret go slowly back to the house, while her flag still fluttered from the stile.

The high tide of Confederate hopes was fast receding now. The army of the Potomac, after Antietam, which overthrew the first Confederate aggressive campaign at the East, was retreating into its Southern stronghold, as was the army of the West after Bragg's abandonment of Mumfordsville, and the rebel retirement had given the provost-marshals in Kentucky full sway. Two hundred Southern sympathizers, under arrest, had been sent into exile north of the Ohio, and large sums of money were levied for guerilla outrages here and there—a heavy sum falling on Major Buford for a vicious murder done in his neighborhood by Daws Dillon and his band on the night of the capture of Daniel Dean and Rebel Jerry. The Major paid the levy with the first mortgage he had ever given in his life, and straightway Jerome Conners, who had been dealing in mules and other Government supplies, took an attitude that was little short of insolence toward his old master, whose farm was passing into the overseer's clutches at last. Only two nights before, another band of guerillas had burned a farm-house, killed a Unionist, and fled to the hills before the incoming Yankees, and the Kentucky Commandant had sworn vengeance after the old Mosaic way on victims already within his power.

That night Chad and Harry were summoned before General Ward. They found him seated with his chin in his hand, looking out the window at the moonlit campus. Without moving, he held out a dirty piece of paper to Chad.

"Read that," he said.

"You have ketched two of my men and I hear as how you mean to hang 'em. If you hang them two men, I'm a-goin' to hang every man of yours I can git my hands on.
                    "DAWS DILLON—Captin."

Chad gave a low laugh and Harry smiled, but the General kept grave.

"You know, of course, that your brother belongs to Morgan's command?"

"I do, sir," said Harry, wonderingly.

"Do you know that his companion—the man Dillon—Jerry Dillon—does?"

"I do not, sir."

"They were captured by a squad that was fighting Daws Dillon. This Jerry Dillon has the same name and you found the two together at General Dean's."

"But they had both just left General Morgan's command," said Harry, indignantly.

"That may be true, but this Daws Dillon has sent a similar message to the Commandant, and he has just been in here again and committed two wanton outrages night before last. The Commandant is enraged and has issued orders for stern retaliation."

"It's a trick of Daws Dillon," said Chad, hotly, "an infamous trick. He hates his Cousin Jerry, he hates me, and he hates the Deans, because they were friends of mine." General Ward looked troubled.

"The Commandant says he has been positively informed that both the men joined Daws Dillon in the fight that night. He has issued orders that not only every guerilla captured shall be hung, but that, whenever a Union citizen has been killed by one of them, four of such marauders are to be taken to the spot and shot in retaliation. It is the only means left, he says."

There was a long silence. The faces of both the lads had turned white as each saw the drift of the General's meaning, and Harry strode forward to his desk.

"Do you mean to say, General Ward——"

The General wheeled in his chair and pointed silently to an order that lay on the desk, and as Harry started to read it, his voice broke. Daniel Dean and Rebel Jerry were to be shot next morning at sunrise.

.   .   .   .

The General spoke very kindly to Harry.

"I have known this all day, but I did not wish to tell you until I had done everything I could. I did not think it would be necessary to tell you at all, for I thought there would be no trouble. I telegraphed the Commandant, but"—he turned again to the window—"I have not been able to get them a trial by court-martial, or even a stay in the execution. You'd better go see your brother—he knows now—and you'd better send word to your mother and sister."

Harry shook his head. His face was so drawn and ghastly

as he stood leaning heavily against the table that Chad moved unconsciously to his side.

"Where is the Commandant?" he asked.

"In Frankfort," said the General. Chad's eyes kindled.

"Will you let me go see him to-night?"

"Certainly, and I will give you a message to him. Perhaps you can yet save the boy, but there is no chance for the man Dillon." The General took up a pen. Harry seemed to sway as he turned to go, and Chad put one arm around him and went with him to the door.

"There have been some surprising desertions from the Confederate ranks," said the General, as he wrote. "That's the trouble." He looked at his watch as he handed the message over his shoulder to Chad. "You have ten hours before sunrise and it is nearly sixty miles there and back. If you are not here with a stay of execution both will be shot. Do you think that you can make it? Of course you need not bring the message back yourself. You can get the Commandant to telegraph—" The slam of a door interrupted him—Chad was gone.

Harry was holding Dixie's bridle when he reached the street and Chad swung into the saddle.

"Don't tell them at home," he said. "I'll be back here on time, or I'll be dead."

The two grasped hands. Harry nodded dumbly and Dixie's feet beat the rhythm of her matchless gallop down the quiet street. The sensitive little mare seemed to catch at once the spirit of her rider. Her haunches quivered. She tossed her head and champed her bit, but not a pound did she pull as she settled into an easy lope that told how well she knew that the ride before her was long and hard. Out they went past the old cemetery, past the shaft to Clay rising from it, silvered with moonlight, out where the picket fires gleamed, and swinging on toward the Capital, unchallenged, for the moon showed the blue of Chad's uniform and his face gave sign that no trivial business, that night, was his. Over quiet fields and into the aisles of sleeping woods beat that musical rhythm ceaselessly, awakening drowsy birds by the wayside, making bridges thunder, beating on and on up hill and down until picket fires shone on the hills that guard the Capital. Through them, with but one challenge, Chad went, down the big hill, past the Armory, and into the town—pulling panting Dixie up before a wondering sentinel who guarded the Commandant's sleeping quarters.

"The Commandant is asleep."

"Wake him up," said Chad, sharply. A staff-officer appeared at the door in answer to the sentinel's knock.

"What is your business?"

"A message from General Ward."

"The Commandant gave orders that he was not to be disturbed."

"He must be," said Chad. "It is a matter of life and death."

Above him a window was suddenly raised and the Commandant's own head was thrust out.

"Stop that noise," he thundered. Chad told his mission and the Commandant straightway was furious.

"How dare General Ward broach that matter again? My orders are given and they will not be changed." As he started to pull the window down, Chad cried:

"But, General—" and at the same time a voice called down the street:

"General!" Two men appeared under the gaslight—one was a sergeant and the other a frightened negro.

"Here is a message, General."

The sash went down, a light appeared behind it, and soon the Commandant, in trousers and slippers, was at the door. He read the note with a frown.

"Where did you get this?"

"A sojer come to my house out on the edge o' town, suh, and said he'd kill me to-morrow if I didn't hand dis note to you pussonally."

The Commandant turned to Chad. Somehow his manner seemed suddenly changed.

"Do *you* know that these men belonged to Morgan's command?"

"I know that Daniel Dean did and that the man Dillon was with him when captured."

Still frowning savagely, the Commandant turned inside to his desk and a moment later the staff-officer brought out a telegram and gave it to Chad.

"You can take this to the telegraph office yourself. It is a stay of execution."

"Thank you."

Chad drew a long breath of relief and gladness and patted Dixie on the neck as he rode slowly toward the low building where he had missed the train on his first trip to the Capital. The telegraph operator dashed to the door as Chad drew up in front of it. He looked pale and excited.

"Send this telegram at once," said Chad.

The operator looked at it.

"Not in that direction to-night," he said, with a strained laugh, "the wires are cut."

Chad almost reeled in his saddle—then the paper was whisked from the astonished operator's hand and horse and rider clattered up the hill.

.   .   .   .

At head-quarters the Commandant was handing the negro's note to a staff-officer. It read:

"You hang those two men at sunrise to-morrow, and I'll hang you at sundown."

It was signed "John Morgan," and the signature was Morgan's own.

"I gave the order only last night. How could Morgan have heard of it so soon, and how could he have got this note to me? Could he have come back?"

"Impossible," said the staff-officer. "He wouldn't dare come back now."

The Commandant shook his head doubtfully, and just then there was a knock at the door and the operator, still pale and excited, spoke his message:

"General, the wires are cut."

The two officers stared at each other in silence.

.   .   .   .

Twenty-seven miles to go and less than three hours before sunrise. There was a race yet for the life of Daniel Dean. The gallant little mare could cover the stretch with nearly an hour to spare, and Chad, thrilled in every nerve, but with calm confidence, raced against the coming dawn.

"The wires are cut."

Who had cut them and where and when and why? No matter—Chad had the paper in his pocket that would save two lives and he would be on time even if Dixie broke her noble heart, but he could not get the words out of his brain—even Dixie's hoofs beat them out ceaselessly:

"The wires are cut—the wires are cut!"

The mystery would have been clear, had Chad known the message that lay on the Commandant's desk back at the Capital, for the boy knew Morgan, and that Morgan's lips never opened for an idle threat. He would have ridden just as hard, had he known, but a different purpose would have been his.

An hour more and there was still no light in the East. An hour more and one red streak had shot upward; then ahead of him gleamed a picket fire—a fire that seemed farther from town than any post he had seen on his way down to the Capital—but he galloped on. Within fifty yards a cry came:

"Halt! Who comes there?"

"Friend," he shouted, reining in. A bullet whizzed past his head as he pulled up outside the edge of the fire and Chad shouted indignantly:

"Don't shoot, you fool! I have a message for General Ward!"

"Oh! All right! Come on!" said the sentinel, but his hesitation and the tone of his voice made the boy alert with suspicion. The other pickets about the fire had risen and grasped their muskets. The wind flared the flames just then and in the leaping light Chad saw that their uniforms were gray.

The boy almost gasped. There was need for quick thought and quick action now.

"Lower that blunderbuss," he called out, jestingly, and kicking loose from one stirrup, he touched Dixie with the spur and pulled her up with an impatient "Whoa," as though he were trying to replace his foot.

"You come on!" said the sentinel, but he dropped his musket to the hollow of his arm, and, before he could throw it to his shoulder again, fire flashed under Dixie's feet and the astonished rebel saw horse and rider rise over the pike-fence. His bullet went overhead as Dixie landed on the other side, and the pickets at the fire joined in a fusillade at the dark shapes speeding across the bluegrass field. A moment later Chad's mocking yell rang from the edge of the woods beyond and the disgusted sentinel split the night with oaths.

"That beats the devil. We never touched him. I swear, I believe that hoss had wings."

Morgan! The flash of that name across his brain cleared the mystery for Chad like magic. Nobody but Morgan and his daredevils could rise out of the ground like that in the very midst of enemies when they were supposed to be hundreds of miles away in Tennessee. Morgan had cut those wires. Morgan had every road around Lexington guarded, no doubt, and was at that hour hemming in Chad's unsuspicious regiment, whose camp was on the other side of town, and unless he could give warning, Morgan would drop like a thunderbolt on it, asleep. He must circle the town now to get around the rebel posts, and that meant several miles more for Dixie.

He stopped and reached down to feel the little mare's flanks. Dixie drew a long breath and dropped her muzzle to tear up a rich mouthful of bluegrass.

"Oh, you beauty!" said the boy, "you wonder!" And on he went, through woodland and field, over gully, log, and fence, bullets ringing after him for nearly every road he crossed.

A RACE BETWEEN DIXIE AND DAWN

Morgan was near. In disgust, when Bragg retreated, he had got permission to leave Kentucky in his own way. That meant wheeling and making straight back to Lexington to surprise the Fourth Ohio Cavalry; representing himself on the way, one night, as his old enemy Wolford, and being guided a short cut through the edge of the Bluegrass by an ardent admirer of the Yankee Colonel—the said admirer giving Morgan the worst tirade possible, meanwhile, and nearly tumbling from his horse when Morgan told him who he was and sarcastically advised him to make sure next time to whom he paid his compliments.

So that while Chad, with the precious message under his jacket, and Dixie were lightly thundering along the road, Morgan's Men were gobbling up pickets around Lexington and making ready for an attack on the sleeping camp at dawn.

The dawn was nearly breaking now, and Harry Dean was pacing to and fro before the old Court-House where Dan and Rebel Jerry lay under guard—pacing to and fro and waiting for his mother and sister to come to say the last good-by to the boy—for Harry had given up hope and had sent for them. At that very hour Richard Hunt was leading his regiment around the Ashland woods where the enemy lay; another regiment was taking its place between the camp and the town, and gray figures were slipping noiselessly on the provost-guard that watched the rebel prisoners who were waiting for death at sunrise. As the dawn broke, the dash came, and Harry Dean was sick at heart as he sharply rallied the startled guard to prevent the rescue of his own brother and straightway delirious with joy when he saw the gray mass sweeping on him and knew that he would fail. A few shots rang out; the far rattle of musketry

[263]

rose between the camp and town; the thunder of the "Bull
Pups" saluted the coming light, and Dan and Rebel Jerry had
suddenly—instead of death—life, liberty, arms, a horse each,
and the sudden pursuit of happiness in a wild dash toward the
Yankee camp, while in a dew-drenched meadow two miles
away, Chad Buford drew Dixie in to listen. The fight was on.

If the rebels won, Dan Dean would be safe; if the Yankees
—then there would still be need of him and the paper over his
heart. He was too late to warn, but not, maybe, to fight—so
he galloped on.

But the end came as he galloped. The amazed Fourth Ohio
threw down its arms at once, and Richard Hunt and his men,
as they sat on their horses outside the camp picking up strag-
glers, saw a lone scout coming at a gallop across the still, gray
fields. His horse was black and his uniform was blue, but he
came straight on, apparently not seeing the rebels behind the
ragged hedge along the road. When within thirty yards, Richard Hunt rode through a roadside gate to meet him and saluted.

"You are my prisoner," he said, courteously.

The Yankee never stopped, but wheeled, almost brushing
the hedge as he turned.

"Prisoner—hell!" he said, clearly, and like a bird was skim-
ming away while the men behind the hedge, paralyzed by his
daring, fired not a shot. Only Dan Dean started through the
gate in pursuit.

"I want him," he said, savagely.

"Who's that?" asked Morgan, who had ridden up.

"That's a Yankee," laughed Colonel Hunt.

"Why didn't you shoot him?" The Colonel laughed again.

"I don't know," he said, looking around at his men, who, too, were smiling.

"That's the fellow who gave us so much trouble in the Green River Country," said a soldier. "It's Chad Buford."

"Well, I'm glad we didn't shoot him," said Colonel Hunt, thinking of Margaret. That was not the way he liked to dispose of a rival.

"Dan will catch him," said an officer. "He wants him bad, and I don't wonder." Just then Chad lifted Dixie over a fence.

"Not much," said Morgan. "I'd rather you'd shot him than that horse."

Dan was gaining now, and Chad, in the middle of the field beyond the fence, turned his head and saw the lone rebel in pursuit. Deliberately he pulled weary Dixie in, faced about, and waited. He drew his pistol, raised it, saw that the rebel was Daniel Dean, and dropped it again to his side. Verily the fortune of that war was strange. Dan's horse refused the fence and the boy, in a rage, lifted his pistol and fired. Again Chad raised his own pistol and again he lowered it just as Dan fired again. This time Chad lurched in his saddle, but recovering himself, turned and galloped slowly away, while Dan—his pistol hanging at his side—stared after him, and the wondering rebels behind the hedge stared hard at Dan.

.   .   .   .

All was over. The Fourth Ohio Cavalry was in rebel hands, and a few minutes later Dan rode with General Morgan and Colonel Hunt toward the Yankee camp. There had been many blunders in the fight. Regiments had fired into each other in the confusion and the "Bull Pups" had kept on pounding the

Yankee camp even while the rebels were taking possession of it. On the way they met Renfrew, the Silent, in his brilliant Zouave jacket.

"Colonel," he said, indignantly—and it was the first time many had ever heard him open his lips—"some officer over there deliberately fired twice at me, though I was holding my arms over my head."

"It was dark," said Colonel Hunt, soothingly. "He didn't know you."

"Ah, Colonel, he might not have known *me*—but he must have known this jacket."

On the outskirts of one group of prisoners was a tall, slender young lieutenant with a streak of blood across one cheek. Dan pulled in his horse and the two met each other's eyes silently. Dan threw himself from his horse.

"Are you hurt, Harry?"

"It's nothing—but you've got me, Dan."

"Why, Harry!" said Morgan. "Is that you? You are paroled, my boy," he added, kindly. "Go home and stay until you are exchanged."

So, Harry, as a prisoner, did what he had not done before —he went home immediately. And home with him went Dan and Colonel Hunt, while they could, for the Yankees would soon be after them from the north, east, south and west. Behind them trotted Rebel Jerry. On the edge of town they saw a negro lashing a pair of horses along the turnpike toward them. Two white-faced women were seated in a carriage behind him, and in a moment Dan was in the arms of his mother and sister and both women were looking, through tears, their speechless gratitude to Richard Hunt.

[266]

A RACE BETWEEN DIXIE AND DAWN

The three Confederates did not stay long at the Deans'. Jerry Dillon was on the lookout, and even while the Deans were at dinner, Rufus ran in with the familiar cry that Yankees were coming. It was a regiment from an adjoining county, but Colonel Hunt finished his coffee, amid all the excitement, most leisurely.

"You'll pardon us for eating and running, won't you, Mrs. Dean?" It was the first time in her life that Mrs. Dean ever speeded a parting guest.

"Oh, do hurry, Colonel—please, please." Dan laughed.

"Good-by, Harry," he said. "We'll give you a week or two at home before we get that exchange."

"Don't make it any longer than necessary, please," said Harry, gravely.

"We're coming back again, Mrs. Dean," said the Colonel, and then in a lower tone to Margaret: "I'm coming often," he added, and Margaret blushed in a way that would not have given very great joy to one Chadwick Buford.

Very leisurely the three rode out to the pike-gate, where they halted and surveyed the advancing column, which was still several hundred yards away, and then with a last wave of their caps, started in a slow gallop for town. The advance guard started suddenly in pursuit, and the Deans saw Dan turn in his saddle and heard his defiant yell. Margaret ran down and fixed her flag in its place on the fence—Harry watching her.

"Mother," he said, sadly, "you don't know what trouble you may be laying up for yourself."

Fate could hardly lay up more than what she already had, but the mother smiled.

"I can do nothing with Margaret," she said.

[267]

In town the Federal flags had been furled and the Stars and Bars thrown out to the wind. Morgan was preparing to march when Dan and Colonel Hunt galloped up to head-quarters.

"They're coming," said Hunt, quietly.

"Yes," said Morgan, "from every direction."

"Ah, John," called an old fellow, who, though a Unionist, believing in keeping peace with both sides, "when we don't expect you—then is the time you come. Going to stay long?"

"Not long," said Morgan, grimly. "In fact, I guess we'll be moving along now."

And he did—back to Dixie with his prisoners, tearing up railroads, burning bridges and trestles, and pursued by enough Yankees to have eaten him and his entire command if they ever could have caught him. As they passed into Dixie, "Lightning" captured a telegraph office and had a last little fling at his Yankee brethren.

"Head-quarters, Telegraph Dept. of Ky., Confederate States of America"—thus he headed his "General Order No. 1" to the various Union authorities throughout the State.

"Hereafter," he clicked, grinning, "an operator will destroy telegraphic instruments and all material in charge when informed that Morgan has crossed the border. Such instances of carelessness as lately have been exhibited in the Bluegrass will be severely dealt with.

> "By order of
>
> "LIGHTNING,
>
> "Gen. Supt. C. S. Tel. Dept."

Just about that time Chad Buford, in a Yankee hospital,

was coming back from the land of ether dreams. An hour later, the surgeon who had taken Dan's bullet from his shoulder, handed him a piece of paper, black with faded blood and scarcely legible.

"I found that in your jacket," he said. "Is it important?"

Chad smiled.

"No," he said. "Not now."

XXV

AFTER DAWS DILLON—GUERILLA

ONCE more, and for the last time, Chadwick Buford jogged along the turnpike from the Ohio to the heart of the Blue-grass. He had filled his empty shoulder-straps with two bars. He had a bullet wound through one shoulder and there was a beautiful sabre cut across his right cheek. He looked the soldier every inch of him; he was, in truth, what he looked; and he was, moreover, a man. Naturally, his face was stern and resolute, if only from habit of authority, but he had known no passion during the war that might have seared its kindness; no other feeling toward his foes than admiration for their unquenchable courage and miserable regret that to such men he must be a foe.

Now, it was coming spring again—the spring of '64, and but one more year of the war to come.

The capture of the Fourth Ohio by Morgan that autumn of '62 had given Chad his long-looked-for chance. He turned Dixie's head toward the foothills to join Wolford, for with Wolford was the work that he loved—that leader being more like Morgan in his method and more daring than any other Federal cavalryman in the field.

Behind him, in Kentucky, he left the State under martial sway once more, and, thereafter, the troubles of rebel sympathizers multiplied steadily, for never again was the State under rebel control. A heavy hand was laid on every rebel roof. Major Buford was sent to prison again. General Dean was in Virginia, fighting, and only the fact that there was no man in the Dean household on whom vengeance could fall, saved Margaret and Mrs. Dean from suffering, but even the time of women was to come.

On the last day of '62, Murfreesboro was fought and the second great effort of the Confederacy at the West was lost. Again Bragg withdrew. On New Year's Day, '63, Lincoln freed the slaves—and no rebel was more indignant than was Chadwick Buford. The Kentucky Unionists, in general, protested: the Confederates had broken the Constitution, they said; the Unionists were helping to maintain that contract and now the Federals had broken the Constitution, and their own high ground was swept from beneath their feet. They protested as bitterly as their foes, be it said, against the Federals breaking up political conventions with bayonets and against the ruin of innocent citizens for the crimes of guerillas, for whose acts nobody was responsible, but all to no avail. The terrorism only grew the more.

When summer came, and while Grant was bisecting the Confederacy at Vicksburg, by opening the Mississippi, and Lee was fighting Gettysburg, Chad, with Wolford, chased Morgan when he gathered his clans for his last daring venture —to cross the Ohio and strike the enemy on its own hearthstones—and thus give him a little taste of what the South had long known from border to border. Pursued by Federals, Morgan got across the river, waving a farewell to his pursuing enemies on the other bank, and struck out. Within three days, one hundred thousand men were after him and his two thousand daredevils, cutting down trees behind him (in case he should return!), flanking him, getting in his front, but on he went, uncaught and spreading terror for a thousand miles, while behind him for six hundred miles country people lined the dusty road, singing "Rally 'round the Flag, Boys," and handing out fried chicken and blackberry-pie to his pursuers. Men taken afterward with typhoid fever sang that song through their delirium and tasted fried chicken no more as long as they lived. Hemmed in as Morgan was, he would have gotten away, but for the fact that a heavy fog made him miss the crossing of the river, and for the further reason that the first rise in the river in that month for twenty years made it impossible for his command to swim. He might have fought out, but his ammunition was gone. Many did escape, and Morgan himself could have gotten away. Chad, himself, saw the rebel chief swimming the river on a powerful horse, followed by a negroservant on another—saw him turn deliberately in the middle of the stream, when it was plain that his command could not escape, and make for the Ohio shore to share the fortunes of his beloved officers who were left behind. Chad heard him shout to the negro:

"Go back, you will be drowned." The negro turned his face and Chad laughed—it was Snowball, grinning and shaking his head:

"No, Mars John, no suh!" he yelled. "It's all right fer *you!* You can git a furlough, but dis nigger ain't gwine to be cotched in no free State. 'Sides, Mars Dan, he gwine to get away, too." And Dan did get away, and Chad, to his shame, saw Morgan and Colonel Hunt loaded on a boat to be sent down to prison in a State penitentiary! It was a grateful surprise to Chad, two months later, to learn from a Federal officer that Morgan with six others had dug out of prison and escaped.

"I was going through that very town," said the officer, "and a fellow, shaved and sheared like a convict, got aboard and sat down in the same seat with me. As we passed the penitentiary, he turned with a yawn—and said, in a matter-of-fact way:

" 'That's where Morgan is kept, isn't it?' and then he drew out a flask. I thought he had wonderfully good manners in spite of his looks, and, so help me, if he didn't wave his hand, bow like a Bayard, and hand it over to me:

" 'Let's drink to the hope that Morgan may always be as safe as he is now.' I drank to his toast with a hearty Amen, and the fellow never cracked a smile. It was Morgan himself."

Early in '64 the order had gone round for negroes to be enrolled as soldiers, and again no rebel felt more outraged than Chadwick Buford. Wolford, his commander, was dishonorably dismissed from the service for bitter protests and harsh open criticism of the Government, and Chad, himself, felt like tearing off with his own hands the straps which he had won with so much bravery and worn with so much pride. But the instinct that led him into the Union service kept his lips sealed when his respect for that service, in his own State, was wellnigh gone—kept him in that State where he thought his duty lay. There was need of him and thousands more like him. For, while active war was now over in Kentucky, its brood of evils was still thickening. Every county in the State was ravaged by a guerilla band—and the ranks of these marauders began to be swelled by Confederates, particularly in the mountains and in the hills that skirt them. Banks, trains, public vaults, stores, were robbed right and left, and murder and revenge were of daily occurrence. Daws Dillon was an open terror both in the mountains and in the Bluegrass. Hitherto the bands had been

Union and Confederate, but now, more and more, men who had been rebels joined them. And Chad Buford could understand. For, many a rebel soldier—"hopeless now for his cause," as Richard Hunt was wont to say, "fighting from pride, bereft of sympathy, aid, and encouragement that he once received, and compelled to wring existence from his own countrymen; a cavalryman on some out-post department, perhaps, without rations, fluttering with rags; shod, if shod at all, with shoes that sucked in rain and cold; sleeping at night under the blanket that kept his saddle by day from his sore-backed horse; paid, if paid at all, with waste paper; hardened into recklessness by war—many a rebel soldier thus became a guerilla—consoling himself, perhaps, with the thought that his desertion was not to the enemy."

Bad as the methods of such men were, they were hardly worse than the means taken in retaliation. At first, Confederate sympathizers were arrested and held as hostages for all persons captured and detained by guerillas. Later, when a citizen was killed by one of these bands, four prisoners, supposed to be chosen from this class of free-booters, were taken from prison and shot to death on the spot where the deed was done. Now it was rare that one of these brigands was ever taken alive, and thus regular soldier after soldier who was a prisoner of war, and entitled to consideration as such, was taken from prison and murdered by the Commandant without even a court-martial. It was such a death that Dan Dean and Rebel Jerry had narrowly escaped. Union men were imprisoned even for protesting against these outrages, so that between guerilla and provost-marshal no citizen, whether Federal or Confederate, in sympathy, felt safe in property, life, or liberty. The better

Unionists were alienated, but worse yet was to come. Hitherto, only the finest chivalry had been shown women and children throughout the war. Women whose brothers and husbands and sons were in the rebel army, or dead on the battle-field, were banished now with their children to Canada under a negro guard, or sent to prison. State authorities became openly arrayed against provost-marshals and their followers. There was almost an open clash. The Governor, a Unionist, threatened even to recall the Kentucky troops from the field to come back and protect their homes. Even the Home Guards got disgusted with their masters, and for a while it seemed as if the State, between guerilla and provost-marshal, would go to pieces. For months the Confederates had repudiated all connection with these free-booters and had joined with Federals in hunting them down, but when the State government tried to raise troops to crush them, the Commandant not only ordered his troops to resist the State, but ordered the muster-out of all State troops then in service.

The Deans little knew then how much trouble Captain Chad Buford, whose daring service against guerillas had given him great power with the Union authorities, had saved them—how he had kept them from arrest and imprisonment on the charge of none other than Jerome Conners, the overseer; how he had ridden out to pay his personal respects to the complainant, and that brave gentleman, seeing him from afar, had mounted his horse and fled, terror-stricken. They never knew that just after this he had got a furlough and gone to see Grant himself, who had sent him on to tell his story to Mr. Lincoln.

"Go back to Kentucky, then," said Grant, with his quiet smile, "and if General Ward has nothing particular for you to do, I want him to send you to me," and Chad had gone from him, dizzy with pride and hope.

"I'm going to do something," said Mr. Lincoln, "and I'm going to do it right away."

And now, in the spring of '64, Chad carried in his breast despatches from the President himself to General Ward at Lexington.

As he rode over the next hill, from which he would get his first glimpse of his old home and the Deans', his heart beat fast and his eyes swept both sides of the road. Both houses—even the Deans'—were shuttered and closed—both tenantless. He saw not even a negro cabin that showed a sign of life.

On he went at a gallop toward Lexington. Not a single rebel flag had he seen since he left the Ohio, nor was he at all surprised; the end could not be far off, and there was no chance that the Federals would ever again lose the State.

On the edge of the town he overtook a Federal officer. It was Harry Dean, pale and thin from long imprisonment and sickness. Harry had been with Sherman, had been captured again, and, in prison, had almost died with fever. He had come home to get well only to find his sister and mother sent as exiles to Canada. Major Buford was still in prison, Miss Lucy was dead, and Jerome Conners seemed master of the house and farm. General Dean had been killed, had been sent home, and was buried in the garden. It was only two days after the burial, Harry said, that Margaret and her mother had to leave their home. Even the bandages that Mrs. Dean had brought out to Chad's wounded sergeant, that night he had captured and lost Dan, had been brought up as proof that she and Margaret were aiding and abetting Confederates. Dan had gone to join Morgan and Colonel Hunt over in southwestern Virginia, where Morgan had at last got a new command only a few months before. Harry made no word of comment, but Chad's heart got bitter as gall as he listened. And this had happened to the Deans while he was gone to serve them. But the bloody Commandant of the State would be removed from power—that much good had been done—as Chad learned when he presented himself, with a black face, to his general.

"I could not help it," said the General, quickly. "He seems to have hated the Deans." And again read the despatches slowly. "You have done good work. There will be less trouble now." Then he paused. "I have had a letter from General Grant. He wants you on his staff." Again he paused, and it took the three past years of discipline to help Chad keep his self-control. "That is, if I have nothing particular for you to do. He seems to know what you have done and to suspect that there may be something more here for you to do. He's right. I want you to destroy Daws Dillon and his band. There will be no peace until he is out of the way. You know the mountains better than anybody. You are the man for the work. You will take one company from Wolford's regiment—he has been re-instated, you know—and go at once. When you have finished that—you can go to General Grant." The General smiled. "You are rather young to be so near a major—perhaps."

A major! The quick joy of the thought left him when he went down the stairs to the portico and saw Harry Dean's thin, sad face, and thought of the new grave in the Deans' garden and those two lonely women in exile. There was one small grain of consolation. It was his old enemy, Daws Dillon, who had slain Joel Turner; Daws who had almost ruined Major

Buford and had sent him to prison—Daws had played no small part in the sorrows of the Deans, and on the heels of Daws Dillon he soon would be.

"I suppose I am to go with you," said Harry.

"Why, yes," said Chad, startled; "how did you know?"

"I didn't know. How far is Dillon's hiding-place from where Morgan is?"

"Across the mountains." Chad understood suddenly. "You won't have to go," he said, quickly.

"I'll go where I am ordered," said Harry Dean.

THE LITTLE SHEPHERD OF KINGDOM COME

Indeed and sent him to prison. Chad had gained no small fame in the arrest of the Dillons and on the death of Mayo, the latter would . . .

XXVI

BROTHER AGAINST BROTHER AT LAST

It was the first warm day of spring and the sunshine was very soothing to Melissa as she sat on the old porch early in the afternoon. Perhaps it was a memory of childhood, perhaps she was thinking of the happy days she and Chad had spent on the river bank long ago, and perhaps it was the sudden thought that, with the little they had to eat in the house and that little the same three times a day, week in and week out, Mother Turner, who had been ailing, would like to have some fish; perhaps it was the primitive hunting instinct that, on such a day, sets a country boy's fingers itching for a squirrel rifle or a cane fishing-pole, but she sprang from her seat, leaving old Jack to doze on the porch, and, in half an hour, was crouched down behind a boulder below the river bend, dropping a wriggling worm into a dark, still pool. As she sat there, contented and luckless, the sun grew so warm that she got drowsy and dozed—how long she did not know—but she awoke with a start and with a frightened sense that someone was near her, though she could hear no sound. But she lay still—her heart beating high—and so sure that her instinct was true that she was not even surprised when she heard a voice in the thicket above—a low voice, but one she knew perfectly well:

"I tell you he's a-comin' up the river now. He's a-goin' to stay with ole Ham Blake ter-night over the mountain an' he'll be a-comin' through Hurricane Gap 'bout daylight ter-morrer or next day, shore. He's got a lot o' men, but we can layway 'em in the Gap an' git away all right." It was Tad Dillon speaking—Daws Dillon, his brother, answered:

"I don't want to kill anybody but that damned Chad—Captain Chad *Buford,* he calls hisself."

"Well, we can git him all right. I heerd that they was a-lookin' fer us an' was goin' to ketch us if they could."

"I wish I knowed that was so," said Daws with an oath. "Nary a one of 'em would git away alive if I just knowed it was *so.* But we'll git *Captain* Chad Buford, shore as hell! You go tell the boys to guard the Gap ter-night. They mought come through afore day." And then the noise of their footsteps fainted out of hearing and Melissa rose and sped back to the house.

From behind a clump of bushes above where she had sat, rose the gigantic figure of Rebel Jerry Dillon. He looked after the flying girl with a grim smile and then dropped his great bulk down on the bed of moss where he had been listening to the plan of his enemies and kinsmen. Jerry had made many expeditions over from Virginia lately and each time he had gone back with a new notch on the murderous knife that he carried in his belt. He had but two personal enemies alive now —Daws Dillon, who had tried to have him shot, and his own brother, Yankee Jake. This was the second time he had been over for Daws, and after his first trip he had persuaded Dan to ask permission from General Morgan to take a company into Kentucky and destroy Daws and his band, and Morgan had given him leave, for Federals and Confederates were chasing down these guerillas now—sometimes even joining forces to further their common purpose. Jerry had been slipping through the woods after Daws, meaning to crawl close enough to kill him and, perhaps, Tad Dillon, too, if necessary, but after hearing their plan he had let them go, for a bigger chance might be at hand. If Chad Buford was in the mountains looking for Daws, Yankee Jake was with him. If he killed Daws now, Chad and his men would hear of his death and would go back, most likely—and that was the thought that checked his finger on the trigger of his pistol. Another thought now lifted him to his feet with surprising quickness and sent him on a run down the river where his horse was hitched in the bushes. He would go over the mountain for Dan. He could lead Dan and his men to Hurricane Gap by daylight. Chad Buford could fight it out with Daws and his gang, and he and Dan would fight it out with the men who won—no matter whether Yankees or guerillas. And a grim smile stayed on Rebel Jerry's face as he climbed.

On the porch of the Turner cabin sat Melissa with her hands clinched and old Jack's head in her lap. There was no use worrying Mother Turner—she feared even to tell her—but what should she do? She might boldly cross the mountain now, for she was known to be a rebel, but the Dillons knowing, too, how close Chad had once been to the Turners might suspect and stop her. No, if she went at all, she must go after night-fall—but how would she get away from Mother Turner, and how could she make her way, undetected, through Hurricane Gap? The cliffs were so steep and close together in one place that she could hardly pass more than forty feet from the road on either side and she could not pass that close to pickets and not be heard. Her brain ached with planning and she was so absorbed as night came on that several times old Mother Turner querulously asked what was ailing her and why she did not pay more heed to her work, and the girl answered her patiently and went on with her planning. Before dark, she knew what she would do, and after the old mother was asleep, she rose softly and slipped out the door without awakening even old Jack, and went to the barn, where she got the sheep-bell that old Beelzebub used to wear and with the clapper caught in one hand, to keep the bell from tinkling, she went swiftly down the road toward Hurricane Gap. Several times she had to dart into the bushes while men on horseback rode by her, and once she came near being caught by three men on foot—all hurrying at Daws Dillon's order to the Gap through which she must go. When the road turned from the river, she went slowly along the edge of it, so that if discovered, she could leap with one spring into the bushes. It was raining—a cold drizzle that began to chill her and set her to coughing so that she was half afraid that she might disclose herself. At the mouth of the Gap she saw a fire on one side of the road and could hear talking, but she had no difficulty passing it, on the other side. But on, where the Gap narrowed—there was the trouble. It must have been an hour before midnight when she tremblingly neared the narrow defile. The rain had ceased, and as she crept around a boulder she could see, by the light of the moon between two black clouds, two sentinels beyond. The crisis was at hand now. She slipped to one side of the road, climbed the cliff as high as she could and crept about it. She was past one picket now, and in her eagerness one foot slipped and she half fell. She almost held her breath and lay still.

"I hear somethin' up thar in the bresh," shouted the second picket. "Halt!"

Melissa tinkled the sheep-bell and pushed a bush to and fro

as though a sheep or a cow might be rubbing itself, and the picket she had passed laughed aloud.

"Goin' to shoot ole Sally Perkins's cow, air you?" he said, jeeringly. "Yes, I heerd her," he added, lying; for, being up all the night before, he had drowsed at his post. A moment later, Melissa moved on, making considerable noise and tinkling her bell constantly. She was near the top now and when she peered out through the bushes, no one was in sight and she leaped into the road and fled down the mountain. At the foot of the spur another ringing cry smote the darkness in front of her:

"Halt! Who goes there?"

"Don't shoot!" she cried, weakly. "It's only me."

"Advance, 'Me,'" said the picket, astonished to hear a woman's voice. And then into the light of his fire stepped a shepherdess with a sheep-bell in her hand, with a beautiful, pale, distressed face, a wet, clinging dress, and masses of yellow hair surging out of the shawl over her head. The startled picket dropped the butt of his musket to the ground and stared.

"I want to see Ch—, your captain," she said, timidly.

"All right," said the soldier, courteously. "He's just below there and I guess he's up. We are getting ready to start now. Come along."

"Oh, no!" said Melissa, hurriedly. "I can't go down there." It had just struck her that Chad must not see her; but the picket thought she naturally did not wish to face a lot of soldiers in her bedraggled and torn dress, and he said quickly:

"All right. Give me your message and I'll take it to him." He smiled. "You can wait here and stand guard."

Melissa told him hurriedly how she had come over the

mountain and what was going on over there, and the picket with a low whistle started down toward his camp without another word.

Chad could not doubt the accuracy of the information—the picket had names and facts.

"A girl, you say?"

"Yes, sir"—the soldier hesitated—"and a very pretty one, too. She came over the mountain alone and on foot through this darkness. She passed the pickets on the other side—pretending to be a sheep. She had a bell in her hand." Chad smiled—he knew that trick.

"Where is she?"

"She's standing guard for me."

The picket turned at a gesture from Chad and led the way. They found no Melissa. She had heard Chad's voice and fled up the mountain. Before daybreak she was descending the mountain on the other side, along the same way, tinkling her sheep-bell and creeping past the pickets. It was raining again now and her cold had grown worse. Several times she had to muffle her face into her shawl to keep her cough from betraying her. As she passed the ford below the Turner cabin, she heard the splash of many horses crossing the river and she ran on, frightened and wondering. Before day broke she had slipped into her bed without arousing Mother Turner, and she did not get up that day, but lay ill abed.

The splashing of those many horses was made by Captain Daniel Dean and his men, guided by Rebel Jerry. High on the mountain side they hid their horses in a ravine and crept toward the Gap on foot—so that while Daws with his gang waited for Chad, the rebels lay in the brush waiting for him. Dan was merry over the prospect:

"We will just let them fight it out," he said, "and then we'll dash in and gobble 'em both up. That was a fine scheme of yours, Jerry."

Rebel Jerry smiled: there was one thing he had not told his captain—who those rebels were. Purposely he had kept that fact hidden. He had seen Dan purposely refrain from killing Chad Buford once and he feared that Dan might think his brother Harry was among the Yankees. All this Rebel Jerry failed to understand, and he wanted nothing known now that might stay anybody's hand. Dawn broke and nothing happened. Not a shot rang out and only the smoke of the guerillas' fire showed in the peaceful mouth of the Gap. Dan wanted to attack the guerillas, but Jerry persuaded him to wait until he could learn how the land lay, and disappeared in the bushes. At noon he came back.

"The Yankees have found out Daws is thar in the Gap," he said, "an' they are goin' to slip over before day ter-morrer and s'prise *him*. Hit don't make no difference to us, which s'prises which—does it?"

So the rebels kept hid through the day in the bushes on the mountain side, and when Chad slipped through the Gap next morning, before day, and took up the guerilla pickets, Dan had moved into the same Gap from the other side, and was lying in the bushes with his men, near the guerillas' fire, waiting for the Yankees to make their attack. He had not long to wait. At the first white streak of dawn overhead, a shout rang through the woods from the Yankees to the startled guerillas.

"Surrender!" A fusillade followed. Again:

"Surrender!" and there was a short silence, broken by low curses from the guerillas, and one stern Yankee voice giving short, quick orders. The guerillas had given up. Rebel Jerry moved restlessly at Dan's side and Dan cautioned him.

"Wait! Let them have time to disarm the prisoners," he whispered.

"Now," he added, a little while later—"creep quietly, boys."

Forward they went like snakes, creeping to the edge of the brush whence they could see the sullen guerillas grouped on one side of the fire—their arms stacked, while a tall figure in blue moved here and there, and gave orders in a voice that all at once seemed strangely familiar to Dan.

"Now, boys," he said, half aloud, "give 'em a volley and charge."

At his word there was a rattling fusillade, and then the rebels leaped from the bushes and dashed on the astonished Yankees and their prisoners. It was pistol to pistol at first and then they closed to knife thrust and musket butt, hand to hand—in a cloud of smoke. At the first fire from the rebels Chad saw his prisoner, Daws Dillon, leap for the stacked arms and disappear. A moment later, as he was emptying his pistol at his charging foes, he felt a bullet clip a lock of hair from the back of his head and he turned to see Daws on the farthest edge of the firelight levelling his pistol for another shot before he ran. Like lightning he wheeled and when his finger pulled the trigger, Daws sank limply, his grinning, malignant face sickening as he fell.

The tall fellow in blue snapped his pistol at Dan, and as Dan, whose pistol, too, was empty, sprang forward and closed with him, he heard a triumphant yell behind him and Rebel Jerry's huge figure flashed past him. With the same glance he saw among the Yankees another giant—who looked like an-

Rebel Jerry and Yankee Jake.

other Jerry—saw his face grow ghastly with fear when Jerry's yell rose, and then grow taut with ferocity as he tugged at his sheath to meet the murderous knife flashing toward him. The terrible Dillon twins were come together at last, and Dan shuddered, but he saw no more, for he was busy with the lithe Yankee in whose arms he was closed. As they struggled, Dan tried to get his knife and the Yankee tugged for his second pistol— each clasping the other's wrist. Not a sound did they make nor could either see the other's face, for Dan had his chin in his opponent's breast and was striving to bend him backward. He had clutched the Yankee's right hand, as it went back for his pistol, just as the Yankee had caught his right in front, feeling for his knife. The advantage would have been all Dan's except that the Yankee suddenly loosed his wrist and gripped him tight about the body in an underhold, so that Dan could not whirl him round; but he could twist that wrist and twist it he did, with both hands and all his strength. Once the Yankee gave a smothered groan of pain and Dan heard him grit his teeth to keep it back. The smoke had lifted now, and, when they fell, it was in the light of the fire. The Yankee had thrown him with a knee-trick that Harry used to try on him when they were boys, but something about the Yankee snapped, as they fell, and he groaned aloud. Clutching him by the throat, Dan threw him off—he could get at his knife now.

"Surrender!" he said, hoarsely.

His answer was a convulsive struggle and then the Yankee lay still.

"Surrender!" said Dan again, lifting his knife above the Yankee's breast, "or, damn you, I'll—" The Yankee had turned his face weakly toward the fire, and Dan, with a cry of horror, threw his knife away and sprang to his feet. Straightway the Yankee's closed eyes opened and he smiled faintly.

"Why, Dan, is that you?" he asked. "I thought it would come," he added, quietly, and then Harry Dean lapsed into unconsciousness.

Thus, at its best, this fratricidal war was being fought out that daybreak in one little hollow of the Kentucky mountains and thus, at its worst, it was being fought out in another little hollow scarcely twenty yards away, where the giant twins— Rebel Jerry and Yankee Jake—who did know they were brothers, sought each other's lives in mutual misconception and mutual hate.

There were a dozen dead Federals and guerillas around the fire, and among them was Daws Dillon with the pallor of death on his face and the hate that life had written there still clinging to it like a shadow. As Dan bent tenderly over his brother Harry, two soldiers brought in a huge body from the bushes, and he turned to see Rebel Jerry Dillon. There were a half a dozen rents in his uniform and a fearful slash under his chin— but he was breathing still. Chad Buford had escaped, and so had Yankee Jake.

XXVII

AT THE HOSPITAL OF MORGAN'S MEN

In May, Grant simply said—Forward! The day he crossed the Rapidan, he said it to Sherman down in Georgia. After the battle of the Wilderness he said it again, and the last brutal resort of hammering down the northern buttress and sea-wall of the rebellion—old Virginia—and Atlanta, the keystone of the Confederate arch, was well under way. Throughout those bloody days Chad was with Grant and Harry Dean was with Sherman on his terrible trisecting march to the sea. For, after the fight between Rebels and Yankees and Daws Dillon's guerilla band, over in Kentucky, Dan, coming back from another raid into the Bluegrass, had found his brother gone. Harry had refused to accept a parole and had escaped. Not a man, Dan was told, fired a shot at him, as he ran. One soldier raised his musket, but Renfrew the Silent struck the muzzle upward.

In September, Atlanta fell and, in that same month, Dan saw his great leader, John Morgan, dead in Tennessee. In December, the Confederacy toppled at the west under Thomas's blows at Nashville. In the spring of '65, one hundred and thirty-five thousand wretched, broken-down rebels, from Richmond to the Rio Grande, confronted Grant's million men, and in April, Five Forks was the beginning of the final end everywhere.

At midnight, Captain Daniel Dean, bearer of dispatches to the great Confederate General in Virginia, rode out of abandoned Richmond with the cavalry of young Fitzhugh Lee.

They had threaded their way amid troops, trains, and artillery across the bridge. The city was on fire. By its light, the stream of humanity was pouring out of town—Davis and his cabinet, citizens, soldiers, down to the mechanics in the armories and workshops. The chief concern with all was the same, a little to eat for a few days; for, with the morning, the enemy would come and Confederate money would be as mist. Afar off the little fleet of Confederate gunboats blazed and the thundering explosions of their magazines split the clear air. Freight depots with supplies were burning. Plunderers were spreading the fires and slipping like ghouls through red light and black shadows. At daybreak the last retreating gun rumbled past and, at sunrise, Dan looked back from the hills on the smoking and deserted city and Grant's blue lines sweeping into it.

Once only he saw his great chief—the next morning before day, when he rode through the chill mist and darkness to find the head-quarters of the commanding General—two little fires of rubbish and two ambulances—with Lee lying on a blanket under the open sky. He rose, as Dan drew near, and the fire-light fell full on his bronzed and mournful face. He looked so sad and so noble that the boy's heart was wrenched, and as Dan turned away, he said, brokenly:

"General, I am General Dean's son, and I want to thank you—" He could get no farther. Lee laid one hand on his shoulder.

"Be as good a man as your father was, my boy," he said, and Dan rode back the pitiable way through the rear of that noble army of Virginia—through ranks of tattered, worn, hungry soldiers, among the broken débris of wagons and abandoned guns, past skeleton horses and skeleton men.

AT THE HOSPITAL OF MORGAN'S MEN

All hope was gone, but Fitz Lee led his cavalry through the Yankee lines and escaped. In that flight Daniel Dean got his only wound in the war—a bullet through the shoulder. When the surrender came, Fitz Lee gave up, too, and led back his command to get Grant's generous terms. But all his men did not go with him, and among the cavalrymen who went on toward southwestern Virginia was Dan—making his way back to Richard Hunt—for now that gallant Morgan was dead, Hunt was general of the old command.

Behind, at Appomattox, Chad was with Grant. He saw the surrender—saw Lee look toward his army, when he came down the steps after he had given up, saw him strike his hands together three times and ride Traveller away through the profound and silent respect of his enemies and the tearful worship of his own men. And Chad got permission straightway to go back to Ohio, and be mustered out with his old regiment, and he, too, started back through Virginia.

Meanwhile, Dan was drawing near the mountains. He was worn out when he reached Abingdon. The wound in his shoulder was festering and he was in a high fever. At the camp of Morgan's Men he found only a hospital left—for General Hunt had gone southward—and a hospital was what he most needed now. As he lay, unconscious with fever, next day, a giant figure, lying near, turned his head and stared at the boy. It was Rebel Jerry Dillon, helpless from a sabre cut and frightfully scarred by the fearful wounds his brother, Yankee Jake, had given him. And thus, Chadwick Buford, making for the Ohio, saw the two strange messmates, a few days later, when he rode into the deserted rebel camp.

All was over. Red Mars had passed beyond the horizon

and the white Star of Peace already shone faintly on the ravaged South. The shattered remnants of Morgan's cavalry, pall-bearers of the Lost Cause—had gone South—bare-footed and in rags—to guard Jefferson Davis to safety, and Chad's heart was wrung when he stepped into the little hospital they had left behind—a space cleared into a thicket of rhododendron. There was not a tent—there was little medicine—little food. The drizzling rain dropped on the group of ragged sick men from the branches above them. Nearly all were youthful, and the youngest was a mere boy, who lay delirious with his head on the root of a tree. As Chad stood looking, the boy opened his eyes and his mouth twitched with pain.

"Hello, you damned Yankee." Again his mouth twitched and again the old dare-devil light that Chad knew so well kindled in his hazy eyes.

"I said," he repeated, distinctly, "Hello, you damned Yank. *Damned* Yank I said." Chad beckoned to two men.

"Go bring a stretcher."

The men shook their heads with a grim smile—they had no stretcher.

The boy talked dreamily.

"Say, Yank, didn't we give you hell in—oh, well, in lots o' places. But you've got me." The two soldiers were lifting him in their arms. "Goin' to take me to prison? Goin' to take me out to shoot me, Yank? You *are* a damned Yank." A hoarse growl rose behind them and the giant lifted himself on one elbow, swaying his head from side to side.

"Let that boy alone!" Dan nodded back at him confidently.

"That's all right, Jerry. This Yank's a friend of mine."

His brow wrinkled. "At any rate he looks like somebody I know. He's goin' to give me something to eat and get me well —like hell," he added to himself—passing off into unconsciousness again. Chad had the lad carried to his own tent, had him stripped, bathed, and bandaged and stood looking down at him. It was hard to believe that the broken, aged youth was the red-cheeked, vigorous lad whom he had known as Daniel Dean. He was ragged, starved, all but bare-footed, wounded, sick, and yet he was as undaunted, as defiant, as when he charged with Morgan's dare-devils at the beginning of the war. Then Chad went back to the hospital—for a blanket and some medicine.

"They are friends," he said to the Confederate surgeon, pointing at a huge gaunt figure.

"I reckon that big fellow has saved that boy's life a dozen times. Yes, they're mess-mates." And Chad stood looking down at Jerry Dillon, one of the giant twins—whose name was a terror throughout the mountains of the middle south. Then he turned and the surgeon followed. There was a rustle of branches on one side when they were gone, and at the sound the wounded man lifted his head. The branches parted and the ox-like face of Yankee Jake peered through. For a full minute, the two brothers stared at each other.

"I reckon you got me, Jake," said Jerry.

"I been lookin' fer ye a long while," said Jake, simply, and he smiled strangely as he moved slowly forward and looked down at his enemy—his heavy head wagging from side to side. Jerry was fumbling at his belt. The big knife flashed, but Jake's hand was as quick as its gleam, and he had the wrist that held it. His great fingers crushed together, the blade dropped on the ground, and again the big twins looked at each other. Slowly, Yankee Jake picked up the knife. The other moved not a muscle and in his fierce eyes was no plea for mercy. The point of the blade moved slowly down—down over the rebel's heart, and was thrust into its sheath again. Then Jake let go the wrist.

"Don't tech it agin," he said, and he strode away. The big fellow lay blinking. He did not open his lips when, in a moment, Yankee Jake slouched in with a canteen of water. When Chad came back, one giant was drawing on the other a pair of socks. The other was still silent and had his face turned the other way. Looking up, Jake met Chad's surprised gaze with a grin.

A day later, Dan came to his senses. A tent was above him, a heavy blanket was beneath him and there were clothes on his body that felt strangely fresh and clean. He looked up to see Chad's face between the flaps of the tent.

"D'you do this?"

"That's all right," said Chad. "This war is over." And he went away to let Dan think it out. When he came again, Dan held out his hand silently.

XXVIII

PALL–BEARERS OF THE LOST CAUSE

THE rain was falling with a steady roar when General Hunt broke camp a few days before. The mountain-tops were black with thunder-clouds, and along the muddy road went Morgan's Men—most of them on mules which had been taken from abandoned wagons when news of the surrender came—without saddles and with blind bridles or rope halters—the rest slopping along through the yellow mud on foot—literally—for few of them had shoes; they were on their way to protect Davis and join Johnston, now that Lee was no more. There was no murmuring, no faltering, and it touched Richard Hunt to observe that they were now more prompt to obedience, when it was optional with them whether they should go or stay, than they had ever been in the proudest days of the Confederacy.

Threatened from Tennessee and cut off from Richmond, Hunt had made up his mind to march eastward to join Lee, when the news of the surrender came. Had the sun at that moment dropped suddenly to the horizon from the heaven above them, those Confederates would have been hardly more startled or plunged into deeper despair. Crowds of infantry threw down their arms and, with the rest, all sense of discipline was lost. Of the cavalry, however, not more than ten men declined to march south, and out they moved through the drenching rain in a silence that was broken only with a single cheer when ninety men from another Kentucky brigade joined them, who, too, felt that as long as the Confederate Government survived, there was work for them to do. So on they went to keep up the

[295]

struggle, if the word was given, skirmishing, fighting and slipping past the enemies that were hemming them in, on with Davis, his cabinet, and General Breckinridge to join Taylor and Forrest in Alabama. Across the border of South Carolina, an irate old lady upbraided Hunt for allowing his soldiers to take forage from her barn.

"You are a gang of thieving Kentuckians," she said, hotly; "you are afraid to go home, while our boys are surrendering decently."

"Madam!"—Renfrew the Silent spoke—spoke from the depths of his once brilliant jacket—"you South Carolinians had a good deal to say about getting up this war, but we Kentuckians have contracted to close it out."

Then came the last Confederate council of war. In turn, each officer spoke of his men and of himself and each to the same effect; the cause was lost and there was no use in prolonging the war.

"We will give our lives to secure your safety, but we cannot urge our men to struggle against a fate that is inevitable, and perhaps thus forfeit all hope of a restoration to their homes and friends."

Davis was affable, dignified, calm, undaunted.

"I will hear of no plan that is concerned only with my safety. A few brave men can prolong the war until this panic has passed, and they will be a nucleus for thousands more."

The answer was silence, as the gaunt, beaten man looked from face to face. He rose with an effort.

"I see all hope is gone," he said, bitterly, and though his calm remained, his bearing was less erect, his face was deathly pale and his step so infirm that he leaned upon General Breckinridge as he neared the door—in the bitterest moment, perhaps, of his life.

So, the old Morgan's Men, so long separated, were united at the end. In a broken voice General Hunt forbade the men who had followed him on foot three hundred miles from Virginia to go farther, but to disperse to their homes; and they wept like children.

In front of him was a big force of Federal cavalry; retreat the way he had come was impossible, and to the left, if he escaped, was the sea; but dauntless Hunt refused to surrender except at the order of a superior, or unless told that all was done that could be done to assure the escape of his President. That order came from Breckinridge.

"Surrender," was the message. "Go back to your homes, I will not have one of these young men encounter one more hazard for my sake."

That night Richard Hunt fought out his fight with himself, pacing to and fro under the stars. He had struggled faithfully for what he believed, still believed, and would, perhaps, always believe, was right. He had fought for the broadest ideal of liberty as he understood it, for citizen, State, and nation. The appeal had gone to the sword and the verdict was against him. He would accept it. He would go home, take the oath of allegiance, resume the law, and, as an American citizen, do his duty. He had no sense of humiliation; he had no apology to make and would never have—he had done his duty. He felt no bitterness, and had no fault to find with his foes, who were brave and had done their duty as they had seen it; for he granted them the right to see a different duty from what he had decided was his. And that was all.

Renfrew the Silent was waiting at the smouldering fire. He neither looked up nor made any comment when General Hunt spoke his determination. His own face grew more sullen and he reached his hand into his breast and pulled from his faded jacket the tattered colors that he once had borne.

"These will never be lowered as long as I live," he said, "nor afterwards if I can prevent it." And lowered they never were. On a little island in the Pacific Ocean, this strange soldier, after leaving his property and his kindred forever, lived out his life among the natives with this blood-stained remnant of the Stars and Bars over his hut, and when he died, the flag was hung over his grave, and above that grave to-day the tattered emblem still sways in southern air.

.   .   .   .

A week earlier, two Rebels and two Yankees started across the mountain together—Chad and Dan and the giant Dillon twins—Chad and Yankee Jake afoot. Up Lonesome they went toward the shaggy flank of Black Mountain where the Great Reaper had mowed down Chad's first friends. The logs of the cabin were still standing, though the roof was caved in and the yard was a tangle of undergrowth. A dull pain settled in Chad's breast, while he looked, and as they were climbing the spur, he choked when he caught sight of the graves under the big poplar.

There was the little pen that he had built over his foster-mother's grave—still undisturbed. He said nothing and, as they went down the spur, across the river and up Pine Mountain, he kept his gnawing memories to himself. Only ten years before, and he seemed an old, old man now. He recognized the very spot where he had slept the first night after he ran away and awakened to that fearful never-forgotten storm at sunrise, which lived in his memory now as a mighty portent of the storms of human passion that had swept around him on many a battle-field. There was the very tree where he had killed the squirrel and the rattlesnake. It was bursting spring now, but the buds of laurel and rhododendron were unbroken. Down Kingdom Come they went. Here was where he had met the old cow, and here was the little hill where Jack had fought Whizzer and he had fought Tad Dillon and where he had first seen Melissa. Again the scarlet of her tattered gown flashed before his eyes. At the bend of the river they parted from the giant twins. Faithful Jake's face was foolish when Chad took him by the hand and spoke to him, as man to man, and Rebel Jerry turned his face quickly when Dan told him that he would never forget him, and made him promise to come to see him, if Jerry ever took another raft down to the capital. Looking back from the hill, Chad saw them slowly moving along a path toward the woods—not looking at each other and speaking not at all.

Beyond rose the smoke of the old Turner cabin. On the porch sat the old Turner mother, her bonnet in her hand, her eyes looking down the river. Dozing at her feet was Jack— old Jack. She had never forgiven Chad, and she could not forgive him now, though Chad saw her eyes soften when she looked at the tattered butternut that Dan wore. But Jack—half-blind and aged—sprang trembling to his feet when he heard Chad's voice and whimpered like a child. Chad sank on the porch with one arm about the old dog's neck. Mother Turner answered all questions shortly.

[299]

Melissa had gone to the "Settlemints." Why? The old woman would not answer. She was coming back, but she was ill. She had never been well since she went afoot, one cold night, to warn some *Yankee* that Daws Dillon was after him. Chad started. It was Melissa who had perhaps saved his life. Tad Dillon had stepped into Daws's shoes, and the war was still going on in the hills. Tom Turner had died in prison. The old mother was waiting for Dolph and Rube to come back—she was looking for them every hour, day and night. She did not know what had become of the school-master—but Chad did, and he told her. The school-master had died, storming breast-works at Gettysburg. The old woman said not a word.

Dan was too weak to ride now. So Chad got Dave Hilton, Melissa's old sweetheart, to take Dixie to Richmond—a little Kentucky town on the edge of the Bluegrass—and leave her there, and he bought the old Turner canoe. She would have no use for it, Mother Turner said—he could have it for nothing; but when Chad thrust a ten-dollar Federal bill into her hands, she broke down and threw her arms around him and cried.

So down the river went Chad and Dan—drifting with the tide—Chad in the stern, Dan lying at full length, with his head on a blue army-coat and looking up at the over-swung branches and the sky and the clouds above them—down, through a mist of memories for Chad—down to the capital.

And Harry Dean, too, was on his way home—coming up from the far South—up through the ravaged land of his own people, past homes and fields which his own hands had helped to lay waste.

XXIX

MELISSA AND MARGARET

THE early spring sunshine lay like a benediction over the Dean household, for Margaret and her mother were home from exile. On the corner of the veranda sat Mrs. Dean, where she always sat, knitting. Under the big weeping willow in the garden was her husband's grave. When she was not seated near it, she was there in the porch, and to it her eyes seemed always to stray when she lifted them from her work.

The mail had just come and Margaret was reading a letter from Dan, and, as she read, her cheeks flushed.

"He took me into his own tent, mother, and put his own clothes on me and nursed me like a brother. And now he is going to take me to you and Margaret, he says, and I shall be strong enough, I hope, to start in a week. I shall be his friend for life."

Neither mother nor daughter spoke when the girl ceased reading. Only Margaret rose soon and walked down the gravelled walk to the stile. Beneath the hill, the creek sparkled. She could see the very pool where her brothers and the queer little stranger from the mountains were fishing the day he came into her life. She remembered the indignant heartbeat with which she had heard him call her "little gal," and she smiled now, but she could recall the very tone of his voice and the steady look in his clear eyes when he offered her the perch he had caught. Even then his spirit appealed unconsciously to her, when he sturdily refused to go up to the house because her brother was "feelin' hard towards him." How strange and far away all that seemed now! Up the creek and around the woods she strolled, deep in memories. For a long while she sat on a stone wall in the sunshine—thinking and dreaming, and it was growing late when she started back to the house. At the stile, she turned for a moment to look at the old Buford home across the fields. As she looked, she saw the pike-gate open and a woman's figure enter, and she kept her eyes idly upon it as she walked on toward the house. The woman came slowly and hesitatingly toward the yard. When she drew nearer, Margaret could see that she wore homespun, home-made shoes, and a poke-bonnet. On her hands were yarn half-mits, and, as she walked, she pushed her bonnet from her eyes with one hand, first to one side, then to the other—looking at the locusts planted along the avenue, the cedars in the yard, the sweep of lawn overspread with springing bluegrass. At the yard gate she stopped, leaning over it—her eyes fixed on the stately white house, with its mighty pillars. Margaret was standing on the steps now, motionless and waiting, and, knowing that she was seen, the woman opened the gate and walked up the gravelled path—never taking her eyes from the figure on the porch. Straight she walked to the foot of the steps, and there she stopped, and, pushing her bonnet back, she said, simply:

"Are you Mar-ga-ret?" pronouncing the name slowly and with great distinctness.

Margaret started.

"Yes," she said.

The girl merely looked at her—long and hard. Once her lips moved:

"Mar-ga-ret," and still she looked. "Do you know whar Chad is?"

Margaret flushed.

"Who are you?"

"Melissy."

Melissa! The two girls looked deep into each other's eyes and, for one flashing moment, each saw the other's heart—bared and beating—and Margaret saw, too, a strange light ebb slowly from the other's face and a strange shadow follow slowly after.

"You mean Major Buford?"

"I mean Chad. Is he dead?"

"No, he is bringing my brother home."

"Harry?"

"No—Dan."

"Dan—here?"

"Yes."

"When?"

"As soon as my brother gets well enough to travel. He is wounded."

Melissa turned her face then. Her mouth twitched and her clasped hands were working in and out. Then she turned again.

"I come up here from the mountains, afoot, jus' to tell ye —to tell *you* that Chad ain't no"—she stopped suddenly, seeing Margaret's quick flush—*"Chad's mother was married. I jus' found it out last week. He ain't no"*—she started fiercely again and stopped again. "But I come here fer *him*—not fer *you*. *You* oughtn't to 'a' keered. Hit wouldn't 'a' been his fault. He never was the same after he come back from here. Hit worried him most to death, an' I know hit was you—*you* he was always thinkin' about. He didn't keer 'cept fer you."

Again that shadow came and deepened. "An' you oughtn't to 'a' keered what he was—and that's why I hate you," she said, calmly—"fer worryin' him an' bein' so high-heeled that you was willin' to let him mighty nigh bust his heart about somethin' that wasn't his fault. I come fer him—you understand —fer *him*. I hate *you!*"

She turned without another word, walked slowly back down the walk and through the gate. Margaret stood dazed, helpless, almost frightened. She heard the girl cough and saw now that she walked as if weak and ill. As she turned into the road, Margaret ran down the steps and across the fields to the turnpike. When she reached the road-fence the girl was coming around the bend with her eyes on the ground, and every now and then she would cough and put her hand to her breast. She looked up quickly, hearing the noise ahead of her, and stopped as Margaret climbed the low stone wall and sprang down.

"Melissa, Melissa! You mustn't hate me. You mustn't hate *me*." Margaret's eyes were streaming and her voice trembled with kindness. She walked up to the girl and put one hand on her shoulder. "You are sick. I know you are, and you must come back to the house."

Melissa gave way then, and breaking from the girl's clasp she leaned against the stone wall and sobbed, while Margaret put her arms about her and waited silently.

"Come now," she said, "let me help you over. There now. You must come back and get something to eat and lie down." And Margaret led Melissa back across the fields.

XXX

PEACE

It was strange to Chad that he should be drifting toward a new life down the river which once before had carried him to a new world. The future then was no darker than now, but he could hardly connect himself with the little fellow in coon-skin cap and moccasins who had floated down on a raft so many years ago, when at every turn of the river his eager eyes looked for a new and thrilling mystery.

They talked of the long fight, the two lads, for, in spite of the war-worn look of them, both were still nothing but boys —and they talked with no bitterness of camp life, night attacks, surprises, escapes, imprisonment, incidents of march and battle. Both spoke little of their boyhood days or of the future. The pall of defeat overhung Dan. To him the world seemed to be nearing an end, while to Chad the outlook was what he had known all his life—nothing to begin with and everything to be done. Once only Dan voiced his own trouble:

"What are you going to do, Chad—now that this infernal war is over? Going into the regular army?"

"No," said Chad, decisively. About his own future Dan volunteered nothing—he only turned his head quickly to the passing woods, as though in fear that Chad might ask some similar question, but Chad was silent. And thus they glided between high cliffs and down into the lowlands until at last, through a little gorge between two swelling river hills, Dan's eye caught sight of an orchard, a leafy woodland, and a pasture of bluegrass. With a cry he raised himself on one elbow.

"Home! I tell you, Chad, we're getting home!" He closed

his eyes and drew the sweet air in as though he were drinking it down like wine. His eyes were sparkling when he opened them again and there was a new color in his face. On they drifted until, toward noon, the black column of smoke that meant the capital loomed against the horizon. There Mrs. Dean was waiting for them, and Chad turned his face aside when the mother took her son in her arms. With a sad smile she held out her hand to Chad.

"You must come home with us," Mrs. Dean said, with quiet decision.

"Where is Margaret, mother?" Chad almost trembled when he heard the name.

"Margaret couldn't come. She is not very well and she is taking care of Harry."

The very station had tragic memories to Chad. There was the long hill which he had twice climbed—once on a lame foot and once on flying Dixie—past the armory and the graveyard. He had seen enough dead since he peered through those iron gates to fill a dozen graveyards the like in size. Going up in the train, he could see the barn where he had slept in the hay-loft the first time he came to the Bluegrass, and the creek-bridge where Major Buford had taken him into his carriage. Major Buford was dead. He had almost died in prison, Mrs. Dean said, and Chad choked and could say nothing. Once, Dan began a series of eager questions about the house and farm, and the servants and the neighbors, but his mother's answers were hesitant and he stopped short. She, too, asked but few questions, and the three were quiet while the train rolled on with little more speed than Chad and Dixie had made on that long ago night-ride to save Dan and Rebel Jerry. About that ride

PEACE

Chad had kept Harry's lips and his own closed, for he wished no such appeal as that to go to Margaret Dean. Margaret was not at the station in Lexington. She was not well, Rufus said; so Chad would not go with them that night, but would come out next day.

"I owe my son's life to you, Captain Buford," said Mrs. Dean, with trembling lip, "and you must make our house your home while you are here. I bring that message to you from Harry and Margaret. I know and they know now all you have done for us and all you have tried to do."

Chad could hardly speak his thanks. He would be in the Bluegrass only a few days, he stammered, but he would go out to see them next day. That night he went to the old inn where the Major had taken him to dinner. Next day he hired a horse from the livery stable where he had bought the old brood mare, and early in the afternoon he rode out the broad turnpike in a nervous tumult of feeling that more than once made him halt in the road. He wore his uniform, which was new, and made him uncomfortable—it looked too much like waving a victorious flag in the face of a beaten enemy—but it was the only stitch of clothes he had, and that he might not explain.

It was the first of May. Just eight years before, Chad with a burning heart had watched Richard Hunt gayly dancing with Margaret, while the dead chieftain, Morgan, gayly fiddled for the merry crowd. Now the sun shone as it did then, the birds sang, the wind shook the happy leaves and trembled through the budding heads of bluegrass to show that nature had known no war and that her mood was never other than of hope and peace. But there were no fat cattle browsing in the Dean pastures now, no flocks of Southdown sheep with frisking lambs.

[307]

The worm fences had lost their riders and were broken down here and there. The gate sagged on its hinges; the fences around yard and garden and orchard had known no whitewash for years; the paint on the noble old house was cracked and peeling, the roof of the barn was sunken in, and the cabins of the quarters were closed, for the hand of war, though unclinched, still lay heavy on the home of the Deans. Snowball came to take his horse. He was respectful, but his white teeth did not flash the welcome Chad once had known. Another horse stood at the hitching-post and on it was a cavalry saddle and a rebel army blanket, and Chad did not have to guess whose it might be. From the porch, Dan shouted and came down to meet him, and Harry hurried to the door, followed by Mrs. Dean. Margaret was not to be seen, and Chad was glad—he would have a little more time for self-control. She did not appear even when they were seated in the porch until Dan shouted for her toward the garden; and then looking toward the gate Chad saw her coming up the garden walk bareheaded, dressed in white, with flowers in her hand; and walking by her side, looking into her face and talking earnestly, was Richard Hunt. The sight of him nerved Chad at once to steel. Margaret did not lift her face until she was half-way to the porch, and then she stopped suddenly.

"Why, there's Major Buford," Chad heard her say, and she came on ahead, walking rapidly. Chad felt the blood in his face again, and as he watched Margaret nearing him—pale, sweet, frank, gracious, unconscious—it seemed that he was living over again another scene in his life when he had come from the mountains to live with old Major Buford; and, with a sudden prayer that his past might now be wiped as clean as it was then, he turned from Margaret's hand-clasp to look into the brave, searching eyes of Richard Hunt and feel his sinewy fingers in a grip that in all frankness told Chad plainly that between them, at least, one war was not quite over yet.

"I am glad to meet you, Major Buford, in these piping times of peace."

"And I am glad to meet you, General Hunt—only in times of peace," Chad said, smiling.

The two measured each other, swiftly, calmly. Chad had a mighty admiration for Richard Hunt. Here was a man who knew no fight but to the finish, who would die as gamely in a drawing-room as on a battle-field. To think of him—a brigadier-general at twenty-seven, as undaunted, as unbeaten as when he heard the first bullet of the war whistle, and, at that moment, as good an American as Chadwick Buford or any Unionist who had given his life for his cause! Such a foe thrilled Chad, and somehow he felt that Margaret was measuring them as they were measuring each other. Against such a man what chance had he?

He would have been comforted could he have known Richard Hunt's thoughts, for that gentleman had gone back to the picture of a ragged mountain boy in old Major Buford's carriage, one court day long ago, and now he was looking that same lad over from the visor of his cap down his superb length to the heels of his riding-boots. His eyes rested long on Chad's face. The change was incredible, but blood had told. The face was highbred, clean, frank, nobly handsome; it had strength and dignity, and the scar on his cheek told a story that was as well known to foe as to friend.

"I have been wanting to thank you, not only for trying to

keep us out of that infernal prison after the Ohio raid, but for trying to get us out. Harry here told me. That was generous."

"That was nothing," said Chad. "You forget, you could have killed me once and—and you didn't." Margaret was listening eagerly.

"You didn't give me time," laughed General Hunt.

"Oh, yes, I did. I saw you lift your pistol and drop it again. I have never ceased to wonder why you did that."

Richard Hunt laughed. "Perhaps I'm sorry sometimes that I did," he said, with a certain dryness.

"Oh, no, you aren't, General," said Margaret.

Thus they chatted and laughed and joked together above the sombre tide of feeling that showed in the face of each if it reached not his tongue, for, when the war was over, the hatchet in Kentucky was buried at once and buried deep. Son came back to father, brother to brother, neighbor to neighbor; political disabilities were removed and the sundered threads, unravelled by the war, were knitted together fast. That is why the post-bellum terrors of reconstruction were practically unknown in the State. The negroes scattered, to be sure, not from disloyalty so much as from a feverish desire to learn whether they really could come and go as they pleased. When they learned that they were really free, most of them drifted back to the quarters where they were born, and meanwhile the white man's hand that had wielded the sword went just as bravely to the plough, and the work of rebuilding war-shattered ruins began at once. Old Mammy appeared, by and by, shook hands with General Hunt and made Chad a curtsey of rather distant dignity. She had gone into exile with her "chile" and her "ole Mistis" and had come home with them to stay, untempted by the doubtful sweets of freedom. "Old Tom, her husband, had remained with Major Buford, was with him on his deathbed," said Margaret, "and was on the place still, too old, he said, to take root elsewhere."

Toward the middle of the afternoon Dan rose and suggested that they take a walk about the place. Margaret had gone in for a moment to attend to some household duty, and as Richard Hunt was going away next day he would stay, he said, with Mrs. Dean, who was tired and could not join them. The three walked toward the dismantled barn where the tournament had taken place and out into the woods. Looking back, Chad saw Margaret and General Hunt going slowly toward the garden, and he knew that some crisis was at hand between the two. He had hard work listening to Dan and Harry as they planned for the future, and recalled to each other and to him the incidents of their boyhood. Harry meant to study law, he said, and practise in Lexington; Dan would stay at home and run the farm. Neither brother mentioned that the old place was heavily mortgaged, but Chad guessed the fact and it made him heartsick to think of the struggle that was before them and of the privations yet in store for Mrs. Dean and Margaret.

"Why don't you, Chad?"

"Do what?"

"Stay here and study law," Harry smiled. "We'll go into partnership."

Chad shook his head. "No," he said, decisively. "I've already made up my mind. I'm going West."

"I'm sorry," said Harry, and no more; he had learned long

[311]

ago how useless it was to combat any purpose of Chadwick Buford.

General Hunt and Margaret were still away when they got back to the house. In fact, the sun was sinking when they came in from the woods, still walking slowly, General Hunt talking earnestly and Margaret with her hands clasped before her and her eyes on the path. The faces of both looked pale, even that far away, but when they neared the porch, the General was joking and Margaret was smiling, nor was anything perceptible to Chad when he said good-by, except a certain tenderness in his tone and manner toward Margaret, and one fleeting look of distress in her clear eyes. He was on his horse now, and was lifting his cap.

"Good-by, Major," he said. "I'm glad you got through the war alive. Perhaps I'll tell you some day why I didn't shoot you that morning." And then he rode away, a gallant, knightly figure, across the pasture. At the gate he waved his cap and at a gallop was gone.

After supper, a heaven-born chance led Mrs. Dean to stroll out into the lovely night. Margaret rose to go too, and Chad followed. The same chance, perhaps, led old Mammy to come out on the porch and call Mrs. Dean back. Chad and Margaret walked on toward the stiles where still hung Margaret's weather-beaten Stars and Bars. The girl smiled and touched the flag.

"That was very nice of you to salute me that morning. I never felt so bitter against Yankees after that day. I'll take it down now," and she detached it and rolled it tenderly about the slender staff.

"That was not my doing," said Chad, "though if I had been

[312]

Grant, and there with the whole Union army, I would have had it salute you. I was under orders, but I went back for help. May I carry it for you?"

"Yes," said Margaret, handing it to him. Chad had started toward the garden, but Margaret turned him toward the stile and they walked now down through the pasture toward the creek that ran like a wind-shaken ribbon of silver under the moon.

"Won't you tell me something about Major Buford? I've been wanting to ask, but I simply hadn't the heart. Can't we go over there to-night? I want to see the old place, and I must leave to-morrow."

"To-morrow!" said Margaret. "Why—I—I was going to take you over there to-morrow, for I—but, of course, you must go to-night if it is to be your only chance."

And so, as they walked along, Margaret told Chad of the old Major's last days, after he was released from prison, and came home to die. She went to see him every day, and she was at his bedside when he breathed his last. He had mortgaged his farm to help the Confederate cause and to pay indemnity for a guerilla raid, and Jerome Conners held his notes for large amounts.

"The lawyer told me that he believed some of the notes were forged, but he couldn't prove it. He says it is doubtful if more than the house and a few acres will be left." A light broke in on Chad's brain.

"He told you?"

Margaret blushed. "He left all he had to me," she said, simply.

"I'm so glad," said Chad.

"Except a horse which belongs to you. The old mare is dead."

"Dear old Major!"

At the stone fence Margaret reached for the flag.

"We'll leave it here until we come back," she said, dropping it in a shadow. Somehow the talk of Major Buford seemed to bring them nearer together—so near that once Chad started to call her by her first name and stopped when it had half passed his lips. Margaret smiled.

"The war is over," she said, and Chad spoke eagerly:

"And you'll call me——"

"Yes, Chad."

The very leaves over Chad's head danced suddenly, and yet the girl was so simple and frank and kind that the springing hope in his breast was as quickly chilled.

"Did he ever speak of me except about business matters?"

"Never at all at first," said Margaret, blushing again incomprehensively, "but he forgave you before he died."

"Thank God for that!"

"And you will see what he did for you—the last thing of his life."

They were crossing the field now.

"I have seen Melissa," said Margaret, suddenly. Chad was so startled that he stopped in the path.

"She came all the way from the mountains to ask if you were dead, and to tell me about—about your mother. She had just learned it, she said, and she did not know that you knew. And I never let her know that I knew, since I supposed you had some reason for not wanting her to know."

"I did," said Chad, sadly, but he did not tell his reason.

Melissa would never have learned the one thing from him as Margaret would not learn the other now.

"She came on foot to ask about you and to defend you against—against me. And she went back afoot. She disappeared one morning before we got up. She seemed very ill, too, and unhappy. She was coughing all the time, and I wakened one night and heard her sobbing, but she was so sullen and fierce that I was almost afraid of her. Next morning she was gone. I would have taken her part of the way home myself. Poor thing!" Chad was walking with his head bent.

"I'm going down to see her before I go West."

"You are going West—to live?"

"Yes."

They had reached the yard gate now which creaked on rusty hinges when Chad pulled it open. The yard was running wild with plantains, the gravelled walk was overgrown, the house was closed, shuttered, and dark, and the spirit of desolation overhung the place, but the ruin looked gentle in the moonlight. Chad's throat hurt and his eyes filled.

"I want to show you now the last thing he did," said Margaret. Her eyes lighted with tenderness and she led him wondering down through the tangled garden to the old family graveyard.

"Climb over and look, Chad," she said, leaning over the wall.

There was the grave of the Major's father which he knew so well; next that, to the left, was a new mound under which rested the Major himself. To the right was a stone marked "Chadwick Buford, born in Virginia, 1750, died in Kentucky" —and then another stone marked simply:

Mary Buford.

"He had both brought from the mountains," said Margaret, softly, "and the last time he was out of the house was when he leaned here to watch them buried there. He said there would always be a place next your mother for you. 'Tell the boy that,' he said." Chad put his arms around the tombstone and then sank on one knee by his mother's grave. It was strewn with withered violets.

"You—*you* did that, Margaret?"

Margaret nodded through her tears.

.   .   .   .

The wonder of it! They stood very still, looking for a long time into each other's eyes. Could the veil of the hereafter have been lifted for them at that moment and they have seen themselves walking that same garden path, hand in hand, their faces seamed with age to other eyes, but changed in not a line to them, the vision would not have added a jot to their perfect faith. They would have nodded to each other and smiled— "Yes, we know, we know!" The night, the rushing earth, the star-swept spaces of the infinite held no greater wonder than was theirs—they held no wonder at all. The moon shone, that night, for them; the wind whispered, leaves danced, flowers nodded, and crickets chirped from the grass for them; the farthest star kept eternal lids apart just for them and beyond, the Maker himself looked down, that night, just to bless them.

Back they went through the old garden, hand in hand. No caress had ever passed between these two. That any man could ever dare even to dream of touching her sacred lips had been beyond the boy's imaginings—such was the reverence in his love for her—and his very soul shook when, at the gate, Margaret's eyes dropped from his to the sabre cut on his cheek and she suddenly lifted her face.

"I know how you got that, Chad," she said, and with her lips she gently touched the scar. Almost timidly the boy drew her to him. Again her lips were lifted in sweet surrender, and every wound that he had known in his life was healed.

*   *   *   *   *   *   *

"I'll show you your horse, Chad."

They did not waken old Tom, but went around to the stable and Chad led out a handsome colt, his satiny coat shining in the moonlight like silver. He lifted his proud head, when he saw Margaret, and whinnied.

"He knows his mistress, Margaret—and he's yours."

"Oh, no, Chad."

"Yes," said Chad, "I've still got Dixie."

"Do you still call her Dixie?"

"All through the war."

Homeward they went through the dewy fields.

"I wish I could have seen the Major before he died. If he could only have known how I suffered at causing him so much sorrow. And if you could have known——"

"He did know and so did I—later. All that is over now."

They had reached the stone wall and Chad picked up the flag again.

"This is the only time I have ever carried this flag, unless I —unless it had been captured."

"You had captured it, Chad."

"There?" Chad pointed to the stile and Margaret nodded.

"There—here—everywhere."

Seated on the porch, Mrs. Dean and Harry and Dan saw them coming across the field and Mrs. Dean sighed.

"Father would not say a word against it, mother," said the elder boy, "if he were here."

"No," said Dan, "not a word."

"Listen, mother," said Harry, and he told the two about Chad's ride for Dan from Frankfort to Lexington. "He asked me not to tell. He did not wish Margaret to know. And listen again, mother. In a skirmish one day we were fighting hand to hand. I saw one man with his pistol levelled at me and another with his sabre lifted on Chad. He saw them both. My pistol was empty, and do you know what he did? He shot the man who was about to shoot me instead of his own assailant. That is how he got that scar. I did tell Margaret that."

"Yes, you must go down in the mountains first," Margaret was saying, "and see if there is anything you can do for the people who were so good to you—and to see Melissa. I am worried about her."

"And then I must come back to you?"

"Yes, you must come back to see me once more, if you can. And then some day you will come again and buy back the Major's farm"—she stopped, blushing. "I think that was his wish, Chad, that you and I—but I would never let him say it."

"And if that should take too long?"

"I will come to you, Chad," said Margaret.

Old Mammy came out on the porch as they were climbing the stile.

"Ole Miss," she said, indignantly, "my Tom say that he can't get nary a triflin' nigger to come out hyeh to wuk, an' ef that sawnfiel' ain't ploughed mighty soon, it's gwine to bu'n up."

PEACE

"How many horses are there on the place, Mammy?" asked Dan.

"Hosses!" sniffed the old woman. "They ain't *nary* a hoss —nothin' but two ole broken-down mules."

"Well, I'll take one and start a plough myself," said Harry.

"And I'll take the other," said Dan.

Mammy groaned.

.   .   .   .

And still the wonder of that night to Chad and Margaret!

"It was General Hunt who taught me to understand—and forgive. Do you know what he said? That every man, on both sides, was right—who did his duty."

"God bless him," said Chad.

XXXI

THE WESTWARD WAY

MOTHER TURNER was sitting in the porch with old Jack at her feet when Chad and Dixie came to the gate—her bonnet off, her eyes turned toward the West. The stillness of death lay over the place, and over the strong old face some preternatural sorrow. She did not rise when she saw Chad, she did not speak when he spoke. She turned merely and looked at him with a look of helpless suffering. She knew the question that was on his lips, for she dumbly motioned toward the door and then put her trembling hands on the railing of the porch and bent her face down on them. With sickening fear, Chad stepped on the threshold—cap in hand—and old Jack followed, whimpering. As his eyes grew accustomed to the dark interior, he could see a sheeted form on a bed in the corner and, on the pillow, a white face.

"Melissa!" he called, brokenly. A groan from the porch answered him, and, as Chad dropped to his knees, the old woman sobbed aloud.

In low tones, as though in fear they might disturb the dead girl's sleep, the two talked on the porch. Brokenly, the old woman told Chad how the girl had sickened and suffered with never a word of complaint. How, all through the war, she had fought his battles so fiercely that no one dared attack him in her hearing. How, sick as she was, she had gone, that night, to save his life. How she had nearly died from the result of cold and exposure and was never the same afterward. How she worked in the house and in the garden to keep their bodies

[320]

He sat there until the sun went down.

and souls together, after the old hunter was shot down and her boys were gone to the war. How she had learned the story of Chad's mother from old Nathan Cherry's daughter and how, when the old woman forbade her going to the Bluegrass, she had slipped away and gone afoot to clear his name. And then the old woman led Chad to where once had grown the rose-bush he had brought Melissa from the Bluegrass, and pointed silently to a box that seemed to have been pressed a few inches into the soft earth, and when Chad lifted it, he saw under it the imprint of a human foot—his own, made that morning when he held out a rose-leaf to her and she had struck it from his hand and turned him, as an enemy, from her door.

Chad silently went inside and threw open the window to let the last sunlight in: and he sat there, with his face as changeless as the still face on the pillow, sat there until the sun went down and the darkness came in and closed softly about her. She had died, the old woman said, with his name on her lips.

.·   .   .   .   .

Dolph and Rube had come back and they would take good care of the old mother until the end of her days. But Jack— what should be done with Jack? The old dog could follow him no longer. He could live hardly more than another year, and the old mother wanted him—to remind her, she said, of Chad and of Melissa, who had loved him. He patted his faithful old friend tenderly and, when he mounted Dixie, late the next afternoon, Jack started to follow him.

"No, Jack," said Chad, and he rode on, with his eyes blurred. On the top of the steep mountain he dismounted, to let his horse rest a moment, and sat on a log, looking toward the sun. He could not go back to Margaret and happiness—not now. It seemed hardly fair to the dead girl down in the valley. He would send Margaret word, and she would understand.

Once again he was starting his life over afresh, with his old capital, a strong body and a stout heart. In his breast still burned the spirit that had led his race to the land, had wrenched it from savage and from king, had made it the high temple of Liberty for the worship of freemen—the Kingdom Come for the oppressed of the earth—and, himself the unconscious Shepherd of that Spirit, he was going to help carry its ideals across a continent Westward to another sea and on—who knows—to the gates of the rising sun. An eagle swept over his head, as he rose, and the soft patter of feet sounded behind him. It was Jack trotting after him. He stooped and took the old dog in his arms.

"Go back home, Jack!" he said.

Without a whimper, old Jack slowly wheeled, but he stopped and turned again and sat on his haunches—looking back.

"Go home, Jack!" Again the old dog trotted down the path and once more he turned.

"Home, Jack!" said Chad.

The eagle was a dim, black speck in the band of yellow that lay over the rim of the sinking sun, and after its flight, horse and rider took the westward way.

MELISSA